I'M SO
(NOT)
OVER YOU

I'M SO (NOT) OVER YOU

KOSOKO JACKSON

JOVE
NEW YORK

A JOVE BOOK
Published by Berkley
An imprint of Penguin Random House LLC
penguinrandomhouse.com

Library of Congress Cataloging-in-Publication Data

Names: Jackson, Kosoko, author.
Title: I'm so (not) over you / Kosoko Jackson.
Other titles: I am so (not) over you
Description: First edition. | New York: Jove, 2022.
Identifiers: LCCN 2021039607 (print) | LCCN 2021039608 (ebook) |
ISBN 9780593334447 (trade paperback) | ISBN 9780593334454 (ebook)
Subjects: LCSH: Gay men—Fiction. | LCGFT: Romance fiction.
Classification: LCC PS3610.A356439 I6 2022 (print) |
LCC PS3610.A356439 (ebook) | DDC 813/.6—dc23
LC record available at https://lccn.loc.gov/2021039607
LC ebook record available at https://lccn.loc.gov/2021039608

First Edition: February 2022

Printed in the United States of America
1st Printing

Book design by Daniel Brount

To Jazmín
Who reminded me how to stand in my power, not in my fear.

ONE

THE FIRST RULE, and only rule, of getting over your ex is not to answer your ex's messages. This can be done in many different ways, depending on the person.

One, change his contact to read: **DO NOT ANSWER**.

Two, block his number.

Three, glue a horrible weave to your scalp, so you look and act like a completely different person.

Four, restart your life as the owner of a mom-and-pop shop in rural Indiana and call it a day. That's one I'm particularly partial to.

All of those are good and valid options. Do what you need to do—no judgment.

And yet, somehow I found a way to break this simple rule. Not just break it, burst it wide open. Shatter it, if you will.

Because it's one thing to open a text and answer it, but it's another to decide to follow through with your ex's request.

Look up *Bad Idea* on Google, and our helpful search engine will bring up, *Did you mean: Kian Andrews's choices whenever they involve Hudson Rivers?*

My phone in my pocket vibrates once. My heart skips a beat. Maybe Hudson will cancel. Or maybe he'll realize the past three months apart have been a mistake and he's going to confess he's still madly in love with me? Maybe . . .

Nope, just Divya.

DIVYA EVANS: Let the record show this is a horrible idea.

"Of course you'd say that," I mutter, forgetting she can't, you know, hear me. And she may be right, but that's not the point.

When I got the text from Hudson a week ago, asking me to meet him at the Watering Hole, Divya was not amused. She scrunched her nose, like she tasted something rancid in the air, which wasn't entirely off.

Because to her, that's exactly what my relationship with Hudson was: rancid. Which, sure, everyone says that about their ex because it makes them feel better.

KIAN ANDREWS: You've said that—multiple times.

DIVYA EVANS: And yet, you still refuse to listen. Remind me, who is getting their law degree from Harvard?

KIAN ANDREWS: Wow . . . we went . . . 12 hours without you bringing up your Harvard degree. That's a new record!

DIVYA EVANS: But seriously, K. This is a bad idea. Closure is not as good as you think it is.

As a lawyer-in-training, she should understand why I need to meet with Hudson: to process what happened, to close that chapter of my life, and to seal it shut with a glue made of truth. The memory of us breaking up is an open wound that never healed. It was a volatile separation, ending with me blocking him on every social media account possible and drinking myself into a stupor that made the two weeks after the breakup a blur.

Maybe that's why Divya's a prosecutor and not a defense attorney. Another vibration, another text.

DIVYA EVANS: I'm only a few blocks away if you need me.

KIAN ANDREWS: What are the chances of that happening? 🖤

Pretty high, if I'm being honest. Divya has always been my rock, no matter what. Whether keeping me from embarrassing myself when I started crying in the club two weeks after my breakup, making sure I got my worthless self out of bed so I didn't lose my partial scholarship, or even finding some men with absolute dump-truck asses to help me get over my head-over-heels obsession with Hudson, Divya has been that ride-or-die friend for me.

So it's reasonable to assume that when I'm about to go through another major, traumatizing Hudson experience, Divya Evans is the big guns I have on speed dial. What's that expression? Behind every great gay guy, there's a badass woman?

Again, my phone pings. I pull it out of my pocket without looking, expecting another (well-deserved) quippy barb from Divya. But instead, an e-mail stares back at me.

FROM: JOBS@SPOTLIGHT.COM
TO: KIAN.ANDREWS@NORTHEASTERN.EDU
SUBJECT: RE: Investigative Journalism Fellowship Application | Andrews, Kian

I stare at the screen for so long, the colorful background of one of the many lighthouses on the North Carolina coast. I want to savor this moment. Hold on to it, keep it in its box, and put it on the top shelf somewhere out of the way. When I'm a famous journalist, with sources sliding into my DMs, begging me to write Pulitzer-winning stories, and I'm giving a guest lecture at Northeastern, they'll ask me, *How did you get started in this competitive, cutthroat business?*

And I'll say, *I got my first job at Spotlight.* Will Spotlight be around twelve years from now? Probably not. News websites cannibalize themselves like bacteria. But it's the hottest place to work in journalism right now. Getting an Investigative Journalism Fellowship there would change my life. It's like . . . do not pass Go; instead, get Park Place on your second turn.

I tap the screen, bringing it back to life. Still, the e-mail alert taunts me. Maybe it's an interview request? Maybe my pitch on the lack of education programs in Appalachia and how it's setting students back several grade levels that I spent all last week making really did impress them, and they are going to offer me a position sight unseen. That's not unreasonable. It happens to white guys all the time. And I have good—no, fucking *great* credentials.

Like Divya says, they would be *lucky* to have me.

But at the same time, as my journalism professor said, *Journalists are a dime a dozen. Why should they pick you over anyone else?*

Which takes us back to Divya Evans, and her exact words: *You're a goddamn star, Kian Andrews.*

I wish I had the same level of confidence as her. I do a good job faking it when I'm around her, at least I think I do. But now? Alone in this café? Doing something stupid like waiting for the boy who broke my heart—who is now seven minutes late—*and* staring at the e-mail that could change my career? That confident facade is pushed far back into the closet; a place I haven't been since middle school.

And I promised I'd never go back there again.

Without overthinking it, I tap on the screen one more time, and then enter my passcode before I can change my mind. One more tap, and the e-mail fills the screen.

Dear Mr. Andrews,

Thank you for your application for the Investigative Journalism Fellowship at Spotlight's Boston branch. At this time, we've decided—

"Shit."

There's no need to read any more. I could do a CTRL-F in my inbox, search for "we've decided," and bring up more than a dozen results. This is no different, despite how badly I want it to be different.

I'm halfway through a text to Divya, informing her about the rejection from Spotlight, which will undoubtedly result in her replying with drinks on me tonight, when a baritone clearing of a throat behind me causes my fingers to stop. The deep voice cuts through the low sensual tones of the Esperanza Spalding cover artist serenading us in the Watering Hole, even if it is as out of place as a Black guy in Boston—aka Me.

But the voice is unmistakable. Even after three months of avoiding everything related to Hudson, the way he speaks effortlessly from the depths of his diaphragm still sends shivers down my spine. And the way his boyish grin plays off his chiseled jaw makes me want to melt.

"Kian?"

I do my best to turn slowly. Eagerness isn't a good look on anyone, especially around your ex when you're trying to act like you've moved on and are living your best single twentysomething life.

But my *God* does he look nice.

No, not nice.

Hot.

"Hey," he says while smirking. "Thanks for coming."

There it is. That smile. The same lopsided grin that he gave me when we were paired together in freshman English to come up with a presentation of *The Bell Jar.* That smile he gave before our first kiss, after almost two years of mutual pining and "will they/won't they"s.

That Southern drawl. The same one that he would make more prominent when we lay in bed on Sunday morning because he knew what it did to me.

Put them together with a dash of traditionally accepted masculine features, a heaping of generational wealth, and you've got Hudson Rivers.

I can already feel the weightlessness taking over. That sickening feeling that's akin to carbon monoxide poisoning. That's what Hudson is: a toxin that makes my best judgment and practical senses go haywire. He's dangerous. He's a mistake. He's going to hurt me.

But he's so damn beautiful. And I miss him. I miss him so fucking much.

"Sure, no problem." *Act relaxed. Act like you don't care.* "I wasn't doing anything anyway. I mean I was in town. I mean I was in the area. I mean I was in the area because I live around here and I wasn't doing anything." *Besides neurotically refreshing my e-mail for a response from Spotlight and obviously looking like an idiot who can't put together a decent sentence to save my life.*

Divya and I went over this, like a witness being prepped for a dangerous cross-examination, multiple times. I have to hold my ground. I have to stay aloof. I have to stay in control. Thirty seconds in, and I'm doing the exact opposite of that.

Hudson just keeps that soft charming grin on his face. It's like he knows my brain is short-circuiting, because he does. He's seen me spiral like this before; multiple times in college when I had too many assignments due and I didn't know where to start. And all those times he let me just talk myself out of the hole I created, smiling at me, maybe rubbing his thumbs over my knuckles in a soft, circular soothing motion.

There's none of those touches this time, though, and that smile, once cute and teasing, now seems like it's twisted into one of mockery. Even if I know that's not true, it's what my head, and my heart, thinks. Funny how when you break up with someone, everything you loved about them turns into everything you hate.

"I don't have much time, though," I add to recover some dignity and take some power back. "So, whatever you want, let's get this over with, yeah?"

"Course, darlin'."

I twitch, like his word is the trigger of a shock collar. He sits, frozen, as though he whispered some command that put a spotlight on him, and shakes his head.

"Sorry. Habit."

"You call a lot of boys that now?" That was uncalled for.

"That's not what I meant, and you know it, K."

"Kian," I remind him. "K is reserved for boyfriends, and you, Hudson, are no longer my boyfriend."

There. I did it. Advantage: Kian. The ball's back in my court. I've taken control of the narrative. Hudson, the smooth-talking Georgian, is not the one who has the power anymore. I . . .

"That's exactly why I called you, actually." Hudson avoids my gaze, fiddling with the sugar packet I ripped open and threw on the counter. He folds it into a nondescript shape, unfolds it, and refolds it again, like some poor man's origami experiment.

I know that tick. He fiddles with things when he's nervous—

truly, actually worried. It's just so rare that I see it. It's . . . about as common as finding a bad picture of Beyoncé.

Is it possible the great Hudson Rivers is more nervous than me?

"Screw it." He tosses the crumpled paper on the counter. "Nothing good comes from beatin' around the bush."

"I'm pretty sure I'm the one who t—"

"I called you here because I want you to be my boyfriend."

And at that moment, I've never been so happy to be Black. Not only because Black don't crack, but because the way the blood rushes to my cheeks would make me look like an overly ripe tomato.

And there is nothing sexy about tomatoes.

TWO

THERE ARE TWO perfect descriptors that come to mind for most people when they mention Hudson Rivers: whiskey and a steel-string guitar.

Whiskey because his voice is as smooth as the alcohol his family famously distills and markets.

And a guitar because, not only is he great at playing it, but there's a soft, alluring twang to his voice that makes the Sirens in the *Odyssey* sound like piss-poor contestants on *The X Factor*.

Does Hudson know he has this effect on people? Absolutely.

Does he use it to his advantage? One hundred percent. I've seen it in action.

Do any of us care? Fuck no.

Because who runs the world? Not girls, but boys with stellar jawlines. And Hudson Rivers has exactly that.

And money—that helps too.

I mean, *come on*, what normal person can pull off a black Henley, with dark jeans, a backward cap, and chunky boots, in a Boston September, and make the fashion look *actually good*? But he makes it look effortless, and I hate him for that. But I also love him for that. Or maybe it's my horniness talking. I guess it could be all three.

If I'm being honest, all those descriptors work for Hudson. On other men they would be nauseating, but Hudson carries the crown well. He's mastered the balance between confident and arrogant like it's his major. He knows he's attractive but doesn't talk about it. I've always told him he looks like Jesse Williams, if he were ten years younger. I still stand by that incredibly accurate statement. Sure, he hates taking selfies, which makes it hard to show a side-by-side photo, and his Instagram is, at most, the occasional picture of some-place he's traveled, or a sunset, or something else mundane (as of sixteen hours ago, according to his account, he finally finished *The Water Dancer* after a year of false starts—good for him). But that doesn't mean I'm wrong! Consider all that, along with the fact he doesn't talk about his family's wealth or influence unless it actually relates to the conversation, and on paper, Hudson Rivers is a good person. Hell, in real life, he's a great person.

You know, besides dumping me at this exact coffee shop—at the exact table we've been sitting at awkwardly for the past ten minutes.

"You look good," he finally says, taking a sip of his Americano.

I let out a quiet scoff that I think goes unnoticed.

I, on the other hand, have changed significantly. Not by choice, mind you. If romantic comedies have taught me anything, it's that after a big breakup, you need a big change. And do not make that big change cutting your own hair in the mirror, because that never turns out well.

For me, change was short-sleeve button-downs replaced by band tee shirts. Coils of short black hair replaced with a small fro under a beanie. Poorly fitting jeans swapped for nicely tailored ones. Dirty

Vans from an off-brand outlet exchanged with cheap yet still fashionable boots.

"Is that such a bad thing to say?" he asks.

"No. Not at all. Thanks." A beat. "You can thank Divya; this was
all her idea."

"How is she doing, by the way?"

"Still wants to punch you in the face."

"So, she's doing great then. Good to hear."

A smile threatens to appear, but I bite my inner cheek until I
taste blood. He doesn't deserve that. No. Absolutely not. He doesn't
deserve any sort of satisfaction or praise. He dumped *me*! Not the
other way around. Not, *Let's talk about it.* Not, *I'm not happy.* Nothing. Completely out of left field. He doesn't get to feel any sort of
relief a smile might give him. He doesn't get to feel like he's off the
hook because *Kian seems to be doing great.*

Keep on task. Keep focused. Get in. Get out.

"Please tell me you didn't reach out to ask me how Divya is doing. You could have checked Instagram for that. What next, gonna
ask me about the weather?"

"The weather is always the same in Boston during the summertime. High eighties, with a thirty percent chance of thunderstorms."

"Don't be cute with me, Hudson."

"But you like it when I'm cute. And if I remember . . ." He leans
forward, strong forearms resting on the table with enough weight
that it wobbles. "You used to also like it when I . . . did that thing
with my tongue on your—"

"Can I get you both anything?"

Out of nowhere, a waitress—Samantha—appears: dark hair, a
too bright smile, a college sophomore or junior, I think, and judging
by the hungry look in her eyes, either she thinks she can get a quick

shag in the bathroom—a rite-of-passage at the Watering Hole—or she thinks Hudson Rivers is new-age royalty.

And technically, with the latter, she wouldn't be wrong.

But Hudson ignores the hungry stares, at least until her standing there becomes so apparent he can't ignore her.

"I'm good, thanks, darling." Samantha opens her mouth, probably to upsell whatever the special is today, but Hudson cuts her off. "But my boyfriend can have whatever he wants."

Her face visibly droops, and it's almost-almost-enough to keep from correcting him.

"Not your boyfriend."

Her face lights up again. Samantha the Waitress is really going on her own personal face journey here.

"Still, get him whatever he wants." Hudson hands her thirty dollars, more than any drink here costs. But it's also blood money—there are strings attached to those bills. Samantha turns to me, unmoving, determined, and stubborn.

"Iced mocha." A moment passes. "Thank you." I've spent the past seven years in Boston, but that doesn't mean I lost my Southern manners.

"Coming right up," she cheerily replies before disappearing.

"There you go again," I mutter.

"Hm?"

"Thinking you can buy people off with money. Us Southerners were supposed to be respectful and hospitable, remember? You're not excluded from that just because you're rich."

"My family is richer than God himself, thank you very much," he says cheekily with a flirtatious wink. "And I gave her thirty dollars on a drink that cost six dollars and gave you a blank check to get whatever you want. That sounds like a good person to me."

"Sounds like someone who just proved my point."

He opens his mouth, closes it, then opens it again. "I'm not even going to dignify that with a response."

"Then answer me this." I rest my forearms on the table and lean forward. I learned in a psychology class that if you want to know if someone's really lying, look in their eyes. Even the best liars have a tell there: a slight widening of the pupils, a blink, a twitch. Reflexive reactions biologically linked to the human decision to withhold the truth.

So, I focus on them, getting lost in his warm, friendly, and inviting brown eyes. Nine times out of ten, when an ex reaches out to you, completely out of the blue, there's only one reason they want to talk to you.

"Did you call me your boyfriend so you could justify asking for makeup sex with me?"

To be honest, and I don't say this with much humility, if Hudson wanted it, he could get it. With his perfect warm Southern drawl, high-end (but comfortable) clothing, and the right amount of cologne that smells like mahogany, he is a dangerous, intoxicating microcosm. Add in the boyish charm you wouldn't expect from someone whose family has met Beyoncé and Jay-Z on multiple occasions, and no one, absolutely no one at Northeastern was immune to his allure.

So why did a smart guy like me do something as stupid as put myself back in this situation?

Simple.

Because I'm still in love with him.

I love his smile. I love the way his eyes look hazy, like early morning in a seaport town, when he first wakes up. I love the way his accent is thicker when he's stressed or tired. And I love his laugh.

Except when it's directed at me.

Like it is right now.

Hudson has that type of laugh that's full-bodied, like an expensive bottle of wine. It's surprisingly deep, and his whole form shudders when he actually finds something hilarious.

And apparently, me asking about makeup sex is the funniest thing he's heard all week.

He continues to shake for the longest ten seconds of my life. With each passing second, white-hot rage boils and threatens to burst, like magma scratching at the top of an awakening volcano. When he stops, which is good for him and his well-being, he wipes tears from his eyes.

"S-sorry. I promise I wasn't laughing *at* you."

"If you say, 'I was laughing *with* you . . .'"

"I mean, come on, that was funny. You were joking, right?"

There it is, the perfect out. Smile and say you're joking, Kian. Fall on your sword; better to look like an idiot for missing a cue, than actually admit you're still pining over the man who broke your heart—in this exact fucking café.

Because the only thing more pathetic than that is . . . well, there's nothing more pathetic than that.

I don't get the chance to lie before Hudson picks up again.

"But, that doesn't matter because, Kian, I do want to date you again."

". . . Okay . . ."

"But only for a day."

Record scratch.

"I'm sorry, what?"

"Maybe three days, tops. I don't think we'll need longer than that."

When-slash-if Hudson Rivers said he made a mistake and wanted me back, I had a whole speech planned out. A metaphorical back-and-forth I've mastered and fine-tuned over the past ninety days to be both romantic and heated. I've planned every comeback, figured out every word I'd use. Enough to cut deep and make him think, but not so much to seem rehearsed. That's what everyone does in the shower: plan arguments.

Besides jerking off, of course. And I've done plenty of that.

But I didn't plan for this. And I'm pretty sure I won't be jerking off to this, either.

"Why three days?"

Hudson fidgets in his chair. His shoulders are stiff, his posture rigid. His eyes seem a little darker and the way he slumps . . . it's like he's trying to make himself smaller. Like he knows what he's thinking or about to offer is wrong.

And I know I'm not going to like this.

"Look," he says finally. "I wouldn't ask this if it wasn't an emergency, you know that, right?"

"Uh-huh . . ."

"And it's not like I planned this. I wouldn't do that to you. Even though we're broken up, you're still . . . still an important person to me, Kian. It's important to me you understand that."

"Just spit it out."

He takes a deep breath.

THREE

"...**AND THAT'S WHEN** I threw the drink in his face."

A day and a half later, I'm far away from Hudson on the other side of town, sitting at a table meant for four but housing five people at the Patriot. It's not often my brother, Jamal, and I get together; he's too busy at Harvard triple-majoring in God-knows-what right now. Something impressive that'll make him a capitalist shill, I'm sure.

But a monthly dinner has been on the books since he started at the Ivy almost two years ago, and we've only done it half a dozen times. Maybe it's fate, or that brotherly connection people rave about; after the mess with Hudson, we find a way to make it work.

"I'm sorry, you need to start from the beginning," Divya says, tilting her drink back, downing the remainder of her Dark 'n Stormy. "Again."

I take three swigs of water to avoid a hangover tomorrow, and to buy me some time. As if some god will pity me and a drunk clown will burst into the bar, distract everyone, and I won't have to repeat myself again.

But there's no such luck because I, Kian Andrews, am not that lucky.

"He asked me to pretend to be his boyfriend. Said his parents are coming in from out of town, and he never told them we broke up and . . ." I take a deep breath and speak on the exhale, ". . . he needs me to cover for him."

I repeat it to the table for the fourth time. The table consisting of Jamal, my brother, who brought his best friend, Emily, with him, plus Divya, who, and I quote, "is simply obsessed with Jamal," so of course she tagged along. And being the secret bleeding heart that Jamal is, Emily's boyfriend, Todd—an entrepreneur trying to open a brewery that specializes in using flowers as the flavor base (aka broke)—is here for the free food.

"That's insane," Divya mutters.

"He's bold," Jamal chimes in.

"Or crazy—wait, we don't use that word anymore, right?" Todd asks.

"It's ableist, babe. Well? What did you say?" Emily asks, leaning forward. She's an English major; romantic misfires interest her far more than they should.

"Of course, he said no," Divya scoffs at Emily, like it was the most ridiculous thing she could have said. "Right?"

"Mhm."

Which isn't entirely accurate. Sure, I didn't actually say the words, but throwing your coffee on a guy is just like saying no, right? Hudson is a smart guy; he got the message. Even if he didn't, it doesn't matter. I've officially blocked him on all platforms—again.

And I've been forbidden from returning to the Watering Hole—worth it.

"As you should have," Jamal adds. He flags down the bartender, and through some secret code, orders us more drinks. Unlike me, Jamal has natural charisma. People like him—no—they adore him when they first meet. Making friends? Easy. Finding a posse? Easy. I feel, as the older, more awkward brother, I should be teaching him things when, in fact, it's often the other way around.

"I wouldn't have gone to see him in the first place," Todd, Emily's blond, muscular Instagram influencer-esque boyfriend, adds while sipping his frothy IPA. "You can't be friends with your ex."

"Whoa," Divya chimes in, looking up from her phone. "I'm the president of the 'I Hate Hudson Club,' but that? False."

"Look, I hate siding with a White Man, but I think Todd's right," Jamal adds.

"*Thank you,*" Todd chimes in.

"Don't get too excited, Colonizer," Jamal replies. "I just don't think it's possible. There's too much baggage there. You two dated for what? Two years?"

"Year and a half," I correct.

"Three if you include the overly dramatic and excessively long pining period," Divya adds.

"No one considers that," I remind her.

"I do and I'm somebody, so it matters." Divya winks cheekily.

"See? That's a long time," Emily adds, chin still in her hand like she's watching her favorite reboot of *Pride and Prejudice*.

"Right. And in gay years? That's what? Two years?" Divya asks.

"Four," Jamal and I say at the same time.

"I'm just saying, there are roots between you two. And to ask you to pretend to date him? That's cruel," Jamal closes.

Divya turns to me. "Why did he ask anyway?"

I'm not as forthcoming with that information. And the truth being? I don't know. Once I decided to leave . . . everything was a blur. I just remember feeling my cheeks burn hot, hearing the blood rushing in my ears, and storming out. The world was like a water-color of rustic browns, sun-ray yellows, and music.

"Some stupid favor." It wasn't a lie. Not completely. Based on the basic principle of Ex-Boyfriend Law, any favor Hudson asked for was, in fact, stupid. Even if I'm not sure of the logic behind it, it doesn't matter. The premise is dumb, so, by default, the ask is flawed.

"I'm just saying." Todd shrugs, reaching over Emily to steal French fries from the communal bowl. "Exes are exes for a reason."

"If I may, I disagree." Of course Emily disagrees. "Some people are meant to be together. Sometimes they get it right on the first try. Sometimes it takes fifty years."

"Are you speaking from experience?" Divya asks.

Emily nods. "My grandparents. Well, my grandma. On my mother's side. Met a guy in high school, dated him, broke up with him in college, married my now-grandfather, my mom's father, divorced him, reconnected with the first man sixty years later." She steals a fry from Todd's plate. "Been happy for the past six years."

"That's an exception, not the rule," I remind her. "Most people, when they break up, that's it. They're done."

"Doesn't mean that's *all* people. Doesn't mean that's you, and . . . what's his name?"

"Hudson," Jamal, Divya, and I say at the same time. Both of them were here for the Hudson Era. Divya was my battering ram and drinking partner. Jamal oscillated between *I told you so* and *I'll drive you back home for the weekend if you want.* Even if back home was a good ten hours.

And, just like any friend would do, I know, deep down, if I told them there was a part of me, a small piece of me, curious about what Hudson needed—and considering helping him—they would drag me outside and douse me with a cold shower like I was drunk. Which, I guess I kinda am. Love drunk.

But not nearly actual BAC-drunk enough.

"Hudson Rivers, if we're being precise," Divya adds, making a disgusted face. "Never trust someone whose name is a proper—"

"Wait, go back," Todd interrupts. "*The* Hudson Rivers?"

Here we go.

This is how every dudebro—especially anyone who works in the beer industry—acts whenever I bring up his name, which hasn't happened in a while. Anyone who drinks IPAs knows the Rivers family. I mean, it's a fair reaction. If you drink beer of any sort, or if you went to a college in America, or took even one econ class as a general education requirement, you probably know of the Rivers & Valleys brand. Discount but still delicious beer, well known for their pale ales, and now, as of two months ago, the most profitable brewing company in the United States. And *still* family-owned.

I don't need to be here for Todd's fanboy moment.

"I'll get our drinks."

I weasel past Divya and move through the crowded bar. The Patriot is a happening place, mostly for Boston's young professionals and those about to enter the workforce. It's swanky and cheap, two distinctions that are hard to come by. Live music, a great happy hour, and ample seating. What more could an overworked, underpaid twentysomething want?

You know, besides debt forgiveness.

I push my way through the crowded bar area and lean against the counter. Most people at the Patriot are with friends, coworkers, and a few groups of students from neighboring colleges. That's the largest segment of patrons here. Tufts, Harvard (which, technically, is in Cambridge, if you want to get fancy), Boston College, Northeastern, MIT. They all funnel their students here or the second, smaller location in Roxbury.

But, unlike most people, I enjoy getting lost in the crowds. I'm short—well, not actually short, but at five-foot-eight-and-a-half, I'm slightly under the average male height of five-foot-nine—so it's easier for me to get lost in these crowds. I like that. I *revel* in that.

It just sucks when you're trying to get a bartender's attention.

Finally, the blond man serving drinks like he has eight hands, with an unfortunate buzz cut on both sides of his head that's a little too close to the alt-right hairstyle for my liking, turns to me.

"The usual for Table Ten," I say, brandishing my card.

"Comin' right up." He presses a few buttons on the cash register. A waitress will bring the order to the table. But instead of taking my card when he returns, he hands me a receipt.

"You're good."

"You're giving us free drinks?"

The man laughs, a deep voice that cuts through the chatter and hum of the bar. "You wish." Instead, he points down the row. "He paid for them."

There's a moment of joy that surges through me when he says that. There's no one, absolutely no one in the world who doesn't find the whole "random stranger paid for a drink to get your attention" trope *not* sexy. Sure, there's the second tsunami wave of emotions that hit to disrupt that joy: What if he spiked the drink? But in that brief, shining moment, it's a Generation X love story.

And if that's not enough logic to bring me down to Earth, the third wave does.

"You have got to be kidding me."

I push through the crowd like an icebreaker ship. By the time I reach him, Hudson's turned his chair to face me, hands up.

"Before you call me a stalker, or bring Divya over here to punch me, I just wanted to say I didn't give you the full story. If you sit down, give me five minutes, I'll explain it all. I promise."

The one thing I know about Hudson Rivers that's still true is that he isn't a liar. So, I do what any curious, slightly drunk, angry ex of an attractive guy with a deep voice who smells a little like pine does.

"Five minutes," I remind him, sitting down. "And another drink. You owe me."

FOUR

"I OWE YOU an apology."

His first words since I sat down come out like molasses. Sweet but thick, cunning but forced. He avoids my gaze when he says it as if he's ashamed, which is what interests me.

Hudson has never been one of those brazen, over-the-top rich boys; though he most certainly has the clout to be one. At the same time, apologies don't come naturally to him, and even when he knows he should give them, they are like puffs of smoke. Faint, barely visible, and gone as quickly as they appear.

So, to hear him say with so much intention and deliberation that he's sorry, that's a surprise.

"For the record, I'm not sorry for pouring my coffee on you," I remind him.

"Fair."

"You deserved it."

"Again, fair."

I catch myself before I say, *And you look nice all wet.* Though I have a lot of experience to support that claim, and even more imagery in the recesses of my overly active imagination, I opt for stubborn indignation instead.

"I'm not a fan of being played, Hudson." Yeah, that sounds confident. Like I'm some badass star of a modern-day queer remix of "Miss Independent" by Kelly Clarkson. Score one for me and my light-on-my-feet thinking.

At least, that's how I hope it came out. In reality, those words were like jagged, sharp rocks that wounded my tongue. How much therapy, how many eighty-dollar payments were exchanged before I could have that one burst of fiery confidence? That never came easily to me. Jamal got those skills.

"I didn't mean to do that. It wasn't . . ." He sighs, taking a long drink of his clear liquid. One might think, because of our location and his family business, he'd be drinking some fancy mixed drink. But as long as I've known Hudson, I've never seen him take a sip of alcohol of any kind. What's in that glass is probably water, or some sparkling water or something similar. But vodka? Nah, that's not Hudson. Maybe it's the same reason people who work at restaurants don't like eating there. I've never asked, and frankly, it's never mattered.

In some ways, a simple thing like him not drinking when his family rules the brewing industry made him . . . attractive? It's the difference. The uniqueness, the stubborn rebellion against his family that makes him special enough to pique my interest.

Because, despite the implication from people who asked what it was like to date Hudson Rivers, it was never about the money, or his connections, or the fact his family is the third richest in the South. It was his softness, his deep baritone voice, his smile and the twinkle in his eyes that always followed.

It was the way his hands felt against me when they were rough. The way they felt when they were smooth.

It was so much more than his bank account. It was the whispered dreams he'd bring up only in the dead of night, when even the city of Boston was still. It was the way he bit his full bottom lip when he lost—for the third time—against a *Skyrim* boss. It was how he said he found musicals boring, but after seeing *Wicked* with me, woke me up the next morning, standing on the couch wearing only boxers, with a blanket draped over him, and belted "Defying Gravity" off-key.

Things like these made Hudson Hudson, not just a Rivers I fell head over heels for. And those memories, the steamy and the sugary, are the reason I'm still here.

"How about we start over again?" he offers. "Please?"

A beat. "Did you follow me here?"

"Well . . . that's one definition of starting over." He takes a sip of his half-drunk clear liquid again, probably to buy himself some time. "How would I know you were coming here, K?"

"Kian. A good guess?"

"Exactly, just that. A guess."

He stares at his glass while I glance over at Divya and the others. No one has looked up to see what's taking me so long with the drinks. Too busy drinking and socializing, which is how it always is. I know Divya loves me. I know Jamal tolerates me, and when we're all together, we have a good time. But I'm not like them. I'm more like Emily, if anything, but she fakes being comfortable around extroverts better than I do.

The only extrovert I ever did well around was . . .

"You owe me more than an apology."

"Hm?"

"An explanation," I add. "I think that's fair."

"I agree. To be fair, you ran out before I could give you one."

"So, you're blaming me? I wasn't the one who . . ."

He holds up his arms, in the "I surrender" gesture.

"Let's take a step back. That was wrong of me to say. Let me try again?"

As if there's a world where I don't give Hudson Rivers as many chances as he wants.

"Explain."

He takes a final sip—a longer one this time. "My parents, they are big deals, you know how they are," he says slowly, a sly way of reminding both of us that our relationship had progressed enough that we'd gotten to the *meeting the parents* phase before it blew up in our faces. "And they expect their children to be, too. You know this."

"I've had more important things to focus on in the past year than your family tree."

Of course I remember. Everyone twenty-one and up, and probably some under, have drunk alcohol the Rivers family touched. Not only do they own Rivers & Valleys, but they also have a substantial stake in two other major alcohol companies, verging on a monopoly in the business. The Rivers distillery they have had in Georgia since Prohibition is a cultural landmark for the Peach State. Mr. Rivers is rumored to be running for office next year, riding on the money he funneled into the state, his Southern charm, and his good nature.

And he's expected to win.

Mrs. Rivers is the business mind behind the operation. Not born into the family business, but she has an MBA and quickly took the Southern chain into international recognition. And Hudson's sister, Olivia? Don't get me started on her. One of the youngest business-women to own over twenty percent of a billion-dollar company.

They were the epitome of a Southern power family.

But he doesn't need to know that I remember everything about him. He doesn't need to know how often I've thought of the last time we met, briefly, during graduation. How his parents looked me up and down and I couldn't pinpoint what they thought of me, or my own family. Did they look down on us? Did they have a problem with him dating a guy? Did they want to know my credit score? Could they smell my measly bank account?

A twinge of panic rises in my chest. Those ten minutes with them in the auditorium were some of the most stressful moments of my life, and there's a chance that whatever Hudson wants me to do, it will involve them. I don't need to think about that. I don't need to focus on how horrible I felt. How . . . not enough I was.

Instead, I concentrate on things I like. The introduction to *Star Trek: The Next Generation* and how *Star Trek: Discovery* pays homage to it. Katie Couric's journalistic voice and how close I am to perfecting it. How Hudson's Southern accent becomes more prominent when he's angry. His secret love for Marvel movies. The way his toes curl when I . . .

Focus, Kian.

Hudson opens his mouth—I'm guessing to start lecturing about his family—before shaking his head. "Doesn't matter. They're coming into town. I got accepted into Tufts's master's program for the spring semester. They're taking me out to dinner to celebrate."

"Congratulations. Sociology, right?"

"Psychology."

I know that. Clinical psychology, to be exact. I know that even though I've blocked him on social media—for my own sanity—it's not hard to make a finsta account and stalk him. Am I proud of it? Not at all. Do I still do it? Of course.

I probably shouldn't feel proud of him, but I can't help it. Hudson doesn't fit the label of "Southern Brewing Royalty" society has boxed him into. He's not a businessman. He doesn't drink. He hates the cutthroat nature of the commercial world. He wants to help fix people's minds. That's what makes him happy. He's willing to walk away from the billion-dollar company and become a psychologist. That's . . . bold.

"My parents think I mess everything up. Especially compared to Livy."

Hudson always had a unique relationship with Olivia. Whenever he speaks her name, it's with the type of disdain that can come only from a sibling relationship. Not someone you actually dislike, but someone who rubs you the wrong way. Like Meredith Grey said to Amelia, *I don't totally like you. But I don't have to because you're family. I love you.*

"She went into the family business. I didn't. She went to the alma mater, Yale; I went up north. She majored in econ, I majored in psychology. Nothing I do is right to them. Except you."

His statement catches me in a mid-sip of my rum and Coke. I cough, the bubbles rocketing up my nose, making my eyes water and nose burn.

"Shit," I hiss, fanning my face like it'll stop the carbonation from eating through my cartilage. Okay, sure, it's not doing that, but I'm nothing if not overly dramatic.

Out of the corner of my eye, I see Hudson hand me a napkin, but I swat it away.

"What did 'except you' mean?"

"Exactly what I said." Hudson takes a moment before continuing. "You were the one right choice I made, Kian. The one good choice. I know that. But most importantly, my parents know that. They still talk about the first time they met you, when they came to surprise me and found us both in bed together when we first started dating."

"Oh *God*," I groan. "Why would you *remind* me of that? That's even more of a reason for me to *not* go with you. There's no way they have any positive thoughts about me."

"You're wrong," he says. "Trust me, my parents are weird people. But my mother hasn't stopped talking about you since graduation. She always asks how you're doing."

"Fine."

"Wonders how the job search is going."

"Horribly."

"You did something right." He finishes his drink in three gulps. "And even if the first meeting wasn't ideal, it wasn't all bad. You looked pretty good with that layer of sweat on you and . . ."

A sharp laugh from a table across the room breaks the moment—thank God. A grad student sporting a Boston College shirt that's a size too small, standing too close to a man in an expensive suit. It's a typical interaction at the Patriot, but my eyes linger on it a moment or two longer than they need to because it's a distraction. One that keeps me from looking at Hudson, from leaning into that iron core like a pit in my gut when Hudson said I was his one right choice.

But it doesn't keep me from reading into how I felt.

Felt. Past tense. Which hurts more than I thought it would. No matter how much I prepared myself.

Because you don't break up with someone who's the right choice; that's not what people do. That's not what the rom-coms and magazines and love stories have told us.

"I have a question," I say.

"And I have an answer."

"I'm guessing you didn't tell them we broke up because you were ashamed?" I ask, still not looking directly at him. I can see him nod from the corner of my eyes, thanking the bartender for refilling.

"It makes sense," I quickly add to soften the blow of how direct and invasive my question is. "You said it before, your sister is the golden child. You're the screwup. No offense."

"None taken. Screwups have more fun, anyway." He smirks lop-sidedly.

"And if you think, if you really think I was the 'one good choice you made,' then breaking up with me and tossing me to the side like a lump of molded potatoes—"

"Overly dramatic but okay . . ."

"—would just be more fuel added to the parents' fire."

He nods, opting for silent agreement rather than using his voice. "You always were smarter than me."

"Are," I correct, but when he looks at me, I make sure to smile to show I'm teasing him. This isn't a time to beat him down. Sure, it would be easy. A well-placed zing lodged between the plates of his Upper Echelon armor is all it would take. It would be game, set, match right there.

But who am I kidding? Despite how much I've cursed Hudson and told Divya, in great detail, what I would do to him if I ever saw him again, the truth is I'm here, listening to him, considering helping him.

I down the drink, ignoring the burning sensation in my throat as I get through each gulp. I push away the glass, watching as it almost falls over, but remains flat. I know I'm going to regret asking this, but . . .

"What do you need from me?"

Hudson turns to me quickly, the legs of his stool wobbling pre-cariously, but he keeps his balance. "Seriously?"

"Don't make me ask again; I might change my—"

"One dinner!" he interjects. "That's it. Two hours. You just need to sit there, look handsome, which you always do, and you know, be . . . boyfriend-y."

"Boyfriend-y . . ." The word doesn't sit well on my tongue, like some sharp, lemon hard candy I want to spit out, but at the same time tastes familiar and sweet. "You know that's not a word, right?"

"It's a word right now."

"You can't just make up words."

"Says who? All words are made up."

"All right, yes, but . . ."

"Shakespeare made up words."

"Are you Shakespeare?"

"No, I'm better-looking."

"And Black."

"Who said Shakespeare wasn't Black?"

"History books?"

"Books also say Jesus was white but he's from Bethlehem, not Sweden. I'm not sure we can trust books written by white people to give Black people credit for anything."

"Valid, but you're not nearly as talented or influential as the Bard."

"That's rude."

"But true."

When I imagine Hudson and me back together, when I let my mind go to that hypothetical place, it's never like this. It's some tearful reunion, passionate sex, kissing under the rain, scenes like that. But this? This awkward, stilted back-and-forth? This feeling like we're both magnetic poles of the same direction, trying to tolerate each other, but knowing we belong apart? This isn't the reunion I expected.

I'm not sure if that makes this favor easier, or if it makes me feel stupid for even agreeing to do it.

"I have something for you in return," Hudson quietly says, cutting through my thoughts. He pulls out his Amex Black Card, because of course he has a Black Card, and hands it to the bartender. "For helping me with this."

"If you tell me you're going to give me a month's supply of Rivers & Valleys, I'm going to have to pass, but thanks."

"You know me better than that," he scoffs, pulling out his phone. A few clicks later he slides it over to me and points. "You know who that is?"

I don't have to look for more than a fraction of a second. "Randall Clements, CEO of Spotlight."

"And a close family friend. Dated Olivia for a few months at University of Michigan. Went to prep school a few years ahead of me, but we were decently close despite that."

"Because rich people keep within their own silos and never let in anyone who doesn't fit their ideals of success?"

"Pretty much. Plus, I think he wants to do some partnership with my parents in the future."

"Go back to the part about him being a close family friend?"

"Right. Well, you help me with this, Kian Andrews, and I'll put in a good word. An actual good word. The type of good word that gets people fellowships and . . ."

"Completely changes a person's life forever."

This is it. The moment I've been waiting for. The big break. These are the things successful people talk about during award speeches or interviews. And all I need to do is have one dinner with Hudson's family?

"You'd do that for me?"

He nods. "A trade, if you will. You help me, I help you. We got a deal?"

Before I can answer, I hear my name yelled.

"Kian!" Divya shouts, loud enough to overcome the multiple parties at the Patriot and the soccer game on TV. "Kian, get your cute ass over here and stay away from Southern men with square jawlines!"

"I think . . ." Hudson starts.

"Mhm." I stand up, just in time to watch Hudson sign the

check—a bill for thirty-five dollars receives a twenty-dollar tip. I glance at the receipt: seltzer water. I knew it. "It's a deal."

"I was hoping you'd say that," Hudson admits with a smirk that's not as wide as before, but makes his dimples show, and my breath hitches. They're a rare sight, those dimples, like a comet or the green burst of light right as the sun sets. I can count on one hand the times I've seen them. It's a real, honest-to-God, Rivers Grin.

But more importantly, I know it's a dangerous smile.

Quickly, almost fast enough for the stool to topple with me, I stand up and step three paces back. Distance from Hudson has, and always will be, the best remedy for being trapped in his cyclone of handsomeness.

"I'm going to go back to my table before I sic Divya on you, and you know she still wants to beat your ass," I say hurriedly. "Text me where you need me to be, and when, and I'll be there. Tomorrow, right?"

He nods in response and opens his mouth to say something. Instead, he grabs one of the small napkins they place drinks on, moves close to me, and slowly wipes the corner of my mouth. He shows me the napkin, stained dark with specks of Coke.

"Better," he whispers in that quiet, husky voice he does. I've never been sure what makes him use that voice. What's the secret code that triggers that sound? That low, almost gravelly depth that makes my spine shiver.

But I know what it does to me. I know from experience, multiple trials, experiments, and case-control studies that prove the hypothesis over and over.

And I don't need it proven again.

"You know this is a bad idea, right?" I ask.

He winks. "The best ideas in the world are, darling. See you tomorrow."

Before I can do something stupid and ruin the moment, I turn around, walk to my table, and sit down, never looking at him. Before Divya can interrogate me, I grab her drink and throw it back . . . instantly regretting putting whatever concoction that was in my mouth. It's like I can feel my brain cells dying.

Which I'm not sure is that bad a thing.

FIVE

BUZZ. BUZZ. BUZZ.

Drinking last night was absolutely the worst choice I could have made. The sharp pounding in my frontal lobe, like a railroad spike drilling in with each pulse, pulls me out of my restless slumber. The sun is bright outside, streaking through the piss-poor excuse for blinds I have in the studio apartment I can barely afford.

"Jesus," I mutter, sitting up. My whole body feels like lead. How much did I fucking drink last night?

Oh. Yeah. That's right—a lot. I lost count after the seventh shot.

Buzz. Buzz. Buzz.

So, it wasn't a dream. I squint, scratching at my chest, and stand. It takes me a few moments to get my bearings. I pat wildly on my bed, using the few senses that have revved to life to find my phone.

Rolling onto my back, I squint, reading it.

HUDSON RIVERS: You awake?

I hate that. It sounds like a booty call text, except it's ten a.m.

I guess you can still have a booty call at ten a.m., sure, but it sounds so much dirtier when you say that.

HUDSON RIVERS: Get dressed. You have 5 minutes.

"Five minutes for what?"

It takes me half a moment to realize, no, Hudson *cannot* hear me talking to myself.

I type my answer back and barely have time to close my eyes before my phone vibrates again.

HUDSON RIVERS: 4 minutes.

Attached is a photo of an Uber, a black line about six blocks away, and the ending destination my apartment. It takes me a second to put two and two together. Hudson is sending an Uber to my place, an Uber he expects me to get into.

"Shit."

What am I going to wear?

————— · —————

TWENTY MINUTES LATER I'm dressed in a light blue button-down that my mother *swears* complements my dark skin perfectly, a pair of matching sky blue shorts and sneakers, thanking Emma for the ride (filled with early 2000s bops) and checking my phone.

"This can't be right."

McLawrens is probably one of the fanciest clothing stores in all of Boston—maybe the whole United States. It's like . . . Gucci mixed with Hugo Boss and a touch of Joseph Abboud. When my parents came to visit a year ago, before graduation, they thought about getting me a custom-tailored dress shirt for interviews (because what working professional who wants to be the Beyoncé of the journalism world doesn't need a fitted dress shirt?).

Turns out just one custom-made shirt easily costs over six hundred dollars.

And that's the story of how I ended up with a two-hundred-dollar Amazon gift card instead.

Just being in the same area as McLawrens makes my skin itch, like a demon stepping too close to a church. There's something so . . . uncomfortable about being in places you feel you don't belong. And it's not that I don't belong. I know my worth. It's that people like me, middle-class people, are looked down upon in places like this. Fold in the fact I'm a Black man and . . . let's just say this isn't the type of place I'd want to go in alone. And Hudson knows that. We've *talked* about it before.

HUDSON RIVERS: Come on inside—they're expecting you.

"This is a hundred percent where he's going to kill me," I mutter, walking across the street. This is just like *Ready or Not*. I'm going to walk in, them sitting around a table, and then there will be some horrific plot twist a third of the way through the movie about how I'm the main course, or how they've made some pact with Satan himself and need to chase me around the restaurant or some shit like that.

But when I enter the boutique clothing store, it's nothing like I imagined. Instead, and maybe this makes it even weirder, there's no one else inside. Just a woman chatting with Hudson.

I'm not sure if that makes me feel worse or better.

The woman, with a perfectly tied bun and sharp Nordic features, gestures to me; Hudson's gaze follows suit. He smiles, waving me over, but comes to me instead of waiting for me to go to him.

"Hey, you." He beams. "Glad you made it. Come over here, I want you to meet someone." Hudson, wearing a nicely fitted light blue polo and a pair of stylish jeans with, of course, boots, gestures to the woman. "Isabella, Kian. Kian, Isabella."

"Hi, nice to meet—"

"This is him?"

Before Hudson can answer, she walks around me in a circle, like a tiger hunting her prey. The movements are slow, the room filled with the clicking of her heels on the marble floor.

It feels like even breathing is the wrong thing to do while Isabella looks me up and down. I don't move, watching as she circles three times before standing in front of us.

"I can work with this," she says, gesturing down the hall to a curtain directly in front of us. "Barely."

"*Barely?*"

"Wait there."

Isabella walks off, disappearing behind curtains to the right. When I turn back to look at Hudson, he's already halfway toward where we've been ordered to wait.

"You might want to listen to her. She's not the type to be messed with."

The room, where we've been told to wait, is larger than my studio. A huge, well-lit circular room, with over five full mirrors, three plush stools in the center, a small table with different chilled fruit waters, and a TV. Without hesitation, Hudson sits on one of the stools. I can't help but stand in awe.

"I don't belong here," I mutter. Hudson glances up from his phone, brow quirked.

"Oh, shut up," he teases and taps the seat next to him. "You belong here as much as anyone else. That's the thing about rich establishments, they try to make you feel like you don't belong, which creates an air of the haves and the have-nots. Remember the scenes in *Pretty Woman* and *Selena*? Embody those badass women and take ownership of your destiny."

"I don't think wearing expensive clothes is my destiny."

He waves his hand. "Look the part, embrace the part, blah blah, come on. Isabella's going to bring you some awesome clothes; you're going to look hot as fuck—no, hotter than fuck, because you always look hot as fuck."

"But I don't need new clothes," I argue. "I'm comfortable in what I have."

"And I like what you wear, trust me, I do. But my parents?" He glances up. "This is all about impressing them enough that they remember why they like you and me together, darling."

"Don't call me that."

"Gotta get used to saying it again, so it sounds natural. You should try it too."

I arch my brow, but he ignores my hesitance.

"Anyway, McLawrens is a good, safe choice. Always. So, relax, enjoy the clothes. And this is on me—go wild."

Relaxing with Hudson while I try to tame a killer hangover doesn't seem like my exact idea of fun, but you know what, I'm going to go with it.

I walk over to the table, pour myself a glass of what looks like raspberry-infused water and take a sip, and survey the room. Hudson's returned to his phone, typing away, completely comfortable, like he belongs.

Meanwhile I feel like Cady Heron did when she went to the Halloween party dressed as something actually scary instead of a seductive bunny.

A few moments later, Isabella walks back in, three different out-fits on each arm. She places one set on a rack close to Hudson and the second set closer to me. "Let me know if these suit you."

"I'm sure they are great," Hudson says without looking up from his phone.

Isabella narrows her eyes and struts over. Before Hudson can look up, she snatches the phone from him, holding it out of reach. And out of reach for Isabella truly means out of reach. I don't think I've ever seen a woman as tall as her.

"When you talk to me, or any service worker, you look at them," she scolds.

Hudson's mouth is slack, and I look down, biting my bottom lip, to avoid him seeing my smirk. I don't know much about Isabella, but I know she's not a woman who takes shit from anyone—their socioeconomic status be damned. I glance up in time to see Hudson open and close his mouth.

"Thank you, Isabella."

"Better." She hands the phone back and turns to me, rolling her eyes. "How do you put up with him? Is he this snappy at home?"

"It's a real struggle, to be honest."

"You need to train him better."

"Do you have any tips? I'm looking for some."

"Actually . . ."

"Okay, okay," Hudson says, holding his hands up. "Enough with the *let's gang up on Hudson* game."

"But it's my favorite game." I smirk.

Isabella smiles too, glancing at Hudson. "I like him."

"I like him too," Hudson adds. "Now, please. Can we have some privacy?"

Isabella nods and directs her gaze at me. "If he gives you any problems . . ."

"I'll find you."

She nods and exits, leaving Hudson to glare—no, not glare—
pout at me.

"Fix your face. It might get stuck like that."

The items Isabella brought me are . . . the highest-quality clothes
I've ever seen. They're simple in style and part of a set: a black jacket
with a white shirt and a pair of slacks. The whole outfit is brought
together by a red thread on the jacket's lapels, the hemline of the
pants, and the collar of the shirt. On the bottom of the right pant
leg and on the breast pocket of the jacket is a stamped M+L—
McLawrens's symbol. The clothes feel different, too. Softer, that's
the right word, and I can't help but wonder if this is how all rich
people's clothes feel.

While taking the jacket off the hanger to examine the stitching,
which is barely visible, the tag reveals itself from its hiding place
inside the pocket.

I shouldn't look, I think. *Nothing good is going to come from looking
at the tag, Kian. You're going to regret it. You know you are. You're . . .*

And of course, I regret it. I very, very, very much regret it.

$2,500.

Twenty-five-fucking-hundred-dollars?! And that's *just* for the
jacket?

I quickly check the shirt and the pants: $1,800 and $2,100, re-
spectively. Almost $6,500 for a set of clothes?

"Um, Hudson," I whisper, my voice coming out hoarse and
crackly.

"Hudson!" I say louder, turning around.

I expect to see Hudson raising his clothes up, comparing them.
That's what rich people do, right? Compare the thread count and
that shit. What is the difference between eight hundred and nine
hundred thread count anyway? Can you really notice the difference?

Your wallet can, I'm sure.

But I come face-to-face with Hudson, his clothes strewn across the floor, standing in nothing but a pair of tight black short-cut boxer briefs—still texting.

"Hm?" he asks, not looking up.

Words. That's what's supposed to come out of my mouth. Words, letters, sounds. But nothing forms. My eyes are too busy taking in every inch, every muscle, every *groove* of Hudson. The flex of his biceps, the strength of his thighs, the length of his legs, the way his abs flex naturally. The perfect sculpting of his chest.

My eyes want to go lower, to focus on the perkiness of his ass, the way his cock fills out his underwear. Was he always that big? Did I forget?

"What is it, K?"

I don't even correct him this time. I'm not sure I could if I wanted to. My body's going into overdrive and focusing all blood and energy on vital functions. Breathing. Heartbeat. Erection.

Wait. What. Shit. *Shit. SHIT!*

This is not the time to get one of those. And of course, of fucking course, Hudson notices. His eyes turn downward, adding more insult to injury by how casually he looks at the swelling in my pants.

And to make it even *worse*, he grins—he has the goddamn audacity to grin. No, not grin—SMIRK!

"Well, hello there."

"Fuck you!" I yell, grabbing my clothes and walking—briskly—past him into the changing room. I draw the curtain firmly and do my best to ignore Hudson's laughter.

TWO HOURS, FOUR outfits, and several cups of fruit-infused water later, we're done.

I have two bags in hand, shoes, socks, a tie included. According to Isabella and Hudson, these clothes are versatile. Three outfits when you mix and match.

"You know we spent several thousand dollars, right?"

"*I* spent several thousand dollars," he reminds me, checking his bags. "Forty thousand, if we're being accurate. But it's worth it."

"Really?"

"My parents will think it is. I used their card anyway."

"Let me guess, your emergency card?"

He shrugs and winks. "This is firmly an emergency. But no. Trust-fund card. Dad might call about the amount, but, well, did you see your fashion before we walked in here?"

"You said you liked my fashion!"

"And I still do! But, *again*, we're playing in the big leagues now. We need to sell this. And that means getting my parents' approval." He shakes the bags for emphasis. "This will get their approval."

"You think your parents care that much?"

"I know they do." He doesn't miss a beat, and there's no hesitation in his voice. "My parents screamed at me when I told them I wanted to major in psychology. They didn't talk to me for a month. They probably thought if they cut me off, I'd change my mind. Trust me. We need my parents to like you."

"Hm."

I start to walk toward the door when Hudson gently grabs my wrist, forcing me to turn to him. "What does *hm* mean?"

I hesitate, looking for the right words, glancing up at the ceiling like they might be written in the plaster. "There are a lot of people who struggle with supportive parents . . ."

"My parents are supportive," he corrects me, responding quickly and defensively. "They accepted me as gay, without question. They funded my education. They never said no."

"They just never give you their blessing if they don't agree and dictate your love life and every other aspect."

That's not what he wants to hear, I know. It's not what he needs to hear, either. But I'm not his boyfriend anymore. It's not my job to be blindly supportive. No matter how much he wants me to be.

"What does that mean?"

"It wasn't hard to understand. Being supportive doesn't just mean not being outwardly against something. It means being supportive—point-blank."

"Did you ever think that . . ." Hudson sighs and pinches the bridge of his nose. He counts backward silently before speaking again. "Look, you're doing me a favor, and I appreciate that, so I'm going to ignore you coming for my parents."

"I didn't—"

He holds his hand up, silencing me. "So, we're going to move on. We have different opinions on how relationships between parents and kids should go."

"Lord knows we've had that talk multiple times."

"Then you should know nothing is going to change."

A moment passes.

"But that's not why I'm here," he adds.

"Nope, you're here to ask me to help clean up a lie you started, just as long as I'm silent and supporting you along the way."

The words come out dripping with poison before I can take them back and filter them. Anger, hurt, and frustration shoot out, burning through Hudson's light brown skin. I know it's wrong, I know it's not that simple, but I don't care. I'm sure Hudson could diagnose my tendency to bottle up emotions with some clinical definition, if asked.

He opens his mouth and closes it, repeating the process three times before any words come out. "You know what? I don't need to put up with this."

"I was thinking the same thing."

He pulls back his hand, yanks out his phone, and presses the screen quickly, probably calling an Uber. "I'm starting to think this was a bad idea."

"Glad you finally understand what I said two days ago."

"You can forget the dinner," he spits out. "I'll make up some excuse why you can't make it."

"Maybe this would be a good time to, you know, come clean with your parents? I dunno, say we broke up."

"Yeah, sounds good."

I push the bags toward him. It's only the right thing to do. But Hudson pushes the bags back at me.

"Keep them. Consider it payment."

"Payment?" I repeat. "Like I'm some sort of . . ."

"If the shoe fits," he replies coldly and brushes past me. "Sorry I wasted your time. Nice to catch up with you, K."

"For the third time it's . . ."

Before I can say anything, he walks out, and his Uber pulls up. He doesn't even look back as he slides inside, and ten seconds later, he's gone.

I stand there in the middle of McLawrens, with my half of the purchase, twenty thousand dollars' worth of clothes, wondering how the conversation went so downhill in the past sixty seconds. Even with the large lobby, the oxygen feels too sparse, too thin, and coupled with the gushing of blood in my ears, everything's dizzying. Jamal would call this a panic attack, but there's no reason I should be having a panic attack now, right?

Jamal. That's who I need right now. I whip out my phone, texting without looking.

KIAN ANDREWS: SOS

By the time I flag down a taxi and tell him to take me home, Jamal texts back.

JAMAL ANDREWS: Starbucks, 20 minutes. Coffee on me, because I know your lightweight ass is hungover.

SIX

JAMAL IS WAITING for me at the Starbucks closest to my house twenty minutes later. He doesn't notice when I walk in at first, but other people do. When you're carrying bags from the most expensive clothing store in the city, you attract attention. I set the bags in the chair diagonally across from him, go to the counter, and get a coffee. Still he doesn't look up.

"Hey." I sit down across from him with my plain black coffee. It's absolutely awful and bitter, but it keeps the sharpness of a hangover at bay.

He nods at me, focused on his phone while sipping his iced drink of some sort.

"You already ordered? I could have gotten that for you."

That's my job, right? I'm the older brother. I should be the one paying for him. It's bad enough I'm reaching out to him for advice, so the least I could do is pay for the drink. This relationship is supposed to be reversed.

But Jamal is the more put-together one. He's the one with suitors and HR headhunters already chomping at the bit to take his hand

and waltz away into the sunset. He's the one at Harvard—with a full ride, mind you. For all intents and purposes, Jamal is the older brother here. Dressed in a button-down that fits perfectly and slacks that accent the subtle tones of his shirt, both of which are a perfect shade for his dark brown skin, maturity in our family seems to have skipped a sibling.

"It's cool; I was nearby." He puts down the phone. Before the screen goes dark, I see a PDF with the Harvard logo on it.

"What class?"

"Terror and Terrorism in Global History."

I take a sip. The coffee is hotter than I'd like, and I hiss in response, cursing at the drink as if it's sentient and to blame for the burn on my tongue. Jamal arches his brow, but I ignore him. I don't need his judgment right now. In fact, I'm not even sure why I called him.

Oh right, because, according to our shared calendar, Divya is in some big meeting right now with a client.

And also, deep down, there's nowhere better than going home when you feel wounded—and since North Carolina is ten-plus hours away, Jamal will have to do.

"That's outside of your major, right? You're majoring in business, I thought?"

"Business with a focus on international finances and econ, but I have a minor in history," he clarifies. "This fills two requirements."

"Ah, gen eds. I hated those." I latch onto that like a child latching onto their mother's leg. Despite both being Black and gay in Boston, there is little that Jamal and I can relate on, so whenever our mutual like, or dislike, for something crosses paths, I run it into the ground. Perhaps to my detriment.

"They don't call them 'gen eds' at Harvard . . ."

Of course they don't.

He takes a deep breath. We share that mannerism. Closing our eyes and breathing out slowly before breathing in deeply to reset.

"Why did you send me an SOS? Is Mom okay?"

"Yeah, last I checked she's fine."

He waits for me to answer the first question, looking at me over the rim of his cup. It's a stalemate between the two of us and a petty one at that, but I don't have the room to be petty. I'm the one who asked him for help. He's the one who answered. For all intents and purposes, Jamal is being the good brother. Just because he doesn't always look up to me, or isn't always at my heels like some younger siblings are with their older siblings, doesn't make our relationship any less real. It's just . . . not cinematic.

And, most importantly, if push comes to shove, I'm sure I can rely on him to be in my corner—like now—but I don't expect that. Because, frankly? I'd rather be pushing and shoving him down a flight of stairs than having to rely on him for anything.

But beggars can't be choosers, and right now, I need someone to gut check against.

He glances at the bags, and his brown eyes linger for a moment or two longer than they need to. "And when did you get the money for *those*?"

"That's the reason I called, actually."

He doesn't hesitate putting two and two together. "Hudson."

"Mhm." A moment passes, but not long enough for him to cast judgment. "I need your advice."

Essentially: asking my younger, more successful brother for help is a fate worse than death and probably a violation of at least seventeen different doctrines in the Geneva Convention. Archaic thinking? Sure. Stupid? Probably. But I'm a Taurus. We're known to be stubborn.

"Well, this is rare," Jamal says, surprise dripping from his voice.

It borders on condescension without crossing into that forbidden territory.

Good, I think. *For both of our sakes.*

Jamal takes a long sip of his drink, one of those obnoxious ones that cause bubbles to gurgle from the cup. I cringe. If Mom saw him do it . . . she would get the switch from the elm tree out back. I shudder at the memory, as if the swipes, which seemed like the worst punishment a seven-year-old could experience, were still fresh.

"Twice as hard," she always used to say. "You and your brother have to work twice as hard to get just as far as your white friends. You can't afford the same mistakes. You can't make the same follies. The world doesn't allow Black boys the same amount of leeway it allows everyone else."

Maybe that's why we're both how we are. Jamal's successful—but because he has to be. There's no choice for him. He's like a shark: If he stops thriving, what else would he do?

Then there's me. I don't even know what the metric of success is. How do I quantify it? Is it by how much money I make? Because right now, I'm barely making anything. Is it by the title I hold? Is ex-intern of one of the top digital news outlets a respectable title? I know the answer to that.

When will I feel like I'm good?

When will I be able to breathe freely?

Not today. Maybe tomorrow.

I wonder if Hudson got the same talk. He's Black, so he should have, but he's also rich. Sure, wealth isn't a shield when you're walking down the street, but wealth does help. It always helps.

But instead of worrying about something that I could write ten think pieces about easily, I force a deep breath and explain it all to Jamal. I don't stop to take another breath until I'm done, afraid that if I do, I won't find the courage to keep going. I tell him about Hudson and me—reiterating facts about our relationship and breakup he already knows. I bore him with the meeting between the two of us earlier this week and about the meeting today.

And most importantly, about what I said to him. The sharpness in my voice. The way I sliced at him and shot across the bow at his family. I don't leave out anything because if I want his honest-to-God opinion, I can't afford it. I can't lie.

"And that's why I'm here," I say fifteen minutes later. "To ask you . . . I dunno, did I go too far?"

Jamal finished his drink ten minutes ago and is leaning back in his chair, arms crossed over his chest. His phone has lit up half a dozen times since we started talking—two texts, a few news alerts, and some e-mails from his Harvard account—but he never even looked away from me toward them. For the first time in a very long time, we actually feel like brothers who have each other's backs.

"Do you want my honest advice?"

"No point if you're not goi—"

"You fucked up, and you're an idiot."

"Well, why don't you say how you really feel?"

He doesn't hesitate or mince words, and his answer feels like a punch to my gut. A strong enough force that I cough up my coffee. I look up, study his face: Maybe there's some subtext I'm missing. But there's nothing—only a stoicism that drips cold honesty.

"You went after the man's family, K."

"I didn't technically go after his family," I argue. "Everything I said was right."

"So, you're technically right. Good for you. Right or not, people aren't logical when their family is involved. You know that. And it's even worse because you know it's a sore subject. You dug your nails into a spot of exposed flesh, a part he only exposed to you *because* you and he have a connection. You took advantage of his vulnerability."

"You're reading into it too much," I defend. "Aren't you a business major? Isn't business all about exploiting your opponent's weakness?"

"Is he the opponent in this discussion?"

I open my mouth to speak, but no words come out. Jamal takes advantage of the opening. "To put it into perspective: What would you do if someone said Mom doesn't support you?"

"Rip his head off right then and there."

There's no hesitation in my voice, and I regret it. Not because what I'm proposing is a crime, but because it validates everything Jamal is arguing. And that's just another notch in his post to prove he's smarter than me.

I really need to go back to therapy.

"Fuck." I groan, slamming my head against the distressed wood of the table. The impact hurts, sending a sharp ripple of pain down my spine, but I ignore it. I deserve to sit in this pain.

"Not your finest moment."

"Obviously."

I think there's a part of me that knew what Jamal was going to say but was hoping for him to be my brother, a ride-or-die friend like Divya. But if I wanted that, I would have gone to her instead. I could have told her I punched Hudson in the face, and he was bleeding on the floor, and she would come up with some plausible alibi—no questions asked.

But I didn't go to her. I went to my incredibly logical, stubborn, Virgo of a brother—who has never done anything wrong or emotion-driven in his whole life. I went to someone who will give me a logical and empirical answer. What did I expect?

I sit back up, rubbing at the warm spot on my forehead.

"I'm going to need to apologize to him, aren't I?"

Jamal shrugs, finally looking at his phone. "Not necessarily."

"What would you do?"

His finger pauses mid-swipe. He glances up at me and narrows his brown eyes, silently asking, *Is this a trap?*

"I want to know," I add. "Thinking with my emotions—"

"Is what got you into this mess and got you making a fool of yourself in front of the boy who broke your heart?"

"That wasn't what I was going to say."

"But it's what you needed to hear." A moment passes as he types a text with one finger. He places his phone on the table, screen side down. "Look. You fucked up. You did what you always do—go overboard with your words."

"I don't *always* do that."

Jamal arches his brow. "Should I bring up the tenth-grade incident with Matthew Blake?"

"Okay, he was giving me gay vibes! *Everyone* in the school thought he was gay!"

"And yet, you put ten pages' worth of original sonnets in his locker, because that's what a normal person does."

I open my mouth to reply with logical, thought-out, and reasonable facts, but Jamal cuts me off.

"My point is: You are a lot. Just . . . a lot with your words. Sometimes they get you in trouble. Sometimes they help you. But we both know what I'm going to say."

I do. "Actions speak louder than words."

"Actions speak louder than words," Jamal says at the same time. "Is there some action you can do that'll show him you're actually sorry?"

Of course there is. I know exactly what that is.

I just don't want to do it.

SEVEN

"**YOU KNOW, I** used to think you were a pretty smart guy, but now? I've come to the conclusion you're stupid as shit."

"Ouch?"

Gotta give it to Divya, she doesn't cut corners when attacking someone's weak spot. But, considering she's the one who volunteered to drive me to the restaurant, without me having to ask, I'm going to let her have this one.

"No." She shakes her head. "No 'ouch.' Don't make me feel bad. I'm your best friend; that means I'm allowed to be offensive as hell to you without you having an issue with it."

"Is that what that means?"

She hits me hard in the arm, giving me dead arm, never looking over at me, no matter how much I hiss.

"That's for being a smart-ass. And me being mean shows I love you. It's also the only way to shake some sense into you. That's part of Best Friend Code."

"What article is that?" I reply teasingly. "Can you—"

The narrowing of her eyes and the way her full lips disappear into a line tell me this isn't the time to joke around. Submissively, I turn away and duck my head.

"Better," she scolds, a beat passing. "Are you *sure* about this?"

"Pretty sure."

"That's . . . not good enough for me to feel comfortable letting you out of this car."

"So, what are you going to do? Lock the doors and . . ."

Instantly, the automatic locks click with a heavy metallic thump. The windows of her Prius roll up, and the car turns still.

"Bitch, try me."

"Oh, for fuck's sake, Divya."

"*Oh, for fuck's sake, Divya,*" she mimics. "No. Not this time. You're the one making the stupid choice, Kian. You're going to get your heart broken, *again*. And not by just any boy; HUDSON MOTHERFUCKING RIVERS."

She says his name with emphasis, like punctuating it will poke through some membrane in my thick skull that separates the logic center of my brain from my emotional one. Maybe in some alternate reality, there's a version of me who, in this exact moment, listens to Divya, drives home, and goes on Grindr for a good, hot lay.

But that's not me. That's never been me. I met Hudson at a house party and thought my life was reenacting the "Thousand Miles" music video by Vanessa Carlton. I'm a romantic at heart, she knows that. And every romantic has to see their story to the end. Or else you end up in a never-ending loop of self-depreciation, self-sabotage. And I'm sure another "self-" word I can't think of.

And what's more romantic than helping your ex who obviously has no more feelings for you? Heathcliff and Mr. Darcy *wish* they were me.

We sit in silence, the soft, muffled sounds of Boston summer in the early evening the only music that fills the space. I wait, expecting her to continue her rant about my poor choices, but nothing follows. And that's what's scary.

Finally, I ask, "Are you angry with me?"

She opens her mouth, closes it, and opens it again. "Angry isn't the right word."

"Please don't say disappointed."

"What am I, your mother?" She doesn't give me a chance to respond to her rhetorical question. "I just don't like seeing you hurt."

"I'm not—"

"And before you lie to me and say you're not, I know you. And I know Hudson. I know how much he means to you. If you could honestly tell me you were completely, one hundred percent over him, then I'd tell you to go forth! But you're not."

"I am," I reply stubbornly.

"Don't lie to me. You know I can tell when you're lying, right?"

"I'm not lying! I'm over him! He's just a guy with a good jawline! Like every other gay boy who can afford a keto diet and an Equinox membership."

Divya turns in her seat, her black pantsuit moving smoothly against the upholstery of the car, all while fluidly pulling her long black hair into a ponytail, as if on autopilot. She narrows her wing-tipped cat eyes, searching my soul for any fraction of weakness she can exploit. I've sat in on her moot court exercises, and she does the same thing to witnesses. There's something compelling about the way she stares into your soul. Something . . . truly terrifying.

"Prove it," she says finally, pulling out her phone.

"I'm sorry, what?"

A few clicks later she hands the phone to me. A tall man in a polo with black hair, leaning more toward what gays would call "having a swimmer's build" than Hudson's muscular body, smiles back at me. He looks older than me, solidly in his early thirties, maybe a little older, but wears it well—GOD, I need to stop thinking of thirties as old.

Anyway.

There's a certain put-together vibe about him. But he doesn't look like a father, just like someone who is comfortable with his life and worked hard to get there. Someone who has their credit in place, their future on track, and knows how to put a fitted sheet on a bed right the first time.

So, the complete opposite of me.

"He's handsome." A diplomatic and honest choice of words. "Who is he?"

"Guy I know from a case. Name's Wallace. He's a lawyer."

"I guessed as much."

"The lawyer or the gay part?"

"What do you think?"

"Never mind what I think. Most importantly: He's single."

"Good for him. I hope . . ." Wait. "You're joking."

"You said you're over Hudson," she insists. "And you just said he's handsome!"

"Yeah, because he is! That doesn't mean I want to screw him. Not every gay guy wants to screw every other handsome gay guy. And besides, how old is he?"

"Thirty-one, and before you say it, that's not that old. He's going to be successful."

"That's eight years older than me."

"Again, an investment. Still not that old and I said *nothing* about screwing anyone . . . but . . ." Divya replies with a singsong voice, "You could use a good dicking. And so could he. See! Equal opportunity love. The best kind of love!"

"DIVYA!"

"Plus, he's seasoned, which means he is obviously a good lover."

"That doesn't mean that at all."

"I have a good source that says he is. And don't ask me who. Attorney-client privilege applies to secondhand booty-call downloads."

I push any thoughts I have about Wallace, and how out of line Divya is, to the back of my brain. Instead I focus on what I'm really doing here. How can helping Hudson make up with his family be the logical decision? Divya's right, I'm not over him, no matter how many times I tell myself I am. At best, I'm going to feel like a doormat. At worst? I'm going back to square one in my recovery plan.

"Hey," Divya says softly, her right hand squeezing my left. "If this is really what you want to do, I support you and I'll be here for you if you need me. You know that, right?"

I nod. She's just looking out for me, I know that. Divya always has my best intentions at heart. Reassuringly, I squeeze her hand back. "Don't you have a shift at the Jaunt?"

"I can skip it; you know Teddy loves me there."

"Teddy wants to sleep with you," I say, correcting her. "Doesn't mean he loves you."

She shrugs. "When it comes to getting shifts changed, it's the same thing. Offer still stands."

Yes, I want to say. *Come with me, be my right-hand woman. Protect me from self-sabotage.* I can feel the words in my throat, just waiting for the right time to pounce.

Instead, I shake my head and force the passenger door open. "I'm good. Thanks, D. Really."

"Anytime." We lean over and kiss each other's cheeks before I slip out of the car.

"Update me?" she asks, holding up her phone. She doesn't wait for an answer and instead speeds down the street, barely making the light before it turns red.

———— · ————

POSEIDON—NOT THE 2006 cult classic starring our queen Ms. Fergalicious Definition—is the type of restaurant people would sell their firstborn child to get a seat at.

Established only four years ago and already part of the 133—the number of restaurants in the world with three Michelin Stars—the wait-list is nearly seven months long, and even then the tables are assigned by lottery. Just standing outside the large periwinkle colonnades makes me feel like Stefan in *The Vampire Diaries* trying to enter Elena's house for the first time.

Halt, plebeian, the chef would say. *Thou poor person cannot enter here! Be gone!*

Wanda Maximoff has Chaos Magic to protect her from literally anything, but I have something more powerful: wealthy friends and a wealthy suit.

I have to give it to Hudson: He knows how to pick an outfit. After talking with Jamal, I ran home, took a shower, trimmed my hair as much as I could, and slipped on the suit Hudson bought me. The plum color with the starkly contrasting light purple shirt with black stripes is a little bold for my taste, but I'm not complaining. It feels odd on my skin, like a second layer that doesn't fit quite right when, in fact, it's the opposite. The fit is perfect, tapers in all the right ways and makes my greatest *ass*et look even better.

Did he do that on purpose? Some personal eye candy to get him through this hellish experience? *I went to dinner with my ex and all I got out of it was a perfect shot of his ass?*

"You've got this," I lie to myself.

I so don't got this.

My phone reads 7:16 p.m. A quarter past the time I was sup-posed to meet them. Hudson has probably already come up with some fancy excuse about how I'm stuck at work or whatever. I can't help but think, in this universe of his where we're still dating, what do I do for a living? What am I like? What do his parents think of me? The first meeting was . . . not how I'd want to meet anyone's parents. No, not the time they walked in on us fucking. That doesn't count. Graduation. That, to me, is the start of my story with Diana and Isaac Rivers.

I know, using my mom as an example, if my boyfriend showed up late to dinner, she would hate him. So, it's reasonable to think they hate me too. Maybe that'll make this whole interaction easier.

Or ten times worse. Rich people don't operate in the same realm as us normal people.

But the truth is, the only way to find out is to swallow my pride and get this over with. Three hours from now, at max, this will be over. I'll have cleared my conscience by making up with Hudson. I'll get an introduction to Randall Clements. I'll get the job of my dreams and this will all be a distant memory. People have done worse things for their career.

I mean, Nicolas Cage did *Face/Off*, for God's sake. I can do this.

I push through the revolving door of Poseidon, regaining my bal-ance after the wall of dizziness that slams right into me the moment I enter. The noise in the establishment Mickey Mouses me, and the smells make my eyes water, like when I enter a hospital. Maybe it's my nerves talking, some psychological fight-or-flight response to re-mind me this is absolutely, totally, completely a bad idea. But still, I push through and force a smile when I reach the hostess.

"Name," she says, not asks, before I can speak. There's a faint British accent in her voice, and I wonder what her story is. Very . . . Emily Charlton realness.

"Kian, Kian Andrews."

Her sharp eyes scan the screen for a beat. "I don't have a reservation for a Kian Andrews."

"Sorry, reservation would be under Rivers."

Her lips push into a thin line, making her cheeks taut. I know, *Ambrosia*, I'm annoyed with me, too. Do us both a favor and release me from this mortal coil.

"You're here with the Rivers party?"

"That's what I said, yeah."

"Diana and Isaac Rivers? Party of five?"

"That's me, number five."

I know where this is going, because it's going the same place it's always going. I keep my lips tight and curtly nod.

Ambrosia glances at me by lifting only her eyes and looks back at her iPad. Seconds at a standstill pass before she caves. "Follow me."

With each step through the massive three-floor room, my heart climbs up my esophagus, threatening to escape through my mouth. The space in the restaurant, with its tall ceilings and the way they've shoved easily three hundred big spenders into the room, is dizzying. How much money and opulence is here? I could throw a shrimp and probably hit at least ten people who have a personal relationship with Zuckerberg.

Constantly three steps ahead of me, thanks to her long legs, Ambrosia leads me up the marble staircase two flights and through a row of tables. At the end, with a view of the New England Aquarium that would make the Property Brothers orgasm, there's a circular table with four people sitting and one free chair. No one sees me approaching, and the hum of Poseidon drowns out their voices.

But I can see that Hudson's laughing. More importantly, it's a forced laugh. The differences are subtle, so subtle his parents might not even notice—they don't seem to anyway (or maybe they don't care). But the way the corners of his eyes don't crinkle, or how he can continue drinking his sparkling water while chuckling when I know for a fact that's a BAD combination, tells me everything I need to know.

Ambrosia, with her tight black bun and matching dark jumpsuit, stands at the table for a moment, going unnoticed. She seems unfazed, used to being an expensive figure in an expensive restaurant to be admired, not considered. That's what people pay for, right? Not just the $220 entrées, or the most elusive bottles of wine, but the ambiance this sort of place gives off, like a frat boy's Axe body spray, and the people.

She waits a moment before clearing her throat, not once, but twice. A man with neatly trimmed salt-and-pepper hair, but not the age to match, looks up.

"Excuse me, Mr. and Mrs. Rivers, but your gu—"

"Kian?"

His deep voice cuts through everything. The sound in the room disappears, and it's like I'm back in middle school, forgetting my lines as Puck in our production of *A Midsummer Night's Dream*. I stand there, dumbfounded.

Hudson's family, his parents and a woman I remember as Olivia from photos when Insta-stalking him, glance at me. The Riverses' range of expressions go from pure surprise (Hudson) to amusement (Olivia), making pit stops at annoyance (his father) and curiosity (his mother).

I can only imagine what expression my face has: stupid.

"Mr. Andrews claims to be part of your party?" Ambrosia asks.

What the fuck? I think. *Claims?* Like I'd lie to get this far? Is it *that* impossible that I could be at the most expensive restaurant in Boston?

I mean, it is. My bank account barely has two hundred dollars in it. But that's not the point. Dress and act like the life you want, not the life you have.

I've got the "dressed" part covered. The attitude, not so much.

So, to compensate for that, I say the only thing that comes to mind. "What's the matter, never seen a broke college graduate in a suit that could most definitely pay for four months of his rent on the black bespoke market?"

EIGHT

WHAT HAPPENS NEXT is like a trailer for some over-the-top performance at the Charles Playhouse.

Olivia drops her fork.

Ambrosia gasps.

His father clears his throat and grumbles something under his breath I can't make out.

His mother shakes her head.

And I want to reenact the Boston Tea Party and fling myself into the river. Posthaste.

But Hudson? Hudson doesn't do any of that. He stands calmly, flashes a stiff smile at the table, walks hurriedly over to me, and grabs my bicep.

"Come with me," he says lowly.

"Yep."

"*Now.*"

"Coming." It's not like I have a choice. His grip will most certainly leave a bruise. Like that one time we were watching a movie together, saw a woman tie her husband to the bed with his belt, and Hudson got the bright idea to try that with me but made—

Nope, not the time to be thinking about that. At all.

We weave through the customers and into a side hallway. At the end of the hallway, servers work diligently to get the top five percent of society their overly priced meals, hopeful for a tip that'll pay their rent for the month.

Hudson ignores them, like I'm sure so many other people do, finally letting me go. With his legs shoulder-length apart, he crosses his strong arms over his chest.

"What are you doing here," he says, more as a statement than a question.

I have my full answer planned out because, if anything, Hudson is predictable. Always has been and always will be. What I didn't expect was how good he would look in his clothes and how distracting it would be.

His suit is a classic black and white, but the black jacket is nowhere to be seen. Instead, the crisp white McLawrens shirt clings to his strong pecs, open just enough to direct the eyes to his hard-earned physique, muscular but not so much that he looks like a Chippendales alum. His dark pants fit snugly, and his dress shoes fully reinforce the age-old idiom: You can tell a lot from a man's shoe size. And that smell? My God, what is he wearing?

"Well?" he asks, raising his eyebrows in expectation. His voice drips with annoyance, and the pulsing of his neck veins tells me he's doing everything he can to keep his quickly melting cool.

I wonder what it would be like if he put that anger to use in the bedroom.

I take a moment to decide what combination of words will help me in this situation; probably not the words I want to say like *the bathroom is right over there* or *your place isn't far from here.* Being on the receiving end of his steeliness makes me want to fold in on myself and at the same time bend myself over. Or bend *him* over. Or . . .

"I don't have all day, Kian. If you're here to—"

"I'm here because I made a promise," I settle on. Honesty is supposed to be the best medicine, right?

He shifts his weight but keeps his arms crossed. Defensive but there's a crack. I can work with that.

"A promise I said you were exempt from, remember?"

"I remember. But I'm not someone who goes back on their word."

"Is this because I offered to connect you with Randall?"

"It has nothing to do with that."

Another brow arch.

"Okay, maybe it has something to do with that."

"I knew it!"

"Hold up one minute. It's not the *only* reason, though!" But come on, I'd be a fool to pass up a chance like this. It's as if Taylor Swift said she would feature you on her next album and all you had to do was attend a Katy Perry concert where you knew she'd miss every note. Suffer now to succeed in the future.

But Hudson isn't buying it. His jaw is tighter than before, and there's a darkness in his eyes that shows me I'm losing him.

Which brings me back to my original thesis: honesty.

"Look." I sigh. "Yes, I gain something in this agreement. No, I don't want to miss out on a once-in-a-lifetime opportunity because I let my pride get in the way. I also admit I was wrong this morning. I shouldn't have said those things about your parents. I was out of line. I'm sorry."

There it is. Like a car shifting into a lower gear, his body relaxes.

Hudson's shoulders move from tense to a slight hunch, and his nails, once digging into his forearms, now rest against them.

Almost there.

"You came to me because you needed my help. You were willing to show your neck with no shame, and that takes guts." I almost add: *Maybe if you had done a little more of that while we dated, we'd still be together and this wouldn't be a lie*, but right now that seems counterintuitive to my goal of getting him not to hate me. "And sure, I might need you more than you need me, but you said it yourself. Your parents are excited to see me again, and you want to make a good impression, so really, we need each other. So how about we put what happened this morning behind us, go out there, and make your parents proud of you, yeah?"

For good measure, I stick out my hand for a gentleman's agreement. Hudson glances down, then back up, before finally grabbing my hand with his large rough one. But instead of shaking, he brings my knuckles to his mouth, letting his full lips burn a kiss against my ridges, keeping his eyes locked on me the whole time.

"Deal," he says, pulling back and looping my arm with his. At least that's what I think he says, because suddenly hypoxia must be more prevalent in Black gay guys than scholars have evidence for.

"For the record?" he whispers, as we walk back to his parents, a faint smell of cinnamon on his breath. "You were always so good at knowing what to do when I bared my neck to you."

I have a witty comeback planned—somewhere—but before my circuits can fire in the right sequence, we're already back at the table. Hudson gives my arm a squeeze.

Showtime.

NINE

WHEN WE RETURN to the table, at first no one says a word. It isn't until the appetizers, which everyone ordered well before I arrived, are plated that Hudson's mother says anything to me.

"Kian, dear, it's been so long." Mrs. Rivers smiles, reaching over the table to squeeze my hand. Well, to be accurate, she extends her hand and just expects me to take it (which I do, of course). "How *are* you?"

She doesn't say it like a normal person would. It's like she knows something I don't know, emphasizing the *are*.

"I'm good?" I say, though it comes off more as a question. "I mean, I'm doing well."

Not fully the truth, but they don't need to know that.

Hudson's mother smiles warmly. She doesn't want to hear any more, which is fair. Her care about my well-being extends only as far as niceties. I don't mind that; she's honest. I'd hate it if we spent twenty minutes pretending we were friends. Nice and kind are two very different things, and the Riverses know how to balance the two.

The conversation falls into a steady rhythm with Hudson's

mother and father, even Olivia chiming in every now and then. It's clear to me that dinners with the Riverses are mostly used to talk business, and even though this is supposed to be Hudson's dinner, it's no exception.

"I just don't understand why Tim decided to pitch *Homes & Gardens* of all places," Hudson's father scolds, scrolling through messages on his phone. "Does he really not understand our demographic? I told you we shouldn't have hired him, Diana. The Yale graduate was a better choice. Yale is *always* a better choice."

"He is trying something new," Hudson's mother replies in a bored tone. She doesn't seem very interested in the conversation—and I don't blame her. I'm guessing this is a discussion she and her husband have had multiple times before. "We need to expand our brand, not pigeonhole it. And you need to get over your hatred of state schools. *I* went to a state school, and you love me."

"Debatable," Hudson mutters under his breath. No one gives him the attention he's asking for. "And besides, Georgia Tech is barely a state school," Hudson interjects. "That's like saying Hopkins is a B-tier school."

"Or Northeastern is a crappy school?" Olivia asks. "Oops, wait, it is."

"I swear to God, if you . . ."

"Enough," Mr. Rivers says, and both children fall silent. He turns to his wife. "Back to your previous statement. Why should we expand our brand? It's worked for the past hundred and forty years. Our financials are great. Our company is thriving—sans this *Homes & Gardens* debacle. I don't see a reason to change."

People said the same thing about slavery, I say in my head while taking a sip of water. But judging by how Hudson almost commits the first case of self-inflicted waterboarding with his Coke, I might've spoken aloud.

"Sorry, dear?" Mrs. Rivers asks. Her question isn't a *come again, I didn't hear you* question. It's more a *he couldn't have said something that stupid* question.

It takes me a fraction of a second to realize everyone is looking at me. "That wasn't in my head, was it?" I whisper.

"*No, it fucking wasn't!*" Hudson hisses before turning to his mother. "Nothing. He didn't say anything."

"No, I'm pretty sure he said something," Mr. Rivers chimes in, glancing at me with curious eyes. "Right?"

"Mhm."

"Mhm?"

"Yes?"

"Where I'm from you say 'Yes, sir' to your elders and those you're trying to impress. We call those manners."

"Strange, my mom taught me respect is something earned, not given just because you were born earlier than me."

"Oh, this will be good," Olivia purrs.

There are times when I want to be the center of attention. This isn't one of them. It feels like being a chicken that fell into a pit with four rabid, starving wolves. Olivia, with her shiny brown hair, raises her glass to me, in a salute not of admiration, but of commiseration. Like she knows exactly what firing squad I've put myself in front of.

"What Kian meant to say was that things sometimes change with the times and maybe we should investigate new—"

"That's not what you were saying, was it, son?" Hudson's father asks.

Son. That word makes my blood curdle almost as much as Hudson calling me "K" does. I don't think Mr. Rivers means it dismissively. Or maybe he does, but intent doesn't matter here, only impact. There's something . . . belittling about a man who knows nothing about me calling me "son." Like he has me all figured out, like just because he owns a multimillion-dollar empire, he can say whatever he wants to me and I'll just take it.

"No, Mr. Rivers, that's not what I meant at all. And my name's Kian. You said it before, so I'm going to assume you know it."

"Oh, for fuck's—"

"Quiet, Hudson. Adults are talking. And don't curse at the dinner table. You might be up here for school, but you still represent the Rivers name everywhere you go." Mr. Rivers doesn't even look at his son as he shuts him down mercilessly. His eyes are locked on me, as if Hudson doesn't exist.

The air is heavy for a moment, like when Tyra Banks holds only one photo while two beautiful girls stand in front of her. The tension between us is equal to two magnets of the same pole trying their hardest to touch one another. I read somewhere it's possible with enough external force—maybe the pressure of two black holes exerted on each magnet.

Well, I'm no physicist, but that hypothesis has nothing on the strain between Mr. Rivers and me right now.

"Go on," he offers, giving me the first attempt to shoot.

His voice is calm. He doesn't think he has anything to worry about. I've known many people like him. It happens when you live within a stone's throw of Harvard. Men who think they are God's gift to the planet. That we mere mortals should be honored to be in their presence; to fly so close to their sun. To revel in the pain that comes when we're eventually burned. *Thank you for the burn, sir*, they expect us to say. *I'll cherish it forever.*

Except I'm not Icarus. I'm the descendent of African kings and queens with their blood flowing through me.

And besides: Black guys don't burn.

Hudson leans over, our shoulders brushing against one another.

"You don't have to do this, babe," he whispers, his hand squeezing my thigh in a silent plea.

My head snaps to look at him, tension rising and quickly subsiding. *Babe*. That's right. This is still a ruse, and he's playing his part expertly. I need to, too.

A part of me considers swallowing my pride and biting the bullet. I'm here for Hudson, not for me. Starting an argument helps no one and puts my reward in this exchange at risk.

But what's the point of doing any of this if I'm going to just . . . bite my tongue and become an Uncle Tom? I'm not going to be one of those journalists who lose themselves for a story.

I squeeze Hudson's hand back, flashing him a smile.

The way his face loses almost all of its light brown color tells me he knows exactly what that means.

"I don't think what I said was hard to understand," I word carefully. "There's nothing wrong with mixing things up. That's called progress."

"Ah." Mr. Rivers nods, sipping his dark alcohol. "I thought so."

"Thought what?"

"You're not a businessman, are you, son?"

"Kian," I correct. "My name is Kian. Not 'son,' and no, I'm not. I'm a journalist."

"A journalist? Have you had any bylines?"

"No, not—"

"So, then you're not a journalist; you're an aspiring journalist."

"Dad," Hudson interjects. "That's not fair."

"Let me give you a little feedback, Kian, about how business works, so if you do ever interview a business professional, you don't stick your foot in your mouth. Progress in the business world is a slow-moving beast. It's not something you can just . . . will into existence. Our company employs thousands of people. Our choices affect more than just ourselves. We can't decide to change things just because of our ethical conscience or whims. Progress, if not handled properly and carefully, can be the death of an industry."

"So, my point still stands. It sounds exactly like an excuse someone would have made when discussing slavery. You're a Black family from the South; I'm sure you know something about that."

"Oh, for Christ's sakes," Mrs. Rivers mutters. "Can we please just order our food?"

The last clause leaves my mouth before I can pull it back, but I don't regret it, even if I should. Olivia's eyes grow wide, but the smile on her face makes my heart calm, even if only slightly. The tightness of Mr. Rivers's jaw brings me joy, too.

I'm definitely going to keep that memory for a while.

A sharp jolt of pain rockets up the nerve of my left leg. I swallow the curse word that almost escapes, glaring at Hudson, who glares back.

Stop, he mouths, a stern expression painting his handsome features. In that moment I can see how he's his father's son, even if only in features. In fact, Hudson is more like his mother if I had to guess.

The waitress returns, interrupting the tit for tat between Mr. Rivers and me. Slowly she rounds the table, clockwise, taking orders.

"The Lobster Thermidor," Mr. Rivers says.

"The cioppino," Mrs. Rivers selects.

"Seafood pappardelle," Olivia chooses.

"Samundari Khazana Curry," Hudson points.

Then it comes to me, the one person at the table who has no idea what they want. A quick scan of the menu makes me dizzy. The prices are insane! How can they be so casual about this? Just the four items they ordered easily cost . . . twelve hundred dollars?!

Olivia clears her throat, motioning with her eyes to the waitress now standing next to me.

Pick something, I urge myself. *Just select anything*. One, two . . .

"Lobster roll, please. With the green beans?"

Not the most elegant choice, but one of the cheaper things on the menu, and I know it'll taste good.

This is probably not the time to say I hate seafood, right? Yeah, definitely not a good time. I'm already on thin ice with Hudson's parents.

The waitress smiles a tight-lipped grin as she scribbles my order. If I were white, my cheeks would be a shade or two darker. The wet-blanket feeling of discomfort is enough to make me want to slither under the table and melt away.

"So, Kian," Mrs. Rivers says after a beat. "It's been so long since we last saw each other, I'm so glad you could join us."

Six months—not that long—but long enough, I guess. How busy is Mrs. Rivers? Running a multimillion-dollar company can't be easy. I remember reading somewhere she's one of the few women who run a company of this size, and the only one in the spirits and alcohol industry, which is usually dominated by men.

"Hudson tells us you're looking for a job? How is the job market for journalists?"

"Poor." That deserves more explanation. "It's not the best time, I guess? One of my teachers warned me even before graduation. 'A dime a dozen,' he called us."

"Oh, dear," Mrs. Rivers says, giving me her full attention. It's as if the world around us doesn't matter, just the concern in her voice and the subtle features on her face that mimic the emotion. It almost makes me feel like she *actually* cares about what we're talking about. Almost. "What are you going to do? If you don't get a job?"

Olivia passes me a bowl of bread and the olive oil that comes with it. I smile a "thanks" to her, take half a rye bread loaf, and pass it to Hudson without looking. I don't need whatever nervous energy is pulsing off him infecting me. I'm barely treading water as it is! One wrong thing, one misstep, and this carefully constructed lie will come crashing down around *both* of us.

No, thank you.

"I'll probably move back to Raleigh. My mom runs a little antique shop there. I'm sure they could use someone to work there. Family business and all."

"Oh?" Diane asks, her eyebrows perking up. "Your mom owns a business?"

"It's adorable," Hudson chimes in, his mouth full of bread. "It's called Uwharrie. Cute little shop."

Mrs. Rivers arches her brows again.

"Named after the Uwharrie River," I explain. "My mom was born in Trinity and spent a lot of time there."

"Ah." She smiles, an actual genuine smile that shows graceful signs of age but also gives her a warm, motherly aura. "A businesswoman who runs her own company *and* one who remembers where she came from. I really appreciate that. Those two things are not easy to find."

"It's nothing like what you do," I add. "I mean, how much money did Rivers & Valleys make last year? Fifty-six million?"

"Fifty-eight and a half," Olivia chimes in.

"You would know that," Hudson mutters, rolling his eyes.

"Is there a problem with keeping up with our family namesake, *Sudson*? Remember, that company is what put you through college *and* grad school."

"Don't call me that," Hudson warns.

"Or what? You gonna psychoanalyze me to death? I'm terrified. Someone protect me."

"Not here," Mrs. Rivers interjects with a singsong tone that's nothing like Divya's. This one is dripping with a threat I know she'll follow through with. Buttering her bread with three fluid swipes of her knife, she turns her attention back to me. "Have you always wanted to be a journalist?"

"Ever since I used to watch Linda Ellerbee on Nick at Nite."

"Following through with your passion. I bet your mother's very proud of you."

"If she isn't, she's done a good job at hiding it from me." I laugh.

Mrs. Rivers chuckles along with me. I'm not sure if she actually finds it funny, or she's just being cordial. "I hope I get to meet her someday."

That'll never happen, I think. But I don't let it show on my face. "I'm sure she'd love to meet you, too. Maybe someday."

Mrs. Rivers flashes a tight-lipped grin back at me, one that has secrets hidden just behind her lips, and dips her face down to focus on her meal as it arrives.

"Maybe someday."

———— · ————

TWO AND A half hours, five and a half thousand dollars, three bottles of Domaine Ramonet Montrachet Grand Cru, and at least twenty-five new grey hairs later, and the dinner is done. Mr. Rivers signs the check while barely looking at it, leaving a tip of eight hundred dollars, like it's nothing.

My throat turns dry just thinking of that type of money. Sure, eight hundred dollars is barely fifteen percent, and in most situations, I'd look down upon people who tip less than twenty. But eight hundred dollars is easily one month's rent for our waitress. I wonder if she's used to getting that type of cash working here.

"Maybe I should be a waiter," I mutter, standing up and slipping my suit jacket back on. Hudson misses, or ignores, my thought, but Olivia smiles at me with a lopsided smirk.

"You're handsome enough to be one; bet you'd rake in some good cash."

Even though I sat next to her for the whole dinner, I didn't get a good look at Olivia until now. If Olivia Pope were about fifteen years younger and from the South, she'd be Olivia Rivers. Softer features, but the same general bone structure, and an air of superiority yet friendliness that makes you feel tense but, at the same time, makes you want to be her friend. Based on the limited research I did before Divya picked me up, and the general disgust from Hudson, Olivia is the exceptional one. The one who will carry on the family name and legacy. Not to mention, she's set for life.

Sure, nepotism had a lot to do with that, but that discounts how damn smart and savvy Olivia is. You don't get to be the headline speaker at World Business Forum or a TED Talk simply because your parents are wealthy.

Okay, maybe you do, but something tells me Olivia didn't get there because of that.

She grabs her Hermès crocodile Birkin and winks at me. "Great to meet you, Kian. My brother was right, you really are an enigma."

"Hudson said that?" I want to add *to you* but catch myself. "I'm not sure if I should take that as a compliment or an insult."

"Definitely a compliment," she promises. With Hudson and her parents out of sight, she moves a little closer to me, the soft, faint scent of her blueberry perfume tickling my nose. "You're not the typical type of person a Rivers brings home. And since our parents pride themselves on the fact they molded us in their image, surprising them is a joy my brother and I share whenever we can." She pulls back and smooths the shoulders of my jacket, adjusting the lapels. "And you, my struggling journalist friend, are just the type to throw my parents for a loop."

"If you're talking about me and your father, I should apologize for that."

Olivia quickly shakes her head. "Absolutely not. Never. Here's a free lesson, Kian. Don't ever apologize. Not for something you're so passionate and proud about. Not for something that's part of your DNA. You are not a mistake, and your convictions are what make you unique. Never concede when it comes to those things."

The phone in Olivia's right hand lights up. Without looking at it, she takes a step back. "I have to take this, but it was great to meet you, Kian."

Before I can return the compliment, she's gone.

The past two hours felt like a blur, and now that I'm standing here at the table, relatively alone, I realize this is the first time in the past two and a half hours I've been able to breathe. Not actually breathing, because if that were the case, I wouldn't need Hudson's help getting a job; I could just apply for the US Olympic swimming team or something else that requires great breath control. But it feels like the world around me isn't as claustrophobic as before.

"Hey," Hudson says, gently tapping my shoulder, a relieved smile on his face. "You ready to go?"

"Absolutely."

I take the lead, heading toward the stairs that'll lead to my freedom, but Hudson clears his throat. When I turn back, his left hand is outstretched, palm facing for me to grab.

"My parents are downstairs," he explains, like that's all he needs to say. "And considering the . . . entrance you gave . . ."

"You're saying I owe you," I finish for him. "To end it on a convincing note."

"You said it, not me."

"But you were thinking it."

A sheepish grin that shows his dimples graces his strong features. "You could always read my mind."

"That's because it's not hard to read."

He puts his free hand over his chest, clenching the white shirt until it wrinkles. "My heart, it burns."

Right then, in that fraction of a second, I forget that Hudson and I are only playing at being boyfriends. It feels like four months ago, when we went to a gallery opening for one of Divya's friends and were just . . . so in sync. He knew what I wanted from the bar even before I was thirsty, and I knew how to play off his jokes to get the crowd roaring. We weren't two separate people, but one entity whose pieces of metal were fused together.

I think that might have been the happiest moment between us.

Without hesitation, I take his hand. I memorize the warmth and every patch of roughness on his palms. Because once this is over, once we walk out that door and out of his parents' eyesight, the agreement is over, and my end of the bargain is fulfilled.

Tomorrow, I'll probably get an e-mail with Randall's e-mail address cc'ed on it, and a short but cordial introduction from Hudson, with a *you can move me to bcc as you two get to know each other*, putting an end to my chapter with Hudson.

That's what I wanted, right? That's why I did all this. It was always the goal.

"K?" Hudson asks. "You ready?"

I don't even correct him this time, only nod and head down the steps with him to say goodbye to his parents.

By the time Hudson and I get downstairs, his parents have already received their car and are tipping the valet with a hundred-dollar bill.

"Chipotle stock is about to see a huge jump in the next few

months, I reckon," Mr. Rivers mutters. "Maybe you should consider starting in investing."

"Is your father always like that?" I whisper to Hudson.

"Always," he says with a tight-lipped reply as his mother approaches.

Mrs. Rivers hugs Hudson tightly. "You have to come home, son. Soon."

"I know, I know. I'll try to come down."

"Great, I'll see you next week."

Hudson frowns. "I'm sorry?"

"Your mom's right, babe. You should visit your parents more often."

Hudson glares at me, without moving his head, only his eyes. As if the conversation with her son is done, Mrs. Rivers turns to me. I expect her to pass the ball to me, as Hudson's boyfriend, to guilt-trip him into coming home next weekend. And why not? If I could go back to North Carolina every weekend, I would—you know, if there weren't half a dozen other reasons to stay in Boston. Besides, I can tell Hudson would rather be straight than go and visit his parents; this final little dose of payback is worth it.

Until it all comes crashing down around me.

"I'm so glad my son has someone like you in his life," Mrs. Rivers says, kissing both of my cheeks, which I return. "It was so great seeing you, Kian."

"I'm happy to have him in mine, Mrs. Rivers."

"Diana, please. You're practically family now."

"I think your husband would say differently," I gently remind her. After our little spat, Mr. Rivers didn't speak to me for the rest of the dinner.

Mrs. Rivers brushes it aside, like my words are nothing more than a summertime gnat bothering her incessantly. "Isaac *thrives* off of conversations like that. And he doesn't have anyone in his life to butt heads with ever since Hudson left to come up north. No one at the company would dare to talk to him like you did. Between you and me, I think he loved it. Which makes this so much easier."

Mrs. Rivers reaches into her purse and pulls out two narrow slips of thick rectangular paper in the shade of purple that screams regality. Without having to see the writing on them, I know exactly what they are, and my heart sinks.

"Mom . . ." Hudson says slowly. "What did you do?"

Still looking only at me, she takes my hands in hers, clasping them together. "Kian. Hudson's cousin is having a wedding next week, and considering you and my son have been together for years, I think it's only fitting for you to come join us!" she says cheerfully, like she just came up with some idea that'll save Rivers & Valleys millions of dollars at the end of the quarter. "Oh, it'll be perfect! You can visit our home, see where Hudson grew up! Meet the rest of the family! You'll love it in Georgia. Have you ever been?"

"I—" So many things are being thrown at me at once. Georgia? Meeting Hudson's family? A wedding? That was *not* part of the agreement! Hudson seems just as dumbstruck as I am, his mouth hanging open and his eyes slightly wide.

"I'm sorry, who is getting married?" Hudson asks.

"Your cousin Nathan. I told you about it."

"You did *not*. Since when?"

"He proposed about six months ago, I believe. Danni, a cute girl. She's run in our circles since college."

Something about how his mother said "runs in our circles" makes me cringe. I think of circles as something ironic. A fake thing that no one REALLY means to be an actual tangible concept. But here the Rivers are, talking about circles as normally as people use the word "summering."

"You'll like her. She's very . . . *normal*," Mrs. Rivers adds.

What does that mean? I think. But deep down, I know what it means. Poor. Or middle class. Probably has a 610 credit score and is proud of that.

"You're going to love Georgia, I promise. And the family is going to love you too! You'll come, won't you? I mean, I know it's last minute, but you'll find a way to make it?"

Absolutely fucking not, I scream in my brain. No, that's not going to happen. One date, a few hours, that's it. I signed this demonic contract with Hudson because I was feeling sentimental and wanted to be a good person. Any more lying and any goodwill I gained from helping my ex goes out the window, yeeted into a pit of icky black subterfuge. I can't afford that, and Hudson knows it. He'll shut her down. He'll handle this. He'll—

"We'll be there," he promises. "Can't wait."

TEN

"YOU'RE MAD AT me, aren't you?"

A few weeks ago, I watched *Lady Bird* with Divya for the first time during our (attempted) monthly movie night.

The scene that jumped out at me the most was in the first five minutes, when Christine "Lady Bird" McPherson threw herself out of the car and broke her arm. I didn't understand, while watching, how anyone could do that. Do white people have such a disregard for their own safety and lives that they just throw themselves out of moving vehicles onto the side of the road? What type of relationship did she have with her mother to make *that* seem like the best solution?

Divya and I spent the rest of the evening arguing about how good the movie was. A Saoirse Ronan stan, Divya thought it was the greatest movie of all time. I, of course, being the *contrarian*, thought it was only okay. Unbelievable and over the top at parts—I used the car scene as an example.

But now, now I understand. Because all I want to do is lunge out of the car, and maybe land, face-first, on the concrete, end up in a coma, wake up twenty years later, and have Hudson Rivers and his lying ass be a distant dream.

Or maybe shove *him* out of the car. But that's manslaughter—or attempted murder? I'll have to ask Divya about that one—and I do not look good in orange.

"K," Hudson begs. "Come on. Say something. You know how much I hate your silent treatment."

"Kian." There's enough bass in my voice that I almost turn myself on. "It's Kian. K. I. A. N. It means 'ancient' or 'wise' or 'grace of God.' It's Gaelic and comes from the name Cian or Kyan."

"Like the color?"

"No, with a K."

"So, you must have Irish in your blood then?"

"What?"

"You just said your name is Gaelic. Did your mom just decide she wanted to give her child an Irish name out of the blue?"

"I don't know, Hudson, did *your* parents just fucking decide they wanted to name you after a New York river that a plane landed in because they thought it was *quirky*?"

"Point taken."

The Uber fills with a heavy silence. The back seat of the—I don't even know what type of car this is, something boxy—is tight. When I shift, my left leg rubs against Hudson's right. He moves away, muttering an apology.

"That's not what you should be saying sorry for and you know it."

In the rearview mirror I see Hudson open his mouth and close it.

"And if you're going to come up with some piss-poor excuse to try and convince me you didn't have any other choice, I'd prefer we just sit in silence."

"I wasn't going to say that. I was going to say you're right."

"I legit *just* said if—wait. What?"

Did I hear that right? Hudson admitting fault? No, maybe there's some neurological disease you can get from bad lobster that's slowly tearing holes in my brain. Hudson Rivers apologizing? Without me prying it out of him? What twisted reality am I—

"But, if I can just say one thing."

There it is.

"I didn't have a choice."

I take off my seatbelt with a loud click, whip my body around, and face him. "How did you not have a choice?"

"Hey," the driver says, a larger Black man with a deep baritone voice. "Seatbelt."

"There were a million things you could have said. We had plans. I was going to be doing a job interview. You had some surprise planned. We couldn't make it. So many things. 'We'll be there, can't wait' isn't even the easiest response!"

"You don't understand my parents," he argues. "They have a way of getting what they want out of people."

"*Seatbelt!*" the driver says again.

"That is the saddest excuse I've ever heard. You're basically saying *I can't stand up to Mummy*. You are a grown-ass adult getting his master's degree, Hudson. You were perfectly fine with lying to her all night. What's one little strike going to hurt?"

Hudson's lips turn into a thin line, his handsome, pronounced jaw becoming even more angular. I see the veins on his left arm protrude as he clenches his large hands open and closed. Truthfully, there's something fucking hot about him when his anger sets in.

I'm almost—almost—petty enough to keep pushing his buttons. Jab him in different ways to get that tanned husk of his to crack open like a porcelain piñata. But I'm not that teenager anymore. I'm an adult. According to a BuzzFeed listicle about "How You Know

You're Over Your Ex," if you can walk away from them, even when you have the chance to taunt and tease them, you're over them.

This is it. This is the final countdown, the final test. As the Uber comes to a rolling halt at a stoplight, I settle back into my seat, clicking the seatbelt tight.

I'm over him. I'm over him. I'm over him, I repeat again and again. *Just let the conversation die. Move on. See it from his side. Take the higher road.*

Fuck that.

"You're always like this," I breathe out under my breath. But it wasn't so low that I expected him not to hear. In fact, I hope he did. So much for being the mature one.

It's Hudson's turn to take his seatbelt off.

"For fuck's sake," the driver groans. "You two are trying to get yourselves killed, aren't you?"

"Excuse me?" Hudson asks.

"I was clear," I spit back. "You always think you know what's best for everyone."

"How many times do I have to tell you I'm sorry, Kian?"

"Until you mean it."

"It just came out."

"Which tells me you don't mean it."

Stillness again, but this one has a crackle to it. Like we're both pulsing out radioactive energy in competition with each other. It's a battle of wills, like any argument with a significant other. Who can hold out the longest. Who will explode first. Or, in the best circumstance, who will start the *I'm sorry; No, I'm sorry* train.

Hudson's phone vibrating breaks the silence. The smooth sound of expensive fabric sliding against expensive fabric fills the air as he reaches into his pocket, quickly tapping the screen. "Mom says she had a great time with you. Can't wait for you to see the family home."

"Of course she does," I grumble. Before he can respond I throw him a curveball. "What if I told her?"

A beat. "Tell her what?"

"What if I told her I'm not coming? Tell her, since you couldn't, that something came up and I won't be able to join you all in Georgia."

"I—"

"Or better yet, what if I told her we lied? I'd take the blame, of course, so you can preserve your good relationship with your mother."

I can feel the venom dripping off my voice. It's not an honest and fair offer. But I don't care. I want him to feel as shitty as I do right now.

Hell hath no fury like a gay Black man dumped by his attractive Southern ex.

"Because the other choice is I tell your parents this is all a lie, and we end this right here and now."

"You wouldn't do that."

There's hurt in his voice, but also hesitation. He's not sure if I have it in me. The old Kian most definitely didn't. The Kian who was head-over-heels in love with Hudson, who stayed up late at night and almost missed a crucial journalism test for just fifteen more minutes with him when he had to go home one week. That Kian lived and died for Hudson Rivers. That Kian was certain they were going to have a future together.

That Kian was an idiot.

"You don't want to bet money on that," I say with fake confidence. I admit, it feels nice to be in control of the situation. Having Hudson against the rails is new. He studies me, with those beautiful warm honey-brown eyes, searching for an ounce of anything that will reveal some truth he can latch onto.

"Déjà vu," I say.

"What?"

"Nothing." No. Not nothing. It's something. It's a big fucking something. "That look you have? That's the same one I gave you when you said we were breaking up. That same hope there was something I could do to change your mind. Some word that was a secret code or whatever to open up our relationship again. I looked and replayed that conversation a dozen—no, two dozen—times to see if there was anything I missed. You made it clear, multiple times: I didn't miss anything."

The Uber picks up again, the jolt into drive smoother than it was before. The driver doesn't yell at either of us to put on our seatbelts this time. I can tell by the quietness in his breathing, he's eavesdropping. I bet he gets spats like this all the time. And you know what? Good for him.

Once I interviewed an Uber driver who said listening to people's conversations was her favorite part of the job. "I get to learn so much about people," she had said while loudly popping gum and singing along, off-key, to some Shakira song on the radio. "Doesn't matter if people know, or don't know, that I'm listening. Within twenty seconds of a discussion, I can know if someone is a good person or a bad one."

What does this guy think about me? Am I the villain or the hero in this story? Is there enough context for him to make a decision? Does standing up for myself make me a bitch, or confident? Is there really a difference?

"I really hurt you, didn't I?"

Hudson's words aren't like a knife or a blade. More like a rocket. They hit me straight in my chest, shattering every bit of armor I have. Shrapnel tears into my flesh, revealing ligaments, muscles, bones, and arteries. I'm in front of him, completely raw, without any defenses.

The master's graduate's version of "pick me, choose me, love me," I suppose.

"Pull over here, please."

The driver looks at me through the rearview mirror. There's a silent exchange between the two of us; a *you sure?* And a reply of *definitely*.

Hudson doesn't fight as the car glides to the side of a busy street and the driver puts it into park. I yank off the seatbelt, the thumping in my chest growing more and more rapid. A heart can't beat this fast. This can't be healthy. This can't be normal.

Well, duh. Nothing about this is normal. Helping your ex lie to his parents isn't normal. Being in an Uber like this with him, so close, like there's nothing between us, isn't normal. I'm not normal.

And I need to get out of here. Now.

"You know the answer to that question," I settle on, pushing the door open harder than needed. I wince, thinking it's going to tear off the hinges and I'm going to be banned from Uber with a five-hundred-dollar bill on my hands.

But it doesn't. It creaks and the driver groans, but it holds strong. At least one thing went right tonight.

"Let me at least pay for an Uber home, Kian."

"I'm fine."

"You don't have to do this."

"I'll walk. It's nice outside."

"Come on, don't be like this. I didn't mean it like that."

"Fuck you, Hudson," I say, turning to him. I bend down, directing as much anger as I can behind my eyelids and into my grip on the top of the door. It's better than letting the hurt seep through. "Conceal, don't feel" and all that bullshit from the 2013 international Disney success *Frozen*.

"Go home. Leave me alone. And get the hell out of my life."

I slam the door before he can attempt to reply and walk briskly down the busy downtown street. Like a spy in a movie, I take a sharp left and head into the Haymarket T station. If I blend into the crowd, I can lose myself in the sea of people; dissolve into just another face in Hudson's life.

And right now? That's for the best. For the both of us.

ELEVEN

"HEY, GOOD-LOOKING. WHAT'S your poison?"

Not far from where Hudson's Uber dropped me off is the General, a bar where Divya bartended through college, law school, and still does every other week. It's just my luck that this is her week on, because that means free alcohol. And right now, that sounds like the best part of my night.

She smiles at me, silently pouring a fountain of clear liquid when I don't answer. "I'm guessing the dinner didn't go as well as you wanted?"

"That would be an understatement. And please don't say, 'I told you so.'" I raise the shot glass to her and give a salute and a silent thanks. She does the same, but her shot is water.

"Wouldn't dream of it. Up to it, down to it, fuck those who don't do it. We do it 'cuz we used to it. So drink, motherfucker, drink," we chant, following the ritual before throwing it back.

"Jesus," I hiss, my whole body and every arterial road feeling like it's filled with fire. "What is this?"

"You like?" she asks, moving like a whisper of smoke around the bar. Patrons don't even tell her to top them off. She just does it, knowing which ones need another, a different drink, or their check before they know it themselves. Even outside the courtroom, reading people is Divya's strength. Which is probably why she gave me whatever hellfire that was. She knew I needed to forget today as quickly as possible.

"It's this new Russian brand; Ian brought it back from his trip. He wants us to try and sell it. Got forty crates in the back."

"It's like drinking radioactive sludge."

"But smooth, yeah?"

"I don't know if that's a good thing?"

"When it comes to alcohol, the smoothness is always a good thing. You dated a brewmaster; you should know these things. And before you correct me, I know Hudson isn't technically a brewmaster, but how often do you get to use that word? Indulge me."

My whole body seizes up as she says that. She sighs, pressing a button on the nozzle, cranberry juice filling a water glass.

"Too soon?"

"Just a bit, yeah."

Leaning over the counter, she firmly presses a kiss on each of my cheeks with such emotive force I'm sure there's an imprint of her purple lips on me, like the comical rosiness of a cartoon character made to look bewildered.

"Hey," a finance bro in his early thirties slurs loudly from six feet away. "What do I have to do to get one of—"

"Bite me," we say in unison.

The customer says something under his breath, but neither of us gives him the time of day. Divya helps another customer, then turns to him. "Now, what do you want?"

I don't hear what he says, but Divya pours him a shot of some dark brown liquid I think is probably rum, before returning to me.

"So, are you going to tell me what happened, or are you gonna make me guess?" she asks, pouring another shot, my third since I arrived. The General has a very Boston vibe to it. If you were transported back to the Boston Tea Party and wanted to drink mead or ale somewhere, you'd come here. Of course, Divya, an Indian American, probably wouldn't be the one serving you, but she's always been the type of person who sees something and gets what she wants. And during college she wanted this job.

"You already know what happened. I'm here, aren't I? Drinking shots with you instead of . . ."

"Instead of getting your back blown out while Hudson says, 'yee-haw'?"

It takes all the control I have not to spit the vodka all over her.

"He's from Georgia, not Texas!"

"Right, right. Lemme try again."

"Please don't."

"Instead of reenacting the peach scene in *Call Me by Your Name*?"

"Oh my God."

"Get it? Georgia peach."

"I get it."

"I don't think you do."

"I hate you so much."

"Nah," she says, shaking her head. "You adore me."

True. I wouldn't be here without Divya. She's always gone out of her way to make me feel at home, for as long as I've known her. When I was calling my mom, trying to decide if I wanted to transfer back to UNC, she sat down at the table across from me, took the phone, and told Mom, *He'll call you back.*

"I don't know you," she'd said, sipping her own iced tea. "But I know one thing. Boston needs more people of color, and I'm not going to let whatever it is that makes you want to leave, run you out."

And the rest is history. I wouldn't still be here without Divya. I wouldn't have graduated from Northeastern without her. I wouldn't have met Hudson if it wasn't for her interfering. Not sure if that's a check in her favor, but that's not the point. Divya's my Person. Not Hudson, not Jamal, not Charlie Hunnam. My hall pass: Divya.

"Standing right beside every gay guy is an equally badass woman."

"Come again?" she asks.

I shake my head. "The dinner was fine."

"Only fine?"

"At first."

"Sounds like the start of a Blumhouse horror movie if I'm being honest."

I can't help but smile at that one. Jordan Peele would probably have fun turning my romantic life into some Lovecraftian horror story. I'd be glad to sell the rights to him if he's looking.

"I mean his parents are great. Well, his mom is. His dad is intense. His sister too."

"Well, they do own a million-dollar company. Sorry, a multibillion-dollar company. You'd be surprised how many dudebros come in here asking for a Rivers & Valleys IPA."

"In Boston? Really?" I feign confusion. Divya grins. Almost like it was foreshadowing, a guy in a backward cap comes up, dressed in Sperrys and chinos.

"Can I get an IPA? Rivers & Valleys, if you got any."

God really does have a sense of humor. Divya throws a knowing look at me before pulling one out of the cooler. "Eight bucks."

The man gives her twelve. She winks and pockets the extra four.

"Anyway, keep spilling. What happened next? Did he make a move on you? Did he confess he actually wanted you there for your kidney? Or even worse! Did he finally decide to go blond? Every gay does that at some point in their gay journey, right? I mean, if I'm using you as an example . . ."

"We said we would never talk about that!"

"It looked cute!"

"My hair was partially *orange*, Divya."

She shrugs. "That's just because you didn't let the dye sit in your hair long enough. Next time . . ."

"There won't be a next time. I like my coils. Besides, I looked like an off-Kmart version of Sisqó."

"Oh, *please*. I would pay *anything* to see you perform 'The Thong Song.' I'm putting that on my list of things for you to do next time you're drunk."

"I would rather watch '2 Girls 1 Cup' again."

"Talk about a throwback."

"Right?"

"All right, then." She puts her hands up in defeat. "Let's make a deal."

I sip the vodka, the warmth starting to burn my whole body in a familiar way, making the sharpness of the alcohol feel smooth. "Those deals never end well for me. I'm starting to think making a promise with a lawyer is a bad idea."

"A horrible idea, but that's not the point. You tell me what happened with Hudson, and I won't bring the hair incident up again. No matter how cute you looked."

I know I'm not going to be able to get around this for long. Divya has a way of getting what she wants out of me, and it's not a toxic or manipulative way. It's just the combination of her charm, her being my best friend, and the skills she paid thousands of dollars to hone. Plus, I can't blame her. Information is her favorite weapon, and once she has it, all of it, she can protect me.

Which is why, shortly after the fresh wound of splitting up had

scabbed over a bit, Divya broke down for me, in her incredibly analytical manner, how she saw it coming. How me fighting with Hudson about always having to be the perfect son, instead of living for
himself, was a recipe for disaster. How, when he threw in my face
that I expected him to be "perfect" and never mess up or stumble,
what he said was completely false. For Hudson Rivers, no matter
how much he likes to pretend, he'll always fall back to the *what will
my family think* question. Every choice, every decision, if he should
breathe or not, centers on that. It's annoying, it's suffocating, and
frankly, I couldn't compete with the Rivers legacy.

And I reminded him. Multiple times; with small jabs, with side
comments . . . and finally, it was just too much.

"Listen," Divya had said that evening. "Are you a lot to handle?
Sure. But should you be with someone who can handle that? Absolutely. Hudson is not that person. Hudson has his own baggage and
shit to deal with. No rich boy is truly as perfect as their Instagram
likes to project. And until Hudson can get his family drama and his
am I worthy of the family name, *Game of Thrones*–level dramatic saga
figured out, he won't be ready for another person. That shit is toxic,
K. You're better off without him. Sometimes, blood is actually
thicker than water."

Now history repeats itself.

"Hudson lied to his parents."

That gets her attention. She raises her eyes, leaning back against
the counter. "Like, lied about . . . ?"

"His mom. She asked me to come visit her and the rest of the
Rivers family in Georgia. Hudson's cousin is getting married or
something."

"And she wants you to meet the rest of the family."

"Mhm."

"Because you're her son's long-term boyfriend."

"Mhm."

"And because she thinks you two will probably get married someday."

"Bingo."

"And . . ."

"He said sure."

"Of course he did." Another shot for free. Another shot I down with ease.

"You're trying to get me drunk, aren't you?"

Divya playfully zips her mouth. "But, in my defense, if I do get you liquored up, it'll be that much easier for you to call Hudson, tell him to fuck off, and for you to move on with your life," she says as she helps a customer close out his tab.

". . . Yeah."

Handing back his card along with a receipt to sign, she arches her right brow. "Right? That's the plan, right, Kian? You're going to finally stand your ground with Hudson and he's out of your life for good?"

I reach over the counter, grab the liquid nozzle, and pour myself a shot of Coke to buy me some time. Divya never stops staring at me, though.

"Don't you have other customers to cater to?"

"They can wait."

Sighing, I down the shot quickly before holding the glass at a forty-five-degree angle, pressing the pad of my right index finger on the rim, and spinning it slowly. "He said something before I got out of the Uber," I mutter. "He said, 'I really hurt you, didn't I?'"

"Were you honest with him?"

"Honest? Of course not! That would be the easy answer."

"And why do anything easy when we can make it hard on ourselves."

"See, you really do get me. I should just date you."

"You can't afford me, darling, but I appreciate the sentiment," Divya promises before shifting back to the question I knew was coming. "Well, did he hurt you?"

"You know the answer to that," I mutter.

"I know it, but do you know it?" she asks. "You know my mother is a psychologist, right? Always used to drive me insane. She used to psychoanalyze me in high school, the absolute *worst* time to do something like that to your teenage daughter. But after a breakup, she told me something I never really understood until now." Divya clears her throat, making her voice an octave higher. "*Divya, life is going to hurt you. A lot. But once you can say it, out loud, admit you were hurt, that's when you can start healing.*"

Of course, Divya's right, even if her advice sounds like it comes from some discount Dr. Phil—who would just be Dr. Phil, but that's not the point. I stop spinning the shot glass, letting her words sink into my skin and etch themselves under my skin, like ink from a tattoo.

"You know your mother doesn't sound anything like that, right?" I ask, smirking coyly. "I've met your mother. She would be ashamed. And your voice cracked at the end."

"Oh, my mother would hundred percent kill me if she heard me talk about her like that. But she's not here and she doesn't need to know. And if you tell her, I *will* kill you. I'm a lawyer, K. I can make sure I get away with the crime."

I appreciate the lightheartedness of the serious subject. Divya can be a bit of a wild card when it comes to conversations like these. Either she's too heavy-handed and sanctimonious, like she's on *America's Next Top Saint* or something, or she's flippant. I've learned to accept both of those as facets of her love. The former is her trying to help me, the latter is her trying to make me ignore whatever pain or frustration I'm feeling in the hopes that it'll just go away. Rarely is either choice the right choice.

But sometimes, she finds a perfect sweet spot, like now. And she reveals a truth I didn't know was right in front of me.

I fish out twenty bucks from my wallet and slide it across the table. Divya notices and shakes her head, pushing the money back.

"Take it," I insist. I feel bad drinking her alcohol. It's technically enough to get her fired, but more than once Divya has read the owner to filth about health- and safety-code violations that I'm not sure are actually even real, telling him if he looks the other way, she will too. Hence why Jamal and I always drink for free here whenever she's on shift.

"You know you don't have to pay me when you come here. Your company is more than enough."

"Then consider this payment for the therapy you just gave me. It's your second job after all."

She hesitates, her manicured brow furrowing as if the question kicks her computer processor of a brain into gear. Finally, she spits out a result, and snatches the money.

"This one time."

"Mhm." I'm not even paying attention to her as I pull out my phone. It's almost 10:30, not too late but not too early either. Isn't visiting someone's home after ten considered bad manners? Like telemarketers calling before nine a.m. or a top not paying for dinner when he fully intends to break a bottom's back?

Doesn't matter. I'm doing it anyway.

A customer to the left clears her throat for the third time. Divya sighs, looking at me with caring eyes, eyes that say she'll leave her shift right now if I ask her to.

"I'm gonna be fine," I promise, stepping back off the stool and heading toward the door. "Hey."

She looks up, in mid-pour, capping the rim right before it runs over.

"That guy you showed me before? Danny?"

"Wallace."

"Same thing. Is he still single?"

"Unless he fell madly in love with someone in the past four hours, I'm pretty sure."

"He's a gay. In Boston. In the summertime. Love has nothing to do with lust. Plus, he's a lawyer. Did I mention that? You've seen how stressed out I am. Imagine that. But in a hot man. In your bed. Well, not your bedroom, your mattress sucks, but you get what I'm saying."

". . . point taken."

The words feel like jagged stones in my mouth. I can't juggle them the right way to spit them into a coherent sentence. So, I do the second-best thing: word vomit.

"Give him my number and see if he's free this week. I'm thinking that Irish pub on Cooper Street."

"You mean the pub literally called That Irish Pub?" she asks. "You sure?"

"About the bar? Yes. About going on a date? No."

A smile spreads over Divya's warm features. She salutes me with three fingers. "Consider it done. I'll let you know when he confirms."

I put two fingers to my lips and gesture toward her.

"Right back at you, hot stuff."

I run out of the bar just in time to see an empty taxi stop at the corner. Before the light turns green, seconds later, I'm comfortably in the back seat.

Well, as comfortable as I can be when I'm going to see my ex—again.

"Beacon Street, please."

TWELVE

I'VE BEEN TO Hudson's brownstone exactly four times. This makes five.

The first time was in college, when he was touring and deciding if he wanted to buy it. It was one of our best dates, if I'm being honest.

"Let's pretend to be snobs," Hudson had suggested as we walked down the street, arm in arm. "You know, the super-rich types who probably get one-percent interest on every loan from the bank and think Gucci is the worst type of clothing you can buy? We can pretend we're going to buy this house."

"Our fifth house," I added. "And this will be our first on the East Coast."

"Oh, I like the way you think, Mr. . . ." His brow furrowed. "What should our last name be?"

"Haberdashery," I said without hesitation. "It sounds pretentious as fuck."

"Haber—what now?"

"Haberdashery, noun. In American English it means men's

clothing and accessories. In British English it means small items used in sewing, such as buttons, zippers, and thread. I played Scrabble with Divya last night," I explained. "It won me seventy-nine points. She challenged me. It's fresh in my mind."

He grinned warmly; his teeth, almost perfectly straight except for a chipped one to the lower right, filled his face. "You're such a dork."

"*Your* dork."

"Always and forever."

The second visit was when Hudson actually decided to buy the place, and he wanted me to help him plan the layout for all his stuff.

"I never liked living in the Northeastern apartments anyway," he'd said to justify it, like I was going to sign off on the purchase of a six-hundred-thousand-dollar house at the age of twenty-one. "And besides, if I get tired of it, I can rent it out! A second income, or you can come live here! Or stay whenever you want! It's a win-win for us both. No more Todd snoring in the other room."

"Or glaring at us when we come out of my room, like his glare is going to summon an express train to hell, where we will burn for all eternity."

Hudson groaned as the Uber came to a halt in front of his newly purchased home. "God, I hate him."

I should have known then he wasn't actually going to buy it. His parents bought it for him, a graduation present. Funny, Diana and Isaac Rivers might not care for their son's chosen profession, but they have no problem spending a shit ton of money on him.

Must be nice to be rich.

The third time was also while we were dating but after he had already purchased the house: I was too drunk to make it home after a Solange concert and gave the driver his address. And the fourth and final time was just before we broke up. It was the first night after he'd moved in, and we fucked in every goddamn room.

"That's what you do," he had said, sauntering toward me in nothing but low rider Levi's, a thin layer of sweat on his body, the air conditioning in his nearly-a-million-dollar house not working. "You gotta show the ghosts who owns this place. Gotta show the house who's boss. Everyone knows this, K. It's chapter four in *Steps You Complete When You Move into a New House: For Dummies.*"

"By putting on a show? What is this, Incorporeal Pornhub?" I asked, doing what we *should've* been doing: unpacking his boxes. The faster we got done, the faster we could relax. Or, you know, do what he wanted to do. What *I* wanted to do, if I'm being honest.

"Oh, that's a good idea," he muttered, his husky voice right against my ear as his rough fingers slid under my tee shirt and rubbed at my sides. "Forget being a journalist, write ghost porn instead. Or better yet, make some porn with me."

We never got those boxes unpacked.

Now, sitting outside his house feels foreign, like I'm in the wrong place at the wrong time, or what I'm sure it feels like to be the only Black person in a horror movie. This is wrong. I shouldn't be here. I have more sense than this. And yet, here I am.

What did I hope to accomplish from this? Did I expect Hudson Rivers, the most Taurus of all Tauruses to apologize to me? Did I expect him to admit he was in the wrong this whole time and confess his feelings for me? Maybe. Yes. No. I don't know, and I'm not sure there is a right, or wrong, answer here. All I know is the taxi driver keeps glancing at me in her rearview mirror, then at the fare, which has risen from $12.50 to $14.10 in the past five minutes.

"Word of advice," the woman says, reaching into the passenger seat to pull out a pencil and a small, worn book with crinkled yellow, stained pages. "No man is worth a booty call when he doesn't care for your fare."

I try my hardest not to smile, even tilt my head down so she can't see the creeping smirk. I guess that's kinda what this is, isn't it? An emotional booty call for sadists who thrive off emotional pain? I mean, I'm a pretty open person when it comes to kinks—to each their own—but I never saw myself as someone into pain.

The more you learn, right?

"A booty call would be easier," I admit. The lights are on at his house, so he's definitely home. A large part of me wished he had doubled back out to hang with his friends for the rest of the evening; then this would have been a failed attempt at . . . whatever it is.

Well, no, I don't want that. Imagining him out at Ruby Slippers or Luscious or Candy Horn, the popular gay bars and clubs in Boston, makes my stomach turn. Imagining some twink rubbing up against him, asking him to say "y'all" or "reckon" or "Do you drink sweet tea?" while flirting with him, makes me want to shove the driver's pencil into my eyes. Of course, I have no control over, or right to know, what Hudson Rivers does with his evenings. It's not like I'm his boyfriend or anything.

But . . . wait, I *am*.

I pull out my phone, quickly tap two buttons, and pull up my e-mail. No introduction to Randall Clements, no text thread between the two of us, no message with a predetermined and arranged meeting and "be well" salutations. Hudson has not completed his end of the bargain, and until that happens, we're still joined at the hip. And that means I'm *fully* in the right to wonder what he's doing at night.

I read a joke somewhere online that said, "Which one of you in the relationship is the neurotic one and which one of you is the go-with-the-flow one?" I don't think anyone would wonder how Hudson and I fell on that spectrum.

"Well, I hope his dick is bomb," the taxi driver says, licking the tip of her pencil. "You look like you could use it." Her eyes flicker, catlike, toward the meter again: $17.00.

"What does that even *mean*?" I ask. "You know, you're the second person in my life to tell me that. I'm starting to take it as an insult."

The driver snorts, reaching into her bag to pull out a slip of paper, then hands it back to me. Before I open it, I know it's one of those proverbs you find in a fortune cookie.

Seize advice like you seize the day, with vigor and zeal. You never know the value it holds.

"I think that was meant for you and not me," she says cheekily, eyes dancing with mirth.

"Oh, screw this. Keep the meter running." Before she can give me any more advice, I jump out of the car and briskly walk toward the cast-iron gate that separates Hudson's property from the cobblestone sidewalk. I don't stop walking until I'm at the front door, hitting the wood harder than necessary. The door vibrates from the force, and I swear even the stone shudders from the impact.

Probably not the best way to approach an almost-million-dollar home at ten o'clock at night. I love Boston, I don't miss North Carolina, but a Black man banging on a door in a rich neighborhood? Not the smartest idea. I like to think I'm a pretty smart guy, but I remember that YouTube video from years ago where a person said, "Dick will make you slap somebody." Aka, a hot guy will make you do stupid shit.

Especially when that dick belongs to Hudson Rivers.

On the tenth bang, the door rips open, so hard the original wood seems like it might actually come off its hinges.

"I don't know what the hell you think you're going to accomplish by banging on my goddamn door at goddamn eleven p.m., but what you're going to get is a boot in the teeth if you don't . . . Kian?"

I stand there for a moment, mouth slightly open like I'm still trying to perfect the smize, frozen in place on his stoop with the out-of-place gaudy mat that says: *Home Is Here.*

"A lot to unpack there," I mutter. "First of all, what even was that?"

"Sometimes my Southern roots come out. You can't take the South out of the boy." Hudson shrugs, raising only his right shoulder. The other is preoccupied, thanks to the important job the left hand has—which leads us to the second bit of unpacking that needs to be done.

The thin layer of water on Hudson's chiseled body would be enough to make my breath hitch. But the way his brown hair is matted to his forehead, not coiffed in a clever pattern or styled to look intentionally messy-cute, makes him look even more real. Sure, bed head is hot, but post-shower head? With the small matching towel that barely reaches the tops of his knees? The way his light brown skin has a hint of red pushing through the surface? That's even hotter.

That's the type of look that, in the past, has gotten us featured on the front page of Incorporeal Pornhub, most likely. But that was another life. Like our problematic emo white king said, "Let the past die. Kill it, if you have to. It's the only way to become what you were meant to be."

"Kian?" he asks in a way that tells me it's his second time saying my name. "What are you doing here?"

Good question. Standing in front of him is like fourth grade, when I fully prepared, all night, the Gettysburg Address, yet it vanished from my brain on that rickety stage at Eagle Borne Elementary. Hudson has that effect on people—on me, mostly. The small things, like the way he bites his full lips, or how there's a slight section missing from his right brow due to running into a wall in high school, or how broad his shoulders are, so broad they almost fill a normal door frame. Each of those things causes my mind to short-circuit. And I let him. I *loved* to let him.

Not this time.

"Do you remember what you said, right before I got out of the car?"

"What?" Hudson steps aside. "Come inside. I don't want to accidentally flash the street."

"I'm good. I won't be here long."

Disappointment passes over Hudson's face. He looks almost puppy-like.

"Answer the question," I repeat. "Do you remember what you asked me?"

"I really did hurt you, didn't I?" he repeats.

Keeps me from having to say it over again. "I didn't answer you before. I want to do that now. Leave no conversation open-ended, you know?"

"We should really go inside, K. It's going to rain. Come on," he urges.

"Kian. My name is Kian. K-I-A-N. Two syllables, four letters—it's not that hard."

There's a sharpness to the words that makes my mouth taste like copper. Hudson's perfect face scrunches together like a first draft of a Picasso painting, before settling on stoic neutrality.

"You're right. You wanted to say something."

That doesn't feel as full as I thought it would. Winning like this feels akin to eating a wafer that tastes like Styrofoam—it's something, all right, but not what you want or need. What I need is to get this off my chest. Anytime you're spilling your heart out, let alone to someone you love, the first words are always the hardest; but once you get past those, the rest is smooth sailing.

"You didn't hurt me. You broke me. I loved you, Hudson. I didn't want to, I didn't need to, but I did. You weaseled your way into my life so fucking easily, and I was happy with that because we just worked. And if we didn't work, if something was broken, we would put it back together. You were the gold that made my wounds and scars and cracks look beautiful. You were my *kintsugi*.

"And you went and ruined it. You took the energy and care I invested—we invested—in this relationship, and you . . . you just threw it away like what I gave was nothing. Because why does it matter when you're the man who can have everything and anything? What other people give, and value, means nothing to you. And I wouldn't have cared if you were just another rich boy. But you weren't. You were Hudson Rivers. The boy with the amazing jawline but also the sweetest heart. The out-of-touch guy who didn't know the price of milk. The guy who would take time when we were walking in the park to play soccer with kids when he saw they'd lost their ball. You were more than just a stereotype people—*I*—put you in. At least I thought you were."

There's no stopping now. It's taking all I have to keep the tears from falling and the wave of emotion from swallowing me whole. Hudson looks like he's about to say something, but if I give him that opening, who knows what'll come next. I can't risk that. I can't shrink my emotions again or deal with them in some unhealthy way that Divya *swears* will be worth it in the long run. This is my new gold. This is my new *kintsugi*, since he can't be it anymore.

"I loved you. I saw a life together with us. Call me dramatic then, call me dramatic now; I don't care, because it wasn't just me anymore. It was me and you. Whatever life that would be. And I was willing to discover that with you. And now—"

"Now that part is over," he interrupts. "That's what you were going to say, right? That it's over? That there's no chance for us to find our way back to each other? To restart what we had?"

"That's exactly what I'm saying."

Is it? I don't know, but the words seemed like the right thing to say. Saying anything else negates the word vomit I spilled all over his freshly washed feet.

Leave, I tell myself. *You said what you meant to say. There's nothing else. You don't need to put yourself through any more pain, Kian. You can let go.*

"Goodbye, Hudson," I say. There's a sense of release in that. Like for this moment, a moment I know I will get past tomorrow, I'm okay with whatever happens next. If Hudson decides not to follow through with his end of the bargain? Fine. If he does and makes sure I get a job at Spotlight? Great. Or if he makes it his life mission to make my life hell? So be it. I'm in control, and that's all that matters.

Well, for about seven seconds while I walk back toward the waiting taxi.

"Wait," he says. I hear him, with soft but heavy footsteps, step off the stoop and make his way across the wet, silvery cobblestones. I turn to face him before he can touch me to turn me around. That might just be too much for me to handle right now.

Hudson doesn't say anything at first. He just looks at me, chewing nervously on his bottom lip. His warm eyes look deep into mine in a way I've never seen before. There are rivers of hurt and pools of regret. There are chasms of longing and notes of desire. There's so much in that galaxy of his.

"I feel like I'm saying this a lot," he mutters, running his fingers through his hair. "I'm sorry. You're right. Everything you just said? You were always better at words than me. But please, Kian . . . I just want you to know I really am sorry for all of that. Even if . . ."

"Even if?"

He opens his mouth and shakes his head. "Adding a 'but' to an apology weakens it. Let's leave it at that."

"Let's leave it at that."

But of course, Hudson Rivers can't just leave anything at that. Good things always have to be pulled apart, like the flesh of a fruit, and devoured. That's what Hudson does.

"And . . . I have no right to ask," he says finally, speaking slowly. "But I can make it worth your while if you come with me to the wedding."

And just like that, all I want to do is be a black hole and rip his galaxy apart.

"Hear me out," he adds quickly. He knows what's coming; it's written all over my face, I'm sure. I can feel the way my features are twisting, telltale signs of anger rising like mountains after a reckoning. That's what Hudson is and nothing more. A reckoning on my life.

"Randall is going to be in Georgia. I checked the guest list when I got home."

Did he just say what I think he said? I hesitate, pushing my anger back into its pot. For now.

"Are you sure?"

"Pretty sure." A moment passes. "One hundred percent sure."

"And he's gonna be at our table?"

"He's going to be sitting right next to you. I'm going to make sure that happens."

This throws a small wrench into Operation: Hudson Rivers Must Die. Well, not a steel wrench. More like a fancy dissolvable one that, in seven to ten days, will disappear, then I can go back to paying for my therapist's second condo. Getting a letter of reference was good. But meeting Randall in person?

Hudson's thinking the same thing. "You were always a people person. Once you get past your own . . ."

"Don't."

He puts his hand up again, nodding in agreement. His voice turns soft. "Let me do this for you."

"And in exchange I keep up this lie for you? This isn't just for me. You get something out of it."

"Doesn't take away from the fact you gain something," he reminds me. "This was always a business arrangement, right?"

"Right."

How, in a span of five minutes, did this turn from me coming over here, being a badass, to once again doing what Hudson wanted because he makes his voice a little husky and he looks good in—and out—of clothing? How do I keep putting myself in situations like this? Why do I keep letting myself fall for his charm?

"I'll think about it."

Before he can respond or try to convince me, I turn on my heels and head to the taxi. Just in time, too. The skies open up, sheets of rain pouring down on me, hand on the door handle.

I'm not sure what made me do it, what made me turn around, like this was *The Notebook* or some other Nicholas Sparks book, and scream my heart out.

"I'm so over you, Hudson Rivers! Don't you forget it!"

Drenched, I slip into the taxi, ignoring the chill of my clothes clinging to me.

"Drive," I say. I don't even look at Hudson. Out of the corner of my eye, I can see he's still there. The joy of knowing he's being soaked doesn't make up for the sinking feeling in my chest.

At least my driver is considerate enough to say nothing and turn off the meter, the red $24.50 reminding me how much my dignity goes for on the Queer Market.

THIRTEEN

HALF A WEEK later, Divya comes through on her promise, like she always does.

"The setting? Dulce's on Twelfth Street. The time? Mid-afternoon. The mood? Hauntingly beautiful. The players? Two hot men, looking for love in all the wrong places," she plays out dramatically over FaceTime, before squealing, while I walk down the street. "This is going to be epic! My two favorite people paired together!"

"I thought Jamal was your favorite person?" I tease, adjusting the collar of my polo. The cotton blend is nice in the extreme Boston heat, and the light pink plays well against my dark skin, but it feels itchy. This is what I get for letting Divya pick outfits for me.

"Don't be jealous. Green doesn't look good on you," she scolds while sipping a Bellini. Judging by her background, she is at home in her downtown loft, filled with glass and distressed wood in a tasteful but still folksy way. Think Chip and Joanna Gaines meets Lady Gaga's futuristic vibe, if you will.

"Are you sure we can't call it off?" I ask, looking both ways before running across the street, only half a block away. "We could say I had an interview! Or I got sick! Yeah! I mean, it's not unreasonable. Summer, Boston? Seafood, food poisoning. Boom. Solution found."

Divya rolls her eyes, keeping one finger extended while finishing her drink. "Kian Andrews, you are not chickening out of this. At worst, you get a free meal with a charming man. At best . . ."

"Let me guess, I get my back blown out?"

A woman next to me clears her throat and covers her daughter's ears, glaring at me.

Sorry, I mouth, giving her my best apologetic smile. She rolls her eyes, pulling her daughter along quickly. I turn my attention back to Divya.

"I was going to say, you find a man who loves you for you and blows your back out on a regular basis, but you got half of it right. Sorry, you're a vers, as you keep reminding me, so you can both blow each other's backs out! From here until eternity! Win-win."

I roll my eyes and round the corner. Dulce's seafoam green sign with cursive lettering is less than fifteen feet in front of me. Now's my chance to turn around. If I'm going to run, this is the time.

No, I tell myself. *You need this. Like Divya said, you have nothing to lose here. Have fun for once.*

"I'll call you once I'm done," I promise, blowing her a kiss. She returns the action before clicking off.

Now alone, I walk the last fifteen steps in silence. I've had a tradition, since high school, that whenever I'm afraid of doing something, I quickly list the things I'm scared of, but through a positive lens. That way, when I enter, I can leave them outside.

You can do this.

You deserve to have a fun date with a guy, no strings attached, no requirements.

You're worthy of being loved.

With my intrusive thoughts left outside to wait like an angry Pomeranian tied to a bike rack, I smile and push my way into the restaurant.

———— · ————

I'M ACTUALLY EARLY and the first to arrive, which isn't uncommon in my life. *If you're on time, you're late, and if you're late, you're fucked.* That's what my mom told me when she dropped me off at Northeastern. Follow that simple rule, and you'll have a leg up no matter where you go.

I guess that's become second nature now. So, when Wallace finally arrives, his brow furrowed with disappointment, I smile reassuringly.

"I was early," I promise. "You're right on time."

"Oh, thank God," he lets out with a sigh. "I thought I kept you waiting."

Wallace looks better in real life than he does in his photo—not that he looked bad in his photo, at all, but it just didn't do him justice. His blond hair is cut short, but still styled in a simple, clean-cut way. His eyes are blue, a bright, almost electric blue. He has some signs of age, minor crow's feet, but he wears it comfortably; not with shame, but pride. For the date, he's wearing a simple button-down shirt, white with dark blue lines in the pattern—a shade that complements his eyes—alongside cream-colored slacks, and loafers. The corner of my mouth twitches. I remember the one time I tried to get Hudson to buy loafers and he compared them to—what was it— "wearing hot dog buns" on his feet.

The way Wallace grins when he sits down tells me he doesn't think about the age difference between us—nearly nine years—as a problem, and he's just here for a good time. A no-strings-attached date.

"Have you been here before?" he asks, scanning the menu. His voice is nice, I note. Soft, but not too soft, still carrying a masculine twang. Different from Hudson's deep, rumbling voice. I'm not sure which one I like more. The softness of his, which makes my shoulders relax, or the baritone of Hudson's, which makes my body shiver.

I bite my inner cheek as punishment—this isn't the time to compare the two of them. That's not why I'm here. I'm here to *get over* Hudson. Not play a horny version of *Love It or List It: The Boyfriend Edition*.

"Never," I say. Waiting too long to respond would make it awkward. "Divya says it has great tapas, though. You work with her, right?"

Of course he does. I've even seen him a few times in the office. But how else am I supposed to break the ice? Divya is Switzerland, neutral ground, a church during wartime. We can settle there until we're comfortable having a meaningful conversation.

Wallace nods, his eyes shifting like a typewriter across the menu. "She's great. A real trouper and smart as heck."

Heck. Did he just say heck? Does this guy not curse? How can he be friends with Divya?

"She's going to take my job one day if I'm not careful," he says with a laugh.

"She doesn't practice divorce law." Unless she made a change that I didn't know about? Divya has never been good with mediating conflict. Her solution whenever one of our friends is having relationship problems? Dump them.

"I imagine if Divya wanted to, she could learn it," Wallace counters. "You know her. She's . . ."

"Brilliant?"

"I was going to go with scary brilliant, but that works too."

Either term is correct, probably Wallace's more so. Divya is one of those people who are naturally talented. Of course she works hard—no one could say she doesn't—but things come easier to her once she puts her mind to them. I wish I had that. Again, I know she works hard, harder than most people, but just once I'd like to work hard and *also* be successful. If only life were actually a meritocracy.

"Kian?" Wallace says, snapping me out of my mental spiral. The waitress smiles respectfully at me. I take a moment to piece the scene together and identify the role I'm playing.

"The sangria, white if you have it?" I ask. "And I'll have the . . . *pan con tomate*, and the *pintxos morunos*."

The waitress's and Wallace's eyes show surprise and pride when they hear my Spanish. As she walks away, I clarify, "I minored in Spanish in college. Thought it would give me a leg up in the job market."

"Ah." Wallace smirks. "So Divya *didn't* pick a Spanish restaurant just so you could impress me with your knowledge of tapas and Spanish wines? That's what you're telling me?"

"I don't pretend to understand her or know her choices. She's her own person."

"Hear, hear."

Stillness settles between us as the low murmur of the restaurant fills the space. It's not a bad feeling, just sitting there, enjoying the warm-but-not-too-warm Boston midafternoon. It's different. I try to recall my first date with Hudson. How we couldn't stop talking, laughing, or joking. How we argued about the best Ellie Goulding song (her cover of "Your Song," obviously) or how we tried to see who could withstand the spiciest of sauces (me). How we bonded for hours, until, in not so many words, the owners said *get the fuck out* at two o'clock in the morning.

This is nothing like that. There's a sense of calm energy, not frantic, passing between us. Wallace isn't trying to fill every second with words, and he seems to find depth in the space that quiet leaves behind. It's refreshing. Scary, but refreshing, because I want to fill it. I want to talk and talk and talk, because that's what I'm used to. Hell, it's the only real-life reference point I have, since flirting on Grindr or Bumble or OkCupid doesn't count.

Maybe there's something to learn from him, I think. Perhaps enjoying the silence and what it offers isn't a bad thing, just a different way of getting to know someone. Because if you can judge a person by how they treat service workers, you can definitely judge a person by how they handle a break in conversation.

"So, Divya tells me you're into journalism?" Wallace asks.

Into journalism sounds like it's some hobby I have. People are *into* video games, knitting, running recreationally. I wouldn't say to him, *You're into law?* But I keep that thought buried. I'm sure he means nothing by it. I hope he means nothing by it. I'm not in the mood to navigate professional elitism today.

Instead, I just nod. "Investigative journalism, yeah."

"Like that piece in the *Atlantic* that came out about for-profit prisons last month?" he asks, thanking the waitress when she brings us bread and olive oil. "Pretty deep stuff. That judge who was funneling kids into the prison system to pad his pockets?"

"Exactly," I confirm, not at all surprised he used that reference. "A classmate of mine wrote that, actually."

Did he hear the jealousy in my voice? Adam secured that job at the *Atlantic* before he even graduated, plus he already had a top story under his belt. Sure, Adam is talented—really talented. And I wish him the best. When one of us succeeds, we all succeed, blah blah blah.

Screw it. I wish I wrote that goddamn article. A white guy writ-

ing about the plight of Black and Brown youth? Did he not see the
irony in that? Of course he didn't. He still profited off the suffering
of Black and Brown kids.

Wallace reaches over and squeezes my wrist. "I'm sure whatever
article you write will be ten times better than his."

My eyes linger on the way his hand touches mine. There's a
spark there, but not a roaring flame. More like the spark that jump-
starts engines. Definitely different than the first time Hudson
touched me.

"Is it that obvious?" I ask.

"Pretty much so. But hey, we all are envious of someone. Wanting to one-up our competition is what makes us human."

"Makes us American."

He raises his glass in a silent gesture of support.

When the food comes, almost twenty minutes later, Wallace
and I are deep in conversation. The nice and unsuspecting thing is
how easily the conversation flows. The pauses seem natural. The way
he actually replies to my questions, and asks his own insightful
ones, makes me pause and think before answering. Not saying I
didn't have that with Hudson, but it feels different. Smoother. How
a first date is supposed to go when things are going well.

"Oh, I don't agree with you on that," I say, sipping the last bit of
my sangria. He doesn't hesitate to wave down the waitress and order
me another one. "I completely think the James Bond franchise could
be revamped to have a woman star."

"Really?" he asks. "Tell me more."

The phone in my pocket vibrates. I pull it out, the screen illumi-
nating with a GIF from Divya that reads *how's it going* in big colorful text, over the image of a kid repeatedly leaning through a
windowsill and falling out. I pocket the phone and turn it to silent.

"007 is a title. It's not a person. The title is passed from person to person, giving them the license to kill. James Bond, now, *that's* a person's name. So, somehow, at some point in history, we conflated the two; that 007 is synonymous with James Bond and vice versa."

Wallace slowly nods. "So, the question is, is our series about James Bond, the person, or the title?"

"Exactly. If it's the former, then sure, Daniel Craig or whoever should continue playing him. But if it's about the title, 007, which I suspect it is, then anyone can play them. Like Lashana Lynch did in *No Time to Die*, which sets the stage for us to have a Latinx Bond or an Asian Bond. It's about time, if you ask me."

"And what are your thoughts?"

"On James Bond, the series?" I ask, thanking the waitress when she arrives with a fresh chilled glass.

"About Daniel Craig," Wallace clarifies. "What are your thoughts on him?"

What a weird question, I think, taking the moment to sip my drink as a distraction. I use the seconds to try and see if there is some ulterior motive behind Wallace's words. Did I miss something in the news that he did? Is he suddenly canceled for doing something in the past twelve hours?

I decide to keep my answer neutral. "I think he's a great actor and has starred in awesome movies, and some duds too."

"Agreed," Wallace says, taking a moment. I can tell he's thinking if he wants to say what's churning through his mind, or if he's going to bite his own tongue. "What about his looks, though? That's what I'm most concerned with."

Another pause. Another beat. And then it all clicks.

I grin, only a fraction of a smile, before pulling my cheeks tight. "I think he's very attractive. I also think you have some similar features to him, which makes you pretty attractive, too. Do people tell you that often?"

"That I look like Daniel Craig?" he says with a laugh, chugging the last of his red sangria before switching to water and drinking half of that. "No? Yes? What's the right answer here? One's a lie, and one makes me sound cocky."

"There's no right answer when it comes to talking yourself up during a date, only the least wrong answer. And right now, I think the least wrong answer is to be honest."

"My mom always told me that's the best policy."

"Mothers have some secret handbook given to them when they have a kid, that no one else gets, I'm certain of it."

"Agreed. Hundred percent."

He grins softly at me. "Well, then yes, I've heard that before. Do you like that about me?"

I think it over for a moment and then nod. "Yeah, I do. I like it a lot."

"Good. Would break my heart if you didn't."

"And why's that?"

"Because then there wouldn't be a chance for a date two, and then what would I do?"

"Cry?" I suggest.

He laughs, a deep, bellowing one. It sends a shiver down my spine, like a familiar chill. I didn't realize, until right then, how much I missed that feeling.

FOURTEEN

"SHOES, SOCKS, BELTS . . ."

Packing is my own personal hell. When I die and Christians are proven right about homosexuals being deviants, and I'm yeeted into a fiery pit with walls of knotty pine, my daily job for eternity is going to be packing bags.

For one, it doesn't make sense. We pack barely enough shirts and pants, but mountains of underwear like we're going to shit ourselves *every single day*? And that's just . . . an acceptable thing? Like, why, for a five-day trip, am I packing eight pairs of underwear? Is there something about my body I don't know about? More importantly, who was the person to start this ritual? Did something tragic happen on a trip that scarred them for life?

I stare at my bed, clothes strewn across it like it's in a bad episode of *Law and Order*. I should be packed by now. I need to get to the airport in the next two and a half hours, and that's pushing it. Luckily, one of those blue van services only needs like a forty-five-minute warning, so I should be fine. But still, I have no idea what to wear.

"Obviously the suit, right?" I ask myself. That would make sense. That's going to be what Hudson expects me to wear. Anything else is just childish. There's a time for being rebellious and then there's a time for—

What is that sound?

It takes me a moment to pinpoint the muffled ringing, and another two rings for me to frantically pat at my bed and find the phone, five rings deep. Without looking at it, I answer.

"I need help deciding what to pack," I say. Divya's probably calling me. She knows I'm leaving soon and since she had an important case dropped in her lap during the middle of last week, she can't be here in person for support. "If you were here, you'd know what to bring. Quit being a lawyer and come be my personal stylist."

There's no sound on the other end of the line, longer than a pause should last. Divya always has the perfect zinger. It's why we're friends. Her silence is . . . off. I pull back the phone to look at the number. My old boss? A recruiter cold-calling me? Sallie Mae?

Nope. Worse.

"Shit."

"Shit? Is that really how you talk to your mother?"

That's not a question, it's a statement. My mother might be a kind woman with a warm smile who runs an antique shop in North Carolina, but she's also a woman who protested the Gulf War in the '90s. She ran for office against a very Republican representative and never backed down, even when she lost by twenty-three points. She started the grassroots support for a petition to get a coffee shop shut down when it refused to serve a trans couple. My mother isn't someone who asks anyone for anything—she demands it, because she knows she's worth it.

I wish I had that same amount of courage.

"Sorry. I thought you were someone else." I slip on my AirPods and continue packing, putting my phone on the counter in my cramped studio so I don't forget it. "What's up?"

"Oh, no. You're not going to dodge the conversation that easily."

Didn't think I was, but I was hopeful.

"What are you packing for?"

"A trip, Mom."

"I know it's a trip," she scolds. "I'm not stupid. Where are you going?"

I hesitate to answer. My mom believes in the Socratic Method. Having finished about three-quarters of her master's in education before having me, she likes to throw a lot of those teachings into our conversations. Usually, though not instantly, the lessons she uses against me come in handy—I guess that's what parenthood is about: finding clever ways to pour all your knowledge into your kids' empty heads—but it also means I have to work my way through the thicket before I see the valley. And I don't have the time or patience for the lecture that's going to come when she realizes why I'm going down south.

"I'm visiting a friend." I've always thought my mom could sniff out a lie, so I learned to live in the comfortable grey area of half-truths. Hudson isn't exactly a friend, but I don't consider him an enemy either. And after all, aren't we taught that everyone is our friend? So, in a manner of speaking, Hudson *is* a friend.

"Mhm," my mom drags out. I can practically see her lips turned into one thin line; her eyes narrowed in that suspicious way she adopts when she smells blood in the water. "Do I know this friend?"

"Yes. You've met them a few times."

"Where does this friend live?"

"Georgia."

That's enough truth for her. A swift right turn down Any Other

Fucking Topic Avenue, and I can buy time until I have to go. "How's the shop doing? You just hired a new employee, right?"

"Oh, don't get me started on her."

For the next ten minutes, Mom drones on and on about the drama in her small town. How the new worker she brought on doesn't know the difference between eighteenth- and nineteenth-century woodworks. How she might buy the shop space next door so she can expand. Local gossip in the town where Jamal and I grew up. While she's talking, I give the occasional "uh-huh" and "that's crazy." Not so much that she'll catch on to me doing other things, but enough that she'll think I'm engaged in the conversation instead of texting Divya outfit choices and reading the replies.

Definitely the red shirt, Divya texts less than ten seconds later. Maybe the black. It's hot in the south, but you look fuckable in it. Very Seal.

"So, business seems to be going well?" I ask.

"What has your father told you?"

"Not everything is a conspiracy, Mom. I'm just asking."

She scoffs, and I hear the sharp clicking of metal against porcelain. She must be home, or in the back of the shop. That's the sound of the cups she loves. I glance over and check the clock: 9:45 a.m. Around time for her morning tea, right on schedule.

"Dad's not working anymore. He can help you at the shop."

"If I need it, I'll ask for it. He knows better."

Mom's always been stubborn. Supposedly I get that from her. The jury is still out on that one.

"So, since you seem to have time to go on trips with your friends, when are you going to come home and see me? You know Jamal came just last month."

Of course he did. Jamal does everything right. Better school.

Better major. Better son. I don't even roll my eyes at that jab. Part of it is true. After graduation I was planning on coming home, but I justified needing to stay in the city for job interviews. I couldn't expect people to do things remotely. But now, there's no reason not to go home. At least for a little bit. Some home cooking. Some time with Mom and Dad. It'll be nice. Maybe it's just what the doctor ordered.

That's what a normal kid would say. But I've never been a normal child.

It's not that I don't enjoy spending time with my mom, I do. A lot. I don't think it's too dramatic to say my bond with my mom is stronger than it is with my dad. Kids, after all, always pick one parent. If you find a twentysomething who has a great relationship with both of their parents, call *The Guinness Book of World Records*.

But going home means fielding questions from Mom, the town, Dad, everyone I knew before I went up north. I can't deal with their disappointment when they realize the boy they thought was going to do such big and great things is nothing more than average. They'll be nice about it, sure, because people there are always nice about uncomfortable things like that. They'll say, *You'll get there someday!* Or, *Struggle makes it all worth it!* Or, even worse, they'll quote a Bible verse at me, making me wish my skin would erupt into hellfire. At least that would be interesting.

No, I can deal with the Southern platitudes. It's the look of disappointment that'll cross their face and stay plastered on their features throughout our whole conversation that I can't handle. It's the way they'll talk about me behind my back, and whisper things when Mom walks in the room or when she leaves. It's the way some of them will feel vindicated by my failure and feast off my inadequacy. I won't put up with that. I won't put my mom through that.

"Soon," I promise, throwing my toiletries into a ziplock bag and lobbing it into the plump suitcase. "I'll come home soon."

"When? Give me a date."

"This fall."

"You mean for Thanksgiving? I would hope so! I swear to God, Kian Andrews, if you are not home for Thanksgiving *and* Christmas . . ."

"I will be, I will be! I promise. Who is going to make those sweet potatoes I love?"

"Exactly. And I want you home next month. Even if it's just for the weekend. All right?"

"I'll have to check my schedule . . . but . . ."

"All right, Kian?" she repeats with a deeper voice.

"All right, Jesus."

"Watch your language. Don't—"

"Use the Lord's name in vain, I know."

"And yet you still do it. See, this is what I'm talking about. You should have stayed close to home. UNC, Duke, Wake Forest. You know you could have gotten into any of those schools. Full ride, too, I bet."

"You know I did," I remind her. It was the pride and joy of her life for a few months. Fully paid tuition to all three, UNC even offering me a room and board stipend. Mom couldn't stop cheering and hollering down the street, calling every family member and friend to tell them. I think—no, I know—she was more excited than I was, but that made me more excited too. There's something about making your parents proud that sinks into your bones like mercury. Something about it that changes you.

I check my phone again. I need to call a blue van soon.

"So, you're coming home . . . when?"

"November," I repeat.

"Promise?"

"Promise."

I don't have the heart to confess everything to my mom. I'm sure Jamal, who loves to have weekly phone calls with Mom, has already done so. It's not that I don't trust her to give me good advice. It's the opposite, really. She'd give me sage wisdom and convince me to give up on Hudson right then and there.

There's no reward worth your dignity, Kian, she would say. *You can't get that back.*

But what she doesn't understand is that dignity doesn't pay the bills. Dignity doesn't give me enough status to get a job at CNBC or the *New York Times*, or wherever I want to go after Spotlight. Dignity won't pay my student loans. I wish those two things weren't exclusive. I wish I could be as bold and strong and confident as she was.

But everything goes back to our small town. I won't return there. I won't be that person who couldn't make it in a big city and has to accept a small, mundane, simple life. That's great for others; more power to those people. That's not me. It'll never be me.

"I need to get going, Mom," I say, sitting on my suitcase and zipping it slowly. "I'll call you when I land in Georgia."

"Okay, baby," she says. "You know I love you, right?"

"I know."

"And you know everything I do is for you and your brother."

"I know, Mom."

"So, when I tell you, you need to dump that boy this moment and cut your losses, you know I only say that because I care about you."

"I know—wait, what?"

Mom sucks her teeth over the phone in disapproval. "A trip to

Georgia? You think I'm that stupid, Kian? I know whose family lives in Georgia."

Of course she does. I roll my eyes, putting on my black UGG slip-ons. Who was I to think I could get something past her?

"You know this is a bad idea, right? No. Not a bad idea. A stupid idea."

"That's the same thing Jamal said."

"I don't say this often, because I love both of you equally, but this time your younger brother might be smarter than you."

"Ouch?" I put my hand over my chest, though she can't see it.

"If you don't want to be called stupid, don't do stupid things. This is a bad idea. Colorado Rivers broke your heart."

"Hudson," I correct. "And it was a mutual breakup."

"HAH!" My mom laughs sharply, so loud that I have to turn down the volume on my AirPods to compensate for the monetary ringing in my ears. "Who names their kid *Hudson*?"

"Better than Colorado," I mutter.

"Want to say that louder?"

"Nothing. I'll be fine, Mom. The breakup is fine. I'm fine."

"Word of advice? When you use 'fine' three times in a sentence, it tells me you're not fine."

My phone vibrates again. Divya's name appears.

DIVYA EVANS: Have you left yet? Traffic in the city is a mess.

"We can talk about this later," I promise. "But I need to get going or I'm going to miss my flight."

"That doesn't sound like the worst thing. But fine. This is your life, not mine. This is actually good."

I can't wait to hear this. "I'll bite. How's that?"

"Because now you can't get mad at me for calling your brother."

"I'm sorry, what?"

I don't get the chance to hear an answer before the heavy pounding of a fist against the metal sliding door of my loft shakes the room.

"Hurry the fuck up, Kian. I'm not going to wait all day."

———— · ————

WHEN I WALK downstairs and poke my head out of the window, sure enough, Jamal and his grey Prius are there. He's sitting in the front seat, texting furiously, but not so absorbed in whatever conversation he's having that he doesn't tell me what to do when I approach the car.

"Get in," he says, putting his phone in his lap. "I'm not going to have Mom blaming me for you being late."

"No *Hi, Kian? How are you doing, Kian? I'm so happy to spend time with you driving you to the airport, Kian?*"

I put my suitcase in the back seat and slide into the passenger side. Much like everything in Jamal's life, the car is perfectly organized. Not a speck of food anywhere, napkins in the front compartment, gum in the middle section. There's even a small black bag for strands of trash, and the car has a soft scent of vanilla like he burned a candle, captured the aroma, and sprayed it on the seats before he jumped in. Which might sound over-the-top, but I wouldn't put it past him.

"What?" I ask, buckling my seatbelt. "What is it now?"

He stares at me, honey-colored eyes narrowed slightly before turning to the street. "Nothing."

"It's obviously something or you wouldn't be scowling at me. What is that thing Mom said? 'Keep your face like that . . .'"

"And it'll get stuck like that," he finishes for me. "You know that's not true, right? Scientifically speaking."

"How do you know? You're a businessman, not a scientist. Maybe there's precedent."

"You're dumb," he says flatly, pulling into traffic and driving toward the airport. Logan International Airport isn't far from my apartment. I could have taken an Uber or the T, or I could have answered Hudson's text when he offered to order me a car (or pick me up himself), but that felt . . . wrong. I'm not exactly sure how to describe it, but taking his charity would have felt like I couldn't afford to get myself to the airport. I'm unemployed, not destitute. I can take care of myself. I have friends and family I can call on, thank you very much.

"Let's be clear," Jamal says, keeping his eyes on the road. "The only reason I'm here is because Mom demanded I come. I would much rather be . . ."

"Studying? Raiding some company for sport and throwing hard-working employees out on the street? Watching PBS?"

"I'm this close to throwing PBS out on the street if you don't appreciate me picking you up."

"To be fair, you're only doing it because Mom forced you to," I remind him, before adding quickly, "But thank you. I appreciate it."

"Thank you. Was that so hard?"

"Deeply."

We drive in silence for the majority of the trip. I don't take cars across town often, so I don't get to see Boston from this level. It's one thing to watch a city pass you by when you're walking, but seeing the landscape blur by, observing the shades blend together like watercolors, is different. There's something beautiful about it, something a step removed. It reminds me why I picked Northeastern. Not just for the education, not for the proximity to New York City and journalism jobs, but because it was different from Raleigh in a way that made me excited. And I still feel the same way.

"Not to make a thing out of this, but are you going to be okay?"

I turn my attention to my brother, who doesn't pull his eyes away from the street. I'm not sure if he's focused on the road because he's a Perfect Driver—like he's perfect at everything else—or for the other, more obvious reason. Emotional moments between the two of us are Awkward.

"Just so you know, by saying, 'Let's not make a thing out of something,' you're making a thing out of something," I reply softly. His eyes flicker over to me. Without saying anything, I offer him a grin. The silent exchange between the two of us speaks volumes.

I'm here for you, his initial statement says.

I know, thank you, my smile says.

If you need me to beat his ass, I'll do it, his glance replies.

"I know, Jamal," I say out loud. "Thank you."

The Prius slides smoothly into a space at Terminal B with fifty-five minutes to spare, more than enough time for a domestic flight. Without a word I get out and open the back seat door, yanking out my suitcase.

"By the way," I start to ask, leaning into the car. Jamal has already gone back to texting. "PBS, what is that? Is that some young gay slang I missed out on?"

"You're only three years older than me. Even you are not ancient in gay years, K," he reminds me. "And PBS stands for Phat Black Stern. I just made it up."

That makes sense. I pat the side of his door and step back. "Keep your career, Jamal. Stand-up isn't for you. Thanks for the ride."

Before he can say something back in retort, I turn my back and walk toward the terminal. But really, the reason I walk so quickly is to keep from chickening out, jumping in his car, and returning home.

FIFTEEN

HUDSON RIVERS: When you arrive, I'll be at the kiosk. You can't miss me.

The purple ticket Mrs. Rivers flashed belongs to Royal Airlines. It's a high-end airline company that boasts that even their economy seats feel like business class, and first class feels like you're flying on a cloud. Of course, for the price of six hundred dollars for a domestic flight between Boston and Atlanta, economy better fucking feel like I'm being courted by Charlie Hunnam on our wedding day.

Flying first class on a normal airline always seemed like an extravagance not worth spending money on. If I'm traveling, would I rather stay in a three-star hotel or sit on a plane for a few hours in style? The former, always. It's like when you choose an apartment: You pick it for the long-term benefits, not the short-term flash.

Or, if you're like me and every other person in Generation Z, you're happy with any apartment you can get.

My fingertips tingle as I approach the purple sign with the golden check mark that designates Royal Airlines kiosks. Every step closer makes me feel out of my element. Obviously, Hudson is going to fly first class. I should be excited. I should be ecstatic. The rumored perks they provide? Astronomical. But I'd be lying if I said it didn't make me feel like an imposter. Or a sex worker. Not that there's anything wrong with sex work; in fact, I fully support it and a person's right to get paid for providing a service—everyone should get paid for their work. But this makes me feel like I'm playing a part I didn't fully sign on to; like I'm a puppet whose strings are being pulled to meet some quota that I didn't know I was filling.

You have no one to blame for this feeling but yourself, my conscience scolds me. *You could have said no. You didn't have to agree. This is a business transaction, remember? You told Hudson that. And in a business transaction, you often have to do things you don't want to do. Just suck it up.*

But deep down, I know it's not that. I've done things I haven't wanted to do plenty of times. Applied for jobs I knew were beneath me. Played up the Gay Card or Black Card to get a foot in the door. Lied to myself, and others, for a moment of solace. I'm not a stranger to compromise. But there's something nagging inside of me telling me this isn't a compromise. This is selling out in a misguided attempt to give myself value by being in Hudson's orbit again and benefiting from the society he so easily disparages.

Or maybe I'm just fucking overthinking it?

How often do people get to fly first class? How often do people get to wear expensive (FREE) suits? How often do people get to play another role where the cost of being discovered is minimal? This should be fun. It's Hudson who has more to lose here, not me. A chance like this won't come again. I'm never going to be someone who makes $400K a year barely blinking an eye. Generational wealth? Top three percent of society? What are those things? I should just sit back, relax, and enjoy the next few days. Take them as they come.

Not everything has to be a Broadway, end-of-first act, "Defying Gravity"–level dramatic moment, Kian.

Also, let's face it, I'm far more a Nessa than an Elphaba, and that's going to take me at least thirty therapy sessions to come to terms with.

Getting through security at Logan is surprisingly easy, and I'm rounding the corner down Terminal B as my phone buzzes with a text from Hudson.

HUDSON RIVERS: You close?

My body shivers. That phrase gives me flashbacks to all my hookups who have used that expression, accompanied with *How big are you? Top? Bottom? DTF? U on PREP?* The last one is valid and important, but it's like those five expressions, spoken in some special order, unlock the secrets to the winning algorithm on *RuPaul's Drag Race* or something.

I type with my free hand without looking: Be there in 3. My phone vibrates again.

HUDSON RIVERS: Royal Lounge on your right. Just give them your name.

I pause in the middle of the hallway, forcing the people walking behind me to move to my left and right like a boulder diverting the flow of a river. I've never been in an airport lounge before. That's always felt like some high society–level luxury. But, for now, I guess I *am* high society.

No autographs at this time, please.

The woman at the lounge entrance, wearing the purple synonymous with Royal Airlines in dress form with a gold trim, smiles brightly. "Welcome to Royal Airlines, where every trip you're treated like a King, Queen, or anything in between!"

Thanks, I hate it.

"Hi. Told I just need to give you my name? Kian? Andrews?"

She nods and quickly types away. Her eyes light up when my name appears. "Welcome, Mr. Andrews! You're with the Rivers party?"

"Yep."

"Right this way! We'll take your bag if you want?"

I look down at my shoulder bag with my laptop and, yes, an extra pair of underwear in it. "This isn't too big or anything, is it? I checked the sizes online."

"Oh no no!" she says apologetically. "More for your comfort. We'll have it in your seat for you when you get on board."

"Ah, the benefits of being rich."

"Sorry?"

"Nothing." I smile quickly and hand over my bag. "Thank you . . . Jackie."

She smiles back and takes my bag, putting a printed-out tag on it that I can see reads: KIAN A.—RIVERS PARTY, before putting it on a conveyor belt. She then taps a button on her screen, and the purple door with the golden emblem in the middle slides open.

"Welcome to the Royal Treatment."

——— · ———

INSIDE THE ROYAL Lounge is like stepping into the Emerald City. Except I guess it would be called the Amethyst City, if I'm being accurate. Purple carpets, golden painted walls. Everyone working dressed in purple-and-gold outfits. The room makes me dizzy, in a good way, like how casinos pump a higher concentration of oxygen into the air to make people euphoric and gamble more.

Or maybe, just maybe, that's the Rivers Effect.

Would I feel the same light-headedness if I had won a trip with Divya on a Royal Airlines flight, and stumbled into this lounge? Maybe. But the fact Hudson is sitting there, with his black, practically painted-on herringbone button-down—slightly open—tucked into his jeans, and his black boots? That doesn't help either.

Once again, I'm a rock in the middle of the stream—a stupid, dumbstruck rock. I've seen individual pieces of that outfit before. I suggested he buy those shoes a few months back. But to see him so effortlessly wearing them all? His dark brown, almost black hair always faded perfectly? His eyes scanning the magazine in his hand like a typewriter?

I've never been a big fan of meet-cute rom-coms, but if anyone wants the rights to my life, as long as they use some drastic artistic license, I'd be down for selling.

Clearing my throat, I remember why I'm here.

Professional Advancement.

Life-changing career opportunities.

Not a hopeful dick appointment.

It takes me sitting down next to him and nudging his shoulder for Hudson to look up from his article, boyish eyes wide with surprise.

"Oh, hey! You're here. Good. Was worried you weren't going to make it, or they weren't going to let you in. And before you make an 'Is it because I'm Black?' joke, no. They're picky if the ticket isn't in your name. Also, that doesn't work on me because I'm also Black."

"Then what makes you think I would make that joke?"

"Because you *always* make that joke."

"It's like how every Black person can tie everything back to—"

"—don't say slavery."

"Slavery."

He rolls his eyes. "Please don't make that joke around my parents. Please. I beg you."

"Because . . . ?"

"Because my parents don't have that type of humor."

I concede. "Fine, I won't. Not because I don't think I should, but because I'm nice."

Hudson grins and gives a fake, seated bow. "I appreciate you, oh benevolent one. Get here okay?"

Do I tell him about the conversation I had with my mom? Do I tell him the support Jamal gave me with no words at all? No. That won't help anyone. Right now, our interactions feel . . . tenuous. That's the word. I don't want to ruin whatever silent agreement we have to pretend my showing up at his doorstep a week ago didn't happen.

"Yeah, no problem at all. What are you reading?"

Hudson raises the magazine to me: *How Isaac Rivers Turned an Empire into an Empire.*

"You're reading an article about your father? Don't you know the answer to that already?"

"If I was Olivia, yes. She probably helped write this article, or at least vet it. But remember, I'm the failure in the family. Might as well have as many advantages as I can before we arrive. I won't have unlimited chances to impress him."

As Hudson turns back to the article, I can't help but feel sorry for him. There are many reasons to be jealous of Hudson. His money, his connections, the fact he is a rich man in America with very above-average looks. But the relationship with his parents isn't one of them. In some ways, if Hudson versus Kian were laid out like one of those presidential policy checklists, I'd have the check in the parental category. My parents and I have always been close. I know I can rely on them when I need them or if I need them. If I wanted to come home, I'd never feel like I had to lie to impress them. Or that I'd have to make up some story about things I'm interested in to get their approval. My parents are always in my corner.

Which, I recognize sounds rich, since I just lied to my mom about where I was going and haven't been home to visit her for fear of letting her down, but it's not the same. It's very different. I don't know how. But it is.

"When you're done, I wanna read that," I say, pulling out my phone. "Might as well be on the same page, right? Isn't that a date's job, to make their significant other look good?"

I don't look up from my phone, but I know Hudson's looking at me, probably with a mixture of a smile and surprise. His broad shoulder nudges mine.

"You're welcome," I say without him having to say thank you. Even if he wanted to, he wouldn't be able to. The front desk staffer announcing flight 514 to Atlanta drowns out everything in the overly purple room.

SIXTEEN

HERE'S THE THING: I'm not a scientist.

I'm a journalist. I believe in the written word. The power of the pen. How words can change the world. I understand that science is a real thing. I love it. I trust it. Usually.

I do not trust planes.

Devil's magic. That's what keeps them up. Not air currents, or the motors that spin and lift us off the ground. Not thousands of metallic pieces working in unison, dozens of cables or years of training from skilled pilots. Devils. Magic. Humans are not meant to be in the air. If we were, we'd have wings.

So, as the Royal Airlines flight roars, gallops across the runway, and giddyups off the ground at a steep angle for about ten minutes, I can't do anything but grip the plush first-class seats so tightly my knuckles turn white. Which isn't easy for a dark-skinned Black guy.

In my head, I recite a song to keep me busy. Specifically, "Heaven Is a Place on Earth" by our '80s pop queen Belinda Carlisle. It's my flight trick. See, "Heaven Is a Place on Earth" is about four minutes long. If I listen to it three times, then we're at cruising altitude by the time it's over, and the hardest part of the trip is over. God has spared me.

But God obviously has a sense of humor, because when I open my eyes, Hudson is sitting across from me, smirking.

"What?"

"Nothing," he teases. "You weren't lying before about hating planes, I see."

I force my right hand to release its grasp on the purple leather seat. The imprint of my grip, like a fossilized echo of the past left for an archaeologist to find, stays for a moment before the leather relaxes and returns to its plump, curved form.

Royal Airlines really didn't spare a single expense when it came to their first-class section. Each pod is about eight feet wide, long enough for two people to sit across from each other and still have leg room. There's a table between us that folds down, with separate screens where we can order anything we want, watch whatever we want, you name it. Each seat has its own chargers, along with a personal button to recline the seats. There's another button to shift the layout of the pod, so you can lie next to the person you're with, a noise-canceling button, a light-dimming button, and one that changes the inside of your pod to make it appear like different places around the world.

I cycle through that button, counting the different options. Lights inside the pod shift and project different scenes on the walls: an island, a winter wonderland, a forest, a desert, a bustling city, a Scottish countryside. Each of them evokes a different feeling, and within five minutes, I forget we're thirty-five thousand feet in the air.

Well, I forgot until right then.

"Will a drink help?" Hudson offers, tapping the screen. A plethora of options, from alcoholic concoctions exclusive to the airline to specialty milkshakes mixed with ingredients I've never even heard of, appear before me.

"I'm partial to a simple pop, if I can suggest something," he says. "Real Mexican cola. Hits the spot. And all free, too."

It's funny how the wealthy always like to point out when things are free. The ones who need it the least capitalize on systems and benefits to spend the least amount of money. But that's not the conversation I should be having with Hudson. I should try to bridge the gap, not build a chasm.

"I'll order the cola if you order . . ." I tap the screen a few times, bringing up the food options. The flight is only three hours, but we'll arrive after lunch. There's no telling what Hudson's family has in store for us.

"The tuna," I settle on.

Hudson's handsome face twists into disgust. "You're serious, aren't you?"

"As serious as a group of gays heading to Fire Island during the summer."

The right corner of his mouth twitches into a grin. He shakes his head and taps the screen three times. I see the order compilation in his right corner say: TUNA.

"See, that wasn't so hard, was it?" I hold up my end of the bargain, typing out the Mexican Coke, throwing a chicken club in there with it.

The skies under us are completely white. The air above us is completely blue. The Royal Airlines plane feels like it's gliding on the air, like there isn't some sinful affront to God at play that keeps us in the air, but actually His grace. If you're into that stuff. I don't know where I stand on religion, but seeing how beautiful it is up here, above the noise and the problems of the city below, makes me want to consider going back to church.

After a moment of staring out the window, I glance over, and Hudson is smiling at me.

"What?"

He shakes his head. "Nothing. You just look . . ."

"Wide-eyed with wonder? Innocent?" I ask, closing the shade. My side of the pod adjusts its light to keep the same warmth and temperature.

"That's not the word I would use," Hudson says in a singsong voice. I swipe my leg quickly under the table, but lucky for him, he moves before we can make contact.

Suddenly, the plane shifts. Not once, but twice. The lady sitting in the pod across from us almost sloshes her wine out of her glass. It's not over, either. The plane continues to rumble as it gallops across the sky, the metal vibrating, threatening to bend and break under the punishment the deceptively clear skies give out.

Hudson barely seems to notice. I, on the other hand, notice every twitch.

I'm going to die here, I think, gripping the chair again. *We're going to fall out of the sky, all of us burning up on impact. Sure, it'll be quick and painless, but I'm going to die at the age of twenty-three. I'm never going to get married. Never going to collect Social Security. Never—*

"Hey." Hudson's voice breaks through the pulsing of blood in my ears. I open one eye, just barely, and see his soft smile looking back at me. His hand slides, slowly, across the table, and rests over mine. He gives it one soft squeeze. "It's just turbulence. Just shifts in air patterns. We'll be okay. The plane can withstand much more than this. Did you know a plane can technically fly without any engines and land? We'll be fine."

"Is that true?"

"Well, technically it can glide and land, it's not going to just drop out of the sky like a rock."

"That . . . doesn't help," I whisper back. "At all."

Hudson frowns and scratches at the faint stubble on his chin. Why did I never notice it before? The soft edges of brown hair, which seem to glow in the pure light that pours down when we're above the skies? Did he have it a week ago, on our "date"? No. I would have pointed it out. I always thought he would look good with some facial hair, but he always said he *liked* being "baby-faced." He'd said it made him young and, "You know how much the gay community loves young gay guys."

"Then how about this," he whispers. "Answer a question for me."

The plane shakes again. Enough for the woman across from us to grab her drink. "Rougher-than-usual flight," she says in her posh voice.

Yeah, we're going to die.

Hudson squeezes my hand, harder this time, turning my attention back to him. "Fine," I say, "what's the question?"

He doesn't hesitate to ask, "Why haven't you changed course? I mean, and I don't mean this the wrong way, but you've been . . ."

Hudson hesitates, but I know what he's getting at. "You can say it."

"Unemployed for a while now. You're smart, you can shift gears. There are plenty of jobs that'll take you or certificate programs you can do to make you marketable for another field. So why keep at it?"

"Are you saying you don't think I can get a job in journalism?"

"No." He shakes his head. "I'm saying when you could do anything, why not take the path of least resistance instead of keep punching a brick wall?"

I want him to know there's a lot of subtext in that statement. Not bad subtext, of course. He's asking a question I've asked myself about a dozen times, especially when I have midnight panic attacks, thinking I'm making a huge mistake. But the fact that someone who could legit have anything they want in the world is asking me why I'm making a choice seems almost tone-deaf, in a way I know Hudson doesn't mean.

But that's the point, isn't it? Hudson's not asking to elevate himself higher than me or make himself feel better. He's asking, on the surface, to keep me distracted from the fact this plane is going to nose-dive into the ground sooner or later. But under that, he's asking because he's actually curious. Because he wants to understand something he just can't seem to wrap his head around.

"I love people," I admit. "I love talking to them, getting to know them, seeing what makes them tick. It's part of the reason I agreed to help you. How often do I get to be in a room with people like your parents?"

"Oh? It wasn't my charming smile and their friends? My muscles, my deep voice?" He accents each word with a comical action: a wide grin, a flexing of his thick biceps, a deepening of his voice in an obnoxious way.

I bite my cheek, but it doesn't stop the grin from breaking through. "I mean, those things might have played a part."

"Oh? So, you admit it? You think I'm pretty?"

"You look sexy with your hair pushed back, yes."

"I knew it." He pulls out his phone. "Hey, Siri, remind me at least once a day that I look sexy with my hair pushed back."

Before she can actually confirm the request, he cancels it and re-pockets the device. "Go on."

Was there any more? Of course there was. Hudson always had that effect on me. Even if I wanted to lie, when he gives that soft grin and his voice is no more than a whiskey whisper, it's nearly impossible for me to be mad, let alone lie to him.

"You've never asked me this question," I admit.

"I know. And that was my fault. I should have. And I know it doesn't matter now . . ."

"Since we aren't actual boyfriends, right?"

". . . Right. But, I think, if we're going to make this work, then I should know. Don't you?"

"I agree." Which means I'm going to have to be honest with him and myself. I look over to the open door of our pod. I press a button, the door slides, and the soft murmurings of first class disappear. Even the low hum of the airplane seems muffled.

"I never told you this, but . . . and it's going to sound dramatic, but I need you to understand when you're thirteen growing up in North Carolina, and you know you're different, and someone says to you, *I see you*, that's all that matters."

"Hey," he whispers, reaching across the table and squeezing my hand. "I'm not going to judge you," he says quietly. "I promise."

I'm not sure why I believe him this time. Hudson made a similar promise when he said "I love you" the first time during that Halsey concert. And look what happened there. But something's different this time. Maybe it's thanks to time, or maybe it's just us being older, or maybe nothing's different at all, but I believe him. Maybe that makes me a fool.

"My aunt, when I was younger, was married. Uncle Hale. I loved him. He was just that uncle that got you without question. He was always there for me. I think he knew I was gay before I knew, and he never judged me when I came out. He was the first person I told. Anyway, him and my aunt got divorced. No discussion, no nothing. Left her heart broken. Left me broken too, since he just . . . left the family. Erased like he never existed."

This is the last chance I have to back out, to create some lie reasonable enough to satisfy Hudson's curiosity. I can't go back once I say this, something I've never told anyone, not even Mom. Might as well have it live and die with this relationship. There's some twisted symbolism in that, I think.

"I never knew why Uncle Hale left. Was it something my aunt did, or, thirteen-year-old logic, something I did? Why did he decide to just . . . up and leave his family and never look back? I don't believe he's another notch in this national stereotype so many "scholars" have about Black men. My uncle was a good guy, from what I can remember. I don't know if that's influenced by being a kid who idolized their uncle, but I know from the way my aunt talked about him that something else was at play there.

"I don't need to know what convinced him to pack up his whole life. I went through my phases of grief already. I don't know if I'm happy he left, or if I still hate him, but I know I'm thankful. Because him leaving helped me find what I wanted to do with my life. Helped me see that I want to understand what influences people, and what makes them decide how to use their choices. What makes an executive decide to commit fraud? What makes an activist want to stand in front of a dozen police officers in no-man's-land?"

"What makes a person want to completely shatter another person's whole existence," Hudson says quietly.

"Exactly."

The plane isn't rumbling anymore. I don't know when it stopped, but we're cruising casually, with the beautiful skies wrapped around us like a blanket of warmth and cold, balanced all at once in a protective layer of air and water.

"Well, I don't know anything about your uncle, but I do know this. I know you're a damn good journalist, Kian. And that's not because your uncle disappeared. That's because you're kind, you're inquisitive. You listen, and you find the good in everyone."

"Except for James from that econ class," I point out.

"Oh, screw him. He's trash, he's an exception," Hudson says.

There's a lightness to his voice, and a warmth to his expression that's open and inviting. But there's something dark behind his eyes.

"You want to say something."

He sighs. "Yeah, but you're not going to like it."

"You know, when you say that, when anyone says that, it's usually worse than the actual thing, so how about you just—" I gesture silently, telling him to spit it out.

Hudson buys himself time by taking a moment to sip his sparkling water, downing the whole can over ten seconds.

"I don't think you should meet with Randall."

And there it is. The other fucking shoe. There's *always* another fucking shoe with him.

"Let me explain."

"Please, do." It takes all I have to say that without gritting my teeth.

Hudson sighs and opens his mouth, but a knock on the pod silences him. The flight attendant places our food in front of us, asks if we need anything else, then slips back out.

"You were saying?" I ask, silently telling him, *Don't you even* think *about eating that food until you tell me what you mean.*

Luckily, he catches on.

"Randall is not a good guy, Kian."

"That's not surprising."

"No." Hudson shakes his head. "You don't understand. I went to school with him. I—"

"Private school," I interject. "And he was two grades ahead of you, I know; you told me this already. And I also know he himself has nearly $1.5 million in net worth."

Hudson frowns. "What does that matter?"

"It matters a lot. Again. He's a successful guy. How many successful people, successful billionaires, do you know who are *actually* good? None. It's nearly impossible to ethically obtain a billion dollars. I don't need him to be good, I need him to help me. And you, also a successful person, whose family has a company worth billions of dollars, are telling me to not accept the chance of a lifetime—to connect with another successful person? I don't get those same opportunities you do, Hudson. Friends from my high school aren't millionaires with trust funds, well-connected mayoral candidates, or business tycoons." I break my own rule and take a sip of the Coke, only to wet my mouth. "I'm a Black, queer, middle-class guy with debt. I have to take every chance I can get to better myself. And Randall? He's that chance. The fact he runs a company I would cut my arm off to work for? That's even better."

Hudson doesn't speak, and, to fill the space between us with *something*, I take a bite of my sandwich. The chicken is perfectly cooked, and the bacon has just the right amount of fat on it. The Coke—Hudson was right about that—is the perfect addition to the meal. Whatever he's going to say next? Might ruin that.

"Are you telling me you don't think my parents are good people?"

"I'm telling you to not judge," I say; half truth, half avoidance.

Say what you want about Hudson staying as far away from his family as possible, both physically and metaphorically, but when Hudson Rivers wants to keep something from you, you can never tell what he's hiding. I'd bet money that's a secret his parents taught him.

"You're right," he says finally, taking a bite of the tuna. His right brow twitches, but he swallows through it. "It's not my place to tell you what you should do to make your life better."

Not the answer I thought, but okay. I watch him struggle to take another bite before I grab our plates and switch them. The way his shoulders relax shows his appreciation without saying a word. I'm not sure whether I would have preferred he said something or not.

"Can I give you one piece of advice, though? You don't have to listen, of course. Just . . . can I?"

I nod.

"You deserve better than whatever Randall is going to offer you. I'm not my sister. My name doesn't carry the same weight as hers does, because she stayed in the industry. She built those connections. If I could use my name to help you, I would. Just promise me you'll be careful around him. Okay?"

The honesty dripping from his words takes me aback. I don't think I've ever seen Hudson be so . . . concerned about someone else. He isn't a selfish person, not usually. But there's not a drop of self-centeredness in what he says. It doesn't come off like he's trying to make himself feel better. Even his body language and facial expression show someone actually concerned with another person's well-being.

Which gives me pause.

Should I listen more deeply to his words? Read between the lines and see what subtext breeds in the dark cavern between his words? Is he trying to tell me something? His puppy-dog expressions don't give away anything. There aren't any red flags or warning bells. I'm good at picking those up; it's one of my strongest skills.

Probably he just wants me to make sure I don't lose myself if I start working for Spotlight, I reason. People have a lot of opinions about digital journalism. It's too much clickbait. It's killing traditional media. Gone are the days of yearlong embedded reporting, unless you're working for some elite, highly well-funded group. I doubt we'll see another Deep Throat scenario in this new day and age. But everyone's got it wrong. Journalism isn't going to hell—it's changing, like everything else in the world.

The work I'd be doing at Spotlight isn't inherently bad just because it doesn't fit what people's preconception of what an acceptable journalist is. But his concern is coming from a good place. No reason to shoot him down now. Instead, I do what many people in relationships do when they reach a stalemate. I concede.

"Thank you for looking out for me," I say. Even if it's misguided, it's appreciated. There's something . . . primally nice about having someone look out for my well-being. Very . . . Kevin Costner in *The Bodyguard* realness, I'd say. "I promise, I'll be careful."

"That's all I ask," he says, taking another bite, his traded sandwich half gone.

"Now you have to answer a question for me."

His brows rise in surprise. "Oh?"

"Are you going to tell me what happened to give you such a bad opinion of Randall?" I ask. "You said you knew him in high school. Did something happen then?"

Hudson opens his mouth, closes it, then opens it again. He pushes the plate to the side and pulls out his distressed leather shoulder bag, tugging at the worn straps.

"I have some work to do before the semester starts," he mutters, putting AirPods in his ears, ending the conversation right then and there. The only sound in our little section is a muffled announcement that we'd be hitting some turbulence once again, and that all passengers should brace themselves accordingly.

SEVENTEEN

"I HAVE A question for you."

We spent the rest of the plane ride in silence. Neither Hudson nor I knew what to say. The few times one of us tried to talk, the other perked up his ears and the talker skittered away. I've never found shyness to be a cute trait in people. I don't know if it's some internalized toxic masculinity in me, but just say what you freakin' want to say. Which is rich coming from me, considering, you know, how I tried and failed to start conversations probably three times during the flight.

I don't look at Hudson when I speak, but I can see his reflection in the window of the limo that picked us up—his attention is turned toward me. Throughout the whole drive, which, as the friendly driver said to Hudson and *not* me—I'm not going to read into that—should only take about thirty-five minutes to get to the Rivers Estate in Decatur, Hudson hasn't attempted to talk. Is that out of respect for me? He's the one who paused the conversation on the plane. I was *happy* to keep going. I love an argument. Live for it, honestly.

"What's up?" he asks, putting away his iPad.

I've never been to Atlanta before. I could use this as an easy out. Throw some stupid historical question at him that obviously wasn't what I intended but neither of us would be brave enough to call me out on. But what would that accomplish? Nothing.

"You asked me about me on the plane; I should do the same." I pull away from the window, shifting in the leather seat that crinkles as I move, and turn to face him.

"Why not follow in your parents' footsteps? I mean, it doesn't have to be working at Rivers & Valleys, maybe it's making your own business empire. You have the world in front of you . . ."

"Yeah, you made that clear on the plane."

Was there a hint of disdain there? Nah, not a hint. A heavy dose of seasoning. It fills the air with bile, but I take a deep breath, inhaling it.

"I deserve that," I admit. "Still. Entertain me?"

Hudson plays with the button on his iPad. He presses it off and on, the screen flashing like Morse code, the background image of him and two other guys posing in front of the Grand Canyon, smiling brightly.

I try to push back the pang of pain that rips through my chest, remembering how the image there used to be a photo of us.

"I think we're kinda similar in our thinking," he mutters. "I like psychology because it helps me understand people. Journalism helps investigate how things happen, and psychology explains why they happen. I'm interested in the why.

"I'm not going to pretend that my money and my family haven't colored how I look at the world. Or how people look at me. I know it. Trust me. I remember when Rivers & Valleys became a top distillery. I remember how students in my classes treated me differently when my parents were wealthy versus when they were Wealthy, with a capital W. People don't give me honest answers. People don't want to disappoint me. Especially here." He gestures to the general area, referring to Atlanta.

"Olivia loves it. I hate it. I want people to be up front with me. It's why I didn't even feel I could ask people to be honest with me, without forcing them. Hell, I . . ." He pauses, face twisting into something suggesting pain and suffering, but a specific type of suffering. The type that comes from reliving a memory that clouds your mind like a sudden thunderstorm.

"Not important. You get what I'm saying. I read an article about reverse psychology in ninth grade and fell in love with the idea that there's a field where even if people are lying to your face, you can see what's under the surface."

"The truth between the lines," I explain.

He nods. "Exactly. So, it's not some Oprah-worthy origin story, but you asked." He shrugs. "And no, before you say anything, I'm not asking for pity. I understand my money, my status, my privilege plays into a lot. I'm lucky to have all that. If the biggest thing in the world I have to deal with is people lying to me? My life is easy. But it doesn't feel any better when I don't know who to trust."

I know the feeling. My mind races, pings of neurons each sending messages to my brain, reminding me how I thought Hudson was The One, and each instance I missed that refuted that. Taking a deep breath, and downing half of the chilled water bottle in the side of the door, I drown those thoughts mercilessly.

Not now, fragile mental state. I'm busy.

"Ten minutes out, sir," the driver says.

"Sir?" I tease, glancing over at him. "You told me you hate being called sir when I proposed it in—"

Before I can finish, his hand covers my mouth. "I have known

Max since I was six. Please do not ruin his image of me being the perfect boy by saying what I think you're about to say."

I smile mischievously under his hand. Hudson presses his grip tighter. Not tight enough to hurt, but tight enough to tell me he's serious. In the end, I nod. Slowly, he pulls his hand back and settles back in the seat, but eyes me cautiously. Like if I act up again he's going to pounce.

Just the thought of that, if I'm being honest, makes me shiver like a cold breeze had slipped into the car. Hudson's strong body on top of me? The weight of his arms pinning mine above my head? The smell of his breath against my skin? The way his voice gets huskier and deeper when he's demanding something . . . ?

"I know what you're thinking," Hudson says, breaking my thoughts. I rub the palms of my hands against my pants, suddenly regretting not dressing nicer. Are we going to meet his extended family as soon as we arrive? Shit. I should have been smarter.

"I promise you; you have no idea what I'm thinking."

"You want to know why he called me sir."

He's cute when he's so confident—and wrong. Loud and wrong, my mom would call it. Except he's rarely loud. When Hudson raises his voice, in any situation, it's a dog whistle to pay attention. Baritone, crackling voice, sure. Demanding voice, absolutely. The type of voice that you have to strain to hear? The type of voice, that when you do hear it, you're in so deep that escaping whatever *Alice in Wonderland* rabbit hole you've fallen into is near impossible? Yeah. That's the Rivers Effect.

Hudson shifts in his seat, just enough for his right pant leg to rise, exposing a bit of his ankle. The skin is paler there, a shade or two lighter, reminding me of the time we went to the beach and Hudson not only got burned but had an uneven gradation of darkness that was comical to say the least. I didn't let him live that down for the whole trip.

"He's part of the family," he says finally. "Been with us for as long as I can remember. He knew me back in school—drove me to practice, to classes, back home—anywhere, you name it. Max was my ticket. When Mom and Dad fought, Max was the one who volunteered to take me for a drive, talked to me about my future, distracted me." Hudson shrugs. "He's more family than the rest of them. He drove me to get my tux fixed the week before prom, without even having to be told or asked. When I wanted to ask you out, he even helped me figure out exactly what to say. Max and I are ride or die."

We take a smooth turn around a curve, so smoothly I barely notice we've changed directions. The houses have shifted too, no longer inches apart; now several feet of land sprawl between each one. As we pass them, the gap gets bigger.

"I think that's the most you've told me about your high school life."

Hudson makes a *psh* sound with his lips.

"I'm serious. You never talked about high school. It's like . . . some big blank dark spot in your history for me."

From the corner of my eye, I notice Max glance at Hudson through his rearview mirror. It's the only time, since we started this drive, that he's made any sort of reference to us back here. But he's not looking at us. He's looking at Hudson, who catches his driver's eyes for only a fraction of a second before looking down at his pants, picking at a rogue fiber.

"What was that?"

"What was what?"

I gesture like a goose trying to warn its Goose People about a hunter in the woods. "That look you and Max exchanged."

"It's nothing."

"Okay, there was nothing 'nothing' about what just happened."

"Just drop it, Kian."

"Okay, but you can admit what—"

"No 'okay buts,'" he bellows, loud enough for the tinted windows in the back to shake. He takes a breath, muttering curse words through his lips, eyes closed. He doesn't open them until metaphorical steam exhales from his mouth and ears. "Seriously. Just drop it. We're here anyway."

As if on command from Hudson's words, the road shifts to gravel, the limo bumping slightly along the rocky river. The weeping willows lining the road bow so low they keep me from making out the house in the distance. From the back seat, all I can see is that it's massive—easily three, no, five times bigger than my home.

Less than a minute later, the limo is parked, and Max is out getting our bags.

This is it, I think. *No turning back now.* Well, if I wanted to turn back, the time probably would have been before we left Boston. I guess, if I wanted to, I could jump out of the car and run all the way back to the airport. I did run track in high school. Then again, what Black poster child in a white-dominated society didn't, at some point, run track, play basketball, or rap? According to the news.

Muted thumps fill the air like a fist hitting fabric as Max takes out the suitcases. I count the bags. How many did Hudson bring? I know I brought only two. We're already up to at least five.

"Hey."

Hudson's rough hand and his voice pull me out of my *One Fish, Two Fish* mantra. I turn to face him, just in time to see his features close in as he scoots closer to me in the back seat. The car is perfectly cool, but the heat coming off his body makes my heart race. Because, obviously, that's the only reason.

"I know, I know. I'm here to impress your family."

"Yes, but—"

"And make you look good."

"Yes, but, Kian, that's not—"

"And you don't want me t—"

"Oh, my fuck, can you just let me ask you if I can kiss you or not?"

Like the side of the Royal Airliner just exploded and oxygen is leaving the cabin, I sit there, dumbfounded, head dizzy. The slam of the trunk snaps my soul back into my body.

"You want to kiss me?" I repeat. Is there a right or wrong answer to the question? Nah, the only wrong answer would be to lie.

"To set the tone," he clarifies quickly.

"Oh." A beat. "You know, help us get into character."

"Exactly. Think of it like that time we went to the dress rehearsal of *Sweeney Todd* at the community theatre for extra credit in that gen ed class."

"I hope this kiss will be better than that."

"Oh, darling," he purrs. "You know for a fact how good my kisses are."

Hudson moves his hand to my thigh, giving it a soft squeeze. I try my best not to twitch; warmth is pooling outward from the touch and spreading through my whole body. Slowly, his hand moves up to my cheek. His rough pads cup it lightly, slowly turning my face to face his. He moves closer again, our bodies pressing against each other so hard it almost feels like we're trying to fuse, like two crystals in a cave. Gently, he leans forward, pulling my face toward his. The few inches between us take only a moment to bridge, but each second feels like an hour.

Softly, his lips press against mine. The kiss starts out chaste, feeling as if a tendril of smoke has passed over me at a cookout. But slowly, the kiss intensifies. Hunger, fervor, and desire take over. Not just for him, but for me too.

He pushes me against the back seat of the car, and I let him. My legs spread, wrapping around him as he slots his body into the space between us. His hands don't know where to go, so instead, he balls my shirt; not tugging on it or trying to rip it off, just holding on to it for dear life. My hands do the same, one finding purchase in his hair, the other against the armrest behind me. It's an awkward position, and I think idly, *I'm going to ache tomorrow.*

But at this rate, it's conceivably possible I might be aching in *multiple* ways tomorrow.

Hudson puts his full weight against me, a surge of pleasure akin to a weighted blanket, but warmer. I push back, adding resistance, the good kind. His tongue slips against my lips, begging entrance into my mouth, and in response, without hesitation, I open. This is what I wanted, and it's clear it's what he wanted too.

Okay, maybe it's not exactly how I pictured it. Winning Hudson back, and living happily ever after as a perfectly upper-middle-class, handsome Black couple in a city like Seattle, or San Bernardino, was actually the goal. Two kids, one golden retriever, two cars. But a good ol' fashion car make-out session—or car sex, if it comes to that—isn't a bad idea, either.

As Hudson's fingers slip across my skin, causing my back to arch like electricity has passed through my spine, I hear a muted thump, just like before. Except this time, it's louder, clearer. It happens again, louder this time.

"Shit," Hudson curses, suddenly pulling back and sitting up. My vision slowly clears, the blur a by-product of Hudson literally taking the energy out of me, like some Dementor in a Men.com porno or something.

I open my mouth, not sure if I intend to scold him for teasing me like that and not finishing the job or make some quippy response to get him back on top of me. But before I can, the door closest to me opens, light spilling into the car . . .

. . . and Olivia stares at us, arms crossed.

"Really?" she scolds. "In the driveway?"

EIGHTEEN

IF I HAD to guess, I'd say the Rivers home would cost somewhere around $3.5 million to $5.5 million. I've spent a lot of time watching *House Hunters*—both the domestic and international versions. It's my mom's favorite show, and back home we would binge-watch episodes, compare the homeowners' (stupid) choices with our own (better) choices, and guess, before the narrator told us their budget, what insane amount of money two beekeepers in the Dakotas made. Even in college, I kept up with it, an addiction I couldn't shake because, when I called Mom every Sunday, we'd talk about it.

But yeah, back to the Rivers home.

The white modern house has sixteen windows on the front, two sets of four on the ground floor and two sets of four on the top floor, with a marble pond the size of most pools. Hedges line the massive plot of land, tiled with cool stone. It's an impressive property for an impressive family.

Hudson isn't even fazed by it. Is that because he and Olivia are loudly arguing with one another? Or is it because this is simply home to him; a building where he grew up, made memories, and left? It's not a mansion to him like it is to me. It's not daunting. It's Christmas presents, and tears shed on the stoop. It's broken windows from a rogue baseball, loud music, stained carpets, and first driving lessons.

But right now? It's just a stage for the Olivia & Hudson Show.

When Olivia opened the car door, I scampered out, almost tripping over myself. Hudson is more relaxed, taking his time, even chatting with Max for a moment before Olivia's throat-clearing forces him to give her his attention.

"What?" he asks calmly.

"You're seriously going to 'what' me?"

"Seems like a pretty normal and accurate response when you're acting like this."

Oh, that won't end well.

Even if he doesn't mean it, those words come out like tone policing, and that's a pretty big no-no in most decent people's books. It's also a low blow in an argument, like calling a Black person who's energetic and passionate about something angry.

Right now, I'm Team Olivia.

"You did not just say that to me."

"Oh, so now what I say is off-limits? That's what offends you?"

"Don't turn this around on me," she interjects, walking around the car, completely ignoring me (which is fine, by the way) to come face-to-face with her brother. "You're the one who—"

"I know, I know. I'm the one who screwed up, right? I'm the one who brought shame to the family name," he says, adding his own overly dramatic air quotes. "This isn't Westeros, Olivia. We're not fighting for the Iron Throne. It's the twenty-first century, we're fine."

"You were . . . *doing it* . . . in front of the house!" she hisses. "In front of *everyone*."

Hudson lets out a deep-throated laugh. The type of condescending laugh that makes my own blood boil. I can only imagine how it makes Olivia feel. Okay, no. I don't need to imagine. I know she wants to beat his ass.

"Who is *everyone*? Mom? Dad? Come on, Livy. You and I have done far worse things. The only difference is Mom and Dad like you better."

That strikes a nerve. "You're seriously going to bring that up here?"

"Where else should I bring it up? You name the time and place, and I'll do it."

Sibling rivalries are always fights for the ages, and this one between Olivia and Hudson feels familiar. Jamal and I were never close enough to fight like these two, but the undercurrent that gives the fight life? Yeah, I know that well. It's how people who love one another solve problems. *Fighting is healthy*, Mom always used to say. *Better to let it out than keep it buried inside. Then it festers.*

But Olivia and Hudson aren't fighting for a constructive purpose. They are throwing punches and slashes with the intent of hurting one another. It started out fun—who doesn't love watching the epitome of a car crash—but now it's just turned unnecessary.

Which is where I step in. Like, literally.

I quickly move around the car and stand between Olivia and Hudson. Like a referee who breaks up two warring opposing soccer players in the middle of overtime. Their vicious volleys pause, Hudson glaring at me, Olivia pursing her lips in disapproval.

"So, I'm getting the feeling you two don't like each other?"

"I don't dislike my brother," Olivia replies.

"No, she hates me," he says.

"And there you go again. Always playing the victim."

"Nope," I interject. "We're not starting this up again. I don't care why you two don't like one another, but we're not here to help heal family trauma. We're here for—" I turn to Hudson and he catches on without me having to ask.

"Nathaniel. My cousin."

"Mine too."

"Nathaniel's wedding. Which means we're going to put him and his fiancée first, right?"

Neither Rivers child answers.

"Right?"

"Sure," they both say, the standoff ending in a truce.

Olivia takes a step back and checks the Apple Watch on her right wrist. "Mom and Dad are almost here. Get whatever that is out of your system, please, and at *least* don't embarrass yourself in front of them?"

Hudson opens his mouth to roar back a response, but Olivia has already checked out of the conversation. She pulls out her phone and answers a call from a man, judging by the photo I glimpse for a split second on the screen.

"I hate her."

"No, you don't."

Somehow, Max has evaded the cross fire. Passing Olivia like a wisp of perfume, he disappears into the home. "Sir. Yours and Mr. Andrews's bags are upstairs."

"Come on." I grab his arm, giving him a tug. Stubbornly, he doesn't move. He's not pouting—Hudson has a very specific look when he doesn't get his way. No, there's a sense of . . . *hiding* on his face right now. Maybe Olivia's words damaged him more than he let on.

"Come on," I say again, tugging harder. His weight shifts, stumbling a few steps forward. Once his ground is broken, I push him forward. "Who's going to give me a tour of the house? This place is so big."

Hudson doesn't snap out of his mood, even if he does walk alongside me. Tough crowd.

"I'm probably going to get lost inside of it," I add. "And no one will find me for days."

Still nothing.

"Until my body starts to smell, and all that's left is bones. And then this turns into a whole *Knives Out* situation."

At the door Hudson glances over at me with a catlike sideways look. "You do know if your body is all bones, it's not going to smell, right? Decomposition is what makes your body smell."

I put my hands up in mock offense. "Wow, careful now, we got a scientist over here. What's next? You're going to tell me Einstein didn't create electricity? Oh no, wait. Don't tell me. Gravity actually really exists?"

Behind Hudson's handsome rich brown eyes, I see the wheels turning, preparing his minute-long monologue. He opens his mouth to lecture me on science before pausing. "Wait. You're joking, aren't you?"

I shrug innocently. "What gave me away?"

Maybe it's because he's Southern, but Hudson has always been a man of simple pleasures. He loved listening to thunderstorms and keeping the windows open when we went to sleep. He was happy with a home-cooked meal, even if it wasn't great. And though he was comfortable at a club, he was just as comfortable watching old reruns of some early 2000s TV show, and laughing at all the cringey jokes, while wearing sweats and a tee from college. I'd have thought he'd be right at home back where he grew up. Home is where the heart is and all that.

But the moment we step over the alcove, whatever thoughts linger about Olivia are gone. His muscles tense and his jaw tightens in a way that makes him look like a right angle. If I was any good at drawing, I'd put those squiggly parentheses around his body, to imitate paralysis.

I stand about three feet away from him, studying his features. Pain passes over his strong jaw, and his fists clench and unclench by his side. What happened here to make coming home such a painful experience? Now I understand why he doesn't talk about his younger life as much. It's not just some quirky "I don't like my parents"–level of angst. Something happened here that feels like a constant, festering thorn in his side.

I reach over, take his right hand, and give it a squeeze.

"Which way to your room?"

———— · ————

"HERE WE ARE."

This bedroom isn't what I'd call a kid's room. This is bigger than some presidential suites at the swankiest hotels in Boston.

The room—or rather, the three rooms—are connected. You enter into the bedroom, large, like a primary bedroom. The room is big enough that in a normal house, it would be the focal point. But here, its just Hudson's bedroom, nothing special. Connected with a sliding door is a walk-in closet, along with a bathroom, a shower, and a tub, off to the side. There's also a small study that overlooks the seemingly endless Rivers land.

But most importantly, there's the elephant in the room.

"There's only one bed."

I blurt out the words without thinking what might follow. Surely Hudson has some idea how to address that, right? He knew. He grew up here! Of course he knew.

He doesn't seem fazed, eyes drifting lazily to the queen-size mattress in the center of the room. "That's not technically true.

There's a daybed," he says, gesturing to the large window directly across. "It pulls out too."

"Is that still considered a daybed then?"

"What else would it be?"

"A pull-out bed? A pull-out couch? A pull-out day . . ."

"Okay, okay." He holds up his hands. "I get it. You're smart and know words. My point is that it shouldn't be a problem. I'll sleep there, you get the bed, we tell my parents we slept together."

I'm quick to pick up on the intended, or unintended, subtext. Not today, Satan. "You don't mean . . ."

"Of course not, Kian," he groans. "Get your mind out of the gutter."

"You grew up here?" I ask while Hudson gets acquainted with his past. I do a quick mental check. When was the last time he came home? Not holidays. He spent those in far-reaching parts of the world or sometimes in Boston. There was talk of him coming home with me and Jamal, of course, but that never happened.

"I mean, I lived here," he clarifies, opening a drawer in the old rosewood dresser. "I don't know if 'grew up here' is the right phrase."

"There's a story there."

Hudson keeps his eyes trained on the dresser. His fingers move against the smooth, polished wood, making patterns that make no sense.

I reach over and press my hand over his, stopping the tracing mid-finish. "You know you can tell me anything, right?" I ask. "I know it might not feel like it, considering, you know, our history—"

"That's the word we're using. History," he muses. "Clever choice."

"Didn't you know? I'm a journalist. We're masters at words," I volley back. "But seriously. You can tell me. And not just because I need to know you inside and out."

"Kinky."

"To sell this lie, but . . . just, you know, because."

Hudson stares at the wood, like there are answers in the swirls. Part of me wishes, hopes, he'll look at me and confide in me. That's what a boyfriend does for another boyfriend, right? That's part of the Ten Commandments of a relationship. If we don't have that, what do we have?

But, again, this isn't a real relationship. It's a contract.

But what if it weren't? What if it could be something real, something more? Have either of us really thought about that?

"I haven't been completely honest with you," he says finally.

That's something no one wants to hear. My body tenses, but I don't let the reaction extend to my hand, which is still on top of his. In fact, somehow, with me missing it, he's moved my hand to be intertwined with his, loosely, but our fingers have still found their way in between one another—and they fit perfectly.

"Sure," I say quietly. Not the right response, Kian. Try again. "I mean, what is it?"

Hudson gives my hand a soft squeeze; a quiet question asking me so much. What exactly the squeeze is asking, I don't know, but I get the general idea.

And I squeeze back.

Before he can tell me, there's a knock on the door. Heavy, rapid, and demanding. Without waiting for a response, Olivia pushes the door open. She's changed her outfit, no longer wearing the white sundress she had on before, but a well-fitted lavender jumpsuit with chunky heels that accent her look. Her hair is in a messy-but-effortless bun.

"At least you're clothed this time," she says. Hudson quickly attempts to reply, probably to tell her we were clothed before, but she interrupts. "They're here. Mom and Dad and the guests. You should come down. Show off your boyfriend."

This time, her eyes slide over to me, studying and taking me apart piece by piece, like an intricate building made of multicolored Legos she wants to understand. "Have you prepared him?"

"Prepared me for what?"

Hudson doesn't answer me. "He'll be fine."

Olivia's lips curl into a smirk. "You're just . . . going to let him flounder out there, huh? That's a funny way to show you care about someone."

"Olivia," he growls. An ice-cold drop of water drips down my spine, and I shiver. Okay. That was hot.

She puts up her hands. "But hey, not my business. It's your relationship."

Again, she gets the last word in, leaning her head from behind the door as she leaves, and winks. "I hope it lasts after this trip."

The hardwood floors that line the house make her heels click like a metronome, until her death march is drowned out by the muffled sounds of the door opening downstairs and the glee that pours in.

"What did she mean by that?"

Hudson sighs, glancing over at me. "Do you really wanna know?"

I weigh the pros and cons in my head. Hudson doesn't need to lay them out for me. Pro: Knowing will help me adapt to whatever's to come. Information is power, and having it will help me fulfill the end of my bargain—which means I'm more likely to succeed, which means more likely to get the job I want, the life I want, and a Pulitzer.

Con: I might psych myself out. The Riverses are like a lake made up of murky water, where the key to my freedom is at the bottom. No, that's not right. A lake made up of murky, acidic water, where the key to my freedom is at the bottom. The longer I stay in there, the more it burns. Reaching the key is impossible without knowing the depths of the lake. If Hudson *does* explain to me whatever Olivia meant, it might do more harm than good. This perfectly constructed facade of a relationship is only as strong as the weakest link. And if we fail, I won't have it be because my nerves got the best of me.

"Never mind."

"Right answer."

NINETEEN

"KIAN! HUDSON! ARE you here? The family is downstairs! Come on down!"

Mrs. Rivers's voice skips through the air like a weightless melody. I'd say she sounds almost exactly like Snow White did when she sat in the forest singing to animals, casually belting out a riff for the gods, but that minimizes the strength Mrs. Rivers's voice holds. It might be flirty, but it demands respect. And the power it has makes me want to jump out the window, grow wings, and fly back north for the summer, fall, winter, and spring. Instead, I settle on:

"I think I'm going to throw up."

That's not the thing most people want to hear, I assume, before you go and meet their extended family. Maybe something like *I'm so excited!* Or *I have the perfect recipe to impress your grandmother!* Or maybe even *I've mastered seamless TikTok transitions; your cousins are going to love me.* But *I'm going to vomit up my chunks,* Exorcist *style?* Yeah, no one finds that attractive.

Okay, I take that back. I think there might be a subset of Pornhub that's actually into that.

Instead, Hudson's face twists into a Picasso-like expression; a perfect mix of confusion and disgust. He scratches the back of his head, the hem of his shirt riding up to expose a bit of taut muscle and a train of hair that extends past his navel and . . . down there.

I believe porn stars call it their "happy trail." I call it the "thank-God-he-doesn't-manscape trail."

"Okay, first of all, you can't do that."

"Can't leave?"

"No! Can't throw up! Wait, are you thinking about leaving?"

"Ignore me. Continue."

He pauses. "My mom paid a lot of money to get these floors redone last year. She would kill you. Then she would kill me, and we don't want that, do we?"

"The jury is still out."

"Bite me. And second of all, that would *not* gain you any points. Which hurts both of us. So let's, you know, not do that?"

Yes, Hudson, I think. *Because the thing I want to do is throw up*. But I hide that fact.

"Try some breathing exercises or something. I have a Headspace subscription if you want to use it? I'm a fan of the Rainday Antiques playlist."

"Okay, first of all, you use Headspace?" I ask, eyebrows raised.

He returns my look with equal surprise. "Is that so unbelievable? I want to be a psychologist. I believe in meditation."

"No, no. It's not that. I just remember—"

"You've suggested it to me before, and I laughed it off," he finishes, nodding. "I've done a lot of dumb things I regret."

In my head all I can think of is that GIF from *Mad Max: Fury Road* of Tom Hardy saying, *That's bait*.

I agree, Max Rockatansky, I fully agree.

"Give me a moment," I say instead.

"Kian . . ."

"I just need a moment. I promise. I'll be down soon. Promise. Just . . . stall."

"Oh, darling," Hudson purrs, drawing out the word in his Southern accent, which has gotten thicker since the moment we landed. "Olivia was right, and you know how much I hate saying that. My mom can smell a stall a mile away."

"Well, it's good that you're her son, right? The Rivers blood runs through you. You must have some of her skills."

"Touché," he says, smiling slightly. "Hurry down, yeah?"

"A boyfriend wouldn't leave his boyfriend to face the wolves by himself. What type of guy would that make me?"

"The worst."

"Exactly."

"And, if I remember anything about you, it's that you're not bad at anything."

With that, he gives me one more look, like he wants to say something, before heading out of the room, leaving me and my thoughts alone.

That doesn't last long.

Quickly, I run into the bathroom, slam the door behind me, lock it, and FaceTime Divya. She answers on the second ring.

"Oh, good, you didn't die from hyperventilation on the—HOLY FUCK!"

Her voice echoes in the marble bathroom, bouncing off the expensive walls, the sharpness of her surprise making my ears ring. I swear, the dozen or so people downstairs must hear her too. To compensate, I turn on the shower, and the three—yes, three—sinks all the way, hoping the gurgling water will drown out her voice.

Like I'm some spy in an early 2000s movie, about to make contact with my American handler while behind enemy lines deep in Moscow.

"Could you *be* any louder?" I snap.

"Oh, I'm sorry, you didn't tell me you were going to a *mansion*. Are you dating—"

"Fake dating."

"Still dating. Are you dating Trevante Rhodes or something? Jesus. Does that bathroom have *three* sinks? Show it to me."

"I didn't call you here to show off the bathroom!"

"Uh-huh. Show it to me while we talk."

Arguing with Divya isn't worth it—especially since she always wins. It would take me longer to try and convince her why she's wasting time, rather than just do what she wants. Conceding, I turn the camera, slowly spanning the sinks.

She whistles loudly. "Is that marble? Change of plans, you're no longer fake dating Hudson. You're going to *for real* date him. Forget Spotlight."

Rolling my eyes, I turn the camera back so we can face one another. "Are you suggesting I give up on my dreams to marry a man just because he's rich?"

"Ah, you fucking bet your perfect round bubble-butt ass I am."

"Isn't that the whole antithesis of everything we believe?"

"Absolutely. I'm a hypocrite when it suits me. You know this about me."

"Didn't you make me reenact that *Grey's Anatomy* scene with you, which is the *complete* opposite of that?"

"Which scene are you talking about? There have been a lot."

True. "The one where Cristina leaves?"

Divya nods. "Yes, yes. The 'he is not the sun' one. Such a good scene," she says, sighing wistfully. Some people watch *Friends*, or

The Office, or *Criminal Minds* (here's looking at you, Jamal). We do *Grey's*.

"But still. Do you know how many people do that? Marry rich now and then marry for love later?"

I shake my head, turning off the sinks before they can overflow, and the shower before it fills the room with thick plumes of steam. "That's not who I am."

"I know," she sighs, leaning back in the chair. I can tell from the lighting and the brown table in the background that she's in her spacious living room. "And it's the most tragic trait about you. You're a 'romantic.'"

"Were those air quotes necessary?"

She shrugs. Any other day I'd want to unpack that, but right now? I don't have the time.

"Are you going to help me, or do you want to see the shower too?"

She opens her mouth to say "Yes," then pauses. "That was a rhetorical question. Sure, what's up?"

"I think I made a horrible mistake."

"Oh, I could have told you that." Before I can verbally scold her from across the digital highway, Divya clarifies: "Look, there is absolutely no situation where helping your ex is a good thing. Especially when you have feelings for him still."

"I don't have feelings for him," I say, just a little too quickly.

Divya deepens her voice to mock me. "'*I don't have feelings for him.*' Boy, be quiet. You can lie to yourself all you want, but lying to me? I deal with liars every day. And you aren't even a good one. Don't get me wrong! Having feelings for him isn't a bad thing. But you need to decide what it means for you, and what type of person you're going to be. Are you going to be someone who looks at the world through fancy rose-colored glasses, who follows their heart knowing they could very well get hurt again, or are you going to be someone who looks at the world through ugly, boring, black-rimmed, analytical glasses?"

Shrill laughter rips through the air from downstairs. The muffled voices I can make out tell me it's some inside joke I wouldn't understand anyway. My phone vibrates, a text from Hudson swiping down from the top.

HUDSON RIVERS: ???

"Which one is the right choice?"

Divya smiles sadly. "That's the point, K. There isn't a right choice. Just the one you're happy with. I'll leave you to decide that one."

——— · ———

DOWNSTAIRS, THE RIVERS home is filled with people, like some gothic *Phantom of the Opera* retelling, with a whole bunch of rich people gathered to sing, "Masquerade! Paper faces on parade . . ."

In crowds like this, where the typical attendee is in a completely different tax bracket or class bracket than me, I'm used to standing out. Usually it's because I'm Black. In Boston, being Black wasn't the most uncommon thing, but it wasn't Common with a capital C. People would look my way in class, do a double take every once in a while. During senior year, in an invite-only journalism seminar, a girl told me, "African American History 400 is down the hall."

It only got worse when I won the Linda Ellerbee Award for Outstanding Journalism Prowess.

But here is different. Hudson's family is also Black, so it doesn't feel as constricting as if I were at a white friend's home. His guests are also Black. There's comfort in that, like being welcomed to a cookout. A very expensive, very wealthy, very privileged cookout.

See, here's the thing I can't forget—and no matter how much I try, I seem to be unable to forget. Hudson is rich. Like, filthy rich. So wealthy that every single fiber of my being feels like I don't belong at this welcome drinks mixer they're throwing for Nathaniel and his bride.

It reminds me of that scene in *Crazy Rich Asians* when Rachel and Nick first arrive in Singapore and Eddie is asking Rachel what family of Chus she belongs to. "Hong Kong telecom Chus? Malaysian packing peanut Chus?" . . . Except here, I'm a nobody. No one notices me. No one ever dares to mistake me for someone else. I'm just a dark shadow, a scorn on the wall.

I adjust the collar of my shirt nervously, weaving through the crowd like some spy making his way through enemy lines. From my position, I clock each of the Rivers family members. Gotta know where every adversary is before I know how to react.

Diana Rivers leans casually against one of the bay windows, sipping what looks like champagne while chatting with a woman in a power suit who looks around Mrs. Rivers's age.

Isaac Rivers, holding a tumbler of scotch in one hand, laughs loudly while clapping the back of a much younger man, who does not look like he's having nearly as much fun, and doesn't seem to be a close relation of anyone in this family. Maybe the guest of a guest?

Olivia, dressed now in a beige halter top with black trim and a pair of fashionable cigarette pants, is holding court in the living room. Three women and one man, a fellow friend of Dorothy, all gather around her. She's talking with her hands, but not in the off-beat way most people do—her hands are a casual accent. And whatever she's saying, her little court is eating it up.

"Where are you?" I whisper, scanning the room for Hudson.

"Drink?" A younger woman appears, dressed in black and white. She offers me a tray with the same liquid Mrs. Rivers is holding.

"Sure. Hey. Can you tell me where Hudson Rivers is?" I pause, adding like I feel I need to, "He's my boyfriend."

Why did I say his last name like that? She didn't ask. It just makes me look more out of place! Luckily for both of us, she doesn't seem to care. The waitress smiles and fluidly points to a room off the side to the right.

"Thank you," I say, fishing out a five-dollar bill. Is that how you handle this? Do you tip party workers? I don't think I've ever been to an event that's had one? Awkward, I put the five-dollar bill on the tray. "Thanks for the drink."

Quickly, I slip through the crowd and head into the side room, keeping close to the walls to avoid the rest of the Rivers family. It's not like I'm afraid of them. No, that would be stupid.

I'm fucking terrified of them.

Hudson is different. He doesn't carry on his shoulders the same weight of superiority and cockiness the rest of them do. And that weight is used against others like a blunt-force weapon. Enough beatings and you'll be flattened into a fraction of your original self. At least, with Hudson by my side, I have some protection.

I slip along the wall, until I come to the sliding door. Carefully, I push it open, half expecting to find Hudson sitting by himself, reading books in his father's study, or on the phone, gabbing about how stupid this party is, or, even more likely, how insufferable his date is. Which, I mean, fair. I can be pretty horrible to put up with, so I'll take that.

But the scene in front of me is the complete opposite.

Instead of finding a lonely Hudson, I see him sitting cross-legged in the center of the floor, half a dozen children, the oldest no older than maybe six, looking up at him like he is some sort of chiseled god. He has an acoustic guitar in his hand, strumming softly.

"Baby shark, doo doo doo doo . . ." he sings quietly, bopping his body to the left and the right. The kids follow suit. Well, some of them do. The others . . . God bless them, they try. That's what Hudson should do his thesis on. Is rhythm taught, or is it inherited, like hair color, the ability to curl your tongue, and tasting cilantro? Some of these children have thirty-year leases in the offbeat.

But that doesn't take away from how cute the scene is. Each child is being their authentic self. Clapping their hands, singing along, dancing in their seated position. Most importantly, Hudson looks actually happy. His shoulders are relaxed; there's that smile that brightens up his whole face. His fingers move over the strings easily, barely touching them before jumping to another one.

He looks like he belongs.

"Who are you?" The voice is direct, confident, and demands respect. A blond child with ponytails purses her lips at me. "We're having music time. Come back later."

Hudson looks up and smiles. "Amelia, be nice. This is my friend . . . my boyfriend. Say hi to Kian."

I wave at them, but the children are more interested in this new piece of information Hudson gave them.

"You have a boyfriend?" asks a freckled boy, like he can't believe it.

Hudson nods.

The freckled boy and Amelia are both quiet, processing the information and pushing it through the necessary filters. Amelia suddenly shrugs. "Can you sing?" she asks me.

"I can try," I offer. I most definitely cannot sing.

Hudson gives me some space next to him and pats it. Amelia stands up, smooths out her dress, walks over to the chairs in the corner. She pulls out one of the pillows, a fully green one, and places it next to Hudson.

"Thank you, Amelia," I say as I sit, crossing my legs.

She shrugs. "I suppose."

"Now, boyfriend," Hudson says with a fake formal accent. "I do believe we owe these fine children a song."

"By George, good man, I do believe you're right!" I say, mimicking him. "What song should we perform for these elegant lads and lasses?"

"'Baby Shark'!" they all say at once.

"Again?" Hudson asks. "This will be the fifth—"

"'Baby Shark'!"

"All right, all right!" He holds up his hands in surrender. "Jeez, tough crowd." Hudson looks at me with a sideways glance and a lopsided smirk. "You ready?"

There are few perfect moments in life. I don't even know if I believe in that idea—of perfection. As a word, sure, I believe in it. As a concept, though? For a relationship? And a person? Soulmates and one true love? All that jazz? I'm not sure it's real. Not anymore.

But in this moment, sitting on the floor, with Hudson's relaxed demeanor as he entertains these children like it's his full-time minimum-wage job and he's happy with it? Maybe perfection does exist.

I reach over and slowly push a strand of hair out of his eyes. "Now I'm ready."

TWENTY

HUDSON AND I continue playing songs for the kids for about fifteen minutes, until the sliding doors quietly open.

"Amelia Maria Elizabeth West, there you are," a woman with too much bronzer and too-bright clothing scolds. "I told you about running off."

You know when you see two people, usually related, and you understand everything about them? That's how I feel when I look at Amelia and her mom. They're spitting images of each other, down to the way the younger version frowns and pushes out her cheeks when her mom reaches for her.

"Amelia," her mom says sternly. "We need to get you cleaned up. You will not embarrass me today."

I glance at the girl, who in the past fifteen minutes has warmed up to me. When I first sat down, she was sitting properly, how I'm sure her mother taught her to sit. But now, she's leaning against me, clapping along with the music. She looks more like an actual kid and less like some mannequin. The concern about embarrassment feels awkward, and I'm sure everyone in the room feels it, even if the other children don't know exactly what the feeling is deep within their stomachs.

The mother keeps looking at both of us, narrowing her eyes a bit, trying to hide whatever it is that's seething behind them. For a moment, I think it's nothing but general annoyance. Parents, especially those with small children, can be pulled to their wit's end. But then I see her eyes, hawklike in nature, how they dart to Hudson's hand on my body with a light but still slightly possessive touch.

And that's all I need to know.

I'm from North Carolina. I'm used to people not being cool around me for being gay. But the way she looks at us? Like her eyes could kill or cut out our gayness if she focuses long enough? It's searing. It's offensive. And it makes me want to shrivel up and fold in on myself.

"Amelia," she says sternly again, reaching forward like she's trying to bridge some cavern of space in an action-romance thriller. She forces her hand open and closed, open and closed.

If my mom were here, she would say something. Divya, too. Even if there weren't any proof—and there isn't. If you see hoofprints, think a horse, not a zebra. Homophobia would be a zebra. Amelia being a child, which is practically synonymous with "dirty," makes so much more sense.

But I'm not crazy. Homophobe Sense is like Peter Parker's—sorry, Miles Morales's Spidey Sense. Or Ben Platt's queerdar. You just know it when you know it.

And I'd know that cold feeling that makes me sink into myself anywhere.

Amelia sighs and slowly stands up. Before anyone, least of all me, can react, she throws her arms around my neck and hugs me tightly. I sneak a glance at her mother, who is wincing. As if I needed more proof.

"Amelia. Come," her mother demands. Amelia pulls back with a sigh.

"You'll play another song for me?" she asks.

"Anytime you want," Hudson promises. "Me and my boyfriend would be honored."

Any other time, I'd call out the way Hudson puts emphasis on the word *boyfriend*. It doesn't sound like marbles in his mouth; instead, it's heavy. Like he wants its weight to be a burden to Amelia's mother.

Does he know? He has to pick up on it. The hate is radiating off of her like a furnace.

Slowly, I feel his hand slide around my waist, gently squeezing my left side. He leans over, pressing a wet, audible, smooch of a kiss on my cheek. The remaining children sitting around us make an array of sounds and faces that could only be described as a firm "EW!"

I'm sure if I were their age, it wouldn't matter who I saw kissing—I'd find it disgusting. Because, let's face it, if you really think about it, swapping spit is a kinda weird thing humans do. I get it, kids! Adults are disgusting. They chastise you for getting dirty in the mud, but they do something as nasty as that? Hypocrites, that's what they are.

Except, here's the thing: It's disgusting until you find the right person to do it with. And maybe you never will—not because of some deep cosmic ulterior motive machine. Maybe you just aren't into kissing other people, and that's A-OK. But I like kissing, and being kissed by, boys. I especially like being kissed by, and kissing, Hudson Rivers.

But even wanting to kiss him back, I don't. I smile weakly, forcing the gears in my cheek to attempt a grin. Hudson's gaze stays on mine. His eyes twitch, his brow furrows for just a moment, silently asking if it was because he did something wrong that I don't return the favor.

"For God's sakes, can't you . . ." Amelia's mother pauses and shakes her head. "Never mind. Come on," she says, snatching her daughter's arm and dragging her through the center of the circle we've made. That's when something clicks inside of me.

Mom always told me it's not about who you think you are, or how you plan to deal with injustice when you come across it. It's all about what you *actually* do. Talk is cheap, especially in the digital age when everyone is a Twitter Warrior. What are you going to do when it's staring you right in the face? That's how you judge someone's character. And for a while now, I haven't been happy with the person I see when I look in the mirror. Why should I be? I'm an unemployed twenty-three-year-old, pining after his ex-boyfriend and trying to make it in one of the most competitive fields imaginable—a field that doesn't promise comfort in life anytime soon. I can't control any of that. I can't go back in time and change my major, or stop dating Hudson, or decide not to help him get back at his parents. But I can do something now. And I fully intend to.

Well, intended to. Hudson beats me to it.

"Ms. West?" he asks, peeling a child off his right-hand side as he stands. Instinctively, he smooths out his pants, getting rid of any phantom creases that might have etched themselves into his expensive denim. "I'm not going to call you homophobic in front of your daughter. But I do know the way you looked at my boyfriend, and I know what that meant."

Ms. West opens her mouth, her eyes becoming twice as large. Is she upset because she's accused of being homophobic, or because she was caught?

Quickly she regains her composure, her jaw clenching tight. "It's nothing personal, dear, I simply . . ."

"Mhm, I don't really care what you think. A bigot's opinion is only as good as far as I can fucking throw them."

The children in the room crackle with whispers and gasps at the curse word. Ms. West puts her hands over Amelia's ears, like that'll protect her, like the words she makes her daughter hear every day aren't viler.

Hudson glances down at Amelia and smiles, mouthing *sorry*, before turning back to her mother. "Which is why I want you to know, I see you, Ms. West. I see how you look at Kian. I see how you look at me. I see more than you want to let on. So, let me be clear," Hudson says, taking one step forward, "if you ever say anything remotely homophobic like that to me or my boyfriend again, or anything close to it, I'm going to make sure the deal you're hoping to get signed with my parents falls through. That's the only reason you're here, right? Because you don't care about Nathaniel."

"I—"

"Don't answer that. It didn't need an answer. Again, I know you. My parents always said your opportunistic streak was what made you and Northwest a great PR agency. But I wonder how great a PR agency it would be if it got around you lost a multibillion dollar contract because you're prejudiced?"

Ms. West's whole body visibly seizes up with that threat.

"Mom, you're hurting me," Amelia whispers, squirming in her mother's grasp. Ms. West doesn't let her go, her eyes locked on Hudson, who isn't backing down.

"So, we're good?"

"Mhm."

"Sorry," Hudson turns his right ear toward her, putting his hand behind it, the international symbol for *I didn't catch that*.

"We're good," she croaks out.

"And?"

Ms. West and Hudson have some silent conversation I'm not privy to, their eyes exchanging the whole conversation without a single word. They seem to come to a conclusion.

"Don't say it to me, I don't care." Hudson gestures to me with his head. "Say it to him."

She sighs, peeking around Hudson's broad body to look at me. "Kian, is it?"

I stand up, repeating Hudson's actions, smoothing out my pants. Seems like the right thing to do. Something a wealthy person would do. Wealthy people are careful with their money. Why take your clothes to the cleaners when you can make sure you don't have to with a simple action like that? When at a Beyoncé concert, you don't stand there and sway side to side, you twerk your ass off. The modern-day "when in Rome."

"I'm . . . sorry."

The bitter bile of cockiness floods my mouth. I should say something, make her work more for my apology. But what's the point? Will she actually change? Do people like her really change? She's the worst type of homophobe: someone who thinks they aren't really one. The type of person who gets appalled when they're called out on it. Because every fiber in their being agrees with their ideals. She probably employs gay people. Or has a gay hair stylist, or a gay friend. As long as they are within a comfortable range of homosexuality for her, she's fine with it. As long as they aren't too close to her, or her daughter, or won't get their gayness on her, she's cool. The type of person who says, around familiar company, *I mean, the gays have marriage, shouldn't they be happy with that?*

And those people don't change.

"It's cool." It isn't, but the room is starting to stink with the thick smell of fakeness. Before she can push, or run out of the room, I do it first.

"Babe, we should meet your parents, yeah? You wanted me to meet your grandma?"

Hudson studies me for a moment, his jaw tight. This silent exchange I understand.

You okay? his eyes say.

Yeah, I reply. *Let's just get out of here.*

You sure? I can make her . . .

Yeah, let's just go.

He nods curtly, smiling broadly at Ms. West. "Well, as my boyfriend said, we're going. We'll see you at the reception, Amelia."

Hudson takes my hand and yanks me out of the room, cupping his hand in mine. As we walk through the foyer toward where his family has gathered, I thread our fingers together and squeeze tightly.

He doesn't look up at me, but squeezes back, silently saying, *I know.*

——— · ———

BLACK FAMILIES ARE naturally large. It's just one thing you associate with them. But the Rivers family? They put even the largest of Black families to shame.

Hudson has one sister, but he also has, like, eight cousins, all of whom are here. Those eight cousins, ten if you include Olivia and him, come from three different pairs of brothers and sisters to Mr. and Mrs. Rivers. Of the eight, five of them have children. There are also three pairs of grandparents.

And that's just the ones who arrived tonight.

"Excuse me?" I ask.

"Oh, yeah. More are coming tomorrow and then the last batch the morning of the wedding." Hudson studies the engravings on the ceiling as we all funnel into the living room, like the answer is written in the intricate designs. He shrugs. "I don't know, you'll be fine! No one expects you to know all of them. *I* don't even know them all."

"That . . . doesn't make me feel any better," I say flatly. "It's my job to make a good example! Not to be like you."

Hudson gasps, putting his large hand over his chest, his mouth slightly open. "And what is so bad about being me, huh? I'm smart. I'm tall. I'm a relatively good person, when I need to be. And most of all, I have—what do you call them—thighs that could probably crush a watermelon? Okay, not a watermelon, probably a grape. Definitely a grape. I should be a catch. You should be honored to be like me. Wait," he says, grabbing my shoulders to force me to look at him. "Is it because I'm, you know, part of the bourgeoisie? I can't do anything about that, Kian."

"It has *nothing* to do with that," I snap. The rest of the family and their guests finish funneling into the room. I do a quick count—only about a third of the people that filled the three rooms when we arrived are here.

"Overflow rooms," Hudson explains, catching my eyes. He pulls out a chair for me.

"Sorry?" I don't argue that I don't need him to act chivalrous for me. Of course, I don't need it, but I'd be lying if I said I dislike the way it sends a shiver down my spine.

"Not everyone can fit in here during the reception. So, we have a room for the kids and then a room for others."

"I thought the point of a reception is to be, you know, intimate?"

"For a normal family, sure, but when did you think we were a normal family?"

That's true; nothing about the Riverses is normal. From their lavish lifestyle to how they treat each other, it's all weird.

"What did you mean by *others* then?"

"Don't say it like that," he quickly retorts, taking his napkin and putting it in his lap with motions that read as automatic. I follow suit. "We just . . . like I said, there isn't enough space."

"And who decides who gets to be in this room, versus the other room?"

"Just like a journalist," Olivia purrs, patting my shoulder as she walks by, taking a seat next to Hudson. A tendril of lavender follows as she moves. "Asking the right questions."

"Be quiet," Hudson says under his breath, turning back to me. "It's nothing. Really. This room is mostly for family members. Mom and Dad's friends, close business partners. Nathaniel's inner circle."

"And his fiancée? What about them?"

"Her family is here . . . Where is she . . ." he mutters, pointing to a petite brunette with a heart-shaped face, a slender form, and an air about her that radiates warmth and kindness, walking in with two middle-aged adults. "There."

"And where are her 'close business partners'?"

"Probably in her dreams," Olivia mutters around the rim of her glass. She doesn't wait for Hudson or me to ask for an explanation. "Look, Kian. You're not dumb, so unlike my brother? I'm going to give it to you straight. This room is reserved for people who can help our parents' company. This wedding is as much a business opportunity as anything else."

My face turns sour at those words. I've taken more than one history class. I also almost had a women's studies minor. I know that marriage, for the longest time, was more about the business and economic benefits than love. Still is, in some places—most places. But not here. I thought that died out years ago.

Olivia picks up on my opinion. "Oh, come on. Don't be so naive. You want to be part of this family? You're going to have to learn that you don't have a multibillion-dollar company without pouncing on every business chance you can." She wipes the corner of her mouth carefully, making sure not to smudge the dark plump lipstick she has on that matches her nails and eyeliner. "The Mitchells? They help us with shipping. The Clydes? International distribution. The Waynes? Domestic distribution. The Andrewses, Rices, and Haroldses? Business advisors and part of the Board of Directors. The Evanses? Agriculture," she lists off, pointing to each one lazily with her right index finger.

"And the Wests?" I ask, looking around. "I don't see them here."

"They are our PR company."

"Were," Hudson says around his glass. From first glance, I'd think the drink was alcohol. But it's in a stout glass, and the bubbles give it away. Ginger ale.

"Were?" Olivia asks.

"I don't want us working with them anymore. Their contract is coming up at the end of the month, yeah?"

I don't think I've ever seen, and didn't think I ever would see, Olivia surprised. But hey, today seems to be a day—or rather, a month—of surprises.

"That's right."

"Cut them. We can find someone else. We should be diversifying anyway. We're in Georgia. Find a Black PR company. We're a Black-led company, we should also be uplifting Black entrepreneurs whenever we can, right? Especially in Atlanta. We're, what, forty percent Black?"

"Fifty-four percent," I interject. "I checked."

"Of course you did," Hudson teases, nudging me. His shoulder stays against mine for a moment. "But, I'm serious, Olivia. We can do this. We can actually help. More than just make our family money and give us a nice fat trust fund. We can actually give back to the community. Mom and Dad always said they wanted to."

"Fifteen years ago," she says, correcting him. "Like it or not, money changes people."

"Doesn't change that that was their goal when they took over."

Olivia rests her elbow on the table, a smirk on her face that makes Hudson and her look like siblings more than ever. Their lopsided grin is even on the same side of their face. "Look at you, taking an interest in the company."

"Hm," Hudson mutters around the rim of his glass again. Under the table, his right leg twitches: up and down, up and down, up and down.

Since when did he develop that nervous tic? I rack my brain to try and remember if it's always been there. Then again, a lot of people don't like coming home.

Discreetly, I place my hand on his thigh and give a soft squeeze, careful not to surprise him or give him any ideas. Hudson doesn't jump, just looks down and then up at me, flashing a reassuring smile.

"It's a good idea," I chime in. Part of a boyfriend's job is to carry the load—no pun at *all* intended. "Help the community, help yourselves. It's a win-win situation."

"How so?" Olivia challenges. "Beyond just, as my egalitarian brother says, it helps our 'brothers and sisters' in arms?"

"The world is changing. This will help bring in a new generation of drinkers. When I'm at a bar and I see people with Rivers & Valleys, it's always the same type of white dudebro."

"That's our demographic."

"So you can change that," I suggest. "Wider markets. More diversity. A Black PR agency could help with that. And I'm sure, though I'm just assuming here, a Black firm might be a little more progressive than Northwest."

I keep it at that. Olivia doesn't need to know any more about what happened. Hudson grins proudly at me, squeezing my hand under the table. With his head turned to me, he mouths *thank you*.

Olivia nods slowly, telling me what I'm saying resonates with her. She takes a slow sip of the champagne as the final guests take their seats. "One more question for you, Kian," she says, lowering her voice an octave. "You mentioned it helps our company. But you also mentioned it's the right thing to do. Do you think something can be a good deed if it benefits yourself in the process?"

I've heard this ethical dilemma before. Once in a philosophy class that I took to fill a humanities gen ed in college. Once when I overheard it during a late-night study session in a coffee shop that was far too hipster for me (never again). And once during a "Which 'Avatar: The Last Airbender' Character Are You?" quiz I took when I smoked weed for the first time and was high out of my mind (also never again).

"A Kobayashi Maru," I say without hesitation.

"Bless you?" Olivia asks.

"It's a Star Trek term," Hudson chimes in. "An unbeatable situation, right?"

"You actually paid attention when I was watching?" I reply, surprised.

Hudson shrugs. "You binge-watched it when you thought I was asleep. I caught bits and pieces."

"What does this have to do with—"

"Your question," Hudson interrupts.

"There's no right answer," I continue. "Which makes it . . ."

"Unwinnable," Hudson and Olivia say at the same time.

"So, you think there's no right answer?"

I pause, thinking over the words. Olivia's eyes are hungry, like a game of chess or a board room is her favorite battlefield. There might not be a right or wrong answer to this question, but if I want to win her favor, there definitely *is* a right and a wrong answer.

No pressure, right?

"I think it depends," I carefully settle on. Each word feels like a ticking time bomb, threatening to explode in my hands. "I think, if a good deed helps another, it doesn't matter what the reason for it is. The receiving party still benefits. But if the original party only does good deeds to help themselves, then they should call it what it is, a one-sided quid pro quo. There's nothing wrong with that. But don't lie about it."

Olivia holds her glass in midair, like her batteries have run out and need changing. She stares blankly at me, never blinking. Her glare feels like it's painlessly peeling back every layer of my skin, trying to reveal some secret mechanism that'll make her go, *Oh, that's why he thinks like this.*

Suddenly, she snaps back into motion. "I suppose." She shrugs. "I'll check in with Michael."

"Advisor to the family," Hudson informs me. "He's been Mom and Dad's right-hand man since . . . as long as I can remember. He's cool. Smart, forward-thinking, pragmatic. I think he'll agree with you."

Before I can even try to say anything witty, Mrs. Rivers enters the dining room, clapping her hands twice to get everyone's attention, which she commands effortlessly.

"Smart answer," Hudson whispers, his proximity like a black hole that consumes every possible sense. Mrs. Rivers's voice no longer commands attention. The rest of the guests are blurry ink blots. The only thing that matters is the weight of Hudson's shoulder against mine, the faint smell of evergreen and wood that makes him seem like a walking *Indie Folk Artist Scratch & Sniff* cover, and his deep rumbling voice. "I knew you would knock this out of the park."

"Oh, so you didn't bring me for my dashing good looks?"

He slowly moves his head, leaning closer to me until his lips brush against my right earlobe. It takes everything to keep from shivering. "That too," he says, his voice deeper than before, which I didn't know was even possible. "But it felt wrong to only focus on your looks when you're the whole package."

"Ladies and gentlemen," Mrs. Rivers says, her silky-smooth voice several decibels higher, like she's specifically trying to get my attention—and it works. "The bride- and groom-to-be."

TWENTY-ONE

I DON'T KNOW if this makes me classist, but rich people have a certain look about them.

It's like the air around them is lighter, like they have the ability to affect gravity or something. I'm sure if I asked Hudson, he'd tell me what scientific principle I'm thinking of. Heat makes molecules move faster, I know that, and air becomes thinner. So maybe that's the analogy I'm looking for. Something related to how rich people burn brighter, faster, and hotter . . .

If Hudson is a zero on the rich scale, and Olivia is a ten, Nathaniel is somewhere closer to a seven. His perfectly coifed hair, his pale blue suit. The three rings he wears on his right hand—one class ring from high school, one from college, and I can't place the last one—complete the outfit. He is, as some people would say, dripped. The way his teeth are unnaturally white and straight doesn't help either. And his smile? Looks fake. No one smiles that widely.

But he looks approachable, like I should want to be his friend, or try to be. His gravity pulls me in, and everyone else in the room. A soft murmur of compliments dance right under the surface.

He's grown into such a nice man.

Danni is so lucky.

Look at him. Always knew he would be a heartbreaker.

Rebecca should be proud.

I take a long sip of water, trying to wash down the sugar over-load. No one is hiding their favoritism for Nathaniel. And I get it. If we were at the Patriot and we locked eyes, I'd hundred percent smile back at him. If he bought me a drink, I'd certainly talk to him. And if he invited me to the bathroom after an hour of flirting? Ah, you bet your ass I'd let him dick me down, or vice versa.

But here's the thing. In the back of my mind, I'd always know he was nothing more than a frivolous, vapid hookup. These people are actually praising him, while saying nothing at the same time. The compliments are as hollow as a ten-calorie rice cake. But they don't know that. Or they do and they don't care?

"He's a good guy," Hudson whispers in my ear, breaking my self-spiraling dive into analytics. "I know he doesn't look like it, but he is. You'll get to know him during the wedding."

"Was I that obvious?"

Hudson gives a smile that is meant to lessen the truth. "I mean, I just know you well. You have a *look* about you when you're judging someone."

I frown.

"Not that he doesn't deserve judgment," Hudson adds quickly. "We all do. Trust me. And I'm not saying you shouldn't judge the shit out of him. But Nathan is a nice guy. He loves Danni. Like, actually loves her."

"Why did you say it like that?" I say, before I can think through whether I want to ask the question. Maybe the answer isn't some-thing I want to unearth.

"Like what?"

"*Actually* loves her. Why did you put the 'actually' in front of it?"

Hudson buys himself a moment, taking a long, deep sip of a ginger ale that has been magically refilled. "No reason."

"Hudson," I say sternly, keeping my voice down. "What did you—"

"Oh, look, here's Danni!"

Every fiber of my being tells me I should push Hudson on this. Since we left Boston, it's felt like he's been speaking in half sentences. Like there's something he wants to say, but when the words are about to leave his mouth, they get yanked back in. Those, to me, are the most important words. The ones I should concern myself with.

Hudson is rich, and rich people know how to speak around a topic. Hudson is no different.

That'll be a conversation for another time, I think. Instead, I remember why I'm here—to help Hudson make a good impression, and to better my life. Those two things cannot exist without one another.

I turn my attention to Danni; a thin woman with thin brown hair. The dress she's wearing matches her tanned skin well. She looks like she belongs, down to the makeup and shoes, but her face doesn't match. Her eyes dart from one person to another, never settling on one face for more than a few moments at a time.

Is it bad to say her nervousness gives me comfort? I think it is, yet I can't help but feel a kinship with her. When her eyes land on me, I give her a small smile, and I can tell we feel the same way. Both of us knowing, gravitating to the same energy frequency we give off that no one else in this room can match.

It's the feeling of not belonging.

Danni is flanked by her parents, same with Nathaniel. Their parents break off, shaking hands and chatting with the right people—the right people being the Riverses.

"Isn't it just so kind of Isaac and Diana?" a woman whispers to her seatmate next to me. "Letting them have dinner here?"

"Well, I'd assume they would," the other woman replies confidently. "Nathan is their nephew, after all. And Randall is hosting the wedding. They're all close, you see." She says the words confidently, like she has a PhD in Wealthy Families of the South or something.

"Right," the other woman whispers hesitantly. "But you know . . . the history they have, right?"

I was only half paying attention to the conversation, if I'm being honest. It blended in with the low murmur of the room. Everyone making their introductions to one another, hoping to say the right words to make a good impression without giving away too much of their true selves, for fear it might turn off the wrong person.

But the way she says "history," with a sharp hush and a hurry in her voice? I know that well. It's a sound that transcends class. You hear it on college campuses, around locker rooms in America, in homes with a broken AC on a Sunday after church.

It's the tone of gossip.

I try my best to lean closer without making it obvious I'm listening.

"No," the other woman says. "What history?"

I expected cattiness and drama when I came down here. There's no family that doesn't have it, since drama isn't reserved for the rich. But, as with everything else, the wealthy do have more access to it. Seems they store it in vats and dump it all out whenever they need to feed their guests. After all, who doesn't love drama?

"I'll tell you later," the woman says, turning her attention to Nathaniel's mother and father across the dinner table. They seem like they belong here; like they are the missing pieces to a puzzle Mr. and Mrs. Rivers paid thousands of dollars to have designed, and each guest represents one piece. If that analogy holds true, then Danni and her parents look like the three pieces rejected during the second or third draft.

But her parents don't seem to care. They have the brightest smiles on their faces I've ever seen, brighter than the way the sun refracts off the painted stained glass of the windows I *just* noticed. How much did those cost?

The dinner goes by pretty uneventfully. Most people talk past me, not to me. Hudson does a good job trying to keep me engaged, leaning over and cueing me in to any inside jokes I'm missing. He's doing his best, and I appreciate that. But even with his little footnotes here and there, most of the conversations over the next two hours fly over me. Not because they are over my head, but because . . . well, I just don't care to apply myself to listen and understand.

That is, until an older woman shuffles over from her seat and waves her hand impatiently.

"Move," says the woman, who is *dripped* in loud and bold fashions.

At first, I think she's talking to me, and without hesitation, I move, like her words are some Pavlovian trigger. But before I can even push out my chair, she glares at me.

"Not *you*," she snarls, pointing a finger at the woman sitting next to me, who never bothered to introduce herself. "*You*."

Whoever this woman is, the effect she had on me, a mere middle-class Black boy from North Carolina, she also has on the woman and her friend. They both stand, shuffling away, quickly speaking words of submission under their breath. No one seems to notice, and most importantly, the woman doesn't seem to care.

Hudson tugs on my shirt just once. "Johannah Rivers. That's my grandmother, on my father's side," he says, quickly and quietly. "Get in her good graces, and we're in the homestretch."

"So, you mean, just debase myself and impress her, leaning into her every whim and need?"

"If that's what it takes, sure."

"I'll do my best," I whisper back.

"I have no doubt."

With that, and a quick kiss on the cheek, Hudson turns away and gives Olivia his full attention, leaving me alone with seemingly the most important person in the Rivers family. Which, I'm assuming, cannot be an easy or fun task for either of us.

No pressure, right?

TWENTY-TWO

I'M NOT A fan of three things in the world. Well, obviously more than three things; for ease we're limiting it to three.

Anything with onions.

Summer.

And old people.

Look, I get it. That's probably not something I should put on, like, a dating profile, but some people don't like babies and we don't fault them for that. I don't like old people. It has nothing to do with their looks or their age—honestly that's an accomplishment. It has everything to do with me.

I feel awkward around them. So, if we're being honest, my discomfort with them stems from my discomfort with myself.

I think my therapist would say it has something to do with the fact that I'm not confident in or proud of myself, so knowing elderly people have lived, generally, a full and happy life makes me feel like I'm not enough. To which I would tell her, *Damn, Karen, no one asked you to be that deep.* But she'd be right.

That's just with the average elderly person. Johannah Rivers is in a completely different league. She carries herself like a duchess, like she pulls the air from around the room, forcing you to lean into her if you want to breathe. And the rest of the room, with its wealth and power and confidence? Drifts away. Not a single strand of her dark hair is out of place, and the dress she wears easily costs ten, maybe twelve rent checks of mine. Her skin is dewy soft, darker than Hudson's, and the perfect example of *Black Don't Crack*.

A 1940s Western has nothing on the standoff between me and Johannah.

"I'm not going to talk first, dear," she says smoothly. "So, unless you want to sit here in silence, which I'm fine to do, I suggest you start the conversation."

"You came over to me?"

"That was me making the first move. Now it's your turn."

She sips her drink slowly, giving me a few seconds to think over what exactly I want to say. Johannah places the cup down so quietly the expensive china doesn't make a sound, and I know this isn't a situation where I want her to ask me again to speak. So I default to what any journalist defaults to—information.

"Your last name is Rivers."

"How observant," she muses. Behind her stylish curls I see a hint of a smile.

I ignore her snark and continue. "Rivers & Valleys is a family-owned business . . ."

"And you want to ask if my husband, or my brother, or my father created the company, yes?"

"If I've learned one thing as a journalist, Mrs. Rivers, it's that history gives men credit they don't deserve when women come up with ideas. I imagine it is more historically accurate that a woman in your family came up with the idea, and your grandfather took credit for it. Am I close?"

Johannah is in mid-sip as she stops, holding the cup about three inches above its coaster. I can feel Hudson's and Olivia's eyes on me, like the focused beam of the sun shot through a magnifying glass burning through the right side of my neck. It's like Hudson's trying his best to pretend he doesn't care what happens between me and his grandmother, but is doing a very bad job at pretending not to care; to such a point his attempts are actually making me self-conscious.

So, there's only one way to fix that; flip the script. I reach discreetly, blindly, under the table and squeeze, aiming for his thigh.

Instead I grab his crotch. His very full, very big crotch.

Because of course I do.

Hudson lets out a *very* high-pitched yelp. He jumps, knees hitting the table, causing it to vibrate and his cup of water to spill all over the tablecloth.

"Jesus," Mr. Rivers mutters. His eyes aren't the only ones staring at Hudson. Nathaniel has a *don't ruin this for me, bro* look on his face. Mrs. Rivers looks actually concerned, and Danni is trying her best to hide her smile. Johannah can't keep her eyes off me—because of my dashing good looks, of course—and Olivia glances between me and Hudson. I don't even question whether she's put two and two together.

"Sorry," Hudson mutters, clearing his throat. "Leg cramp."

"You should get that checked out," says a woman across the table. "I know an amazing doctor in Atlanta. I can get you his contact."

"Pretty sure that's a porno plot."

"Sorry, dear?"

"Nothing," Hudson says gruffly, sitting down. "Sorry about the table."

Mrs. Rivers waves it off. "Water dries."

Almost immediately the low murmur of conversation resumes,

the small interruption nothing to the top one percent of the South. Except for Johannah Rivers. She takes one final sip, dabs the corners of her mouth, and pushes out her chair. "Walk with me."

Johannah doesn't even look to see if I follow. She doesn't seem like the type of person people say no to. I glance over at Hudson, who speaks before I can talk.

"We'll talk about it later," he adds. "Go."

"What if I don't want to talk about it?"

The words escape my mouth before I can reel them back in. Hudson's face cracks, a mixture of surprise, interest, and confusion painting his handsome features. Which, I mean, honestly: same. I don't think if he asked me to clarify I could. Or I would even want to. Because the words sound foolish when I play them back in my head, but also they don't sound half bad.

"I'm going to go."

"Yeah, probably best."

I catch up with Johannah before she reaches the back door. Without waiting, I extend my right arm to her; a simple courteous action. She glances at it, then back at me.

"I'm old, Kian, not an invalid. I can walk down three steps by myself."

Summer in Atlanta is just like summers in North Carolina: sticky, hot, and humid. But there's something beautiful about the expansive landscape of the Rivers property. You can't see it when you drive up, but the land is never-ending. Trees line the perimeter, leading into a deep forest on both sides, but forward it's like we're walking into the sun. There's a stillness the atmosphere provides, like a thin blanket over my shoulders, that can't be replicated simply by spending a few hours in Boston Common. The air is cleaner and richer too.

My mind can't help but think about the different lives Hudson and I had. What's it like to grow up here? Sure, he has his problems—everyone does—but there's a certain level of ease that comes with living like this. That head start changes you, health-wise, anxiety-wise, financially. This life automatically puts you a few rungs ahead of other people. Despite how relatable I think he is, how down-to-earth and detached from his family wealth, there are experiences Hudson has had that make him inherently different.

But is that a bad thing? He's not someone who flaunts these advantages, and I certainly didn't grow up poor. Mom always said we were solidly middle-class. I never wanted for anything, though I wasn't getting a brand-new car for my sixteenth birthday or a top-of-the-line laptop. I can't play the *look how hard my life was* card.

"Beautiful, isn't it?" Johannah has the same expression on her face I have: serene peace. "My father bought this house when Rivers & Valleys made their first million. Did you know this property used to be a plantation? He bought it because of that. Tore everything down and built anew on it. Said he wanted to reclaim a piece of our legacy and make it his own. Daddy used to say, 'Imagine, Johannah, how those old white men and women would be rolling in their graves if they knew Black folks had as much money as we did and erased their whole legacy.'"

There's a twinkle in her eyes, like telling their story gives her joy. I have to admit, I can't help but want to punch the air.

"When I was younger, we took a tour of a plantation for high school history class. There's a lot of them in North Carolina. It was just history to most of the people in my class."

"Except for us," she says. "For us, it's more than just words on a page. It's our life. It's the reason we don't have the ability to trace our lineage."

"It's painful."

"Exactly." She nods, pausing for a moment. "So you understand why my daddy bought it."

"Absolutely. And I understand why you kept it in the family. Why you wanted to turn it into something else. Something"—I gesture—"that would erase that legacy. You want the only history of this house to be Rivers & Valleys, not the broken, hurtful past."

I should probably stop talking there, but something keeps me going.

"And there's power in that, you know? How many people pretty much get to say 'F you' to those who hurt them? Few. And you're able to do that. Through money and whatever means you got it."

"I can sense a 'but' coming . . ."

"But." I pause. "I mean, I said this to your grandson before. There's no such thing as an ethical billionaire."

"I don't disagree with you."

"Which makes me wonder what people you hurt to get your family's company to where it is."

After saying something as . . . impassioned as that, I'd usually expect people to cheer, have some sort of uncomfortable reaction, or reply with a *well, actually* . . . Hell, I've experienced all three of those responses. But Johannah doesn't do any of them. She just quietly stares at me, her face as stoic as it was before and always has been.

As a journalist, I know silence is a tool, a weapon to get your source to talk. If you wait long enough, people will always give up something, even if that something is only a small crack for you to expand. I've just never had it used against me.

"I hope that wasn't overstepping."

"I value honesty in every aspect of my life, Kian."

"Do you really, though?" Another comment I wish I had kept in my mouth. "I mean, when people say that, they don't always mean it."

"One thing you'll learn about me, if you become part of this family, is that I am very honest with my words. I don't have the luxury of time to beat around the bush. And frankly, it's boring. Which leads me to my next question: Do you love my grandson?"

"You're not going to answer my first one?"

"You'll earn that answer in time. But I'll tell you this: Everything I've done I've done for my family, and I don't regret any of that. Now, answer."

"That's a steep shift, don't you think? A jump from a conversation about a system of capitalism that made America what it is today, for better or for worse, to a pointed question about my feelings for a boy?"

She shrugs. "I enjoy being unpredictable. Keeps me young and keeps people afraid of me."

"Wouldn't you rather be respected? Isn't that how that expression goes?"

"Maybe if you're stupid, sure."

I can't help but smile back at Johannah. She's not nearly as scary as Hudson made me think she was. Or maybe that's her charm.

"Well, do you love my grandson?" she asks again. I can tell she's a woman who doesn't like asking things a second time. "Even if he personifies everything you just mentioned, which I don't disagree with, mind you. When I heard what you said to Olivia, I knew you were different. That's why I came over to talk to you. So, I'll ask you again: Do you love my grandson? Because I think he loves you."

Murmurs from the party bleeding into the foyer trickle outside. They're soft and muted, thanks to the glass doors, but over my shoulder I see the crowd flowing out. Danni, Nathaniel, and Hudson are talking, Hudson talking furiously with his hands. It looks like he's explaining some sort of story, excitedly. His eyes catch mine a moment later, and he winks, flashing me a thumbs-up, with a clenched grin.

Everything going well? the expression asks silently.

I don't smile back or give him an answer. Instead, I turn to Johannah. "I don't know."

That doesn't seem to faze her. "That's all right. You have time."

And then we stand there, looking out, as if the answer will come galloping over the hills, delivered to me on horseback.

TWENTY-THREE

"SO, HOW DID it go?"

Hudson and I spend the rest of the afternoon like two planets in orbit, never touching. After talking with Johannah, I spent some time on the grounds by myself. By the time I came back inside, Hudson was off with his father in the study, and I caught only a glimpse of him before the door closed. The conversation looked serious, but I didn't have time to linger and let the what-ifs fester before a gaggle of kids came running up and did what kids do best—*lovingly* pester me.

My general hot take consists of "we have too many children on the planet" and all the corresponding conversations that spiderweb off that incredibly witty thesis statement, but those kids are all right.

Later that evening, closer to 9:30, after making a beeline for the shower, Hudson comes in and flops on the bed, unceremoniously. He has the forethought, God bless him, *not* to come out in just a towel or underwear; instead, he wears black short-shorts, like the ones you might see at the gym, and a matching dark tank with thin shoulder straps covering his upper body. If I didn't know better, I'd think it's painted on. Hudson isn't that bold, though. He's not one of those gays. He's more of a . . . "checks 'Boy Next Door' on Grindr when selecting his tribe, but one hundred percent can throw it down in the club to 'Toxic' if it comes on but would *never* admit it" gay.

"Johannah," he clarifies, shaking his mop of brown hair. Droplets of water spray the expensive pillows, and of course me, speckling the book I'm reading with dark-tinged dots.

I want to be mad at him, bark about how expensive this book is—first editions aren't cheap, you know?—especially since I got it out of his parents' library at his mother's firm suggestion. But the boyish, lopsided smile sends flutters through my heart and makes my chest feel warm. It makes me forget, for a moment, about everything in our past. The way his muscles dip and bulge, the smell of faint soap, and the warmth radiating off his body—it all pulls me in.

"It went fine," I say, closing the book and putting it on the nightstand on my side. "She's—"

"Terrifying? Will probably kill you in your sleep? Is planning your demise and is a half a dozen steps ahead and there's nothing you can do about it?"

". . . seems nice."

"Oh, we are not talking about the same woman." He sits up, pressing the back of his hand against my forehead. "Did you drink too much? You sure *you're* Kian? Who are you and what have you done with my boyfriend?"

I swat his hand away, but I can feel the smile forming on my lips. "Hypothetically, if I *was* an imposter, what would you do?"

"Sounds like something an imposter would say," he mutters, narrowing his eyes playfully. "I'd probably fight you, until I get Kian's real location out of you."

I arch my brow. Hudson doesn't hesitate to push.

"What, you don't think I can fight?"

"I'm not saying you can't!"

"Your face said it all! Here. I'll show you."

Hudson sits up on his knees, grabs my shoulders, and, in one easy movement, throws me to the bed. Before I can relax, one hand moves to wrap around my wrists, pinning them above my head, both knees on either side of my hips.

I squirm under the pressure, trying to get his weight off me, his body thick—the exact body I remember spending many nights jerking off to. For some reason, I can't help but hear the Commodores' 1977 classic playing in my head.

A second passes. Then another twenty or so, but Hudson doesn't move. His grip doesn't loosen either. He just stares down at me, shifting his weight slightly, like he's trying to get comfortable or . . . no . . . like he's trying to slow his body against mine, just trying to find the right Osiris to make our bodies fit like puzzle pieces.

My heart begins to beat harder, and my body naturally squirms back. Hudson notices, and through his wet shutter-like hair, I see his eyes grow wider. And then that signature fucking smirk.

That goddamn smirk.

He adds intentional pressure. My crotch presses against his ass while he leans down, his minty breath against my ear.

"My word, Mr. Andrews," he whispers. "Is that a—"

"NOPE!"

Where the strength comes from, I have no idea, but in one easy swoop I buck my hips up and twist my body. Without preparing for it, Hudson's body reacts in kind. You know, the whole of Daddy Newton's third law: Every action has an equal and opposite reaction.

Hudson flies off the side of the bed, his legs and arms comically flailing. His body makes a heavy thump, his form crumpled on itself over the right-hand side.

Crisis averted. And by crisis, I mean my erection.

I use the moment to cover myself before rolling over and looking over the bed. Hudson hasn't moved, he just . . . is *there*, like a poorly folded lawn chair.

"You deserved that, you know that, right?"

"Mhm."

"You need some help up?"

"Nnhm."

"Can you move?"

"Nnhm."

"You're fine," I say, rolling onto my back. It's not long before I feel Hudson's eyes looking at me over the side of the bed.

"You assaulted me," he accuses.

"No one would believe you. You're like four inches taller than me. And wider. Thicker, I'd say. You have the advantage."

"I demand something in return for this offense against my person."

I try to keep a smile from breaking through. I turn, resting the side of my head against my palm. "What do you have in mind? I wouldn't want your honor to be sullied."

"Hmmm." He strokes his chin. "The possibilities are endless."

"Nothing illegal. I don't like you that much."

"Well, now you're just being a party pooper."

Another moment passes before he stands up. "Meet me downstairs in five minutes," he says. "And don't ask why. It's a surprise."

He knows what's coming next. Haven't we had enough surprises over the past two weeks? Before I can reply, he sprints off, doubles back, and runs into the bathroom.

"I gotta get dressed first . . . unless . . . you know . . ."

"Get dressed."

Hudson nods. "Wise choice," he says, and closes the door. "Wait till I leave to start counting!"

Moments later he emerges from the bathroom, in a light grey Henley, showing off just enough chest hair to be tasteful but also teasing, a pair of jeans, and boots. Not cowboy boots—trust me, I checked—just normal boots. Would cowboy boots look hot on Hudson? Who am I kidding? Everything looks hot on him.

"All right, you can start counting now! Wait, you're not . . . *never mind*!"

"Not what?"

"Nope, not gonna ask. Just meet me downstairs."

The door closes, leaving me alone in the spacious room. I sit up in the air, noticing the stillness. Without Hudson here, even with all the oddities here and there, there's no life in this room. Listening closer, I don't hear any laughter, loud music, or arguing parents. It's quiet and cold, even in Georgia during the summertime.

I think I understand what he meant before.

I wait the exact five minutes before throwing on a faded Beyoncé tee shirt, slipping on my sneakers, and heading downstairs. Hudson is texting furiously in front of the door, sitting in a go-kart.

Nothing good comes from a go-kart.

"Are you going to tell me now where we're going? I don't know how to play golf, by the way."

"Oh please, do you think I'd expect you to play golf?" He scoffs. "It's . . ."

"Barely a sport," we say at the same time. Hudson smiles more brightly, dimples showing.

"Right?" he asks.

"How is hitting a small ball while standing in place a sport? Don't you have to sweat for something to be a sport?"

"And those are the same people who say cheerleading isn't a sport."

"You know why?"

"Misogyny," we say together again. Hudson hits me with his shoulder before starting up the go-kart, the small machine rumbling to life before it gives off a low hum.

Hudson zooms off, driving effortlessly over the cobblestone and shifting to the grass with a thump.

"Shouldn't we take the path?" I point. The moon is out, and even without headlights, the delineation between the two is easy to see. "I don't think your father is going to enjoy tire tracks on the lawn."

"Fuck my father. I mean, don't actually fuck my father. If you're going to fuck anyone, it should be me."

"*Excuse me?*"

"God bless you."

The light catches Hudson's profile in a special way. The vein in his neck is more pronounced, and, at this angle, there's almost a glow to him, like the moon knows he's worth spotlighting. As if she's telling me, *Pay attention, Kian, this one is a keeper.*

The faint smile on his face doesn't help either. It makes him look like a boy in a candy store, as if the forest, as we go further into it, is his happiest place on Earth. It makes me want to smile myself. Something inside of me feels warmer than it has in a long time. And that scares me.

I'm not sure I would say coming here with Hudson was a mistake. I've made a lot of mistakes in my life, Lord knows I have, but this doesn't feel like one of them.

A mistake feels cold and hollow on the inside, like it's swallowing you whole. Like there's no way to get out, as you sink deeper and deeper into the icky blackness of generally your own creation. But in this go-kart with Hudson, all of the mistakes I've made in the past week or two weeks or month, all the mistakes surrounding him in my life and my job and my friends . . . they don't matter.

He makes them not matter.

He's the only thing that matters.

And if we could stay like this forever, in this rickety old go-kart in a place where I feel uncomfortable but comfortable at the same time, it would be worth it, because I'm here with him.

TWENTY-FOUR

FOR THE FIRST half of the trip through the forest, we ride in silence; for the second half, I swing my hand over and place it on top of Hudson's again. This time, without hesitation, he maneuvers my hand so it's underneath his. The smile on his face grows even brighter, and the warmth inside me grows too.

We ride until the grass turns into uneven pavement of small pebbles that make the ground shift under the wheels of the go-kart.

"Here we are," he says, jumping out. Hudson runs around the side of the cart and pretends to open the door like it's a chariot.

It takes me a second to realize where we are. The forest has given way to an open space, maybe half a mile in diameter. The moon above shines down so the whole area seems to glow with white light. There's a lake in front of us, silvery and inhabited by a duck or something in the distance—I can't make it out for sure, but there are no other humans here. It's quiet and cool.

"Hear ye, hear ye," Hudson says loudly, in a fake British accent that is worse than any Michael Scott impression I've ever heard. His voice skips over the emptiness. "Lord Andrews of the House of North Carolina has arrived. All bow before him."

"You know no one can hear you?" I ask, getting out of the go-kart. "And let's be honest, that's probably for the best." But I play along and bow in return.

"The ducks can hear me, and trust me, if the ducks respect you, you're well on your way to having everyone in Georgia respect you."

"Step one, gain the ducks' trust—"

"No, step one is gaining my grandmother's admiration, which you did," he says, correcting me. "Step two is gaining the ducks' trust. Then step three is profit."

"Can't forget about the profit." I nod seriously. "The most important step."

"See, you're well on your way to being a capitalist."

"There are worse things in the world you could be." I shrug and walk toward the lake.

The lake reminds me of one back home. Mom and I used to spend every weekend there during the summer. It wasn't far from our house, so we could walk or sometimes bike, but usually we drove. It was the time my mom and I became closest, sitting by the water in the tall grass, letting heat soak into our dark skin and cover us with a layer of sweat that felt as right as it did wrong. We were most at peace then. This was before my mom met Jamal's father. We still went together after they became an item, but it just wasn't the same.

Maybe it's possible for me to make new memories at a new lake with Hudson. Maybe those memories will be just as powerful, just as good, just as strong. Maybe they'll even be better.

I look over at Hudson, who shares my wistful expression as he gazes out at the water. What is he thinking about? What type of memories does the lake hold for him? Before I can ask, he tells me:

"My mom and I used to come here all the time. It was my safe haven away from the house, when Olivia and Dad went down their business rabbit hole and I felt excluded. I love it here because I feel like I can be myself, among the water and the trees and the stillness." He doesn't break his gaze outward, as if something across the lake has his attention. "I don't know if I'm making any sense."

"You're making perfect sense," I reassure him. I give his hand a longer squeeze, like a dot in Morse code, and don't pull my hand back. "I don't believe in spirituality, but I do think there is something healing about being at a lake."

Hudson glances over at me. "What about us?"

"Hm?"

"Do you think it can heal us?"

My breath catches in the center of my throat and expands, refusing to leave, like it's a squatter in my trachea. What am I supposed to say to that? How am I supposed to answer that? Instead, I find myself staring at Hudson, noticing the sharp angles of his jaw, the tightness of his neck, the fullness of his lips. The way his familiar warm brown eyes sparkle when they reflect the moon, which reflects off the darkness. I notice how his large body is tense with hesitation and most of all . . . just maybe . . . filled with the weight of fear.

I turn to him, giving him my full attention, and swallow hard, forcing air into my lungs. "Do you think we need healing?"

Hudson turns back to me, his face heavy with intent. It looks like he's grappling with something, something deep behind his skin, his muscles, his bones—like there's something fighting for dominance. A question or a truth that he's wrestling with, deciding if he truly believes or not. I know that look, I know that feeling, I know that truth, because, since he contacted me a few weeks ago, I've been wrestling with the same dilemma.

"You tell me," he says.

"That's not an answer."

"Yeah." He shrugs. "But you've always been the smartest one between us."

"Wait, wait." I pull out my phone, tap twice, and bring up the Voice Memos app. "Say that again, loud and clear so I can get a good reading."

Hudson rolls his eyes and mutters something under his breath that I can't quite pick up. But knowing him—and I feel like I know him pretty well—I think I can discern what he's saying. *There Kian goes again. Using comedy as a wall to keep from dealing with actual real human emotions. Good ol' predictable Kian.*

But even if that's what he's thinking, he doesn't say it. Hudson takes a step forward, bridging the space between us, erasing any sense of personal space I might have. His strong chest presses against mine, my phone squished between the two of us like a small child trying to weasel his way to the front row of a *Yo Gabba Gabba!* concert. In response, I take a step back.

It's not that I don't like being close to him—the opposite, actually. Being within his orbit is intoxicating. Hudson Rivers has what so many successful people have, that X factor synonymous with radioactive charisma. It's dangerous to be too close. Side effects include neediness, horniness, bad judgment, and more.

"Sorry, I didn't quite get that," I say, waving the phone, reminding him of the game we're playing. As long as I can keep playing this game, pretending what I think is about to happen isn't actually going to happen anywhere but inside my head . . . then I can't get hurt again. Because I can make up the rules in my head. And in my head, Hudson and I live happily ever after. Or we go our separate ways after this wedding. No feelings. No nothing. No . . .

Hudson gently reaches forward and grabs my wrist, bringing my phone close to his mouth. The bottom seal of my hand rests against clavicle bone, and I notice the strength of his pecs. I didn't notice it before, or maybe I didn't want to notice it before, or maybe I didn't want to notice it before and that's why I didn't notice. But it doesn't matter because I fucking notice now. How strong they are, how defined his body is, how . . .

"I, Hudson Rivers, fully admit, in sound mind and body, to the fact that Kian Andrews is much smarter than me."

"That's better—"

"I'm not finished yet," he says. "And I, Hudson Rivers, also fully admit, in sound mind and body, that I want so fucking badly to push Kian Andrews against one of these trees and kiss him until he doesn't know what day it is anymore. If he'll let me."

And there it is. The one thing I did *and* didn't want to hear.

How do you answer a question like that? I suppose in the most literal sense, it wasn't really a question. It was a statement. As a journalist, I should know the difference. But the semantics of what tribe of grammatical structure the statement belonged to don't fucking matter. A hot man is standing in front of me, asking to kiss me, and all I can think about is the difference between a declarative sentence and a question.

"So," he asks finally, lowering my hand gently. "What do you think?"

I could go on a tangent about how this is a bad idea. I could push him away, storm back to the go-kart, and let bygones be bygones. Hudson is not stupid—he would get the message loud and clear. But is that really what I want to do? Do I really want to send the message that there's no chance of us getting back together? I remember what Johannah asked me while we stood outside the house, just hours ago.

Do you love him? A forward question that I don't think, frankly, she had the right to ask. But just as forward as she was, I avoided giving an answer.

Until now.

I don't wait for Hudson to make the first move. I push him against the tree, forcefully, but not so hard that it'll hurt him. I take a step forward, bridging the space between us, our hips sliding together like puzzle pieces. My hands grab his shoulders, and pushing up on the tips of my toes, I press my lips hard against his.

It doesn't feel like before in the car. This is different. There's no roughness, no struggle for dominance; in fact, it feels like our bodies are melding together. Like two chemicals in chemistry class displaying homogeneous properties. His hands slide down my side, gripping my hips to keep me in place. He opens his mouth, begging for entry, his wet, warm tongue sliding toward mine, engaging in a dance that I know the steps to, even if I don't remember how to do them. His broad chest heaves, expands, and retracts, a silent *fucking finally* said without any words.

Instinctively, I push my hips up, my barely covered cock sliding against Hudson's. I wrap my body around his, his hips moving in the opposite direction. A shudder leaves my body as his fingers slide under my shirt, rough pads pressing against my skin like he's trying to activate an eight-digit code to open the door. A thought briefly enters my mind: Should it be this easy? Doesn't this give in to every stereotype the media has told us about gay people: two men who can't keep their pants on, lesbians who move in together within one week of meeting, and so forth? Are we—kissing, gyrating, panting like this against a tree—just reinforcing every negative thing people have said about us and ours since the dawn of time? Shouldn't I be concerned with that?

Probably, I think. But right now, it doesn't matter. Right now, I'm happy, and that should be enough. I've earned this. But more importantly, I *want* this, and who cares what society thinks? It's about time I grab what I want and hold on to it tight.

But Hudson has other ideas.

"No," he whispers. He doesn't have to push me back; I move on my own accord. My pulse skyrockets at Hudson's words. My mind starts to wander, no, *race* to conclusions. Is this where he tells me he doesn't like me like that anymore? Or did the kiss prove to him there's no spark between us? I think over every Instagram photo from the past three months, trying to piece together if there's another man in Hudson's life who I have conveniently erased from my memories. That would be typical. Always a bridesmaid, never a bride.

Or, in gay terms, always the one holding the camera in the Fire Island gang bang, never the one in the center getting Eiffel Towered.

"Look, if I took it too far—"

"It's not that."

"Or if you have someone else . . ."

"What? No, fuck no. That's not it at all." He takes my hands and squeezes them, tight enough to get my attention. "Look at me," he whispers, and I oblige. "There is no one else, there will be no one else, ever," he promises. "It's been you since we met at the party. Hell, it was you before that, when I asked my friends who you were when I saw you in the cafeteria during sophomore year. This . . . despite how romantic it is, isn't how I pictured it."

"We've had sex before," I remind him. "Multiple times."

"But not like this," he argues. "Call me a romantic or superstitious, but I want this to mean something. I don't want the first time we . . . get intimate . . . to be in the dirt or something. We're better than . . ." He pauses, and I know he's looking for some pop culture reference to make it all come together.

"Sookie and Bill fucking in the grave?"

"I was going to say Elio and Oliver, but sure. Wait. Am I Sookie or Bill in that analogy?"

"Am I Elio or Oliver?"

He arches his brow. "Who do you *want* to be?"

"How about we say who we think we are on three?" I suggest. "Think of it as a compatibility test."

Hudson pouts in an adorable, boyish way, his full lips actually turned downward. "Seems fishy."

"Indulge me," I urge.

A moment passes before he shrugs. "Only for you. One . . . two . . . three . . ."

I open my mouth to say my answer, but no words escape. Well, words do, but they're swallowed into Hudson's mouth as he steals a quick kiss, one hand coming up to cup my cheek. My body melts into his, whatever audible protests I try to give disappearing with my thoughts. My mind is as still as the lake, focusing only on the Southern man in front of me.

Slowly, he pulls back, resting his forehead against mine. "Let's go back," he whispers. "I'm getting cold. That okay with you?"

I want to say *I'll follow you anywhere you lead me*, but that feels a little too . . . "My Heart Will Go On."

"Yeah, it's chilly," I settle on instead. "But this time, I'm driving."

TWENTY-FIVE

I'M NOT A fan of admitting that I'm wrong. I'm even less of a fan of admitting that I'm not good at something. But driving a go-kart? That takes a specific type of skill. A skill that God did not give me when he was deciding what talents I would have before yeeting me off the cloud and throwing me down to Earth to fend for myself.

Honestly, I'm surprised we even make it back alive. Between almost hitting a tree, nearly tipping over when I ran into a divot, and driving for literally ten minutes yet somehow ending up back at the lake, finally we park the cart in the car port, per Hudson's directions.

"Oh, sweet Jesus," Hudson says, stepping out and kneeling on the ground, kissing it. "I'm alive. I actually survived."

"It wasn't *that* bad."

Hudson arches a brow at me. "You know there's a stereotype that gay guys can't drive, right? I'm starting to think you fit that."

"You really want to start our relationship off again with offending me? You really think that's smart?"

"Once again, I always said you were the smart one."

"And what does that make you?" I ask.

"The charming one with a big dick, a perfect smile, a deep voice, and debonair charm."

I roll my eyes, but it's just an excuse to keep him from seeing the burning on my cheeks. Sure, I'm too dark for any blush to show, but that doesn't stop me from trying to save face. Hudson could read the phone book and my body would turn muddy. No reason to make it any easier for him.

"I like how you put your cock size first," I settle on.

He shrugs. "It's my best quality."

"You have a lot better qualities."

"Really now? Don't stop, keep flattering me. Flattery will get you everywhere."

Some people get off on being good people. Some get off on being bad people. And others, a small sect of us, get off on surprising people. I fall into that third category.

As I list off his good traits, watching Hudson's face change from a confident, lopsided smirk to a look of surprise and unguardedness is worth its weight in gold   or no, a job offer with Spotlight, since that's more valuable.

"Note to self," Hudson says when he finally returns from whatever surprised realm his mind was dancing in. "Never let you get away with some sweet words. That's too easy for you. You're going to have to work harder to woo me."

"Of course," I agree, nodding seriously, and adding in a salute to show him how "serious" I actually am. "Wouldn't dream of it."

Hudson rolls his eyes, nudging me with his shoulder. "Insufferable, that's what you are."

"Accurate."

"And you're going to be the death of me."

"Also accurate."

"Well, if I'm going to die, can we at least make sure I die comfortably? In the bed?"

"The bed you fell out of?" I remind him.

Hudson groans. "You're never going to let me live that down, are you?"

"Maybe in five years. We'll see. Now be quiet. We don't want to—"

"Wake my parents? First of all, I'm not a kid who is sneaking inside. I'm coming in. With my boyfriend. At a fairly reasonable hour. Second of all . . ."

I have to admit, the way Hudson pulls me close is smooth. His arm is around my waist before I can pull away, and his lips are against mine, again, within a fraction of a moment. There's something . . . so simple about kissing Hudson. I don't know exactly what it is—maybe just the familiarity of his body, or maybe it's some higher cosmic romantic connection, like when you find your soulmate after searching for them for dozens of years.

Or maybe he's just fucking hot and that's enough for right now.

I don't need to overthink everything. If I've learned anything from this trip, it's that not everything is some piece of a greater cosmic plan. Sure, every decision may have an equal and opposite reaction but—and I'm being completely honest here—it's tiring to always try to be one step ahead of the universe. Maybe it's time I let things be and stop trying to control everything. Maybe it's time I jump off the cliff and not worry about how deep the water is. Maybe it's time I fall into it, *lean* into it, and hope for the best. If I'm going to fall into something, falling into Hudson's arms seems like a perfect place to start.

Hudson pulls back, barely an inch from my lips, and whispers, "My parents don't fucking tell me what to do."

The space between us widens more as Hudson turns around fluidly, walking inside. My heart is racing so fast I can feel the blood pumping in my ears, making the whole world blend together like a watercolor painting splashed with lukewarm liquid.

I pride myself in being, as any magazine would describe it, a strong Black man who don't need no man. Hashtag #Singleladies. Hashtag #YouMustNotKnowBoutMe. Hashtag #TheGiftfeaturingBeyoncé.

I'm not proud of how eagerly I follow Hudson, like if the space between us grows, I'm going to miss out on something secret and I'm just dying to be in the know.

We take the stairs two at a time, bouncing on the balls of our feet as if putting too much weight on them would trigger an alarm. Quietly and quickly, we slip into his room, locking the door behind us.

"You know," he says, finally speaking while toeing off his shoes, tossing them into the corner. "I was never able to have a sleepover when I was younger. My parents didn't want kids sneaking around the house. Everything is 'too expensive,'" he says with air quotes and a bad impression of his father's deep voice.

I can't help but frown, even as I try to correct my face. But, with my luck, Hudson notices.

"I know, it's pretty much a crime, not letting a kid have a sleepover," he teases, opening the closet and pulling out a blanket from the top shelf. It's easy for him to reach, and his shirt rides up, revealing his strong lower muscles and his back, with its constellations of freckles.

"Sleepovers are an important part of socializing kids."

"I went to private school with the same kids I would be sleeping over with. Trust me, I'm happy my parents didn't let me. I never wanted to spend more time with them than I needed to, anyway."

He shuffles over to the daybed, tossing the throw pillows onto the floor. It takes me half a moment to figure out what Hudson is doing. But then I remember, the bed is mine. The daybed is his. An agreement we settled on when this contract was created and we started this seventy-percent-on-Rotten-Tomatoes rom-comedy of errors.

But everything has changed since then, right? We're not just two marbles circling each other. We're not faking it anymore. We're fully in deep. Like, no-lube-level deep. Code name: Prostate Stimulation Deep. Adele "Rolling in the Deep" . . . deep.

"You can sleep with me," I blurt out. Hudson's talking about something . . . wealthy. Something about the private school he attended and how much he hates the people he met, I don't know, and I really don't care about the woes of the affluent—which totally sounds like an A24 film.

Have you ever seen someone become the human embodiment of something? Like, when you were a kid and you played freeze tag and some kids were really good at it and looked like statues? If there were a way to embody a record scratch, Hudson just did it.

His whole body turns quickly to me and stops suddenly. "I'm sorry, repeat that again."

"You can sleep—"

"Slower. I want to savor it."

"You . . ."

"Oh yeah."

"Can . . ."

"That's the stuff."

"Sleep . . ."

"Keep going . . ."

"With . . ."

"Almost there."

"Me . . ."

"Oh fuck, Kian!" he cries out, like he's faking an orgasm. He throws the blankets in the air for dramatic effect and falls backward, once again, on the bed.

Except this time his head comes dangerously close to hitting the corner of the bench at the foot of it.

"You're dumb, you know that," I mutter. But I don't fight the feeling anymore. A hot guy like Hudson, lying in my bed? I would be dumb to resist that. And this is more than just any hot guy. More than just *the* Hudson Rivers. He's *my* Hudson Rivers. My boyfriend. Right?

Wait.

We never technically agreed on those exact words. *Boyfriend* is a specific title. A contract that isn't easily broken, not something you can brush aside. Well, I mean you *can*, and people do all the time. But that's not the current phobia of the day. Today's phobia is reserved for six simple words.

We. Never. Said. We. Were. Official.

In hindsight, worrying about whether Hudson and I were official seems kind of silly. *Official* is such an early 2000s thing. When being "Facebook official," or "Instagram official," were the markers of a solid relationship. I wonder how many of those actually ended happily. Probably not many.

But wanting Hudson to tell me, to my face, that we are actually dating, that we're actually boyfriends in it for the long haul, doesn't make me weak. It doesn't make me less than or vapid or any other words people use to describe people who are overly emotional. And usually, the people who make those decisions are those we in the community call "fuck boys."

Caring where you stand with someone doesn't make you weak.

Wanting to have clarity on your relationship doesn't make you clingy.

Making sure that a person you're tying your future to—long term or short term—is on the same page as you, doesn't mean you have a problem.

And fuck anyone who thinks that.

"Hey."

Hudson's voice brings me back to reality. He has that look on his face like he said something very important in the past ten seconds and I completely missed it. Between the fake orgasm that I'm sure woke the whole house—I'm waiting for his parents to come bursting in with a Bible and holy water—and my own little journey down Overthinking Lane, he's found his way to the bed and under the covers.

"Where did you go?" he asks, reaching over, grabbing the cuff of my shirt and pulling me down onto the bed. "And next time you have to take me with you. That's one of the Boyfriend Commandments."

Hudson doesn't help me when my knees buckle. He sits up quickly and grabs me, bracing his body and using it like a cushion so I fall on top of him. He has a stupid boyish grin on his face, while mine has all the signs of a familiar scowl.

"Oh, come on," he groans, pinching my sides. "You loved that. I was smooth as hell."

Hudson keeps rubbing his hands up and down my sides in a soothing motion. With each wave, I find it harder and harder to be annoyed at him, the sharpness of my scalp weakening with each passing moment. But also, the walls inside me, which keep at bay the words that could either make or break us, have begun to crumble.

I'm not going into this relationship with a lie. I'm not going into this relationship like before, second-guessing everything, thinking I'm not worthy enough, but also always worried that something I do or say will drive Hudson away. That's not a relationship; it's a gilded cage.

The silence between us feels heavy, like it's expanding with heat and pushing us away from each other. Hudson seems to feel the same thing, because the boyish, lopsided grin that makes my heart flutter slowly dissolves into a look of curiosity, then worry, then more immediate concern.

"All right," he says, sitting up and pulling me with him. "What's up? And don't try and lie to me. You suck at it."

I could spend probably another three to five minutes dodging his question. Hudson may be right about me being a bad liar, but I am a journalist, and we are good at getting information and dodging questions when we want to. But if Hudson is willing to give his all to be open in this relationship, then so am I.

As the Basic Bro Boys of our generation, who gave us hits like "Closer" and "#Selfie," said, "If we go down, then we go down together."

"Do you want to be my boyfriend?" I finally say. "I know it sounds like a dumb question. But—"

Hudson sighs and takes my hands in his. He brings them up to his lips, kissing each of the knucklebones, one after the other, while maintaining eye contact with me. The action is simple; there's nothing sexual or sexy about it. But that doesn't mean that each kiss doesn't feel like lightning going up my spine and striking just the right nerves in my brain to hold me in place.

"You're right. It was a dumb question. But I'm used to you asking dumb questions. Most smart boys usually do."

"You know what, never mind." I try to pull my hand away from Hudson's grasp, but his hands are like a vice around my own, holding them in his lap. The small flicker of a smile that plays off his full lips makes me want to punch him. Or kiss him. Or punch him and then kiss him. I'm not really sure which, and I'm not really sure it matters.

"Listen," he whispers. "You want me to say it? Is that what you need? Because I will. I want to be your boyfriend. I want to give us another try. I want to stop *thinking* about you every waking moment, and actually *know* you're mine every waking moment. I want to be yours. I want to be that couple that floods everyone's feeds with photos, and makes inside jokes over texts. I want to make everyone uncomfortable with how much we like each other's company. I want to know you inside and out, not just, you know, in the bedroom, but actually know you.

"And that doesn't happen by being your fuck buddy, or your friend with benefits, or whatever other term we can use to dance around what we're feeling. I want to be my most vulnerable self around you, Kian. I want to know, even when I'm my darkest, my smallest, my most broken, you'll be there to shine a light, to hold my hand and light the way. And I want to be the same for you. I *know*, if you give me the chance, I can. Just . . . let me prove it to you. One more time."

I had prepared myself for a lot of different things that Hudson might say. I was ready for him to beat around the bush, for me to have to dissect his words and read between the lines to find a kernel of truth that I could use to extrapolate. But I wasn't prepared for such an honest, emotional, and—frankly—fucking sexy truth from the man I've spent multiple nights thinking about, texting, jerking off to, and, of course, crying over.

"Now, are you going to keep asking stupid questions, or are you going to let me hold you while we sleep?"

"Probably going to keep asking stupid questions," I quip with a flickering smile. Hudson groans, wraps his muscular arms around me, and uses his stronger build to flip me over so my back is against his chest, his grip keeping me in place.

"Shut up and go to sleep," he whispers, face nuzzled into my head. The hot air against the nape of my neck makes me shiver with each breath of his. Never really understood the attraction of spooning. One person always ends up with a dead arm, usually the same person who ends up suffocating in another person's hair. And for the spooned, it feels like you're in a straitjacket made of human flesh, which is honestly a terrifying thought.

But then again, as with everything else in life, it seems that when you're doing it with the right person, the perfect person, none of those thoughts really matter anymore. It just feels . . . right.

So, I relax, letting my bones slide into place and my form relax in Hudson's arms. He shifts a fraction of an inch to get comfortable and sighs contentedly.

"Alexa, turn off the lights."

Obediently, and silently, the room turns dark.

"You know, smart technology is going to . . ."

"For fuck's sake, Kian, please, and I say this as nicely as I can, shut the fuck up for once in your life and just . . . be with me."

Any other time, if anyone else had said that to me—except maybe my mother or Divya—I would've punched them in the face. But Hudson has wormed his way into the elite group of people that I'm not sure even Jamal belongs to, who can talk to me like that and make me want to whisper *Yes, sir.*

But I'm not trying to keep us up all night.

Moments pass as the quiet hum of the house starts to lull me to sleep. But right before I swan-dive into dreamland, I want to get something off my chest.

"K," I whisper.

"Hm?" Hudson replies, voice filled with sleep.

"You can call me K."

His grip around me tightens, and I don't mind it. Not one fucking bit.

TWENTY-SIX

THERE'S ONLY ONE way to describe the way I feel waking up the next morning, and I'm not exactly proud of this description, but hey, this is the year of living our best, true, authentic lives:

Today, I woke up feeling like a goddamn Disney princess.

Now, which princess you identify with is the most important question of all time. More important than your sun sign, your Harry Potter house, or even your *Avatar* bending style. Because we all know, when the big bad copyright-manipulating M-I-C-K-E-Y becomes our rodent overlord, people will be sorted into Disney Princess houses, wage war, and eventually have a class uprising. So knowing where you stand, whom you can trust, and whom you'll need to fight in the streets is very, very important.

As a gay born in 1999, I spent a lot of time watching those movies, then thinking about and debating which princess I would be. After much deliberation and soul-searching, I've settled on an answer that I don't think most people would choose for me:

Ariel.

I know, not the most common of picks. When I was younger, a

hundred percent it would have been Belle, but I'm much more of a redhead with no legs.

First of all, I would look *fire* with red hair—no pun intended. Second of all, much like Ariel (because, you know, she doesn't have legs), I can't run. Like, I *can*, but I absolutely hate doing it. The only time you should be running is if a bear is chasing you. And third and finally, I would give anything—and have—for the things I want.

Hudson. Spotlight. Moving up to Boston for school when North Carolina was a much better financial choice. I get our favorite heroine to the Atlantican throne.

How Ariel felt when she knew that she and Prince Eric were going to spend their lives together is exactly how I feel when I wake up the next morning and turn around to face Hudson. For the first time since this whole insane lie started, I don't feel like I'm trying to play catch-up, or that I'm two moves away from being exposed as a fraud. I feel like I actually belong somewhere, with someone, and that's a damn good fucking feeling.

You know what isn't a good feeling? Thinking you're going to roll over and see someone sleeping next to you, only to find the bed empty.

It takes a moment for my brain to process that Hudson Rivers is not there next to me. It takes me another moment to put two and two together that he isn't in the bathroom either. That his phone is gone, and the shoes he took off by the door? Gone too.

I sit up in the bed, dumbstruck, doing the one thing Generation Z is exceptionally good at: blowing things out of proportion. But the lessons of my sixty-dollar-an-hour therapist kick in.

Deep breaths, Kian. Think this through. The most logical answer is probably the right answer. Work the problem, don't let the problem work you.

Note to self: "Werq the Problem" would be a really fucking good rap song. Future Kian, e-mail Megan Thee Stallion and team up with her to make this idea profitable.

Where is he?

Judging by the fact his shoes and shit are gone, he's probably not far.

Did his mother call him down?

After all, we are here for a wedding, not just to sleep in bed and kiss under the starlight by a pond like some *The Princess Diaries 3: The Gay Edition*.

But that kiss was nice. Like . . . really, really nice.

Focus.

Maybe he's . . . cleaning the car?

Does Hudson seem like someone who has cleaned a car, even once in his life, or even knows how to clean a car?

Point taken.

My mind, the id and the ego (I think?), goes back and forth debating all the possibilities that could explain where Hudson is. But as we eliminate different options, the most logical—or rather the most *illogical*, but for me that's the same thing—option shines through.

He's left me. He got up in the middle of the night, once I fell asleep, slept in the living room, and went away to live his life before I even woke up, because he doesn't want to see my ugly face.

With each word that balloons in my mind, my pulse quickens until I feel a thin line of sweat appear on my brow that isn't from the Georgia summer heat. Of course this would happen. Of course I would let Hudson back into my life, give him another chance and he would do this to me. He was so smooth too. Fool me once, shame on you; fool me twice—

"Hey! You're up."

Hudson's deep and cheerful voice breaks through the clouds of darkness swirling around my mind. His voice is like a bullet train of light, striking through the darkness my anxiety creates. It ripples off him, pulsing out warmth. He's like Gandalf the Grey fighting the Balrog. Or the stag the Darkling killed in *Shadow and Bone*.

But Hudson is hotter than Gandalf or Mal or even the Darkling. More of an Emmett Cullen, but Southern. And Black. More of a Southern himbo.

He flops on the bed, his full weight making the bed creak. He's dressed in a light blue button-down that fills out his pecs well. His hair is washed and slicked but not too styled, and the jeans are designer but fit his ass and thighs perfectly. A little too perfectly.

He reaches over, running his fingers through my unruly curls. "How did you sleep?"

"Fine—no, great actually." A moment passes as my heart calms. "Your bed is really comfortable. You're really comfortable."

"First of all, you can thank my mother for the first compliment. Hell, you can thank her and her DNA for the second one, too. I'll make sure to give her them. She'll love you; she lives off of praise after all. Keep that in mind."

"Noted," I tease. "Gotta make sure the boyfriend's mother loves you. What psychological principle is that, again?"

"Mama's Boy Syndrome." He nods seriously. "Documented in 1953 when a young dandy boy returned from war and moved in with his parents."

Silence and a stoic expression on Hudson's face fill the space between us. "Wait, you're joking, right?"

He shrugs. "Maybe? Maybe not."

"I don't know if I can trust you or not."

"Well, I am a psychologist. If you needed to talk to someone about some disorder, you'd contact me as an expert. Why is this any different?"

"Because you get off on tricking me."

Hudson gives me a wink and a finger gun. "You got me there, Daddy-o."

I cringe, my body visibly coiling in on itself. Hudson, again, smirks, like it's a permanent expression on his handsome face and million-dollar cheekbones.

"You like that?" he asks. Before I can respond, Hudson pushes me back on the bed, resuming his position on top of me from last night. Except this time, I don't fight him when he pins me to the bed.

This time, I don't struggle when he leans down low and presses his lips gently against my neck.

This time, I push my body up, quietly asking him to do more.

"We never followed up on that kiss from before," I whisper, feeling heat radiate from my body and his.

"Oh?" he asks, voice muffled in my neck, typing our Morse code with his soft lips. "I don't know what you're talking about; can you give me more details?"

"You're an ass."

"My ass is very nice and thick, yes." He grins.

"It's not that nice, I've seen better."

"Oh, fuck off," he says with a laugh, shoving me with his open palm. "And to think I was going to be nice to you and take you somewhere. But no, you had to go and insult me."

Well, that piqued my interest. I let my body sway with the motion of him pushing me, like a bobblehead, before sitting back up. "No one is saying you can't still take me somewhere."

"Why should I take someone who treats me like an ass?"

"Isn't it obvious?" I quickly rebut. I lean forward and steal a kiss. "Because I'm cute."

He opens and closes his mouth twice, his shoulders collapsing like a deck of cards, but the grin that makes everything feel better never disappears from his face.

"All right, all right." He waves it off. "You got me. I'll take you— *but*—you have to be punished somehow."

"You have a dirty mind, and I'm not going to indulge it," I say.

But Hudson speaks at the same time, adding, "And I've determined that punishment is going to be you not knowing where we're going."

Never before have I actually seen a stalemate like in the Westerns. Two cowboys, staring each other down in the middle of a town at high noon. But that's what it looks like with me and Hudson right now. Except our stare-down is much more us just being incredibly surprised at one another, and less trying to predict who is going to draw their gun first.

"You know what?" he says, walking backward. "I'm going to let you sit there and think about what you just said. For ten minutes. Use that time to go get ready. And no, I'm still not telling you where we're going. I'll be in the car waiting," he adds, half his body hidden by the door. "And for the record? You have no idea how dirty I can get."

———·———

"OKAY, I KNOW I said I didn't feel like I belonged at your home, but I certainly don't belong here."

I don't think Hudson will leave me—he's taking *me* on an adventure after all—but that doesn't mean I want to risk it. Nine minutes later, I'm in the car. Thirty minutes later, with no clearer idea about where we're going, we finally pull up to the destination.

And when I tell you I had no idea this is where we were going, I mean I truly had no fucking idea.

The iron gates of the Rivers & Valleys Brewing Company head-quarters loom in front of me like the gates of a castle the Scooby gang would have to infiltrate. But beyond the iron gates, you can see a beautiful modern building, more like where the Cullens lived in Forks.

Personally, I think the two styles play against one another, not together. Hudson leans out of the car to press a button, the gates opening, and says what's on my mind before I can make a pithy comment myself.

"It's like my family, isn't it?" he asks, letting the car roll slowly. "Prickly on the outside, modern and chic on the inside?"

"Most people juxtapose prickly with something soft, you know."

"Do you think my family is soft?"

"Oh, absolutely not."

"Then I rest my case."

He speeds up a bit; the long driveway, about a quarter of a mile, is lined with shrubbery that passes us by. The lawn, from what I can tell, has a winding cobblestone path through the landscape, probably for workers to have some sort of walking breaks between shifts.

Without thinking, Hudson pulls into one of the three parking spots up front, spots marked with white writing against the black pavement: FOR THE RIVERS FAMILY.

We step out of the car—well, Hudson steps out, with a swagger like he belongs. I just slither out, my neck arched so much I swear I'm going to need a chiropractor to realign my bones like some sort of Rubik's Cube. I bet Hudson's parents have a chiro on call. That seems like the type of over-the-top expense they would have.

"Trust me, it's not as bad as it looks," he says sheepishly. I glance over at him with a sideways look, seeing the way his shoulders slightly fold in on him.

I take a moment to study him. He can't be embarrassed, right? I mean, I get it, having money—or not having it, or your parents having it—can be a sore subject, but come on now, Hudson. You know me better than that.

The words feel like scolding when I play them over in my head. Instead, I reach forward and take his hand in mine, squeezing it tightly, and give his arm a hard tug. Not so hard as to pull his arm out of the socket, like he's some raggedy doll with loose stuffing and frayed fabric stitches, but firm enough to make his body take a step forward, a step closer to me.

"What makes you think I won't steal the secret family recipe, hm? You're putting a lot of trust in me."

"Trust me, I'm not worried."

"Why? Don't think I'm cut out to be a thief?"

He shrugs and pulls me closer to him, so our shoulders connect. His hand slips out of mine to wrap itself around my shoulder. "Oh, trust me. You're a journalist. You bitches are cutthroat. I've seen several documentaries about how journalists have shifted the tide of history."

"You don't . . ."

"Just let me have this, I'm giving you a compliment."

I mimic zipping my mouth.

"Gosh. Thank you." He smirks. "But, like I was saying before I was *so rudely* interrupted, I'm more than confident that, if you wanted to, you could steal from our family. I mean, you have me wrapped around your finger—if you asked nicely enough, I'm sure I would just fucking give it to you. But what I really meant was, I know you wouldn't hurt me. I know you would do nothing to make my life worse with my parents. I mean, hell, you were willing to lie to their faces, possibly endure humiliation by being the butt of their jokes, and be a sacrificial lamb if I wanted you to, all to help me out."

"I did it for a job," I remind him. "And when you put it like that, you make it sound like I might have made a bad choice."

"Nah, I think I'm a pretty good choice," he says, pressing his lips against my cheek like he's burning an imprint of his mouth onto my skin before pulling back.

"And I think I made a good choice in you too," I say without a hint of hesitation or a lie.

"Of course you did. I mean, I'm me. Who could be better?"

"John Stamos, Charlie Hunnam, Chris Evans, John David Washington, Justin Trudeau . . ."

"Okay, okay, okay, way to bruise a man's ego. Come on, let's go inside," he says, waving at the camera. A moment passes before the cast-iron gates slowly push open.

"'One short day in the Emerald City,'" I mutter under my breath.

"Hm?"

"Nothing."

Hudson isn't gay enough for that.

TWENTY-SEVEN

I DON'T HAVE an extensive amount of experience wandering around breweries, but I can tell from the get-go that Rivers & Valleys is not like others.

Hudson's parents have tried to balance, even if I'm not sure they did it successfully, the idea of two different business principles: the family-owned company and the corporate powerhouse. When you enter the brewery on the first floor, the layout is very much like an Apple Store. There's a social aspect to it, a flow similar to the Valhalla of shopping (IKEA) that kind of pushes you through like a gentle stream. The first floor is also the most public-facing floor. It's where all the examples of Rivers & Valleys' successes are: a display about the company's history, tasting stations, the gift shop. If you have any interest in brewing, this is the floor for you.

"It's based off of the Guinness factory in Dublin," Hudson says. "Every Rivers kid, or extended family member, who intends to work for the company has gone to the Guinness factory. It's some sickening and twisted top one percent rite of passage. Some families have boxing, others have board games, some of them have spades—ours have flying halfway across the world for a weekend to visit a god-damn brewery. If that doesn't tell you everything you need to know about my family, I don't know what else can."

The second and third basement floors are dedicated to offices—boring things like administration and HR and so on and so forth. The branches of running a business that no one thinks about and, therefore, do not deserve to get vitamin D on a regular basis.

The second and third levels above the first floor are also dedicated to office space, but these are the ivory towers of offices. Outreach, communications, PR, and the Rivers family suite.

Hudson doesn't let the elevator stop there.

"There's nothing for us to see," he says curtly. "Just a whole bunch of boring offices. When you've seen one, you've seen them all."

Nine times out of ten, when someone says there's nothing to see, there's something for you to see. It's like when the police tell you to move along—you know they're probably committing some type of attack on our civil liberties. But we're not ready to get into that.

Hudson takes us across a glass walkway, which leads to a scout building about three stories tall. The moment we enter the room, we're hit with the smell of hops, the warmth of the burners, and the tingle of carbonation in the air. The rooms are starkly different from the five public-facing floors we just left. These have a brassy color to them, instead of a monotone hue. There's less liveliness, more of a mechanical, almost steampunk feeling. There's no personality; it's devoid of any sort of heart. Here, everything is pure capitalism. In some ways, it reminds me of what Willy Wonka's factory would have been, if he had been allowed to keep it after the children he terrorized took him to court and forced his factory to be an aboveboard legit business.

Okay, maybe that analysis is a little creepier than I wanted.

"Welcome to one of many locations where the magic happens," Hudson muses with a sweeping hand motion.

"And by magic you mean . . ."

"Twenty billion dollars."

"Actually, closer to twenty-five billion," a familiar, confident voice says. "Our best year yet."

Olivia Rivers is one of those people who command attention when they walk into the room. It isn't the clicking of her heels against the concrete floor, or the way her white cigarette pants lay perfectly against her long legs, or the way the chiffon top falls perfectly against her body. It certainly isn't the perfectly placed makeup that accents her sharp cheekbones, or the way her brown hair shimmers as if it has gotten a keratin treatment just moments before.

All of those things are good. All of those things are also true. But Olivia has something Hudson doesn't have: a sense of authority and demand for respect.

It doesn't help that following behind her are two familiar faces: Nathaniel and Danni.

"What are you doing here?" Hudson asks accusatorially.

Olivia arches her brow, the Hermès bag she carries loosely dangling over her crossed arms. "Not *Hello, sister. How are you doing, sister? It's so nice to see you, sister.*"

"I'll get to that next."

"Hudson was showing me around the facility," I say, holding up three fingers in a scout's honor sign. "Promise I'm not going to steal your family recipe."

She arches her brow. "Is that something we should be concerned with? Are you a thief, Kian? I mean, you already stole my brother's heart, it seems. Is our family fortune next?"

That hits me like a dump truck in the chest, and I know, for a fact, I do a *horrible* job of covering up my reaction. Look, I get it. The Riverses are fucking rich. And I am a random outsider whom Olivia probably doesn't know much about. But being called a gold digger is like when there's a murder on your street. Or when someone you know is arrested. It's one of those things that you acknowledge can happen, but you always think will happen to someone else. It will never happen to you.

In short, being called a gold digger fucking hurts.

Hudson takes half a step forward, his larger body acting like a metaphorical shield against Olivia. "Look, I know we don't get along—and that's fine—but letting you throw accusations at my boyfriend? Not cool."

"Not *cool*?" she asks, using air quotes. "How old are we, Hudson?"

Olivia and Hudson could be an allegory for some great war we're taught in high school. I think World War II, or maybe the Cuban Missile Crisis, would be a good comparison—neither of them are willing to back down, and they are inching closer and closer to mutually assured destruction. I glance over Hudson's shoulder, and Danni and I lock eyes. It's like we understand each other and what we need to do. Like two members of some circus troupe who have practiced their routine so many times it's second nature.

Wait, did I just call myself a clown? That's a discussion for another day.

"Hey," I say, stepping up and gripping Hudson's shoulder. "Look, I'm always here for a good free brawl, because HBO is too super fucking expensive to watch boxing matches, but we're here to relax, not give one of us a heart attack, yeah?"

Danni plays off my words easily. "And I don't want the last thing I see before getting married to be a fight. That has to be bad luck, right? Blood before the wedding and all? There's some Nordic warning about that, I'm sure."

"I'm pretty sure I read that somewhere."

"See?" she says. "Kian seems like a smart guy; we should listen to him."

Danni glances over her shoulder at Nathaniel, I guess expecting him to throw his vote of support behind her. Instead, he shrugs, going back to messing with the lapel of his off-white coat, which complements his periwinkle shirt perfectly. "I don't care either way."

"Of course you don't," Danni and I say at the same time. We grin at each other, like two mischievous Thing One and Thing Two siblings. Simpatico achieved.

Olivia's the first of the two warring sides at the Battle of Rivers to take a step back. Her arms uncross and she lets out a loud sigh through puffed cheeks, made, I'm sure, for dramatic effect. "I've wanted to talk to you anyway," she says to her brother. "So, let's just call it fate or kismet or whatever you want."

"Hell? The worst day of my life? Punishment for something I did in my last reincarnation? The Devil testing me?" Hudson rattles off.

"Babe," I say sternly. The word catches me off guard. Not because Hudson technically (or literally, actually) isn't my babe. Because what I really meant to say was his name. Even in my head, I thought the two-syllable word *Hudson* was what came out. But nope. It was *babe*. Such an easy and casual pet name that means so much and costs so little.

Hudson's face is the physical manifestation of my surprise. But the way his features warm up in a boyish, hopeful way also reflects how good the word feels being said out loud. Like a secret I've been holding on to for months I can finally share with the world.

"Fine," he says. "But only because my gold digger of a boyfriend insists. The office?" he suggests.

Olivia nods, turning to us. "Can you three keep yourselves busy and out of trouble?"

Nathaniel holds up his phone. "I have a work call."

"We'll be fine," Danni promises. "Plus, it gives me time to get to know Kian."

"Which is frankly more interesting than a tour of our family brewery," Hudson mutters, winking at me. "I won't be long."

"Take your time," I promise.

Hudson and Olivia take the stairs together, while Nathaniel gives Danni a quick peck on her cheek before wandering down through the brewing stations, his voice becoming more and more distant with each passing second until it's swallowed by the constant hum of fermented capitalism.

Danni turns to me and smiles. "Guess it's just you and me."

"I like girls more than boys anyway, so this is a win-win in my book."

"And I like gay guys more than straight guys. So, I guess we both win. Want to get a drink?"

"In a brewery, is that even allowed? Or possible?"

She laughs, a mix between Hudson's full laugh and Olivia's airy one. "I like you. Come on, I'm sure we can find a beer or two."

———— · ————

AS DANNI PROMISED, locating beer is not a problem. We go back to the lobby and find a cooler full of Rivers & Valleys' different flavors and proofs. Danni quickly gravitates to one of the bottles with a purple ribbon around it.

"Elderberry?" I ask, weighing two different options for myself: blueberry or original. I put back the one with the blue ribbon. Probably should stick with the OG.

"You've never had it?" she asks, pulling her credit card out of her purse. She doesn't even give me a chance to offer to pay, which makes me feel a certain way. This is Danni's weekend, not mine. She's the one getting married. Aren't you supposed to, as a bride, let people wait on you hand and foot? Isn't that the benefit of being a bride?

"All right, you have to try it. I'm demanding it of you," she teases. "And you can't say no to me."

"Because it's your wedding weekend?"

"Yes, and because who would want to say no to this face?" She weaves her fingers together and places her chin in the cradle, gently cocking her head and batting her eyes in an angelic manner. A loud laugh, originating from the depths of my belly, bursts into the air. My abs hurt from how hard I'm laughing.

"And because I made you laugh that hard! Humor like that doesn't come for free. Come on. I've heard the grounds are even more beautiful than the building."

Danni leads us to the first floor of the brewery like she owns the place. And though I can tell she doesn't actually own the place (that would be a real season two plot twist, wouldn't it?), I'm sure she has some connection to the Rivers family. Which leads me to wonder, is Nathaniel involved with the family business? Is that how they met each other?

They both seemed fairly familiar with Olivia and the rest of the family. I mean, familiar enough that Isaac and Diana Rivers let them use their home for the reception. That requires a certain level of trust and closeness. Or maybe I'm just reading too much into it. Does it really matter either way? I'm here for Hudson, not for Danni, not for Nathaniel, not to be a reporter. I'm here for my boyfriend.

Boyfriend. I still haven't gotten used to saying that again, even in my head.

We push open the glass door, which leads to a giant patio with circular tables overlooking the grounds. If I had to imagine how Google's campus looks, the Rivers & Valleys headquarters would resemble that. Much like the expensive landscape of the Rivers home, but the headquarters has even more acreage. I can't even see where it ends.

Danni picks a table that's far enough away from everyone else, yet close to the railing, giving us the best view possible. But more so, it gives me a chance to really look at her. The light pink sundress she's wearing nicely complements her skin with its pink undertones. She's thin, almost model thin, but not so much that it looks sickly— more like someone who has the world's best metabolism. Her hair is pulled into a messy bun, and she has minimal makeup on her round face, but the general air of relaxation and calmness she carries more than compensates for it.

"Am I that beautiful?" she asks after a moment. "I mean, please tell me if I am. I'm a Scorpio; we love praise, supposedly, but you've been staring for a while." She leans forward, faking a whisper. "I won't tell my fiancé if you won't."

"I have a feeling if I tried to take you from Nathan, he would punch my face in," I say. I give her half a second to worm her way into the conversation, if she has any inclination to correct me. She doesn't take the bait. "But no, that's not what I was thinking about. I mean, you are beautiful. Very beautiful in fact. Like model-tier beautiful."

"Oh, stop." She playfully flicks her hand. "But no, keep going. Please, keep going."

"I was more wondering . . . and this might sound wrong . . . so I don't mean to offend you . . ."

"You're trying to figure out why I'm marrying someone like Nathan," she finishes for me.

A beat. "Yeah, that's about it."

Danni takes a long sip of her elderberry beer, and I follow suit with my bottle of the original flavor. This isn't the first time I've had Rivers & Valleys, but after Hudson and I broke up, I swore off the brand. Seeing it at the Patriot, or in the store, or at friends' parties was a knife to the chest that could reopen old wounds over and over again, just when I thought I was healing.

But now, I think I can try it again.

I wasn't a big beer drinker before I met Hudson; about as much as any college student is a drinker. Beer is cheap, even a high-end brand like this one, and it's easy to get drunk off it. So, in a nutshell, almost every college student is a professional beer drinker. But the hoppy flavor in the beer? I approve.

Danni grins over the lip of her beer. "Here," she says, gesturing to her bottle. "Try it. I think you'll like it."

"And if I don't? What do I get in return?"

Danni pushes her perfectly manicured brows into a thin line. I can see the gears turning in the back of her head, like three dots appearing above her while she thinks.

"I have an idea," I suggest. "One fact."

"That's it? What's the catch?"

"No catch; scout's honor," I say, holding up three fingers.

Danni reaches over, grabbing my beer and drinking half of it. How can she tolerate those bubbles? I have no idea. Finally, she puts down the drink and extends her hand; her decision made. "Deal."

We shake on it before I take the elderberry drink and sip it slowly. The bubbles aren't as strong as the original formula, and the taste of fruit is light and airy. If I had my way, I'd probably make the fruit more prominent, and reduce the hoppy aftertaste. Maybe reduce the bubbles too. Maybe I'll suggest that to Hudson. Get in his parents' good graces by helping their company. Everyone loves money, right? Help the company, help the family. Save the cheerleader, save the world.

"Well?" Danni asks. "What do you think?"

The logical and fair answer would be to tell the truth—tell her I love it because, well, I do. But then, I wouldn't get the information I want from her. This is a chance to understand the Riverses from an outsider's perspective; someone like me. To understand how she actually got in their good graces. Do I want to marry Hudson? I don't know yet; but I do know I want them to like me. And I can't do that if I don't understand the inner workings.

"It's all right." That's a perfect middle ground. Not great, but not a full lie. But enough of a lie for me to declare a win. That's what politicians do, right? Live comfortably in that morally grey area.

Danni isn't easy to fool, though; not as easy as I thought she'd be. "You're lying."

I shrug. "It's only all right, not bad, not great," I say, pushing the bottle back. "I prefer the original."

"Oh, you fucker," she scolds, snatching the bottle. "You played me, didn't you?"

"I can neither confirm nor deny that."

"I should have known you'd backstab me."

"Again, I can neither confirm nor deny that. But you made a deal."

Danni takes a long sip of her drink, probably to buy time as she leans back in the chair. Her eyes narrow, studying me, searching for a way out of the agreement. The silence between us is like a stalemate in some wartime drama.

Finally, she caves.

"All right, fine, you win," she concedes. Danni leans forward and waves her hand dismissively. "One fact—that's all you get. One. Fact."

Part of me didn't think this would ever happen. All she had to say was no, and that would have been that. I can't *force* her to tell me anything, and it's not like we're close enough for me to pull any *remember that time you promised me . . .* or *you owe me because . . .* arguments. I don't let the surprise appear on my face. Instead, I say the one thing that has been in the back of my head this whole time. And not just since I met Danni or since Hudson and I became a "couple"—but ever since Mom divorced my father and married Ja-mal's father.

"How did you know Nathaniel was the one?"

Danni isn't looking at me at first; the landscape is pulling her attention away from me. But the question? Something about it has weight, and her eyes snap to me.

"Excuse me?" There's a tinge of venom in her voice that strikes between my ribs and makes me hiss. Quickly, I backtrack.

"I mean, you're marrying him, yeah?" I say. "So, you must have known he's the one for some time. I'm just curious. What made you think he's 'the one.'" I use air quotes for emphasis. "Everyone has a story, right? That 'when did I know' moment. What was yours?"

"I didn't. I don't."

"I'm sorry?"

Danni doesn't hesitate with her answer, though part of me wishes she had. There's no way that's the true answer. She's marry-ing someone. She's committing herself to another person. Of *course* she knows he's the one! Why would she marry him if she didn't?

My poker face must be worse than I thought, because she elabo-rates without me having to say anything.

She sighs, finishing off the rest of the bottle. "What the hell, right? Might as well say it to someone—I'm getting married in a matter of days."

"You don't sound happy about that?" I suggest. "Not as happy as you should, at least."

Danni finishes her beer in a few gulps and reaches toward mine. "You mind?"

I wave my hand, giving her permission. She doesn't go through the annoying back-and-forth of the *are you sure* dance some people do. She just takes the drink and polishes it off, too. Two bottles of beer in less than ten minutes.

In journalism, that's what we would call a great story.

"I met Nathaniel in college. Emory," she starts. "Same dorm floor. And we had three classes together. Business 201, Art History, and English 200."

"You're a business major?"

"Was," she corrected. "I run an art studio downtown. Hence the art history. A passion for me."

"An easy gen ed for him?"

She tilts the drink to me. "You get it."

"Boys are always the same," I say, like I'm not one.

She smiles and continues. "It was a very typical boy-meets-girl. Boy sleeps with girl at a party. Girl falls for boy. Boy wants to sow his oats and live his life in college. Boy and girl have a passionate four-year-long off-and-on relationship."

"Most of those stories don't end in marriage," I remind her.

"Most of those stories don't involve Nathan Wilcox, the heir to one of the largest telecom companies in the South," she reminds me.

My turn to drink to her.

Danni continues. "It honestly was chance, really. During graduation two years ago, my parents came to campus. The same day Nathan and I returned all the stuff we had of each other's. A new start, you know? Wiping the slate and . . ." She pauses, drifting off as her voice loses its tenor. I arch my brow in response and lean forward. Danni opens her mouth, closes it, then opens it again like the words got caught in the back of her throat.

That can only mean one thing.

"And then you two had sex, didn't you?"

"I mean . . ." she bashfully mutters.

"Hey, get yours, girl. Nathaniel's hot," I say. "He has a very . . . Chuck Bass vibe to him; if Chuck Bass was six inches taller, had more muscles, didn't use so much gel . . ."

"And wasn't a misogynistic asshole?"

"That too."

"But that would have been the end of the story, you know. That was my plan. A goodbye fuck, a good one at that, and then move on with my life. Go to art school, open up a gallery—two things I did, actually—and just . . . find a nice, creative guy on my same wavelength. But then my parents walked in."

"Oh no!" I yell, leaning back in my chair like I'm listening to some *Real Housewives of Atlanta* summary. "They didn't!"

She nods. "Oh, they did. And let me tell you, the only thing more embarrassing than your parents walking in on you, half-clothed with a guy, is them realizing who the guy is and putting two and two together that their artistic daughter, who is a failure in their eyes, could have her life set if she changed the trajectory just a little bit."

At first, Danni's words sound like some sort of exaggeration; like she's saying this because her parents embarrassed her in front of Nathaniel. But the way Danni carries herself, the way her shoulders fold like she's trying to make herself smaller, is Basic Psychology 101.

And then, it all clicks.

"Wait. You're not saying what I think you're saying?"

She smiles sadly.

"Let me get this straight," I say, leaning forward, resting my arms against the table to bridge the space between us. "Your parents convinced you to marry a guy you're not in love with because it would be better for your career and for them? Is that what you're telling me?"

Danni doesn't answer at first, but the sharpness and darkness in her face tells me all I need to know. The words make sense when they're said aloud, but at the same time, they don't fit; like pieces of a puzzle forced together, not naturally aligned.

"Why?" asks the journalist in me. "Why would they do that?"

Danni chuckles. "My parents didn't grow up like Nathan's or like Olivia's and Hudson's. I'm imagining neither did yours."

"My mom owns an antique shop in North Carolina," I confirm.

"My parents are teachers at a Montessori school," she adds. "So, you understand that this life is so far out of our reach . . . and my parents just wanted me to be set for life."

"But not happy?"

"I think happiness is something that Americans focus on too much. It's more important to be secure," she says.

"Is that what you think or what your parents think?"

A moment passes. "Does it matter?"

"I'd say it does; it's your life, not theirs. When they are dead and gone—which I'm hoping won't be soon—you have to live with your choices. So, I'm going to ask you, Danni, do you love Nathan?"

I regret asking her such a loaded question. Not because I don't think she should be able to answer it, but asking someone on the spot, the day before their wedding, whether they love the person they are supposed to marry, seems . . . unfair. If she says yes, and she's telling the truth, then it makes me sound insensitive. If she says no, or says yes and she's lying, then it'll fester and grow inside of her like a cancer.

"I do," she says, nodding. "Nathan is a good person. His family is good, and we're a good match. He'll make me happy, and he'll be good for me."

I'm not convinced, and I'm not fully sure she is either. I can see the shifting of the floorboards behind her. From the warm grip on my shoulder and the way Danni looks past me, I know who's behind me.

"What are you two gossiping about?" Hudson asks. Nathaniel moves close to Danni and kisses her cheek, letting his lips linger.

Instinctively, I watch as she goes through the motions, turning her head toward him with a soft smile that doesn't reach her eyes. She grips his hand, threading her fingers between his, and squeezes.

How many times has she done things like that? How many times has she done those soft, small actions to convince her fiancé-to-be she truly, actually, fully loves him? How many times has she lied to herself, and him? Does she really believe her words, or are they thick like molasses in her throat, strangling her?

"I think we should head back, if you're ready to go?" Danni says.

"Sure, love." Nathaniel smiles. "Let's go—maybe to that café?"

"That sounds great," she says, which sounds honest. Danni stands, lets Nathaniel wrap his arm around her waist, and turns to me and Hudson.

"It was nice to see you both, and nice to chat with you, Kian. We'll see you both at the wedding rehearsal?"

"Wouldn't miss it for the world," Hudson says. "I'll bring my dance moves."

"Please," Nathaniel groans. "Leave those at home."

"Ass."

"Fucker."

They both grin and clap each other on the shoulder, as bros do, before breaking apart; Nathaniel and Danni blend in with the growing crowd as they walk out. I keep my eyes trained on Danni's back, wondering if, like in the movies, she might look back at me, giving me some glimpse into what she's thinking—and whether our conversation somehow made her think differently.

But this isn't like the movies. Our lives aren't cinematic. They're real. They have consequences and paths—even with others flitting into and out of our story, we have to walk alone.

Hudson mimics Nathaniel's actions, sliding his body against mine. He presses his lips to the top of my head.

"You ready to go?" Hudson asks. "I know you wanted to see the distillery, but I have a few other surprises planned for the day, if you're game? Plus, we have all the time in the world to see this place."

I turn to look up at Hudson, memorizing each of his features. The growing stubble, the angle of his jaw. The darkness and lightness within his eyes. Everything I want to remember for as long as I possibly can. For a moment, I don't understand what he means. We're only going to be here for a few more days. But then I remember, he's thinking about the future. A future of us together; our future.

"Are they good surprises or bad surprises?"

"Do I seem like someone who gives bad surprises?"

"Should I remind you of that time you waited outside my communications lecture and surprised me with . . ."

"Okay, okay." He holds up his hand. "Point taken. But this is going to be a good one. Do you trust me?"

I don't hesitate to answer. "Always."

TWENTY-EIGHT

"OKAY, WHAT'S WRONG?"

Hudson and I continued our previous day's activities of saying *so long, suckers* to his family and spent the whole new day together. While yesterday consisted of the hole-in-the-wall things no tourist in Atlanta would be caught dead doing, today Hudson and I did all the touristy things. According to him, it was a requirement.

"You've never been to Atlanta," he said that morning while spooning me, tracing constellations on my arms. "And sure, I'm sure we'll come back again soon, but might as well make the most of it now and pretend to be tourists, yeah? Plus, I'm the best tour guide. I'm handsome, I know what you like, and I'm free."

Hudson made sure, throughout the day, that we got in as much of Atlanta as we could during our nine hours out, with our phones turned off—Hudson's only demand. Georgia Aquarium, World of Coca-Cola, and, of course, the Botanical Garden took up our morning and early afternoon. Then we had a late lunch at Bones and dinner at Aria's. The trip wasn't complete without visiting McLawrens either, for one more set of clothes, which Hudson insisted might come in handy at some point during the wedding.

"My parents are not above demanding we do outfit changes," he warned while I tried on a maroon suit. "I know, it's a lot, but better to be safe than sorry, right?"

And despite the fact that trying on more clothes and spending more money seemed like the most outrageous thing to me, especially after we spent so much before, that wasn't what left me unsettled.

"It's the extravagance, isn't it?" he asked as we sat in the parking lot, now filled with more than two dozen Buicks, Teslas, Range Rovers, and more. "See, I don't know if you caught on, but that was part of my plan. We don't need to be here for this. I was hoping we'd miss it."

"This" being the rehearsal dinner. When we ran out earlier that morning like two six-year-old children sneaking out to the river, Hudson's mother *made us promise* we would be home in time for the dinner. She knew her son. I'm sure she knew that when he promised he literally had his fingers twisted behind his back in the age old hand gesture indicating a lie.

I mean, why else would you have your phone off for the whole day besides not wanting to hear your parents' wrath?

"That's not it."

"Was it the salad? The mozzarella was supposed to be fresh at Bones, I swear. I know how much you love a fresh salad and . . ."

"Not that either."

To be honest, there wasn't a part of the trip that I didn't enjoy. It was fun to see Hudson's stomping grounds. To see the way his eyes lit up at every single spot where a memory was attached to the location. Some of them good, some of them bad, and some of them seemingly bittersweet. But each one gave me a bit more insight into Hudson Rivers. Each one cracked open his shell a little more, revealing a soft inner flesh that was worth its weight in gold.

For that, I was happy I came along.

I couldn't say the same about myself, though. This trip, and excursion, should've been a time for us to bond. Hudson was doing his part, trying to meet me halfway, but the interactions with Danni from yesterday have been filling my mind like a thicket, making it impossible for me to see the forest for the trees, or the trees at all for that matter. All I kept thinking of was how Danni seemed okay with settling for Nathaniel. That was wrong, wasn't it? Someone shouldn't make a decision like marriage just because their parents wanted them to, or because it made their life "better." This isn't the 1800s anymore; marriage should be based on feeling, not financials.

I thought I did a good job hiding those thoughts from Hudson throughout the day, interjecting *yeah*s and *uh-huh*s and, of course, the occasional *that sounds great* at all the right moments. But judging by how Hudson locks the door, unbuckles his seatbelt, and turns to me when we reach his house again, strands of twilight barely visible in the jet-black horizon, I realize his lack of prying didn't mean I was fooling him. Quite the opposite, actually. It meant he was giving me space, like a boyfriend should, waiting for me to come to him.

I guess he's tired of waiting.

"Hello?" he says, waving his hand in front of my face. "Paging Kian Andrews. I repeat: paging Kian Andrews."

"Hm?" I ask, feigning ignorance.

Hudson's face remains deadpan. "Really? You're going to try that with me?"

"Worth a try." I shrug. "It's nothing, really."

"Every time anyone says it's nothing, it's always something, K.

You're no exception to that. In fact, if anything, you're probably the rule itself." He laughs.

I arch my brow in a silent question.

"You're a journalist," he says. "And you always have an opinion. That's not a bad thing! It's what makes you a damn good investigator. But what I know is that when you have an opinion, and you don't have a way to express it, it festers inside of you. The silent treatment I've been getting for the past four hours is just one example of that. And you don't need to tell me what's bothering you. If you don't want to, I understand. Everyone deserves their secrets, and everyone deserves their time alone. But if there's something I can do to make you feel better, if it's something I did that put you in this mood, I would like to know. Hell, even if you don't want to tell me, just tell me it was my fault and I'll apologize. I'll do whatever I can to make it okay."

I study Hudson's features, seeing if there's any ounce of manipulation or mendacity hidden in the crevices of his pronounced cheekbones. But there isn't: It's more like Hudson is laying it all out on the table. Like he actually wants to help, and actually wants to use whatever powers, gifts, or money he has to make me feel better. Like my mood, and my hurt, is his hurt to share.

I keep quiet, long enough for the engine of the cooling car to shift from a low rumble to silence. Finally, I lick my lips and push the words out of my mouth.

"Is this what a real relationship is supposed to feel like?" I laugh, trying to keep the moment light. "Caring for each other, and you know . . ."

"Carrying the load?" he asks.

"No pun intended, right?"

"Oh, pun completely intended." He waggles his brow. "I'd be honored to carry you—"

"Don't you dare!" I quickly push my hand against his mouth,

covering his lips tightly. His mouth might be hidden, but the mirth dancing behind his eyes sparkles like firecrackers.

"We are on your property," I whisper. "Who knows who might hear you. Olivia already saw us making out yesterday; I don't want a repeat like that again, okay?"

He nods slowly, eyes never blinking. I hold my hand there for a moment longer before slowly pulling back.

"So, you don't want to hear about how I'm more than happy to carry your load?" he says quickly.

"Oh, my fucking God, Hudson!" I yell, hitting him several times. Each hit is met with a full-bodied laugh. His arms jerk up, attempting to block my hits. Like tentacles of an octopus, our four arms flail around each other. Eventually, his fingers interlace with mine, holding our hands together. He brings me close; I don't fight him. Our lips gently press against one another. He's right here. And I can tell, deep down, this time, he isn't going to leave.

Without any hesitation, I push back the middle console. Hudson helps by pulling me through the space between us, sitting me firmly in his lap. His free hand moves to my hip, to hold me in place. The movement is seamless, our lips working together in harmony. My heart pulses in my chest; each pulse like some sort of sonar. Each vibration a single-word directive.

Harder.

Faster.

More.

It's funny how easily Hudson and I go back to the same moment. Neither of us needs to ask the other, neither of us waits for the right opportunity to get our hands on each other. It just happens. And when it does, it's effortless. Maybe that's because Hudson and I have history? Or maybe it's because we are simpatico with one another and we just work well together? The journalist in me wants to know the reason behind our success.

The horny twentysomething in me just wants to get his clothes off and remember every divot, valley, hump, and firm part of his body that I love so much.

As Hudson pushes his tongue into my mouth, working his way around, a part of me just wants to say, *Fuck it, who cares if anyone sees us.* The Jeep's windows are tinted. Who is going to look at a car parked in the car port and see who's inside?

"Wait," I whisper.

Hudson stops immediately. He doesn't try to push a second longer or convince me that waiting isn't really what I want. His hands instantly snap back like a magnet, yanked six inches away. He pulls away his mouth and looks at me with his curious, concerned puppy-dog eyes that say both *Are you okay?* and *What did I do wrong?*

"You did nothing wrong," I promise. "It's just . . . it's been a long time, you know?"

The logistics of car sex begin to make the moment feel less romantic. Hudson is a big guy, not only in height and width but . . . well, in dick size.

"Since we had sex?" he asks. "Yeah, I remember."

"No. Since . . ."

It takes him a moment, but finally he puts two and two together. "*Oh.*"

"Mhm. Plus, I mean do we really want our first time again to be in a car?"

"We've already made out in a car, this seems like a logical progression to me," he says, smirking.

"I'm serious."

Hudson's answer is a shrug, his hands resting on my thighs in a non-sexual manner. "I don't really care where we do it if I'm being honest, I'm just happy to be doing it with you . . . but . . ."

He looks over my shoulder, through the tinted window toward the house. Dozens of people were supposed to arrive for the rehearsal dinner, and the sun is now fully set. Behind the river is the mansion, which has a sort of yellowish-orange glow to it, probably coming from the tent and lanterns set out in the large, expensive courtyard where the rehearsal dinner will be held. A twinge in the pit of my stomach starts to bubble up, like poisonous bile.

"We shouldn't be late—again," I remind him, stealing a kiss, this time planting my lips against his forehead. "Remember, we're still here to impress your parents. And being *extraordinarily* late to this rehearsal dinner doesn't pass the vibe check."

"One, we're already so late my mother is going to skin me alive and use me as a blanket, I'm sure."

"That was your plan, wasn't it?"

"To be late and miss everything? Hopefully, yes. You saw how the cocktail party was a few days ago. Absolutely horrific. To be skinned alive? I'm not into that type of kink play, babe, but if you wanted to explore, I dunno, some impact play . . ."

"And number two?" I interrupt.

Hudson smirks, that wild mirth dancing in his eyes. "Number two is, no one our age says 'vibe check' and you sound like you've been spending too much time on Facebook."

"Am I wrong, though?"

He shakes his head, squeezing my hips gently. "Not at all; then again, you're rarely ever wrong. But . . . I think they can wait a minute, don't you?"

"Hudson," I warn.

"Shush," he teases, squeezing my sides a little tighter. "You said earlier today you trust me. That still true?"

I nod. "Of course."

He opens the side of the car and hoists me out before getting out himself, leaving the bags in the car. "Then follow me."

———— · ————

IF THE *GREAT* *Gatsby* movie was set in the South, and they used the same modern-day style they did for the 2013 version, but made it in 2024, the Riverses' rehearsal dinner afterparty would be a good blueprint for it.

Did people actually change their clothes since I last saw them? It would seem so! I count at least three hundred thousand dollars' worth of jewelry on one person, and that was only three pieces. And was that . . .

"Come on," Hudson urges, tugging me as I stand in the middle of the foyer. "You're going to cause a traffic jam."

"Did I just see . . ."

"Rachel Maddow? Probably."

"How—"

"Family friend," he says, without turning back, weaving through the crowd effortlessly.

"Wait, hold on, you just . . . know Rachel Maddow?"

"I don't, my parents do."

"Are you going to explain that one?"

"Maybe. But not now. We have more important business."

I have no idea where Hudson is leading me, but within a matter of seconds we're near the same room where we babysat the kids yesterday. He looks around once and pulls open the door, shoves us both inside, and turns on the light.

"A bathroom?" I ask.

"A bathroom." He grins, wildly.

"Okay, Hudson: You're very dreamy, and I appreciate you, but

Rachel fucking Maddow is here, and as a journalist . . . wait . . . what are you doing?"

He sinks to his knees before I can say another word. The buckle on my pants comes undone, the loud click audible despite the sounds of the party leaking into the bathroom. Hudson smirks up at me, unzipping my pants slowly.

"Do you want me to stop?" he asks in a husky whisper.

My heart pounding in my ears makes it so I can't hear my own response. Judging from how he reacts, continuing to unzip my pants until he can pull them down to my mid-thighs, boxer briefs included, my answer doesn't give him any inclination to stop.

And, if I'm being honest, I'm glad he doesn't.

His warm hand wraps around my cock, giving it a few strokes to make it harder. Hudson lets out a groan in the back of his throat.

"Fuck," he mutters, pressing hot kisses against my inner thigh. "Fucking hell, I missed this."

A jolt of electricity goes up my legs as he mouths at my balls, taking the right one into his mouth and sucking on it slowly, leisurely, almost like he's worshipping it. My toes curl, back arching. His free hand moves up, pressing against my abs, keeping my hips pinned to the wall.

"Nope," he says, his voice muffled with his mouth full, his eyes never leaving me. "Still," he says.

His voice is soft, and it doesn't have any power to it. But that's what makes it even hotter. It's not a command, not in the traditional sense, but I don't dare to move. I do the opposite, actually, forcing my hips back against the wall, keeping them there as best I can.

"Good boy." Hudson's mouth shifts to my other ball, sucking on it a bit harder this time, groaning to make his mouth vibrate.

"Shit!" I hiss, reaching up with one hand to bite my thumb. I taste blood, but I don't care. The other hand grabs the back of his head, clutching his hair—not enough to damage it but enough to hold on to something, something to ground me.

Hudson pulls back, chuckling. "Someone hasn't gotten head in a while."

"Technically y-you're not . . . you're n-not . . ."

"Shut up," he teases. "This isn't the time to be a know-it-all. This is the time to enjoy."

Hudson dips his head back down, but this time focuses on my cock instead. His tongue—broad, wet, and warm—drags across the underside of it, from hilt to tip. Reaching the head, he wraps his hand around the shaft again, spitting on it, while jerking me off with steady, constant pumps of his fist.

And Hudson Rivers has a fucking great grip.

"Shit, shit, shit," I mutter. The goal was to keep my hips against the wall—I'm good at following orders, after all—but the sensation that comes from him jerking me off? I can't help but push my hips forward in time with each pump.

He's right. It's been a while since I've had sex—since we broke up. And sex was never as good as it was with Hudson. There's something so different about being with someone who knows you. Someone who has your body memorized like their own telephone number. Someone who—

"Oh my GOD."

At some point, during my mental thought and trying to hold on to sanity for dear life, Hudson's mouth found its way to my cock. Mouthing it, kissing it, swiftly taking the full length into his mouth without hesitation.

His mouth tight, warm, and wet, he lets out a wanton moan as he bobs his head up and down. His slick mouth coats my cock, moving with a rhythm that makes my eyes cross. I shudder. Legs threatening to bow and break, I hold on to his head. My panting and his sounds of wet suction fill the air, drowning out the sound of the party. Faster and faster. Further and further down my cock he goes, then I feel the head hitting the back of his throat.

"Jesus," I hiss. I also curse myself mentally, biting my cheek. I want to scream, but that is absolutely the wrong thing—the worst thing—to do. Hudson knows this. I know this. So, I do my best to enjoy the ride. For as long as I can, as best I can.

Which isn't long.

If this were some sort of animation or a porno on Brazzers, I probably would have pulled out a patch of Hudson's hair. But I'm smarter than that, better than that. I think. Might depend on whom you ask.

Instead, I force his face down on my cock as deep as it will go. I moan into my arm, hoping that muffles the sound enough as my thighs shake so much I swear my hamstring is going to snap like a rubber band.

But hey, at least I got off, right?

Hudson doesn't fight it. He gags a little, squirms a little, moves his head to a more comfortable position. But more importantly, he takes it all. Every twitch, every shudder, every drop—he swallows around my cock, pulling back and wiping his mouth.

"I forgot how good you—"

"If you say what I think you're going to say I one hundred percent will kick you."

He laughs, standing up and kissing me slowly. I can taste myself on him. There's something strangely hot about that.

"I vote we stay in here forever," he mutters.

"If you want me to blow you back, just ask. You don't have to wax poetically."

"I mean." He shrugs. "I'm not against that, but more saying . . . I like this. I like us."

Us. I'm smart enough not to break the moment and ask him what "us" is to him, but my hesitation, instead of instantly replying with "I like us too," gets the point across.

"You don't have to say it back," he whispers, kissing my nose. "But know I do love you. I always have loved you, and I'm going to keep loving you. I'm willing to work to get to the point where you're comfortable saying that again. And if you know me, you know I'm persistent."

"To a fault."

"To a fault," he repeats. Hudson takes his time, like a watchmaker carefully putting together something precious, to lift my pants and underwear, zip them up, and press out any creases as best he can.

"See? Good as new. No one would know you just got the best blow job ever."

"Eh." I shrug, making a seesaw motion with my hand. "I'd say it was a nine out of ten."

"Excuse me?!"

I turn my back to him—the best way to drive someone insane is to ignore them—and open the door. I had a complete plan in my head. Ignore him until we reached wherever his parents were. Turn around, let him kiss me, have everyone see how in love we are, make a good impression with his parents.

That goes out the window when the familiar blond man appears in front of us with the million-dollar smile and *Vogue* magazine-worthy cheekbones.

All of which belong to Randall Clements.

"Did I interrupt something?"

TWENTY-NINE

RANDALL CLEMENTS LOOKS different from his photos when I see him up close and personal. He's far lankier in his photos than he is in real life. I thought the camera was supposed to add, like, fifteen pounds? If anything, he's better-looking up close.

The quintessential rich person's attire hangs off his body effortlessly: an expensive Hermès shirt in a black and gold pattern, complementary pants, loafers, a belt I can tell costs more than my rent, and a few adorning bracelets and such. The small nugget of an expensive gem lodged in his right ear completes the outfit.

No, that's not true. The confident smirk completes the outfit.

"Well, well, well," he muses, stepping aside for me and Hudson to move by him. "I go looking for a bathroom, and I find the beginnings of a porno? Looks like this wedding was a good investment of my time after all."

Hudson adjusts his shirt and quickly wipes his mouth, which I feel is completely unnecessary, of course, but that doesn't stop him from doing it—and it doesn't stop me from blushing hard, hard enough that when I discreetly feel my cheeks, they burn; I'm sure it's evident even with my dark skin. Great first impression, Kian.

But Hudson, thank God for Hudson, doesn't let the moment get away from him. He extends his hand, pulling Randall into his gravity well of bro-ness with a warm shake and a clasp of his other hand on Randall's back.

"You wish," he teases. "Maybe if you weren't so ugly I could get you into one."

"Hey, hey," Randall chides as he pulls back, poking Hudson in an accusatory manner in his chest. "The boys and girls in Amsterdam, Ibiza, and Paris would beg to differ."

There's something unsettlingly nauseating about hearing someone talk, with such confidence, about their sexual conquests. Sure, Randall is conventionally attractive. High cheekbones, perfect skin, conditioned hair, overly white teeth. He's the product of wealth—be it old money or new money. Of course, people lust after him and want him. That doesn't seem impossible to me at all.

But talking about it so brazenly and openly? That feels like salt in a wound in a way I can't exactly explain. But, Randall is Hudson's friend—and the fucking CEO of Spotlight—so he's a means to an end. And no one is perfect.

I mean, unless you consider Michael B. Jordan, but then again, he's a god, so he gets an exemption.

Hudson picks up on my tension and squeezes my arm.

"Well, we can discuss your conquests later. This is the guy I was talking about."

Randall's face doesn't register that he understands what Hudson is referring to. Great, talk about a confidence booster.

"The guy I e-mailed you about? And texted? And called?" Hudson tries to clarify. "The one applying for the Spotlight position?"

That seems to help. Randall snaps his fingers. "Ah yes, him," he says. "This him?"

This him. What is that supposed to mean? Do I not feel like someone who could secure a god-tier position? Or is it because he caught me with my pants down—literally—and now his opinion of me is completely jaded?

I mean, ideally, I'm just reading into his words. That sounds like me. But the panic thumping in my chest won't let me know peace. All I can think of is how I've ruined my chances of making something out of myself. I'm going to end up like Danni, marrying Hudson in three or four years just because that's the smartest choice, not because it's the choice I want and . . .

Calm down, I tell myself. I take a deep breath in and out, forcing the world around me, which is starting to blend together like a ruined watercolor painting, to be distinct and establish its own borders.

This will be fine.

I will be fine.

Everything will be fine.

Hudson seems to pick up on my nervousness and squeezes my shoulder discreetly. To be fair, it's only discreet because Randall seems to be completely oblivious of the world around him. His eyes are sharp and slightly glassy. I'm not sure if it's how he normally looks, or if this glassiness is from alcohol or something stronger he consumed to get through the party. To be honest, I wouldn't blame him either way.

There's a part of me that cannot wait to get back to Boston. Maybe that's just because I'll have Hudson to myself and, selfishly, I won't have to share him with everyone else. Maybe it's because I'm looking forward to an end to pretending and needing to act as stiff as an over-starched shirt. Maybe it's a mix of both.

Probably a mix of both.

"You're not gonna find a better worker than Kian here," Hudson promises. "He's smart, a quick thinker, has great creative ideas, and . . ."

"Good-looking," Randall interrupts. "That's where you were going, yeah?"

Hudson shrugs. "I'm a little biased, but yeah, I agree. That can only help in getting sources to talk."

"You're not wrong," Randall says, taking a long sip of his drink.

I hesitate to insert myself into the conversation. There's something weird about being called hot; I don't know how to describe it. I know Hudson means well. He's simply trying to chat me up like a good hype man/boyfriend is supposed to. But the way the words fall out of his mouth and linger in the air makes me uncomfortable, if not nauseous. I don't pretend to understand what women feel like when they are objectified, and even though I'm a Black gay man, I still embody a certain amount of privilege, enough that I'll never understand what it's like to be a woman in a room. But I think I'm pretty close to understanding right now.

It's not the way that Hudson talks that feels grating against my skin, like there's an itch right under the surface I can't scratch; it's the way Randall looks at me over the rim of his glass. His eyes, a rich brown, peer into mine, like he can see something I can't. Or like he's trying to find something that he can claim as his own and hold over me like a carrot on a stick. It makes me feel dirty in my shirt, makes me want to squirm and escape his gaze.

His eyes, his wealth, his demeanor—they combine to act like an oppressive force I can't get out of. It weighs me down, breaks my bones, tears down my walls, and exposes a part of me that isn't worth exposing. Nothing is worth feeling this . . . raw and used just from the way he stares, like he has the right to see what's under my clothes and is trying to figure out how to demand that transactional payment.

I hate every second of it.

For a moment I wonder, *Is it worth it?* The job is a job, and in the end I'm leaving this party with Hudson on my arm, working toward any future together. I didn't attend this event intending to become Hudson's boyfriend, but that win is bigger than any job win. I can find another job, I can find another company to work for, and if I'm being honest, Hudson would probably help me get a position anywhere that I want. It doesn't have to be at Spotlight.

In short, I don't have to put up with this.

But I've wanted this for so long, and it's within reach. Just one conversation, that's it. One time to charm him. This is good practice. People are assholes, and I'll have to put up with them in my career; people worse and more brazen than Randall. *So, suck it up, survive the next fifteen minutes, and take hold of the life you've always fucking wanted, Kian.*

Hudson squeezes my shoulder a little harder this time, snapping me out of my thoughts. My vision focuses in, seeing the worried expression on Hudson's face, the puzzled and half-bored expression on Randall's. I take half a second to put two and two together and filter through the muted memories of the partly remembered discussion from just moments ago.

"Yeah, sure, let's have a talk," I settle on, smiling at Hudson. "I'll catch up with you in a bit?"

Hudson kisses my cheek quickly but doesn't pull away.

"You're going to do great," he whispers. "And maybe there'll be more in store for you after you crush this."

My cheeks burn again, but the sensation is a welcome distraction from the nervous thumping in my chest. I squeeze Hudson's right ass cheek discreetly. The yelp he makes when I do it? Not so discreet.

Before he can argue with me or get the final word in, I trot after

Randall, trying to remember every talking point, accolade, and fact about Spotlight I can.

———— · ————

RANDALL LEADS ME down the hallway and up the stairs. We turn sharply left and head halfway down, passing half a dozen partygoers along the way. Most of them I have seen in passing—one of them, a woman of Asian descent, sat across from me during the reception. About half of them nod at me or give me some sort of recognition.

Better than when I first arrived, I think. Beforehand, I wasn't even worth the time of day. Give it a little bit longer and they'll know my name.

Be still my beating heart.

"This seems good," Randall says. It isn't a question, or a statement wondering if I want to enter the room with him, or if this room is actually good—it's more of a declarative sentence. This room or none at all. His way or the highway.

Usually confidence like that would be alluring to me. It's one of the reasons why I fell in love with Hudson; that alpha swagger he has without being alpha with a capital A, easily straddling the line between alpha and beta. But on Randall, it's sickening. Almost like sugar that's far too sweet, so it makes you nauseous. Or the sound of nails against a chalkboard. I force myself to smile, nod silently in agreement, and enter the room with him.

When the heavy redwood door closes behind me, the soft scent of peach fills the air, which I realize comes from an air freshener inconspicuously tucked into the corner. But the heaviness of the old wooden walls blocks any noise from the outside. The party is muffled, as if we are hearing it through three layers of glass, hundreds of feet under the ocean.

"Looks like it's just you and me," he says, making his way over to the drink set on the mantle.

"Looks like."

Without pausing, or any question of whether he should, Randall starts making himself a drink. He raises the glass to me in a silent question. I shake my head.

"So, Hudson tells me you want to work in journalism."

"Specifically, Spotlight," I say. *Finally.* "I've wanted to work there since—"

"You're not one of those fanboys, are you?" he interrupts, taking a long sip of his bronze-colored drink. "Fucking hate fanboys."

How do I answer that question? Is it bad to be passionate? Aren't you supposed to want to work for the company you're applying for? That's not weird, right?

I seize the moment while Randall takes another swig to come up with my answer. "I've loved the work that Spotlight does on investigative storytelling," I say carefully. "The work you did on the teachers' union five years ago? I want to write stories like that. Are there ways the site can grow? Of course, but I think it's a great stepping-stone."

"Ah. So, you're one of those."

Shit.

"One of those people who wants to use a job as a step to the next level."

Shit shit shit.

"That's not what I meant," I quickly backtrack. "I mean, no, I don't think I'll be at Spotlight forever . . ." *Abort!* "But I don't see myself leaving instantly. It's not a bad place to work but not great either." *ABORT!* "What I'm trying to say is . . . I mean . . . you understand . . . I think. . . ."

I can see my hopes and dreams of working for Spotlight burning right in front of my eyes. Who wants to hire a journalist who can't even put together a fucking sentence? I'll be lucky if I get a job at Wawa once I'm done here. Randall Clements is going to smear my name up and down the East Coast. And the ink will bleed across the heartland and gather on the West Coast. The whole United States of Prospects in Journalism poisoned by this one interaction.

Goodbye, Pulitzer.

Goodbye, student loan repayments.

Goodbye, GLAAD Media Awards for hard-hitting journalism and lunch with Martha Stewart after interviewing her on the twenty-year release-from-prison-versary.

My mind starts to fracture as I see my life destroy itself in front of me. I feel like Thanos just snapped his fingers and I'm watching every piece of myself wither away in the ass. But suddenly I feel Randall's hand on my shoulder.

"It's okay," he coos soothingly. I have to admit, Randall has a calming air about him. His cockiness is at times—and by *at times* I mean almost all the time—more impressive than Hudson's. But handsome men have a way of making you feel weak in the knees. To make you feel like your problems aren't really problems, because, in that moment, someone as attractive and suave as Randall Clements is giving you the time of day. And there's a part of me that feels . . . like I'm worth something be—

"Excuse me?"

I don't mean to have so much confusion and downright disdain in my voice, but the words Randall said, which were previously in the back of my mind, finally ring clear.

I'm sure we can find a way to get to know each other better. Maybe between the sheets, or in the closet if that's more your thing.

Randall couldn't have said what I think he said. My mind is playing tricks on me. He's not that . . . brazen? Is that the word I'm looking for? Maybe *stupid* is a better word.

"Sorry," I say. Why am I the one apologizing? "I just . . . don't think I heard you right?"

Ending that sentence in a question gives him an out. Offering him a way to make up for what he just said. A silent way of admitting it, of giving him an opportunity to recover, so I can pretend this didn't happen.

"I think I was pretty clear," he says, taking a step forward. In response, I take a step back. "I mean, come on. You could have me or you could have Hudson. Hell, you can have both of us and he doesn't have to know. I'm not the kiss-and-tell type."

If that wasn't bad enough, Randall fixes his mouth to say something that takes me a moment to fully comprehend:

"Besides, I've never slept with a Black guy before."

In that moment, it's like everything slows down and nothing seems to matter. The grandfather clock in the corner strikes five seconds. One second after the other. But each tick takes longer and longer to echo before there's nothing but the ringing in my ears.

He really said that.

He really fucking said that.

I'm not sure if I'm angry, upset, freaked out, or some mix of all of those emotions. Randall doesn't seem to pick up on it. Oblivious like a white man who has never had to fight for anything in his life, I suppose.

"I mean . . ." His hands move to my side, caressing me like I'm some sort of fragile being. "Come on, when's the last time you really got fucked," he says in a hushed voice I assume he thinks is sexy.

Spoiler: It's not.

"I am much better in bed than Hudson. Trust me, I heard what guys said about him at Edmonton."

In that moment, I'm not thinking about Randall. I already know it's gonna happen, I'm gonna punch him in the fucking face, the question is just *when* it will happen. Now, I'm more thinking about what Hudson said when we were coming to his house. He tried to steer me away from meeting Randall. Did he know this was gonna happen? No. I refuse to believe that. If he did, he wouldn't have let me walk into the situation. At worst, he thought Randall would be handsy, I'm guessing. Maybe say a few off-color things.

But try and get me to fuck him for a job?

"So, what do you say?" he whispers, leaning forward, his minty breath skimming against my neck. "I can bend you over the table right there. We'll be quick."

I don't bother wasting words on him. I don't bother to weigh the pros and cons, about how it's going to ruin my chance to get into Spotlight, or what my future might become if I assault the heir to one of the biggest digital journalism platforms known to man. Instead, I quickly place both of my hands against his chest, put all my energy into my movement, and shove him as hard as I can . . .

. . . hard enough for him to stumble backward, arms flailing, colliding with the freestanding bookshelf. A loud boom echoes through the study as dozens of books come tumbling down on him, burying him like the Wicked Witch of the East.

Never before in my whole life have I felt more like a friend of Dorothy.

THIRTY

IN MOVIES, A man fighting for you is supposed to be a romantic thing. There's masculinity wrapped up in valor, with a dash of cockiness all rolled into one. Fix that with a man who's willing to lay down hands for you, and it's actually a pretty hot thing. I don't think it's something every person gets to experience, but if you have the chance to let a guy fight for you, I say, let them.

At least, that was my assumption before it actually happened.

Fights, up close and personal, are far different from how they are in the movies or TV. They're not as dramatic or as flair-filled as the media wants you to think. They don't rise with consistent escalation. Have some Western-style ultimatum, with the good guy and the bad guy facing each other down the street. Honestly, when that happens? It's just two people pissed off at each other with the inability to solve their problem with anything except fists.

The noise from Randall hitting the bookshelf alerts not only Hudson but a small gathering of people who were outside; Hudson is just the first to enter the room. Was he outside listening? I stare at him with an expression painted on my face that I know can't be good. Or was he just in the right place—or the wrong place—at the right—or wrong—time?

Either way, as Randall stands, curses dripping from his mouth, I'm thankful that I'm not alone and there's a crowd here to witness.

I'm even more thankful Hudson doesn't decide to check up on his boarding school buddy over me.

"What happened?" Concern is heavy in his voice. He uses his thumb to trace the outline of my face, as if he can feel for any imperfections that weren't there before.

"I'm fine."

"That doesn't answer the question. What happened, K?"

"Nothing," Randall says. "I just stepped wrong. Always two left feet, you know? Your boy—"

"Shut the fuck up, Randall," Hudson snarls coldly, never taking his eyes off me. "Or, I swear to God, I'll make you shut up." Again he asks, his voice quieter this time, like it's only meant for me to hear, "What happened?"

I'm hesitant to give him the true answer, but a lie feels worse than just being up front. A part of me wonders if Hudson will believe me. I don't know how close he and Randall are, but I know a bond between friends who have been through shit is hard to break. What if he picks him over me? What if Randall talks his way into convincing Hudson I'm lying, or I came onto him?

That's just a risk I'll have to take.

"He came onto me." Without any emotion. Definitive. Direct. Declarative. That's the best way to deliver a statement like that. Don't get bogged down with tears. Don't try and explain how it was your fault or wasn't. Just give the facts and let the chips fall as they may. "He told me if . . ."

"He's a fucking liar!" Randall barks.

"*Hey!*" Hudson booms louder before I can defend myself. His head turns so quickly I think it runs the risk of snapping off his neck. "If you open your fucking mouth one more time, I swear to God, I'll rip your jaw off its hinges. Try me, Randall. Fucking try me."

Randall falls silent, obviously not trying him. Hudson turns back to me, squeezing my shoulder once; a silent request for me to continue.

"He told me if I had sex with him he'd give me a job at Spotlight," I force out in one quick breath. Each passing second the words feel thicker in my throat and I can feel my pulse.

This isn't my fault.

What happened wasn't my fault.

I didn't ask for this. I didn't want this to happen. I didn't lead him on or make any suggestions or—

Or did I?

I play the moment over again in my head, dozens of times in a fraction of a second, trying to find any part of me that even hinted toward such an exchange.

Hudson tightens his grip around my shoulders when the words set in, like water seeping through porous stone. He's become larger, like a peacock flexing its presence. He turns to face Randall, who instinctively takes a step back.

"You did fucking what?"

Hudson seems like he's getting taller, like the anger pulsing through his body is a tsunami that's pulling in everything it can to grow in size. Hudson might be only a half- or quarter-inch taller, but right now, he dwarfs Randall, who is nothing more than an out-of-place child who poked a bear and expected there to be no consequences.

"Hey, calm down," Randall chides, brushing it off.

"Don't fucking tell me to calm down," Hudson seethes. "Pull

some shit like that, coming on to my boyfriend, trying to convince him to have sex with you, and you want *me* to calm down?"

Hudson encroaches on Randall's space, his chest and Randall's pushing up against each other like bumper cars.

In response, Randall shoves him. "Listen, I don't know what that bitch told—"

I have half a mind to yell back at Randall. To challenge him when he calls me a bitch. I'm not the most violent of people, nor am I trained in karate or any of those other physical arts, but I know how to scrap. I know that if someone comes for you and you don't push back, the comeback is twofold. But Hudson jumps in before I can defend my own honor.

Hudson delivers a right hook so fast I don't even see him cock his arm back and swing. When it collides with Randall's cheek, it sounds like a Southern thunderstorm, crisp air crackling through the room.

Randall falls to the floor, once again struggling to stand on the pile of books that move like sand under his feet. Blood drips down his chin, his busted lip swelling. The red mark on his jaw is already beginning to spread thanks to the paleness of his skin. His ten-thousand-dollar outfit, now riddled with wrinkles and a few specks of blood, looks more like a bargain-bin find he threw together last minute for a community theatre production of *Les Mis*.

Hudson takes a step forward, one leg between Randall's sprawled-out legs. He leans down, grabbing Randall's collar, and hoists him up; his position on the floor giving Randall a huge disadvantage.

"Call him that again, and I swear to God . . ."

Using the moment to surprise Hudson and throw him off-balance, Randall crudely slams his forehead forward. Hudson stumbles back, barely standing, grabbing his nose.

"Shit, you—" Blood stains the floor as it comes out of his nose, which may be broken. Randall uses the moment to gain the advantage, shoving Hudson against the wall, holding him by his shoulder.

"You swear to God what, Hudson?" Randall asks. "What are you going to do? Sucker punch me again? This is a familiar sight, isn't it? Remind you of senior year at Edmonton? Tell me, when's the last time you had a drink?"

Have you ever stepped into a conversation midway through, knowing there is a backstory six feet deep? So deep you can't see the bottom of it? That's what it feels like for me, and I'm assuming the dozens of other people watching the fight happening in front of them. I see Hudson tighten his grip on Randall's shirt, see him steady his stance against the ground like he's gearing up for a more powerful swing, and I know that whatever Randall is referencing hit a nerve.

But it did more than that—it gave Randall the advantage he wanted.

The whole scene happens in a blur. Hudson ignores the pain, pushing against Randall's chest. The two scuffle, Hudson once again getting the advantage, grabbing Randall by his collar and shoving him against the wall. A scream comes from the crowd. Randall grabs Hudson's shirt, using his body to throw him against the table. One punch, two punches . . . the third punch would have connected if Hudson hadn't raised his knee and shoved Randall back, both of them hitting the floor hard.

The two of them toss and turn like animals, fighting and scrapping while rolling around. If there weren't a crowd or tension in the air, I might think he and Randall were play fighting. Like dogs or kids. But the mutters and the curses, the growls and the sounds, as body parts collide?

You remember that scene in *Twilight* where the Cullens are playing baseball and "Supermassive Black Hole" is jamming in the background? That's what this is like. We're just missing the thunder—

"That's ENOUGH!"

Ah, there's the thunder.

A voice breaks through the room like a sonic boom. It's that super masculine type of shout where you're like, *oh my God* but also like, *that's kinda hot*, all at the same time. The type of voice that when you turn to see who screamed, you know you're going to be super turned on or super disappointed. It could go either way. This time, it's disappointment.

Isaac Rivers stands there, and the crowd of people, none of whom tried to stop the fighting, parts like the sea. He's taken off his suit jacket, and his tie is slightly undone, relaxing for the evening like any normal person would when a party is a success and they can revel in their glory.

Then Hudson went and ruined it. That's what the look of anger and disappointment dripping off his face says.

Hudson and Randall scurry to stand, separating from each other. The buttons on Randall's expensive shirt are ripped, but it's Hudson who has come away worse; a busted nose, bruised lips, and an eye that might be blackened—TBD on that one.

And he did it all for me.

Look, in theory, yes, someone fighting for your honor is a hot thing. In practice, it's barbaric. But to know that Hudson went through all of that just because someone tried to . . . what's the word . . . accost me? Would I want him to do that again? Absolutely not. Am I happy he stood up for me? Absolutely.

Love, and lust, is a confusing thing.

"Mr. Rivers, I—" Randall stutters.

"I suggest if you want me to not press charges, you get the hell off of my property right now," Mr. Rivers says coolly. "And I don't expect to see you at the wedding tomorrow either."

"Excuse me?"

"You heard me," Mr. Rivers warns. "You know the reach I have, Randall. You should be honored that's the only punishment I see fit for you hitting my son. Do you want to try my patience, Randall?"

I watch the emotions cross Randall's face as he tries to weigh the pros and cons of standing up to Mr. Rivers. Is he actually rich enough to buy his property? Will he follow through on the threat?

I don't know him well enough, but there's nothing about the Rivers patriarch that makes me think he's joking—or at the very least, that he wouldn't actually try to buy the property.

Randall says nothing, making his way past me and Hudson. He almost hits Mr. Rivers's shoulder. Almost. Mr. Rivers doesn't turn his head to make sure Randall leaves. He's too busy staring at his son, who isn't far behind Randall. Which means I'm not far behind Hudson.

"Hudson," Mr. Rivers says, his voice like cold steel. It lacks any of the softness I'd expect after seeing his son with a bloody nose, but I guess kicking Randall out of the wedding is his way of showing he cares.

"Don't. Just don't." Hudson turns to me. "You coming?"

It's then I realize I haven't moved since Mr. Rivers came in. It's like my legs refused to follow any sort of command. Until now.

Ride or die, I think. Hudson and I are ride or die for each other. If he wants to go and brush off his father, then that's what I'll do.

"Coming," I say, trotting after him.

Plus, I need to get him to a medic. A black eye might be sexy, but looking like you got hit by a semi? Not so much.

THIRTY-ONE

"YOU HAVE GOT to sit still."

Hudson and I quickly make our way out of the room and down the hall, heading to the most secluded area I can think of—the cupboard. This tight room right off the kitchen is bigger than the cupboard in an average house . . . because everything about the Rivers family is above average. If I pulled out an imaginary ruler and measured it, the pantry where they keep their dried goods would be about the size of a small New York apartment; one a college student would consider home for the next two years while working an unpaid internship and trying to make their name in the big city.

In other words, it's decently sized.

Hudson won't stop moving, squirming all around on the makeshift seat (an upside-down bucket), like a child getting ready for a shot or trying to decide what to say on the stand during their parents' divorce proceedings. The blood from the punch to his lip is mostly dried, thank God. The good news: He's not badly injured, just looks like he broke some blood vessels. The bad news? He has a few scuffs here and there from the hits Randall got on him, a bruised cheek, a busted lip. The expression "you should see the other guy"? Not sure that applies here; both of them are a mess.

"How bad is it?" he asks, not looking directly at me. I firmly grab his shoulders, attempting to keep him from moving.

"You could have gotten off worse."

"That's not an answer."

"You look . . . charming."

He looks up. "John Wayne charming or Marlon Brando charming?"

"Definitely Brando. I'm not into guys like that. Plus, I'm pretty sure John Wayne was a Republican."

"And you're not into Republicans?"

I give him a look that says everything I need to say.

"Point taken."

I squat down in front of him, examining the wounds. They'll leave a mark, but it won't be bad. What's worse and unfixable is the mess we created in front of everyone. If the goal was to make a good impression, starting a fight probably didn't do that. I drag my thumb slowly over his face, outlining his strong features.

Hudson winces, grabbing my right hand with his left one, looking at me with warm eyes.

"Sorry."

"It's fine," he says, kissing the heel of my hand. "Do you think you can get me some ice, though? Kitchen."

"Yeah, sure." I nod. "You'll stay here?"

"Where else would I go?"

"To punch him again?"

"Hm." He taps his chin. "That's a good idea. But no, I think I'm going to stay here. I'm liking being close to the ground."

I groan. "Please don't tell me you have a concussion."

"If I do, will you carry me to the hospital?"

"You're big, but I'll try."

"Big in all the right—"

I close the door before he can finish that sentence. I know exactly what he's going to say, and there's no time for that here. I have only one goal, get the ice and get back to him without being stopped by his parents, or a guest, or worse: Randall.

A cold shiver goes down my spine just thinking about what would happen if Randall found me. I know I'm being melodramatic, considering nothing really happened, but just remembering the words that he said feels like a nasty warmness flowing over my body. It's like that muggy type of feeling you get when it's hot outside but not hot enough? It's like lukewarm sweat or stepping in a puddle of standing water, except it feels like that all over.

I'm lucky Hudson was there to help me. I'm lucky that Hudson took my side. I'm just lucky to have Hudson in general.

I'm so lost in my own thoughts that I don't notice the man standing behind me until I start doubling back, having walked too far and shot straight past the kitchen.

"Sorry," he says, an apologetic smile on his lips. "Didn't mean to scare you."

"You didn't." That's a lie, but he doesn't need to know that. "Sorry, stopping in the middle of a hallway probably isn't good form."

"Not at all," he says with a laugh. "But I won't tell anyone if you answer a question for me."

That gives me pause. It's like when someone says *are you in a place to receive bad news* or something similar. But I shrug. What's the worst that could happen?

"You're Hudson's boyfriend, right?"

I nod without hesitation. The mysterious man puts up his hands defensively and flashes an apologetic smile.

"I'm Collin," he says, extending his hand. "Collin Miller. I'm a friend of the family. Well, a friend of Olivia's, if I'm being more accurate. I heard what happened . . . you know . . ."

I cringe at the thought of how much of a spectacle I just made. I bet Collin isn't the only one who saw what happened and is talking about it. These people are too nice to say it directly to your face. They're going to stare at me for the rest of the night. Judge me silently for months, if not years.

"Hey," Collin says gently, squeezing my shoulder. "No worries. Hell, between you and me, I'm sure these stuffy rich bozos are probably excited they got to see some action. But more importantly, I'm a doctor. General surgery resident, actually."

"Like Meredith Grey?"

"But hotter." He winks. "Can I see Hudson? Looks like he took a few good punches. Randall has a good right hook. I can help. Make him look . . . decent." He shows the shoulder bag he has with him. "Plus, I'm that weirdo who always carries a first aid kit."

There's no reason not to trust Collin. He seems honest, genuine, and, most of all, a Brother. Plus, what can I do without his help? It's an example of pros and cons.

"Come on."

I head down the hall and to the closet. Hudson groans in response, a mix of "go away" and "what."

"I have someone who can help," I say, pushing the door open. Three people in the walk-in pantry isn't a great idea, but neither was getting punched in the face.

Hudson looks up with a bored expression, but his eyes light up when he sees Collin.

"You got yourself beat up? Again?" Collin teases.

"Again?" I ask.

"Don't listen to him, he's a liar," Hudson says, standing and giving Collin a bro hug, two quick claps on the back. He sits back down without having to be told.

Collin doesn't hesitate getting right to work, unzipping his bag and pulling out the kit that has more tools than any first aid kit I've ever seen.

"Well," he says after a moment, dabbing at the wounds with an alcohol wipe. "The good news is you're going to keep your devilish good looks and you won't have a scar."

"The bad news?" Hudson snarls, looking over at me and winking, like I'm a distraction or someone who needs coddling while their boyfriend gets fixed. "There's always bad news."

"You caused a mess."

"Oh, that's not bad news," Hudson huffs. "I love being the life of the party."

"People think you started it," Collin adds.

"Does it matter who started it? Only who ended it."

"Your father ended it," I remind him.

"Hey! Whose side are you on?" Hudson scowls. "Fuck! Can you be more careful?"

"Just two more stickies," Collin promises, putting two adhesive tabs on the different cuts. "They'll be better by tomorrow. Put ice on it when you go to bed, though. Helps with the bruising."

"Thanks, man. Really. How's work?"

Collin shakes his head. "I'm here for the party and as Olivia's plus-one. Please do not talk about the hospital with me."

Hudson puts his hand up defensively. "All right, all right. Don't let my sister bleed you dry. She's a fun suck you know."

"You and Olivia need to stop being like this to one another and appreciate each other more. You never know how much time you have."

"All right, Dr. Death," Hudson says, pushing Collin out gently. "I'm going to enjoy the rest of the night with my boyfriend."

"And not get into any more fights?" he asks.

Hudson puts up three fingers, like he's making a scout's honor sign.

"That's not reassuring," he warns.

"I'll make sure he doesn't," I promise. "You can trust me."

"And you can't trust me?"

"No," both Collin and I say at the same time. We grin at one another, Collin nodding to me.

"Enjoy your time here. And don't let this one get out of control. He's a lot to handle."

"Bite me!"

"You're not my type," Collin says, waving at us before leaving.

"I hate him," Hudson pouts.

"You don't hate him, stop being like that."

He mutters something nondescript under his breath, aka more pouting, before hip-checking me gently and turning on his heels to stand in front of me.

"Let's go."

"Back to the party?" I ask, frowning. "I don't think that's the right idea. Unless you're up for it."

Hudson shakes his head. He stands and leans forward, resting the full weight of his body against me, effectively pressing me into the wall behind me. His strong chest pushes against mine, his body inhaling and exhaling like a hot air balloon as he does. His heavy breathing further pushes me against the hard wall, but I don't mind. His weight feels good against me. Really fucking good.

But not as good as him leaning down and pressing his lips against my own. The kiss is slow, and even him nibbling on my bottom lip doesn't irk me. I move my hands up, sliding them around his neck, letting his hips slot against mine and grind, just slowly.

We should stop, I think. We're in a fucking cupboard. I can *hear* everyone, less than twenty feet away.

But I don't actually stop. I keep going, keep pushing my own hips forward, keep pulling him closer, keep sucking his tongue that finds its way into my mouth without hesitation.

Until he pulls back.

"Let's go back to my room," he whispers seductively. "You cool with that?"

"Yes," I say without hesitation. Trying not to come off too needy, I clear my throat. "I mean, sure."

Hudson grins; that handsome, boyish lopsided smirk I fell in love with the first time I saw it. He takes my hand, threading my fingers between his, and yanks me gently.

"I like the enthusiasm. But then again, I like a lot about you."

"I—"

"I know," he says, kissing my cheek. "I know."

THIRTY-TWO

HUDSON SPENDS ALMOST a full thirty minutes in the bathroom when we reach his room. I hear the water running from the sink, a shower, and a string of curses throughout the whole time. Eventually, whispers of steam leave the bathroom, and Hudson wanders out, toweling off his hair, wearing only a pair of low-hanging sweats that show off the v of his hips.

"Okay, be honest with me, how does my face look?" He turns to the left, then the right, showing off his profile. "My nose is okay, yeah?"

"You look great."

"Are you sure?" He walks over to the mirror hanging on the wall, leaning in close. "You don't think my nose is crooked? He didn't break it at least."

"I promise, you look fine."

"See, you said 'great' the first time and now you said 'fine,' and I'm worried. Do you mean great or do you mean . . ."

"Oh my God, can you *please* just join me in the bed? You're verging on giving Narcissus a run for his money."

Hudson continues to study himself in the mirror, before finally sighing and crawling onto the bed on his hands and knees; he rolls onto his back, arms behind his head, ankles crossed. His long sinewy body is on display, the curves of his chest muscles and abs perfectly visible. It's the simple things about Hudson that still make me shudder. The flush on his light brown skin from the hot shower. The way every freckle, every muscle accents his whole vibe.

"Are you okay?" I ask after a pause. "Like, not physically but, like . . . that was a lot."

"I'm fine."

"That answer came a bit too quickly, don't you think? Wanna try again?"

Hudson sighs, wiggling his toes like a nervous tic in the process. He's silent, his chiseled facial features turning sharper as he purses his lips.

"I don't want you to judge me," he says finally, his voice low, almost like a whisper. "And I'm afraid you will. That you might . . ."

"Look at you differently? You punched a guy for me, Hudson. I think the least I could do is be open-minded to whatever you're hiding."

"That's what everyone says," he mutters. Sighing, he sits up, sitting cross-legged and tapping his fingers against his right knee. "You sure?"

Reaching over, I squeeze his right hand, rubbing my fingers over his knuckles. "Ready."

Hudson smiles weakly. "Randall mentioned something. An incident that happened?" he says, glancing at me without moving his head. "Back during senior year of high school, I drank. A lot. I could come up with a hundred excuses: school was stressful, family was stressful, following in my parents' footsteps and their expectations, the fact alcohol isn't that hard to get if you know the right people."

Hudson flourishes his hands in an expressive motion to generally express *you know what I mean.*

"It became a problem. On the way back from prom, I got carried away and drove my car into someone's garage, completely totaled the door. I don't even remember leaving the party, I just remember waking up in the hospital."

Hudson takes another breath, a thicker one that's almost audible. I squeeze his hand again, tighter and firmer this time, holding the grip and acting as an anchor. Hudson isn't looking directly at me, avoiding my gaze as he continues speaking.

"My parents paid for my rehab. They covered up everything. The damage to the house, the damage to the car, landscaping, the fence, even paid off anyone who might have seen what happened. Effectively my parents made it so my fuckup was completely erased."

"That should be a good thing, right?" I ask. "I mean, you don't drink anymore. I haven't seen you drink, at least."

"Six years sober this November," Hudson mutters. "But that's not the point. The point is that my parents had the ability to do it. If I were anybody else, this would have gone down very differently. I'd probably be in jail. I most certainly wouldn't be at Tufts. The only reason why I am where I am is because my parents had enough money and power to make everything go away. Do you know what that's like? To feel like the only reason your story is different than so many other people's is because of your family's wealth?"

I have no idea. Hudson's right. If he were anyone else, he'd probably be in jail; not only for underage drinking, but for the property damage. It's an age old story, especially for Black people. How one incident can change our whole lives. This would have been what Hudson was known for. Not his smile, not his wit, not his jokes. That one accident.

I think back to what Hudson said on the plane, how Randall's a bad person, and it all clicks. The quid pro quo he suggested, the way he threw it in Hudson's face. That's not a guy I want to work for. That's not a guy I want within two hundred feet of me.

"You're quiet," Hudson whispers, nudging me with his shoulder. "Look, if you don't want to date a recovering alcoholic . . ."

"I never said that," I say quickly. "So let's put an end to that right now. You're more than what happened to you. I've never seen you take a drink, never saw you relapse. I don't know the first thing about dealing with those demons, but I know you're one of the strongest people I know, Hudson. Especially considering your family works in alcohol. That takes some steely confidence. So I think the better question is, why would I be an idiot and not want to date someone who is as strong as you are?"

Hudson smiles at me again. This time the smile fully reaches his eyes, making them twinkle almost like some precious gems catching the light. Slowly, he leans forward, sitting up on his elbows and arching his neck slightly to reach me. His lips graze mine, mouthing against them as if he's muttering some type of spell under his breath.

"You really do always know the right thing to say, don't you?" he says, voice barely a whisper.

It feels like his body is taking my ability to speak. With each subtle movement of his lips, my body becomes more rigid. I'm not paralyzed with fear; it's the exact opposite of that. It's like if I move, Hudson might stop. His lips might start up and move onto mine. In this moment, nothing matters, not even the fight, or my failed career at Spotlight before it even started, or anything else.

The only thing that matters, the only thing that ever matters, is Hudson.

I raise my hand to cup his cheek. Hudson responds in kind, fully sitting up. Gently, he pushes his hands against my shoulders, once again putting me on my back. Except this time, he doesn't pin me. He moves on top, straddling my chest, hands sliding to be on either side of me.

"I don't say this enough," he whispers, "but you're beautiful, you know that?"

"You've said it before," I remind him.

"Mhm. But not recently." He leans forward, peppering kisses against the corner of my lips, my cheeks, then down my neck. "I think I should say it more often. You're beautiful, you're beautiful, you're beautiful . . ."

Each statement is complemented with a kiss. Placement after placement, burning touch after burning touch, my body arches; just slightly at first. His hands move deftly, and without much hurry, slipping under my untucked dress shirt, dancing against my skin like he's feeling his way through darkness and knows exactly what he's doing and where he's going.

His hands slip from under my shirt, moving to the front, slowly undoing each button. His lips, now at my collarbone, stop. He glances up at me, my eyes slightly lidded.

"You okay?" he asks, stopping at the mid buttons. "You okay with me continuing?"

I nod, words not processing; my brain short-circuiting.

"I want to hear you say it, Kian," he mutters, pressing a firmer kiss against where my neck meets my shoulder. "I need to know you—"

"I want this," I say softly, nodding. Maybe the nod was overkill, but I felt like I needed to reassure myself. "I want you to fuck me."

The words almost, *almost* feel crude, but it's not like Hudson and I don't have history together. He smiles, a flicker of mirth in his eyes for just a fraction of a moment.

"Say less," he mutters. His fingers finish undoing my shirt, push-ing it to the side and off my shoulders. Once my shirt is off and tossed aside, Hudson moves to my pants. His fingers pull the button apart slowly, unzipping them like he's unwrapping a present. Pull-ing my pants down, he helps arch my back before throwing them in a wrinkled heap with the rest of the clothes, his sweats and boxers soon removed too.

Hudson's body is everything I remember it being. Even with the sneak peeks here and there with him shirtless and pant-less at McLawrens, or him walking out of the bathroom. Broad shoulders with just the right amount of muscles to fill out his body. He's not quite as muscular as I recall, not when we used to fuck around like this, but he's found a perfect common ground between firm and thick, while also being lean in all the right places.

And I would be lying if I said he didn't look hot, sitting there on his knees, cock erectly pointing at me.

"I sound like a first-timer asking this, but do you have condoms and lube?"

"Do I have lube and a condom?" He scoffs. "What do I look like, an amateur?" He leans over me, chest almost flush with mine, and opens the drawer. With one hand he pulls them both out, returning to his kneeling position. With his eyes locked on me, he slowly ap-plies the lube to his right hand, coating two fingers.

"It's been a while, yeah?" he whispers, slipping his hand between my legs. Gently, he rubs the slightly sticky liquid against my hole. I shudder, back arching a bit, toes curling into the bed. Hudson doesn't stop, but he doesn't increase the pressure either. His fingers circle me, his eyes focused on me, being careful and deliberate with each movement.

"If you ever want to stop, you let me know," he says, pushing his middle finger inside me. There's a moment of burning, just a fraction of a second, before I breathe through it, my body relaxing. I'm not sure if it's muscle memory, remembering how to bottom, or recalling what it's like to be with Hudson, but everything just feels . . . right.

He wiggles his finger in and out, pushing it a bit deeper each time. Once he's almost knuckle deep, he pulls it out. With lidded eyes, I watch him roll the condom over his cock and cover it with lube. He slides his body over mine, one hand propping himself up over me as he lines his cock up against my entrance.

"You ready?" he says quietly, leaning down, pressing a kiss against my lips. "You and me, Kian," he says. "You and me forever."

Before I can respond, the burning returns. Hudson's body slowly lurches forward, pushing inside of me. I shudder for a moment, only a moment, my hips pulling back to keep some distance between us. He's thicker than I remember. But after a second, my mind begins to relax. The pressure becomes a good kind of pressure. I push my hips forward, letting his motions guide me. We get into a nice steady rhythm with one another, our bodies in some type of sensual tango in the bed.

There's still a party going on downstairs, I'm very conscious of that. His mother could come in, or a lost guest looking for the bathroom, his sister; anyone. But with each of Hudson's thrusts and each roll of my hips, I find myself not caring. I find myself more focused on him. How his eyes cross a bit when I move my hips a specific way, how his face looks flush with pleasure, letting me know he's enjoying this as much as I am.

I remember when I was younger, struggling with the idea of bottoming. Not because it hurt or anything, but because of how society often views men who take it instead of giving it. How people might think it makes me "less of a man." But why should I care about them? It took me a long time to get to this point. Sometimes

I like to top, sometimes I like to bottom; Hudson was never some-one who rallied against that, never tried to change me.

I thought it was the most romantic thing in the world and yet one of the simplest of things.

Rolling my hips once again, I grab Hudson's shoulders and use the momentum to turn us over. He slips out of me for a moment as I adjust, straddling his lap with my cock on his lower abs, dribbling precum. He doesn't question what I'm doing, doesn't force me to do anything else. Instead, he grins like a guy who just won the lottery.

"You're so fucking hot," he whispers.

That was something I always loved about Hudson, how he looked at me like he was screwing a celebrity or the most beautiful man on the planet. It wasn't ever *you're hot, but you have some acne here* or *you're a seven, but you could be a ten if you lost fifteen pounds*. He just smiles up at me, almost stupidly, like he's the happiest person on the planet.

Slowly, I roll my hips, making figure eights with them and other shapes. Hudson's eyes almost instantly roll back, grabbing my hips as if he's holding on for dear life.

"Jesus fuck, K . . ." he growls deeply in the back of his throat. His hips roll in time with mine, once again matching our movements. His actions are slow, almost sporadic, like he's afraid if he moves too much I'll leave.

When in fact, it's the exact opposite.

Leaning forward I lose myself in the pleasure, letting the warmth fall over me. I grab the headboard with one hand, his shoulder with the other, digging in hard enough to leave some marks. I push my hips all the way down, until my ass is flush with his hips, and move my hips faster, harder, taking him in deeper.

"Fuck, fuck, fuck," I chant, my body feeling like it's on fire, but a good fire. The pleasure from riding Hudson radiates from my hips outward to my whole body. The faster I go, the longer I ride him, the only thing I'm feeling is formed. Even the sounds downstairs turn muffled, the unison of our panting and the sound of skin sliding against skin, the only thing I hear. Hudson's breath hitches for a bit, a louder moan almost escaping his mouth. But before it can, I move my hand from his shoulder, clapping it over his mouth, almost to the point I'm afraid I might cut off his breathing.

"Shit, sorry," I mutter, pulling my hand back and slowing down. Quickly, his hand grabs mine, moving it to his throat, eyes serious and locked with mine.

"Squeeze here," he says. "And don't you fucking stop riding me, Kian. I'm serious."

It takes me a moment to understand he's asking me to choke him. Not too hard, since I've never done something like that before; for all my sardonic jokes, I consider myself pretty vanilla.

Hudson must have picked up on my hesitation.

"I don't want to leave a mark. We have—"

"Fuck the wedding. Maybe we should fuck through the wedding. Maybe we shouldn't go." Based on how the light dances in his eyes, I know it's only pillow talk.

"You won't hurt me, I promise," he says. "Plus, I'm bigger than you; in every sense of the word. Even if you had the chance to hurt me, I think I'd be fine."

Of course he'd make a joke now. Rolling my eyes, I follow his instruction and wrap my fingers around his throat. I squeeze only a bit, Hudson letting out a satisfied groan from the back of his throat.

Rolling my hips in different shapes, I let the pleasure act like hunger. It's like there's an itch I can't scratch, and if I can get just a little closer, if I can arch my hips in just the right motion, shift our position in just the right way, I'll be able to get it.

The world melts away while I focus on giving myself—and

Hudson—as much pleasure as possible. I feel his fingers dig into my hips. The pleasure, the passion, the need all course through me and back through him like a complete feedback loop.

And that excitement leads to his thighs shaking, his hips thrusting almost desperately into mine manically as he comes.

It's like a chain reaction: me making Hudson come, which makes his hips jolt, which makes his cock slide against my prostate, which makes *me* see stars, which then makes *me* come all over his lower chest, ropes of white hitting all the way up to his neck. I ride out the wave, feeling the weightlessness inside me reach its highest peak, colors and sounds heightened for a fraction of a second before my mind grounds itself again.

The sweat on my body mixing with his feels damp and sticky. Hudson doesn't move at first, my hand sliding down from his neck. Leaning forward, I kiss his lips chastely, letting the moment last as long as possible.

"Holy shit," he pants, slowly rolling out from under me. He stands carefully, walking with wobbly legs, and gets us two towels: one to wipe himself down and one to wipe me down. He tosses the condom in the trash can before flopping back on the bed, still panting.

For a moment, we both lie still, lost in our own thoughts, replaying what just happened. I glance over at him; no marks on his throat that seem like they'll linger tomorrow. Good. The silence between us is welcome, each of us processing what took place. I'm not sure either of us knows exactly what to say. Which isn't a bad thing. A little silence never hurt anyone.

Thirty seconds turns into a minute. A minute into two before, finally, I turn to look at him and speak.

"You wanna go again?"

I don't think I've seen Hudson move so fast in his entire life.

THIRTY-THREE

HUDSON AND I spent the rest of the night, well . . . not sleeping. Another round of fucking, some pillow talk, another round of fucking, sneaking downstairs to get some food, more fucking, more pillow talk. It wasn't until around four a.m. that we both fell asleep, his arm draped over my chest, the weight of his body like a weighted blanket, but not nearly as fucking expensive as the one you would get at Bed Bath & Beyond.

The next morning, I wake to the smell of buttered toast, eggs, and a fruit smoothie by the nightstand, and the hissing sound of the bathroom shower. I stare at the food, half not knowing where it came from, half knowing but thinking it has to be a dream.

But it isn't a dream. Hudson kissing me wasn't a dream. Hudson moaning my name in the night; our sex, a blend of primal fury but also laughter, wasn't a dream. And him stepping out of the shower, towel riding low on his hips, showing off that v he worked so hard for, his body covered in a thin layer of sweat and water, hair matted to his forehead like a dog . . . that isn't a dream either.

Hudson stands there at the door, leaning against it, one leg crossed over the other. He has a wiry smile on his face as water drips down his forehead, landing on his abs and rolling down slowly.

"You shouldn't look that sexy," I mutter. "No one should look that sexy when they get out of the shower."

He rolls his eyes and puts his knees on the bed, slowly kissing me in the process. I nibble on his bottom lip, tugging on it just slightly, until he hisses and pulls back.

"For the record, I am *not* into pain play," he warns, rubbing at his lip.

"Not even for me?"

"Are you telling me you *are* into pain play? Because, if so, I mean, maybe I'll try it."

"For me?"

He nods. "For you."

My stomach and my chest swell with a warmth that makes me feel dizzy and sick. This can't be happening. It's too good to be true. I know it's probably my anxiety speaking, finding a way to sabotage any good thing in my life, but what did I do to deserve this? Seems like a pretty simple question to answer.

So, I ask.

Hudson, who is looking through his closet for whatever he's going to wear today, glances over his shoulder at me. "What do you mean? Also, blue or black?"

"Blue," I say immediately. "You can't wear black to a wedding."

"Who says that?"

"It's bad luck."

"Again, who says that?"

"People?" I argue, reaching over and grabbing a slice of toast.

"People?" He uses air quotes, having pulled out a light blue shirt that I can already tell will show off his muscles perfectly, and a pair of tight grey slacks that do the same. Slip-on dress shoes complete the outfit. "Where can I find these people?"

"Probably in the same place you can find your sense of style," I say teasingly. "Take away the fact that black is seen as the color of death—"

"Can we take a moment to unpack that?" he asks. "Black magic, black death, why is black always seen as bad? Who . . ."

"You know who made that decision," I say plainly. "Anyway, back to the important question at hand. Who wants to wear black in the summertime, anyway? It's hot as hell down here. Hotter than Boston."

"Right, but I look great in black, do you disagree?"

I open my mouth to say something, but nothing comes out. Hudson just smirks and mimes the action of plucking the words out of his mouth and tossing them into the trash can, symbolizing he'll never say them again. "Three-pointer . . . and the crowd goes wild," he says, smirking.

Before I can make a quippy response about how he wouldn't make that shot, he turns to me.

"To address your first question, and I want the record to show this is the last time I'm going to answer this, I like you. I love you. I've loved you since I first met you, I loved you through a breakup, I loved you through our fights, and I loved you when I came to you with my tail between my legs asking you to come to this wedding with me."

"Are you telling me that you hoped this would happen?"

"By this you mean . . . sleeping together? Having this conversation? Getting back together?"

"Yes."

Hudson pauses and then shrugs. "Yeah, I did. I mean, I didn't think it would, but I'm happy it did. Are you?"

"Of course." I don't even have to think about it.

"Then let's not overthink anything else. Let's get through this wedding and spend the rest of the night doing something fun. Anything you want to do!"

"Anything?" I ask.

"Anything."

"Pain play," I say without hesitation.

"Oh, fuck you!" he yells, rolling his eyes and walking out. "I'm going downstairs before you say something like, I dunno, you're into balloon play."

"What's that?"

"Better that you don't know," he says, closing the door halfway behind him.

"Wait."

He pauses, poking his head back in, eyes wide and childlike.

"I love you."

Hudson's eyes stay wide, a slow smile turning into a big one that shows his dimples and white teeth.

"I love you, too."

———— · ————

I'VE ONLY BEEN to small weddings before. I mean, my parents' wasn't a big one. They both agreed they didn't wanna waste money on a big venue. The backyard was good enough for them. Because they get the family handicap, I rank that a B+.

Divya's cousin had a wedding in DC about two years ago. I was excited to go to a traditional Indian wedding, but she was marrying into a white family, so they got married in a fancy hotel and had bland food, Glenn dancing, and watered-down alcohol because the groom's parents wanted to be cheap. I rank that a C-.

Ten months ago, about a week before I met Hudson, I had just come back from a high school friend's wedding. It was . . . decent. If your idea of a wedding is in a field somewhere in North Carolina, with all of your cousins and brothers shooting off shotguns as you kiss the bride, then sure. I rank that one a D-.

But this wedding throws the curve completely out of sync.

Randall's house isn't as big as Hudson's, but I am guessing few houses are. But he does have a beautiful setup with cobblestones, an archway, and a beautiful pond with a water fixture in the center. You can tell that he's taken influences from other cities to add a sophisticated vibe. Probably to try and make up for the sliminess of him as a person.

I shake off that thought and push the idea of Randall out of my head. I'm not here for him. I'm here for Danni and Hudson. I'm just happy the wedding is outside instead of inside. More points of egress, if it comes to that.

Hudson and I arrive early-ish. Of course, his parents and Olivia are already there, sitting on the left-hand side with the groom's family, about a quarter of a mile away from where the vows will take place in front of the water fixture. Many of the seats, maybe two-thirds, are already filled up. I only recognize about half of the faces, but I can tell more than fifty percent of the people coming to this wedding are from Nathaniel's side of the family. You can see a sharp difference between those who come from the groom's walk of life versus those from the bride's.

Pangs of guilt fill my stomach again. I can't help but think about the conversation I had with Danni at the brewery yesterday. But, in the long run, whatever choice she makes is exactly that—her choice, not mine.

"Hey," Hudson whispers, nudging me when we take our seats. "I was thinking, maybe we take a drive after this? Leave a little early? Go to Mississippi or something. My parents own . . ."

"I'm going to stop you right there," I whisper back. "I'll do a lot for you, and I know there is a lot of great work being done in Mississippi by Black leaders and activists, but you won't catch me there—especially for a wedding. I don't care how nice your lake house is. I don't care how much land you have. I am not going to be the victim of some *Lovecraft Country* spin-off, okay?"

Hudson stares owlishly at me, as if the dagger in my voice throws him off-balance. Olivia, dressed in the same light blue that Hudson is wearing (but no one is going to mention that), with her hair pulled back into an elegant bun, does her best not to laugh, while pretending she isn't listening in on our conversation.

"Well, then, since you feel so strongly about Mississippi."

"Very strongly," I say.

"How about we take a flight to, I don't know, San Francisco?"

San Francisco? Did he just pull that city out of a hat? Or did he actually remember?

Slowly, he reaches over and gives my hand a squeeze, lacing his fingers with mine. "You always said you wanted to go, right? We never got around to it. Might as well do it now. Sooner is better than later, and we have time to make up for."

Before I can answer, the room rustles with noise like a crackling fire, and the wedding begins.

All weddings are the same when it comes to the basics. The couple walk down the aisle, they say their vows, they make promises to each other, the officiator goes on and on about some bond they have to each other. Both people kiss, and we're on our way. No more than thirty minutes, maybe forty. Like everyone who has any sort of brain will admit, the ceremony part of the wedding is the most boring part. We all live for the party, for the dancing, for the music, and especially for the food. But sitting here, crammed together, watching two people do a ceremony that we've seen hundreds of times before, be it in person or on TV? All of us just want this to be over with. But no one's going to say that. Not now, not ever.

But this wedding is a bit more personal to me. When Nathaniel walks down the hallway, I notice how proud and excited he is. He looks like a boy getting his first car or taking a girl out on a date for the first time. His back is straight, his chin is held proudly, and in that moment, I notice that this truly is the happiest moment of his life. And marrying Danni will make him the happiest man in the world.

Which is why I study Danni so much more critically when she and her father walk down the aisle.

The white dress she's wearing—with its intricate design, sleeves, neckline, and hem—fits her perfectly. Her hair is pulled up in a tight black bun similar to the one Olivia has, which I'm sure does little to quell Olivia's ego. Danni looks like some sort of elf from *The Lord of the Rings*, warning Frodo about the dangers he'll face if he continues his journey toward the mountain.

But the most important thing is that, in studying her face, I can't help guessing what she's thinking. I like to consider myself a good judge of character, someone who can easily pick up subtle clues and understand what someone is thinking, truly thinking. It's one of my strongest skills. But ever since coming here and meeting Hudson, I've found myself out of my element. Like I'm not as good at reading others and figuring them out as I thought. That my little fishbowl of Boston *isn't* representative of the world at large.

Who would have thought?

I try to catch Danni's eyes in those last final seconds before she approaches the man she's going to marry, to make sure she's okay. I can't tell if she is avoiding me intentionally or if she's just so focused in the moment that she can't see me or anyone else. I like to think it's the latter. Everyone says your wedding day goes by in a blur, that a bride is thinking about one million things and her happiness is usually the last of the million. The wedding day is something you remember in hindsight, not while you experience it in person. And if I'm being honest, the conversation she had with me, a man she had just met a few hours earlier, probably isn't the first thing on her mind.

"Pre-wedding jitters," I mumble.

Hudson leans over, nudging me. It's an old, silent way of asking what I said.

"Nothing," I promise quietly, squeezing his hand and turning back just in time to see the bride take her place.

The priest is an older man I haven't seen before, with sunken eyes and droopy skin, but dressed to the nines. He clears his throat. The Welcoming and the Gathering of Words all fade into the background as I sit there, doing my best to concentrate. I don't know these people, which makes the wedding even harder to care about. Hudson's thumb traces over my knuckle, making circular motions, keeping me grounded and focused enough so my mind doesn't completely wander.

"Dearly beloved. We are gathered here today to join this man and this woman in holy matrimony," he says with a surprisingly smooth, liquor-like voice. The priest turns half his body to face Nathaniel. "Nathan, do you take this woman to be your wife, to live together in holy matrimony, to love her, to honor her, to comfort her, and to keep her in sickness and in health, forsaking all others, for as long as you both shall live?"

"I do," Nathaniel says without hesitation. He brings Danni's hands up to kiss her fingertips. "Sorry, Priest, I just couldn't wait," he adds.

The corner of the priest's lips twitch with annoyance, for only a fraction of a second.

"Father John is who we'll use," Hudson whispers to me. "For our wedding."

"Aren't you getting a little ahead of yourself?"

He shrugs and kisses my cheek quickly. "I think I've earned the right to dream, don't you?"

Father John turns to Danni. "Danni, do you take this man to be your husband, to live together in holy matrimony, to love him, to honor him, to comfort him, and to keep him in sickness and in health, forsaking all others, for as long as you both shall live?"

She doesn't answer as quickly as Nathaniel did. In fact, the pause is longer than any natural pause should be, and it keeps going. The space between the question and the intended answer of *I do* only grows larger and larger, like a gaping hole between the two of them, so large that people start to fidget in their seats. Nathaniel's face begins to twist in confusion.

"Danni," Father John asks. "Did you . . ."

"I heard you," she says quietly, but still clearly. Slowly, she turns her head, to glance into the crowd. To the untrained eye, it would seem like she's looking at all of us, how actors look above people's heads to give the impression that each audience member is the only person in the room. But to me, to Hudson, and I'm sure to the rest of the Riverses, it's pretty obvious she's looking directly at me. And though there's warmth and acceptance in her face, the way that our eyes lock sends an ice-cold shiver down my spine.

"You were right," she says, clearly enough for me and every other person at the wedding to hear. Now, if there was any doubt she was talking to me—that's fucking gone.

Danni pulls her hand away from Nathaniel and finally gives her answer. "No. I don't."

Though everyone in the room, rightfully so, is focused on the declaration of refusal Danni just gave Nathaniel, the only thing I notice is how Hudson pulls his hand out of my grasp.

Shit.

Fucking shit.

THIRTY-FOUR

IF LOOKS COULD kill, I would be fucking dead.

The way Hudson's family looks at me when the crowd starts murmuring and rumbling with discomfort, thanks to Danni's declaration? That's painful. I mean, it's fair when you think about it. People paid hundreds, if not thousands of dollars to come to this wedding, and Danni just went . . . and canceled it? Ended its life with one simple sentence?

I'd be mad, too.

And her *thanking* me in public? That didn't help either. Just think of the optics of that! The two "outsiders" of the group, teaming up to take down the big rich families of the South? What is this, a reboot of *Revenge*?

Danni's smart enough to know that she doesn't belong here anymore.

"I'm sorry," she says, loud enough for Nathaniel and the rest of the wedding-goers to hear. "I'm really sorry."

With that, she steps down off the platform and leaves, a blur of white running down the aisle. Where she's going? Who knows! But hopefully it's far away from here.

At least, if I were in her position, that's what I would do.

No one follows her; not even Nathaniel. He's still dumbstruck, standing on the platform, like his heart was just ripped out of his chest and thrown to the wolves. Which, in some way, I suppose it was.

Being turned down for a date? Bad.

Being stood up for a hookup when you just douched? Horrible.

Being left at the altar? Even worse.

And it's my fault—at least, that's the logical progression thanks to Danni's statement. Which also means it's time for me to act like Danni and get the fuck out of here.

I weasel my way through the now-standing wedding-goers, turning my body to the side and quickly pushing through the rows of befuddled rich people. Each second that passes I feel the nonexistent walls of the tent closing in on me. Did I really ruin this wedding? Did I really give Danni the idea that she was better off alone? That wasn't my point. I'm not to blame.

I'm not to blame.

I'm not to blame.

I barely make it out from under the tent, barely make it out into the free air of the space with no walls, before I hear a familiar voice that grounds me.

"Where do you think you're going?"

My feet are fixed to the ground like they're stuck in cement. Olivia's smooth but sharp voice is heavy, like an arrow that pierces my shadow and keeps me rooted in place.

Olivia doesn't even give me time to turn around before she walks in front of me, arms crossed over her chest. My body tenses when I take in her nonverbal cues. Tight jaw, flexed arms, pursed lips, narrowed eyes.

This is not a good position to be in.

"Look, I know what you think you saw, but—"

"Don't fucking bullshit me, Kian," she snaps. "What. Did. You. Do?"

The subtle anger—no, it's not fucking subtle. The way Olivia's face screws into anger doesn't look natural, like her features aren't made to be angry. The pissed-off aura she gives off is more than enough to make my skin prickly.

I chew on my bottom lip, debating the pros and cons of telling the truth. Behind her I see Hudson standing a few feet away, as if he's hesitant whether he should join in while she berates me or if he should stop his sister from approaching the nuclear level she's steadily approaching.

"Look, I don't know what happened," I say honestly. "I talked with Danni at the brewery and then . . ." I gestured. "I don't know how she got from our conversation to this."

"Of course you don't." Olivia rolls her eyes. "Are you happy now? Feel like you got what you came here for?"

"Excuse me?"

"Oh, cut the crap," she says, her voice louder. "I know you and my brother aren't actually dating. I'm not stupid."

The words are like a jab right into my heart. I tense up so tightly I think my muscles are going to snap. Again, I glance over my shoulder at Hudson; he's just . . . standing there. Now the crowd is larger; half the wedding guests are gathered around the edges of the tent. I can even see Hudson's mom and dad watching.

Olivia takes a step forward. "Let me guess. My brother said he could get you a job at Spotlight? I looked you up before you came. Read your online articles on Medium. You're a good writer but a stupid strategist. You really thought, what, you could lie your way into our family?"

I take a step back, but Olivia takes one forward in kind. "And then when you got what you wanted, when you weaseled your way into my brother's heart, you thought, why not cause some mess as payback for dumping you before?"

"That's not what happened at . . ."

"Yeah, I don't care, really. You can say what you want, but I know deep down you felt angry about how my brother treated you. Which, fair. My brother is a mess. But to take that rage out and execute some revenge fantasy on my family?"

Olivia stands close to me, so close that no one but me can hear the icy words that leave her mouth. "So I'm going to give you twenty minutes to get back to the house, pack your bags, and leave. And maybe, just maybe, I won't do everything in my power to blacklist you from every media outlet in the country. You want to see if I can do that? Try me. I'm not my brother, Kian."

Olivia pulls back, just for a moment, to show me how serious she is. There isn't a doubt in my mind that the panic cord of fear wound tightly in my chest isn't an illusion. Olivia will fully follow through on her threat.

"I don't want to see your face again," she says. "Ever."

With that, she turns and storms into the tent, walking by Hudson.

"Deal with it," she says, loud enough for me to hear. Not *him*. Not *Kian*. *It*.

The crowd disperses slowly along with Olivia, with Hudson's mother and father the last to leave now that the show is done. I'm still standing there, rooted to the ground, unable to force my legs to move. Slowly Hudson moves toward me, crossing his arms over his chest.

"Look, I don't—" I start to say, but Hudson raises his hand.

"Is it true?"

"What?"

"Answer me honestly, Kian. Is what Olivia said true? Did you have a talk with Danni about leaving Nathaniel?"

"I don't need to tell you," I say slowly. "But I'm going to do it anyway. People are their own individuals. They can make their own choices. Just because I . . ."

"Cut the fucking crap, Kian!" he booms. His voice is loud enough that I know, without looking, people are watching. I mean, if I'm going to be famous, why couldn't I be famous for something positive? Not for being the main player of some twisted queer soap opera.

There was a time when Hudson could say these things to me, and I'd put up with it. When I'd thought I deserved it.

This is not one of those times.

"So, we're doing this?" I ask. "Here?"

"All I'm asking you to do is tell me the truth. What the hell just happened in there?"

"I think it's pretty obvious," I growl. "Danni didn't want to marry Nathan."

"I can see that. And what role did you have to play in that?"

"What do you want to hear, Hudson?"

"The *truth*!" he yells again. "That's all I've ever wanted from you. Why is it so hard for you to tell it?"

A beat. "I'm sorry, what?"

Hudson pinches his nose. "Never mind. Just answer the question."

"No, I think that's something we—"

"Answer the fucking question, Kian."

I've always believed in honesty. I'm a journalist, after all. It's important to lean into the facts. So I might as well be honest with

Hudson here. We love each other. We're going to spend our life together. We'll get through this.

"I talked with Danni," I say. "While you and Olivia were doing whatever you two were doing at the distillery, we . . . chatted."

"Chatted?"

I nod. "She told me she wasn't sure about marrying Nathan."

"Jesus," he whispers, hands on his hips. "And what did you say?"

A moment passes. Then another.

"Kian. What did you say?"

"From the outside it might look like I told her she shouldn't marry him," I say slowly. "But—"

"Oh, for fuck's sakes!" he shouts. "You did it, didn't you? Congratulations. I hope you're happy now. You win."

Okay, wait. That wasn't what I anticipated from him. Talk about going right when I expected him to go left.

"I'm sorry," I say slowly. "I won . . . what exactly? Was there some game we're playing I didn't know? Are you talking about the Game? 'Cause I thought we stopped playing that in . . ."

"Can you for once be serious, or is that something you aren't capable of?"

I pause, letting the words Hudson just said sink in. It takes all my energy not to bark back; two wrongs don't make a right, so I just take a deep breath, hold it, and reply.

"Okay, let's pause before we say something we regret."

"Oh, trust me, we're already there."

All right, then, I think. *Sure, let's go. Post up.*

"Why don't you say what's actually on your mind?" I shoot back. "Maybe you should speak up for once. Your parents aren't around. You don't have to be the lesser Rivers anymore. Come on, you can do it. Be more like your sister. Rip into me like she just did. I know you have it in you."

There it is. That's the button. Hudson's face contorts, for a fraction of a second, into the personification of anger that Dalí *wishes*
he could paint. His fists ball by his side, holding all his anger in
them before flexing his fingers, releasing it.

"You always have to be right," he says slowly. "Let me guess, you
wanted to get the last word in, huh? Humiliate me in front of my
family? Is this really revenge for me breaking up with you? Olivia
was right."

"Fuck you," I say through broken words. "Fuck you, Hudson."

"Yeah, we won't be doing that again."

"Sounds good to me."

I push past him quickly, using the full force of my shoulder.
Hudson predicts it and steps to the side, leading me to stumble past
him and almost fall forward. Not the most graceful of exits, but I
just need to get out of here. Doesn't matter if my clothes are at his
parents' place. It doesn't matter that I'm stuck in this uncomfortable
suit. It doesn't matter that I don't have any money to get home.

I just need to get out of Atlanta and far from Hudson.

While walking with my hands shaking, I pull out my phone.
Blurry eyes keep me from seeing the number I'm typing, but my
actions are like second nature. Two rings later, Divya picks up.

"I need a favor," I force out. "A four-hundred-dollar favor. I'll
pay you back."

Divya doesn't ask any questions. She doesn't even hesitate. "Give
me fifteen minutes. Economy work for you?"

THIRTY-FIVE

"IF I'M BEING honest, I was surprised to hear from you."

Two months later, not much has changed.

Okay, that's a fucking lie. A lot has changed, I just don't want to admit that because it hasn't changed in the way I wanted it to.

Let's approach it in the only true way a journalist can—with the Five Ws and the H.

Who: My name is Kian Andrews. I'm twenty-three years old.

What: I'm a journalist who graduated from Northeastern University with a 3.7 GPA, with a double major in journalism and sociology, with more than half a dozen articles under my belt, over $90K in student loans, a 595 credit score, and not a single job prospect in my future.

Where: I'm from a small town in North Carolina, about thirty minutes east of Raleigh, and I live in Boston, Massachusetts; but right now, specifically, I'm sitting in the Watering Hole.

When: My life has been at this weird middle-of-the-road standstill for the past two months, ever since I left Atlanta and blocked Hudson on every platform possible.

Why: I'd much rather NOT answer that one, thanks.

How: Oh, that's simple. I got here by being an asshole.

I smile at Wallace, thanking him as he opens the door for me. If I'm being honest, now that I'm out from under the Rivers Spell, I can see undertone features that make Wallace look more appealing. Thirty-one really isn't that old; he's only eight years older than me, after all. He doesn't act like he's thirty-one—what does that even mean?—and he was the one who reached out first, not even *asking* why I left him before at the restaurant. He let me have my own secrets and life and didn't judge me. So why not give him another chance?

"What can I say, I'm a man of surprises."

"That's for sure," Wallace says, chuckling. "I've never been here before, what's good?"

"It's a café shop like any other shop, you can't go wrong with a croissant and a drip coffee or . . ."

"Latte," we both say at the same time. He grins at me, with the few bags under his eyes that I imagine are normal for someone in his line of work. I smile back—there's something infectious about his smile.

Like Hudson's . . . but different.

I shake my head, sure I look like a mad person, but redirect the conversation quickly. "I can promise you the coffee here is better than at the hospital."

"And if it's not? What are you going to give me?"

I lean back in my chair, not even opening my menu. I know what I'm going to order. It's the same every time: two buttermilk pancakes with blackberry jelly, some turkey bacon, and coffee.

"How about a kiss? How does that sound?"

Wallace looks up at the ceiling, holding his tilted position for one, two, three seconds. "I think that's a valid payment method."

The waitress—the same as before, when Hudson and I

reconnected—comes over to the table, this time with hot-red high-lights in her hair. I clock that bold and bright hair dye anywhere—Good Dye Young by Hayley Williams.

Hudson and I were going to try green dye a few years back.

Again, I push the feeling down and lean my elbows forward, giving Wallace my full attention. As long as I keep him in the center of my vision, as long as I only focus on him, making him my light at the end of the tunnel, I can get through this. I can get over Hudson. It's been only two months. That's not that long. They say it takes three times as long as you dated someone to get over them; that means I need about three months to get over Hudson. I'm two-thirds of the way there. I can do this. I can—

"Excuse me, do you mind if I steal Kian for a moment?"

There are many odd things I expect to happen in life that no one else does. An asteroid causing another extinction-level event within our lifetime? Check. Vampires to be discovered as real? Check. Our first queer president? Rainbow check.

But seeing Olivia Rivers, standing there with her lavender shawl, cream-colored dress, and shades, in Boston, in the Watering Hole, with her Hermès purse draped over one arm? That *was not* on my bingo card.

And neither were the words that left my mouth before I could stop them.

"I'm sorry, what in the *actual fuck* are you doing here?"

——— · ———

I DON'T KNOW where that meme came from, but the one of Diddy in a staring contest with that Black singer from *The Four*? Neither of them breaking eye contact? That's exactly what Olivia and I look like right now.

Who is Diddy and who is the no-name guy, Elijah? You tell me.

"That's no way to greet a friend, is it, Kian?"

"I don't know if we would call each other friends."

"Then what would you call us?"

"People? That sounds about right."

Olivia pushes her lips into a thin line, her way of looking hurt, I assume. She turns to Wallace and flashes a practiced smile. "Do you mind?"

"Not at all," he says, standing up and gesturing to his seat. "Seems you two have some things to discuss."

"Oh, Jesus. Wallace, you don't—"

"I'm going to check on my patients," he says, waving his phone. "Be back in fifteen?"

"That should be more than enough time, thank you," Olivia says for me, without even looking up, and takes off her shades, gently resting them on the corner of the table.

Ten seconds later, even though the Watering Hole is crowded, it's like we're alone.

My body tenses and my form becomes defensive, arms crossed over one another, leaning back in my chair. Olivia doesn't speak; her eyes flit all around the menu, like she's actually going to order something.

"This place is . . . quaint," she finally says. "Seems like a nice place to have a quiet peaceful Sunday meal."

"What do you want, Olivia?" I ask. "Here to yell at me again?"

She closes the menu, crossing one leg over the other, resting her hands on her top knee. "Closing a deal tomorrow for the company. We're going to be the primary beer provider for Fenway Park."

"Congratulations."

"Thank you," she says, not picking up on my sarcasm or, more probably, not caring. "It truly is a huge get for the company. But that's not the only reason why I'm here."

"Want to know all the hot spots of Boston? I'm more than happy to e-mail you some links."

She shakes her head, moving the menu and Wallace's utensils around until they are perfectly straight. A nervous tic or low-grade OCD?

"I'm here to talk some sense into you because, if I'm being honest, for someone so smart, Kian—and you are exceptionally smart—you are very, very dumb."

My attention becomes the bodily personification of the phrase *wait, hold up* in the City High classic, "What Would You Do?" Olivia doesn't seem fazed, but she takes my interest as an invitation to continue.

"Ever since you and Hudson . . . what's the word I'm looking for . . . orchestrated that elaborate hoax at the wedding, Hudson has been more invested in the company."

That's not what I expected her to say. I expected her to apologize. But sure, I'll go with this. "That doesn't sound like Hudson."

"Well, people do odd things when their hearts are broken."

"Now you're just being dramatic," I mutter, sipping my water.

"Am I? Come now, Kian, you're a journalist, you can read people. You read Danni well. And, by the way, she's doing *amazing*. Nathan, not so much, but between you and me, I never liked him much anyway. But, whatever you said to her . . . you were right. If she was here right now, in America, I'm sure she'd tell you."

The waitress returns, confused by the change in gender of the person sitting across from me. Olivia doesn't even look at her as she raises her hand. "Give us five minutes."

I look at the waitress, smiling apologetically. She disappears without a single word.

"Let me ask you a question," she says. "Do you think Hudson actually cares about you? Truly, not a jaded answer based on your hurt feelings, but in your actual heart."

That's a hard one to answer. I sit quietly, shifting every now and then, as if a new position will give me insight into the answer I didn't have before. The mental pros and cons list about Hudson I'm writing is already a dozen entries long on each side, and I'd be lying if I said it wasn't affected by our recent and more far-reaching past.

"That's a complicated answer."

"Love is complicated," she says. "Real love, at least. I'll answer the question for you, then, how does that sound?"

"I feel like you were going to do that anyway."

"I think Hudson loves you. Is he perfect? Absolutely not. But are you? No. You went along with his lie. You meddled in someone else's affairs. He said things he shouldn't have said. But can you say you were faultless in that situation?"

She pauses, giving me room to answer, knowing I'm not going to. "So that leaves me with two questions. One: Do you love Hudson Rivers? And two: Do you think you can see a life with him? Because I can answer for my brother both answers: absolutely yes. And if you agree, then I'm asking you to do something that isn't exactly fair, but hopefully, in the long term, will be a blip in your future: be the bigger man and reach out to him. Does he deserve it? No. But you know my brother. He would rather sulk than actually apologize. That's part of the reason it took my parents coming up to visit him for him to reach out to you; he needed a reason, more than it being the right thing to do. You know how men are." She smiles.

Olivia's dominating this conversation; I can feel myself getting smaller. But that's just being in the orbit of a Rivers. They command the room, and their orbit is impressive. But that doesn't make her wrong. I do love Hudson, but plenty of people love people who aren't right for them. Plenty of great love stories have been written about that. This is no different.

Instead, I ask her a question.

"Why is it up to me?" I ask. "You said it yourself, Hudson said horrible things. He should come apologize to me."

"My brother is a man," she says with a sigh. "And by that, I mean he still has the problem all men have—being in touch with their emotions—and my father's upbringing didn't help. He's not going to come to you when he's a wounded dog who feels he has nothing to gain. Maybe if you had more time . . ."

"Is he dying or something?"

"In some ways, I would say yes," she says. "He's moving back home with me."

I instantly sit up straight. "I'm sorry, what? You should have *started* with that lede."

Olivia doesn't seem fazed by my reaction. "It's the other reason why I'm here. Ever since you broke his heart, he's been talking with Father. Going back home seems to be the right solution. Working for Rivers & Valleys is the best choice. He agrees."

"There's no way he wants to do that."

"Why does that matter?" she asks. "He only stayed here for you, you know that, right? This isn't the first time Father has offered him a position in the company. But something always kept him here in Boston. It wasn't the weather, school, or the people, I can promise you that. He could get a master's in psychology anywhere in the country; no, the world. He's here because of you."

From the corner of my eye, I see Wallace pacing outside the large bay window on the phone. Our eyes catch, and he smiles at me, giving me a thumbs-up. I do my best to return the action, but the half-a-second linger in his glance tells me I didn't do the best job convincing him everything is okay.

Because everything is one hundred percent not A-OK.

"When does his plane leave?"

"Are you considering going to talk to him?"

"I'm not saying that," I add. "Just asking."

Olivia checks the Apple Watch on her wrist. "The limo will pick him up in forty-five minutes. But considering it's my flight and my ticket, I'm sure I can give you another hour if you need it. So, I'm going to ask you again. Are you going to talk to my brother?"

"I have a question for you in return before I answer that."

"Always the journalist," she says, sighing again and gesturing for me to continue.

"Why?" I ask. "You were, how do I put this nicely . . ."

"A raging bitch to you at the wedding?"

"I would never call a woman that, but if that's the choice you want to use . . ."

Olivia adjusts her shawl and grabs her purse, standing up slowly. "I care about my family, Kian. It will always be my top priority. That's why I lashed out at you. Family above everything else, especially when I see something or someone threatening it. No matter what. I don't care how people view me, so long as my family succeeds. Family is the most important thing. And Hudson, no matter our relationship, is my family. Unlike the rest of us, his success comes from his happiness. You make him happy, so in turn, I care about you.

"Plus, I think you'd make a pretty good brother-in-law. At least someone who can keep up with me. That will be refreshing," she says, grinning as she walks around to me, resting her hand on my shoulder. "He's home. I'm not going to tell you what choice to make, the ball's in your court. Make the choice which is right for you."

Olivia walks halfway to the door before pausing and turning to me. "And Kian?" Something vulnerable flashes over her face, something soft and gentle.

"I'm sorry for how I treated you. Truly. If you're going to be as big a part of the family as I hope you will be, I don't want that version of me to be the only version you know."

And like that, as silently as she came, she's gone.

The world passes me by like a Michelle Branch music video, everything blurry as if it moves in long exposure. I see Wallace return, observe his lips moving as he sits down, read some of the words: *heart failure*, *seizure*, *double shift*, and something about some guy at his hospital driving him insane. But none of it matters. Because it's not Hudson. He's not Hudson. I'm not at the Watering Hole with Hudson.

And right now, wherever he is, is the only place I want to be because, to quote the world-famous Natalie Imbruglia, *Nothing's fine, I'm torn.*

"I have to go," I say in one breath, already prepared to make up some excuse about Divya being sick or Jamal needing me or . . .

"It's the other guy, isn't it? Dallas or something?"

I pause. "Hudson."

"Ah, yes, I knew it was a Texas city," he says with a grin. "Divya told me about him. Said I had some competition ahead. Looks like I lost."

"I'm sorry," I say after a moment. "It's not you. Truly. I want you to know that."

He waves his hand. "Please, I'm a catch. I'll be fine." He smiles. "You should go get your man before he leaves. Here." He fishes out thirty dollars. "Brunch is on me, but take this. Get a cab."

"I can pay for my . . ."

"Get a cab," he urges. "Consider me a romantic who loves a grand gesture. Just promise me you'll invite me to the wedding, if it happens?"

I take the money, stand, and walk over, kissing him on the cheek. "I promise," I say before running out, hailing the first taxi I can find, my heart racing so hard I barely feel when my knuckles hit the heavy metal buckle.

Like all the greats in pain play say, no pain, no game.

THIRTY-SIX

$25.56

$26.14

$27.87

$29.01

I sit in front of Hudson's house, just watching the meter tick away, every sixth of a minute the price going up more and more, for no goddamn reason besides my own panic and my own terror.

For someone who doesn't have a job and is just living off the kindness of their friends, their minimal savings, what money their parents can give them, and odds-and-ends TaskRabbit jobs, I sure am flippant with my income.

But no matter how much I want to move, I can't will myself to do it.

Is this a bad idea? Probably. No, most definitely. Hudson's life isn't my concern anymore. What he wants to do with it—wherever it is—is up to him, not me. I need to remember that. Mind my business. Mind my place.

"Are you getting out here or what?" says the driver, a brown-skinned man of distant Arab descent chewing cud with his mouth full. He rolls down his window and spits a blob of brown out, and I cringe. Part of me wants to get out of the car because it means getting away from this level of masculine chaotic energy. But you know that whole expression about *the devil you know*? Yeah, that applies right now.

"Can I ask you a question?"

He shrugs. "Your money, not mine."

"Are you married or dating someone?"

He raises his right hand and shows a basic silver ring. "Fourteen years."

"And if you could go back in time and change anything, like having a life without her, would you?"

The driver looks at me through the rearview mirror, his eyes, sullen with sleep and bagginess, locked with mine. He chews slowly, and spits again before speaking. "I love my wife. Good times and bad times, my friend. That's what makes up a relationship. You and this girl—"

"Boy," I interject.

Our eyes lock again, and I wonder if I've said too much. Queer kids have to constantly come out to people—it's a never-ending cycle, and you never know how anyone is going to react.

This guy doesn't seem fazed.

"You and this guy have to try. There's no other way to know if you don't try."

"A sound and solid answer," I mutter, looking out the window. What's the worst that could happen? My emotions and mental well-being shattering? I'm used to that.

My driver is right—I have to try.

I check the meter again—$32.17—and hand him thirty-six dollars, all the cash I have, before jumping out of the car.

"My friend," he says, leaning out the window to give me a thumbs-up. I return the gesture, a wave of (short-lived) confidence rippling over me.

The human body is nothing more than a complex machine, and like any machine, sometimes you have to force commands. Walking to Hudson's door is one of those commands.

One foot over the other. One foot over the other. Repeat this set of two, twelve times. The heavy wooden door on the expensive brownstone looks even more imposing when I know it's the only thing separating me from changing my whole life. What happens in the next five, ten, or even thirty seconds could completely alter my trajectory.

I just have to be brave and trust. Which I'm not good at.

But this time, I have to be.

I raise my fist and knock twice on the door, each time matching the heavy thumps in my chest. I don't know why, but in my ears all I can hear is Taylor Swift's "Mirrorball": "You'll find me on my tallest tiptoes, spinning in my highest heels, love, shining just for you."

"Coming, coming!" I hear Hudson's voice through the wood. The heavy lock thumps as the door groans open, my voice disappearing with the vacuum.

"I know, I know, I'm not packed. I should be. Sue me. And no, I'm not going to get on the plane dressed like this," he says without looking, gesturing for me to come in. For a moment, it feels like the life I've been living for the past few months is a complex illusion of my own creation, that I'm coming home to Hudson and we're happy and the past two months never happened.

What a beautiful dream.

"Hi," I say, the only word I can form.

Hudson, dressed in a casual, ratty Northeastern tee and some well-fitting jeans, turns around quickly, his eyes wide and surprised—matching my own expression, I'm sure.

"Hi yourself," he whispers.

We stand at an impasse, silence besides the street noise and the low music coming from his iPhone lulling in the background in the fully packed and bare brownstone.

I don't do well with silence. Never have and never will. It's why I usually put my foot in my mouth. This time is no different.

"What's a guy gotta do to get a drink here?"

——— · ———

"I DON'T HAVE much to drink, is water okay?" Hudson asks, leading me into the kitchen. "I have sparkling or still."

"Sparkling. Flavored?"

"Cherry or lemon-lime," he says, looking into the fridge.

"Let's go with lemon-lime."

"You got it," he says, pouring two glasses. The sound of the liquid at least fills the air with something. I let my senses wander: My eyes notice that Hudson's hair is now long enough to curl behind his ears; my ears notice the music playing is the 1975, one of their older albums; my nose notices the brownstone smells like antiseptic, a deep clean that I wonder if he or a cleaning service did. And my heart notices, without fail, the lump in my chest.

"Thanks," I say when he passes the drink to me. "So, you're finally doing it, huh?"

He raises his brow while he sips.

"Going back home to Georgia. You're really doing it."

Hudson's face goes through a rapid journey before settling on the answer, putting his drink down. "Olivia."

I shrug. "She might have crossed paths with me."

"I'm sorry about that."

"Why are you sorry?"

His turn to shrug. "She forced you to come here. Somehow. She has a way with people like that. I know you didn't want to."

"What makes you say that?"

"Maybe you blocking me on every platform imaginable, as well as my phone number?"

I open my mouth and close it three times, trying to think of an answer but only the truth comes out. "I was hurt."

"I know."

"Really hurt."

"I know." He takes another sip. "I . . . fucked up, badly."

I shrug again. "You're fine."

Hudson shakes his head. "Don't do that."

"Do what?"

"Downplay what I did. The things I said to you, and how I lashed out? You had every right to block me, and frankly I'm surprised to see you here. If the situation was reversed I'd still be fuming. You're a bigger man than me."

A part of me wants to throw in some steamy joke, like, *in more ways than one*, but instead I keep this open dialogue going. "Have you talked with Nathan or Danni? How are they doing?"

Hudson takes another sip. "Danni is good—she is in London right now, finding herself. Always wanted to do it and saw this as the perfect time, I guess."

"I mean, what better time to take an international trip than when you ditch a guy at the altar?"

Hudson raises his glass in agreement. "Nathan is . . . doing okay. He just downloaded Bumble today. I helped him set up a profile this morning."

I arch my brows. "You always said you hated dating apps."

"Still do. I think they're impersonal. But they work for some people." He pauses, looking over the rim of his glass. "Do they work for you?"

"What does that . . ."

Oh. I see. That was subtle.

My heart beats faster and threatens to break out of my rib cage. The moment of truth. How am I going to answer?

Again: with truth. Lying is what got us into this situation. Might as well be honest.

"No, they don't." I pause, then add in one steady and quick breath, "The guy I want thinks dating apps are too impersonal."

"Oh? Who might . . ." Hudson interrupts himself, his right cheek rising into a wry smile. Slowly, he puts his glass down and walks around to my side of the counter. In response, I turn my chair to face him, his large frame slotting itself between my legs. "Who might that be?"

I stare up at Hudson, noticing every additional change he's undergone in the past two months. His stubble is growing, his chin a bit more defined. He's put on a little weight, but he wears it well. But, at the same time, his eyes look darker; there are more bags under his eyes and that constant wry look he has, that coy *I know a secret you don't*, is muted.

I never thought I could yearn to see something as simple as that again.

I move my fingers up his side, tracing and re-familiarizing myself with each groove of muscle and mold of flesh on him. Each passing second makes the yearning more intense.

But mixed with the yearning is another feeling that swallows my desire whole in one bite: fear. And my fingers stopping right at his hip is the manifestation of that, a manifestation Hudson picks up on.

He moves his hand down to grab mine, bringing my fingers up to his lips. Again, like before in Georgia, he kisses each of them.

But this time, the touch lasts longer, as though he's trying to commit the taste to memory, while also transferring up my arm some sort of silent admission of guilt and feeling.

"I know," he whispers, followed by another kiss. "Trust me, I know. I know you're worried that I'm going to hurt you again, a third time. I know you're thinking you're being an idiot and not listening to that voice in the back of your head. I'm sure Divya has told you not to trust me, and she'd be right. I don't think I would trust me either."

"You're not doing much to sell yourself here."

"I'm being honest, which is more important." He smiles. "I can't promise you'll be happy forever. I can't promise you that we won't have our ups and downs, but what I can promise you are these three things. One: I can promise you that every day, I'll do my very best to show you that my life is better with you by my side. Two: I can promise you I'll continue to grow, to try new things, and to admit that I'm not always going to succeed, but that doesn't mean I won't stop trying.

"And most importantly," he whispers, stepping closer, gently grabbing both sides of my head and tilting it up to look at him. "I can promise to put you and our relationship first. To put us bettering each other and growing together first, over everything else. To be that ride-or-die person you've asked me to be. To live up to your expectations, every day that I can, if you'll let me prove myself to you one more time."

Hudson's breath smells faintly of mint. During his speech, that's all I can think about, because if I focus on his words, or his eyes, or the way a strand of hair is in front of his face, I'll collapse. I have to be objective here. I have to think with my head, not my heart. I have to put logic—

What am I fucking saying? No, I don't. This isn't the time to be logical. Because logic is what got us into this mess—me thinking about my career, about my future, about the pros and cons of profiting off my ex's pain, played a part in this . . . this shitstorm we're navigating like Dorothy when she's landing in Oz.

But at the same time, being completely illogical is what made us break up in the first place. Expecting Hudson to be perfect, to always succeed, to be able to read my mind, to be my knight in shining armor—that is why we're here.

I don't need a knight. I'm Kian fucking Andrews. I'm my own knight. But wanting to have someone to ride alongside me? There's nothing wrong with that.

"My turn," I whisper, pushing against him gently so I can stand up. "I'm going to promise you these three things."

"Kian," he interrupts. "I appreciate it, really, but you don't . . ."

I put my finger to his lips. "Shhh," I say. "I'm talking."

He blinks owlishly, focusing on the tip of my finger, closing his eyes adorably, before falling silent.

"One: I promise I'll always give you space to be yourself, the good, the bad, and the ugly. Two: I promise to always be in your corner. If that means giving you advice, or telling you when you're wrong, or being your cheerleader, I'll continue to do that—and even when you fall, I'll be there to pick you up and let you fall a hundred more times if you need to. And three," I whisper, pulling my finger back, and pulling him closer. "I promise to always let you call me K, because that's what my boyfriends call me."

Our hips collide as I pull us closer, Hudson's lips barely an inch from mine. Naturally, his hands move up to my waist, wrapping around me and holding me securely—a feeling of safety I didn't know I needed until now.

"So, we're doing this, huh?" he whispers, forehead against my own.

"I guess we are," I whisper back.

Hudson smiles, slowly leans forward, and presses his lips against my own, kissing me slowly and letting our lips melt together. I wrap my arms around his shoulders, pulling us so close our bodies feel like they're forming into one.

Look up *Love Story* on Google, and our friendly sidekick will bring up, *Did you mean: Kian Andrews and Hudson Rivers?*

And right then, nothing else, not my professional or financial life, matters. Only Hudson's lips against mine and the future we're going to build—together—one step at a time. Not bad for a Black boy from North Carolina with his life completely out of whack, huh?

Not bad at all.

EPILOGUE

"NO, I'M NOT sure we can do that."

It's been almost eight months to the day since my last date with Wallace. And besides having to survive another hellish Boston winter, which truly is something that should earn me hazard pay, it's been good. Like, actually good.

"I mean, it's not the worst idea in the world," Amy says, her voice laced with hurt.

I sigh, checking both ways before I cross the street. My phone vibrates again.

HUDSON: ???

I'm not far from the Patriot—only four blocks—so Hudson can wait.

"No, you're right, it wasn't a bad idea. But I think we can do something better this summer. I mean, it's Pride Month. We should really go all out."

It feels weird to stand up for myself, especially over the phone. I mean, just eight months ago I was begging for a job at Spotlight, pretending I had a boyfriend, and wondering if I was going to be able to pay rent.

Now, I'm a Cultural Reporter for the new Condé Nast digital-only magazine for Generation X and millennials called—you guessed it—*Generation Millennial*.

Oh, how quickly our lives can change.

And because it's such a new and fresh magazine, job titles really mean nothing. At another outlet, a reporter would just be that: someone who writes stories. But here, I am also the mentor for three junior-level reporters and I help steer *Generation Millennial*'s Culture section in a direction we think best suits the magazine. I guess some people would say I'm an editor, but we at *GM* don't believe in strict titles like that.

The junior-level reporters on the other end of the line rustle and mutter incoherent words that blur with the sounds of Boston traffic. A pang of guilt floods my body like the opposite of a beer buzz.

I should be with them, I think. They're my team. I shouldn't be going out for drinks with Hudson. But, as Hudson reminded me during one of our daily pillow-talk sessions last month, I deserve to take a break.

"Nothing at *Generation Millennial* is going to fall apart without you. You're a manager now, babe. You get to take breaks and go out to lunch and leave early. Now, trust your team and turn off your fucking phone."

And he's right. The only thing on my calendar today that I didn't accomplish? Start planning for our Pride Month video.

Pride Month, which is in two months. I got time.

"Listen," I say as I cross the street. "How about we do this? We each take the night and think it over. We come back with three ideas tomorrow and we regroup. Cool?"

"Sounds good," Amy says.

"I'm cool with it," Blake adds.

"Right on," Dave cheers. Dave always loves to leave early. Then again, Dave also comes in late, so . . .

I see the Patriot in the distance and know that Divya got a table by the window. I also know that if she, my brother, or Hudson see me on my phone, it's going to be my job to pay for everyone's drinks—a ploy they put together to help me establish work-life balance. And also to get free drinks out of me, now that I can afford them.

I'll be damned if I let that happen.

"All right, so we're in agreement, and you all are going home. 'Night everybody, and great work today."

I hang up less than fifty feet from the door and have my phone pocketed by the time I walk in and find the table where Divya, Jamal, and Hudson should be sitting. It's the same table every time, closest to the window for the best light for taking selfies, Divya says.

And of course, that's exactly what she's doing.

Jamal is leaning against her body, his head at a forty-five degree angle as he looks up at the camera. Divya kisses his cheek in a very faux-romantic, but also flirty, but also friendly pose. They look happy together, and I can already imagine the amount of likes they'll get on that photo.

In another life, they'd be best friends and I'd be the third wheel. Nine months ago, that would have sent me on a Selina Kyle–level (the Michelle Pfeiffer version, not Halle Berry) rampage through the streets.

A lot can change in nine months.

The Patriot is always super crowded. That is a truth that we can always rely on, just like we can rely on the fact that white people will always vote to maintain the status quo, spinach will never be a good vegetable, and Pepsi is the superior cola.

But why does it have to be a fact that in such a crowded area, a feeling of claustrophobia comes with it? It's a specific type of claustrophobia, the one generated when another body is deliberately impinging on your space. That's what I'm feeling right now, and whoever it is isn't even trying to respect Personal Boundaries. I can feel his chest skimming against my back. The way his breath skips over the nape of my neck.

And most disgustingly, the feeling of his crotch against my lower back.

With my first paycheck from Condé Nast, besides starting to be an actual contributing member of society and paying off my student loans and credit cards, I joined a gym. And not just any gym, the Tier Gay Gym: Equinox. Just last week, we were taught four points of self-defense.

When will I ever use this? I remember thinking.

The universe right now is probably like, *bitch you thought*.

I go through the motions in my head: back step, elbow, grab, and flip. I prepare myself for the aftermath of throwing a man to the ground, knowing Divya and Jamal will hopefully come to my aid and defend me. At least if I get charged with something, I know I have a good lawyer. And it'll be pro bono! I think . . . I hope. I don't make enough money to afford Divya's retainer.

"What do you think the caption is going to be?" a familiar voice says over the hum of the bar.

Immediately, my body relaxes. Fluidly, I spin around on my feet, coming face-to-face with the slightly taller man I have spent almost every evening of the past nine months with. Hudson's hair has grown a little longer since nine months ago; it's shaggier, and he started to take on some stubble that connects with his mustache. He's dressed perfectly still, every piece of clothing complementing the other, but he's leaning more into his Southern roots.

A flannel button-down shirt, with only three buttons buttoned and the sleeves rolled up, a pair of jeans, and still-expensive sneakers. On his right wrist is a black cobalt beaded bracelet I gave him about four months ago for his birthday. On his left forearm, peeking out from under the sleeve, is the start of a tattoo he got inked about a week ago. The first of many, he told me, proudly.

We've both changed. The wedding, the date that followed, the past three-quarters of a year, have tested people in different ways. Hudson is a lot more confident in himself, separate from the identity of his parents.

And I'm far more brazen. Well, I've always been brazen, but more intentionally brazen. That's key.

"Oh, we're totally fucking tonight," I say.

He arches his brow and lets out a laugh, wrapping his arms around my waist and pulling me close. "That's not what I think they're going to caption that photo, but hey, I'm not against you and I making a video with that title if you want."

He quickly kisses my lips once, then kisses them again a little slower. Then this time, he lets his lips linger against mine for longer. Long enough for our breathing to become in sync. When he pulls back, not only do his teeth catch my bottom lip, but he also pulls my breath out with him, like he's a fishing line and my sanity is the fish.

When he finally calls me back and I regain some semblance of consciousness, all I can do is dumbly say, "Hi."

"Hi yourself," he whispers, hands still around my waist. "Come on, I just ordered; you want to help me bring the drinks over? I got your favorite."

"Oh, you can't carry a few drinks yourself?" I tease. "What is that gym membership going toward?"

"Keeping my stamina up so I can keep up with you," he says without missing a beat. "Plus, maybe I like hanging out with you, and I want as much time as I can have with you. Did you ever think about that?"

"Sounds fishy."

"Mhm."

I follow Hudson over to the bar, getting everyone's drinks and helping him carry the four drinks to the table. By the time we get back, Divya and Jamal have engaged in a heated conversation about some legal doctrine. Hudson gestures with his hand in an *after you* sort of manner, allowing me to sit next to Divya as he passes out the drinks. A rum and Coke for Jamal. A vodka cranberry for Divya. Sparkling water for Hudson. And for me, a Rivers & Valleys hard cider that I helped create with Olivia over the summer.

Is there some type of psychological phenomenon where your favorite thing is something of your creation? Probably, but I'm not going to worry about that for now.

"I'm telling you," Jamal says. "*Hamilton v. Carrows* is a good choice."

"Whoa, whoa, whoa," Divya interrupts, taking a sip of her drink. "Number one: When did you become a legal scholar? Number two: You didn't go to law school. Number three: Hi, K, you're late."

"I got held up at work," I explain. "We're launching this new—"

Divya looks at me with pure confusion. "I'm sorry, was there any part of what I said that made you think I wanted to hear an excuse? No. Here. Give me your drink, you don't deserve that."

"What? No!"

Before I can grab the stout glass, Divya already has it in her hand and has drunk, in three large gulps, a third of the glass. She wipes her mouth and kisses my cheek quickly . . .

. . . and burps directly in my ear.

"Oh, my fucking God!" I groan. "You are *disgusting*."

"Oh, calm down," Hudson teases. "It wasn't like she licked you or anything."

"She's done that," I mutter, wiping my face.

"Accurate," Divya says proudly. "But like I was saying . . ."

"Oh, I thought you forgot whatever ludicrous list this was and were going to spare us. Darn," Jamal mumbles around the rim of his drink, glancing over at Hudson. "Thanks for the drink."

"Anytime."

Divya goes back on her rant, listing three other reasons why Jamal is wrong about whatever they are going on about. But as she talks, I find myself zoning out, thoughts of *Generation Millennial* fluttering in the back of my head, questions about whether I actually locked the door before I left this morning (an answer I still haven't settled on), but more importantly, and probably most importantly, I find myself focusing on the handsome man in front of me. How easily he inserted himself into my life, how quickly Jamal and Divya gave him a second chance because I asked them to, and how seriously he became part of our inner circle. How happy I am to spend so much time with him, to wake up next to him, to call his name, and frankly sometimes scream it multiple times a night . . .

I don't think I've said it often in my twenty-three years of existence, but I think I'm pretty lucky. No, I *know* I'm really fucking lucky.

The feeling of Hudson's hand wrapping around mine brings me back into the conversation. When my eyes focus, he's staring back at me, but not in an oppressive way; in a soft, loving way that makes me squeeze his hand.

"Good day?" he asks. It's the statement he usually asks me whenever we see one another.

"Good day," I reply. "You?"

Hudson nods. Eight months ago, he decided staying in Boston was the best choice. Standing up to his parents was a weeklong event that required him to go back home, and it gave us time to decide if this was really something that we wanted to pursue after such a great date that night. But when he came back, Hudson was a different person. He was confident in himself, and he went headfirst into his master's program. And now, with only a semester left, he's deciding exactly what type of practice he wants to run.

And where he wants to run it.

That's a topic I haven't even discussed with Divya or Jamal yet. Leaving Boston seems like such a big life change. I met Hudson here. I went to Northeastern here. I made a life here and became who I am today in this Katy Perry *hot and cold* (and a little bit racist) city. Leaving it feels . . . wrong.

Maybe it's time to start a new chapter. For every good memory here there's two bad ones, although that tapestry makes up a significant part of my life and I wouldn't be who I am today without all of those pieces coming together. Starting fresh with Hudson somewhere else isn't a bad thing; it's just . . . a thing.

And that's okay.

Hudson slides his hand across the table and squeezes mine in a tight grip. It's like the beginning, middle, and end of an elaborate Morse code message. The fraction of a second where our skin connects, and our pulses are one, says everything I need to know about this moment. And about everything that will follow.

No matter what happens, we will be okay.

The tone in the bar changes. About three or four months ago, the Patriot added a makeshift dance floor to the bar in the back. The goal was to attract more customers, and to make it more of a friendly, collegiate atmosphere. My ever-so-astute business-minded brother had some thoughts about that choice. But then again, he was always one of the first to get on the dance floor.

It seems this time, though, fate has another idea.

"Oh, fuck yes," Divya says, pushing her body against me, trying to force me out of the booth. "This. Is. My. Fucking. Jam."

I can't make out exactly what the song is, but it's sung by some chorus of girls. I strain my ear to listen, squinting my eyes as if that will help my ears pick up more of the bass line. "Is this . . ."

"A club remix of 'Work from Home'? Yes, it is. Is it the best song in existence?"

"Yes, it is," Hudson chimes in. Now *that* is a surprise. He also shimmies out of the seat, giving his glass one final swig. "Divya. You. Me. Dance floor. Now."

I step out of Divya's way before she has to demand I move. She smooths out her skirt, adjusting her strapless top. "You think you can keep up with me?"

"I should ask you the same thing. I've got . . ." He does the wave with his arms. "Moves."

Divya arches her brow and glances over at me. I shrug innocently. "He says he has moves. Trust me, you'll be surprised."

"If these are the type of moves he has in the bedroom . . ."

"Hey! No insulting my fucking skills in public. Come on!"

"You're very good at fucking, babe," I promise.

"Oh my God," Jamal groans, thumping his forehead on the table. "Kill me."

"Later," Divya promises, grabbing Hudson's hand. "Come on.

Show me these moves you speak so proudly of." She pulls him close, looking over her shoulder at me, a silent ask if I'm coming.

"In a bit," I promise, raising my glass. "I want to make some headway on this."

"Don't wait too long," Hudson says. "You can't leave me alone with her."

"Oh, you should be *so lucky* to be alone with me!" Divya barks before giving him another tug, the two of them disappearing into the crowd.

"Make good choices!" I shout to them, like an overbearing mother. Divya turns around and sticks out her tongue. Hudson gives me the middle finger, though the smile never leaves his face.

I watch two of the three closest people in my life spend time together. Loving Hudson and him loving me back is as important as it should be in any relationship. In fact, how you and your significant other view and value each other is probably the most important part of any relationship and the secret to long-term success. But a close second is how your friends and confidants feel about the person in your life. And I'm not sure I could live with Divya or Jamal hating Hudson.

Thankfully, I don't have to worry about that. Judging him harshly and giving him shit at every corner? That's just something he'll have to deal with. Especially with Divya; it's how she shows her affection.

"I have a question for you," Jamal suddenly asks, breaking the comfortable silence between the two of us. I've learned over the past few months that forcing him to have a conversation isn't the way to get close to him. We're different, and there's nothing wrong with that. It just took me years to realize that the type of brotherly relationship I saw in movies and TV shows was not the type I was going to have with Jamal. Our relationship looks different, and that doesn't make it any worse or any better than anyone else's. Once I realized that, we became a lot stronger.

Another thing I have Hudson to thank for. The past eight months of being in a relationship, an actual loving relationship with its ups and downs and complexities and learnings, has bled into every single relationship that I have. My relationship with Divya is stronger; my relationship with my parents and Jamal is better than it's ever been.

"Shoot." I lean down, resting my elbows on the table, and blow bubbles in my drink.

"Are you happy?"

The question would catch most people off guard, but I'm used to these deep existential questions from Jamal. Another reason why he and I are so different, and it took me so long to understand him. Jamal is more than just a power-hungry corporate capitalist who is on track to be top of his graduating class from an Ivy League. He's hungry, he's curious, and most of all, he's trying to understand the world around him. Maybe as an older brother, I can help him in that regard.

So, a question like *are you happy* isn't really what he's asking. The subtext is deeper than the Mariana Trench. What he's really asking is, *How do I get happy like you?*

And that's a question I don't have the answer to.

"Yeah," I say finally, watching Hudson and Divya try to match their different dancing wavelengths to no avail. Divya is smooth and fluid, while Hudson is lucky if he can even hit the offbeat. But that doesn't make it any less adorable. "I am. I really am."

I take three more gulps of my drink, ignoring the burn from the alcohol and the bubbles before standing up. "Come on, let's dance. We deserve it."

Jamal doesn't fight me like I thought he would—always up for the surprises, I see. He takes a sip and wipes his mouth with the back of his hand, following me into the crowd as we join Divya and Hudson, dancing the night away, and pushing away worries about school, happiness, where our lives will take us, and so many other thoughts until tomorrow.

And for right now, we all make a promise to be, in this moment, happy.

ACKNOWLEDGMENTS

This book is the true by-product of the expression "it takes a village." There are so many people, in big and small ways, that made this dream a reality. There are so many people that I'm sure I'm going to forget, so I'm going to do my best.

First of all, Leah Johnson. I feel like I've included you in every book dedication at this point. You were the first person who read the pitch for this book, and your texting me *"inject it into my veins"* made this book possible.

To my friend, fellow Athena stan, and icon Brendon Zatirka, who read the first fifty pages and gave amazing notes, thank you so much for giving me the courage, support, and cheering to write a queer male rom-com.

To my agent, Jim McCarthy, who, when I e-mailed, *"I think I want to write an adult rom-com"* with no adult rom-com or adult novel experience, responded with, *"sure, let's give it a try,"* thank you. Your constant support and unwavering dedication and trust in my abilities are some things I love about you. Every author deserves an agent who believes in them as much as you believe in me. I'll never be able to thank you enough.

To Mary Averling, whose insight into how to edit a book and make it clean is always, always unparalleled. I cannot wait to see you shine.

To Jen DeLuca, Casey McQuiston, Sasha Smith, Julia Whelan, Nisha Sharma, Denise Williams, and Christina Lauren, I couldn't have found better supporters and kinder people to help introduce me to the world of rom-coms. Each of you, in different ways, has helped make this book a reality. I love this community so much, and I want to thank you for welcoming me with open arms.

To my Berkley team, Kristine Swartz, Mary Baker, Brittanie Black, and Jessica Mangicaro, thank you for taking a chance on a boy with a dream, a cute plot, and some decent writing ability. This book and its success is as much your win as mine.

I'm very proud of this book. I'm proud of my team and proud of what it represents—how far the industry has come in supporting books by queer authors about queer stories. Deep down, I hope this story makes you feel just a little bit joyous inside. If it does, no matter the success, I've done my job.

Photo by Louisa Wells

KOSOKO JACKSON is a digital media specialist who lives in the New York Metro Area and spends too much time listening to Halsey and Taylor Swift. *I'm So (Not) Over You* is his debut rom-com, published by Jove.

Ready to find
your next great read?

Let us help.

Visit prh.com/nextread

Penguin
Random
House